About the Author

Calvin Clarke graduated in Science from the Open University and worked for a pharmaceutical company. He now teaches in a London school and has coached a girls' football team. Calvin enjoys playing guitar and has run a sub-three hour marathon. Having lost a daughter to a rare lung condition he now campaigns for the Pulmonary Hypertension Association.

Dedication

I would like to thank Alison Grist, whose expertise led me in new directions. For Vincent Mills, who supplied me with enough copy to keep me going for years. Actually it was years! For Deborah, John and Naomi, who must have wondered what I've been doing all this time. Thanks for being patient. And for Lucy, whose light now shines in glory.

Calvin J Clarke

EXTRA TIME

ISBN 978 1 78455 844 4 (Paperback)
ISBN 978 1 78455 846 8 (Hardback)

www.austinmacauley.com

First Published (2015)
Austin Macauley Publishers Ltd.
25 Canada Square
Canary Wharf
London
E14 5LQ

Printed and bound in Great Britain

Acknowledgments

The commentaries of Kenneth Wolstenholme and Wally Barnes reproduced here were televised by the British Broadcasting Corporation.

The lyrics of Pink Floyd, reproduced here, were written by Syd Barrett, David Gilmour, Nick Mason, Roger Waters and Rick Wright.

The song World Cup Willie was performed by Lonnie Donegan.

Time is an illusion

Albert Einstein

Prologue

Saturday 14th October 1066

The ancient stone dolmen that stood among the mighty oaks was little Freya's secret place. She had found it one day when searching the hidden tracks that wound deep into the forest. That was two years ago. Now she was ten.

Freya Aylwin woke early with a sense of adventure. Leaving her family croft she began scaling the grassy incline that led to the edge of the wood; her long, dark hair caught in the autumn breeze. Black crows flapped into the air sending raucous screams across the fields. She whistled for Hengist, a huge scraggly wolfhound with wiry grey fur and keen eyes. He came bounding up to her and standing beside her stood almost to the girl's shoulders. They raced up the slope towards the summit. All around, the rolling hills of southern England glowed emerald in the first rays of dawn.

As they came to the crest of Senlac Ridge, a small glebe opened up where large standing stones had been erected. Freya did not understand their purpose but had grown to love the mystery of their existence. A large rectangular slab lay across two chiselled rocks like a giant troll's table. Freya hauled herself on top. She laid her face on the rough stone and ran her tiny fingers over the yellow-green lichen that covered its surface.

Standing tall, she raised her wooden sword above her head and cried: 'Freya for King and Country.' Hengist bounced around below, barking and throwing his head in the air.

But then the slim girl realised she was shivering and found her arms covered in goose pimples. A breeze had picked up. Her eyes sharpened knowing something was about to happen. The very air around her seemed to carry hidden messages that she could sense.

Freya usually felt charged and alive at this moment playing on the stones in her secret place. Today she felt a growing suspense as if her destiny was about to be made known. It wasn't just the wind rustling the branches of the lofty trees that heightened her awareness. Hengist had also frozen as he looked up quizzically towards Freya.

The world she knew was changing. The sky darkened and a drizzle started to fall.

'What is it Hengist?' she whispered through clenched teeth. She could hear something, like the sound of a distant rumble, almost inaudible, rhythmic, the breathing of a sleeping giant stirring from a dream. Freya jumped down and pushed her way through some undergrowth towards the noise. What she saw next took her breath away.

Spanning the entire length of a wide field, she saw a vast and mighty army. They carried banners, swords and axes. On their heads they wore leather helmets. Freya's dark eyes widened, so stunned was she at their number, stretching out of sight around the foot of Senlac Ridge. Upon a sturdy horse the colour of charcoal sat their commander, his eyes scouring anxiously south towards the distant coast. King Harold!

Little Freya did not know that Harold and his army had been battling invaders to the north of England. If she'd listened to the stories running rife in the land she would have known that his army had just seen to the Vikings at York, finally quelling them at Stamford Bridge. Then came unwelcomed news of an imminent attack from across the sea. *Why now?* the King had said. *Is God against me?* The return march from the north alone had taken almost two weeks and had drained the strength of Harold's army.

Freya saw him now, sat wearily upon his warhorse with the flag of St George flying in the wind. She could see a distant gathering from Hastings. The sun glinted on the Normans' armour as they advanced; the colours of their banners high above, their horses' hooves clattered as they pounded the stony ground.

From her vantage point Freya watched open-mouthed. She had played war games all the time, much to the dismay of her parents. But here, in her quiet corner of the realm had two armies come face-to-face ready to do battle. It was beyond her wildest dreams and her sense of excitement grew with every second.

She saw King Harold speaking with his generals and imagined them discussing battle plans and strategy. She saw the generals disperse, riding to their battalions, waiting for the King's command.

Freya knew this was the best day of her life. The wolfhound placed his head in her lap and whimpered. Freya stroked him tenderly, 'Don't be afraid, Hengist.'

She watched the enemy assemble, with archers, foot soldiers, wagons, chariots and cavalry. Stretching field after field to the horizon were contingents of Normans, Bretons and Flemish. They came like ants marching in procession, like a river flowing through the valley, like a cancer consuming flesh. Finally, the venomous eyes of the foot-soldiers faced the English. Among the throng, upon his steed, rode William, Duke of Normandy.

In a stand-off they faced each other; hardly a word was spoken, each gauging the other in psychological foreplay. Then Freya heard a Saxon war cry rise into the sky. The noise was chilling as they taunted the Normans by beating their shields with swords in a crashing rhythm like thunder.

'God-e-mite, God-e-mite, God-e-mite,' they cried. 'God Almighty, God Almighty, God Almighty...'

Two furlongs distant, the Normans replied in kind, beating louder and chanting with equal fervour. And so it continued for half-an-hour until a silence came over the place. Then, all that could be heard was the wind sighing in the trees and the crows screeching overhead.

Freya was astonished to see a minstrel in colourful costume appear from among the ranks of Norman archers. He was a most unlikely warrior, prancing absurdly across the gulf between the two armies. He skipped and danced and played a piccolo as he came closer to the jeering Saxon line. The English looked incensed, hammering their shields in wild provocation. Then a huge footman leapt forward and with one swift blow felled the tiny jester with his sword. Freya gasped, her hands automatically reached to cup her pale face. Then a hissing sound came from above and the sky filled with arrows arcing across the divide. Norman archers had sent their first volley into the phalanx of Saxon soldiers and she witnessed hundreds fall at once.

The battle had begun.

From her secret place, Freya watched the two armies crash like violent waves smashing a rocky shore. She heard cries of agony, the metallic clash and clang of sword upon sword and the drumming hooves of Norman cavalry. To her growing distress she saw the killing on both sides. A bloody ooze began to carpet the battlefield. She heard the generals marshalling the troops with huge bear-like voices. And behind the rear-guard, upon his grey horse, she saw King Harold, watching and waiting. England's future lay on his shoulders.

Then, amidst the height of battle, Freya sensed something close behind her. She heard a twig crack, crushed under a heavy foot. She spun round with her wooden sword out ready to defend herself. Two men stood there, dressed in long black coats. One held a staff, his dark tangled hair fell over his shoulders; Freya immediately thought of Merlin the Magician. Her heart thumped. *What did they want?* Freya could see her hands shaking in front of her. *Has my time come?*

'Young lady,' said the one with the staff, his voice strong and appealing, 'we need your help. There's a mission only you can do. It will change the course of history. Come with us if you have the courage.'

Two hours after midday, on the 14th October 1066, there was a lull in the Battle of Hastings.

Both armies retreated to a distance of a furlong apart, carrying their dead and injured with them. They took up station facing each other; a wearied silence filling the void. Then, from a clearing in the nearby wood, came a noise no soldier had heard before. What seemed to be some kind of chariot came speeding into view and moved into the gulf separating the Norman and Saxon lines. Without the need for strong horses it moved with ease across the rutted ground. The surface of the vehicle was a dull grey and green which caused it to blend into the forest from where it had appeared. It rode over divots and furrows on its four black wheels with its engine roaring like a lion. From the front there came two lights so bright that no one had seen such radiance in daytime, save from the sun itself. Both Norman and English looked on in disbelief.

'Elijah comes to save us!' one Saxon yelled.

The Land Rover came to a halt, the doors opened and two men, a girl and a wolfhound stepped onto the pitted battlefield. They stood for a moment and surveyed the vast assembly that encompassed them. Freya took a deep breath and shivered.

'Men of England,' shouted the tallest, propping himself against his long staff, 'Men of Normandy, now is the time to put aside war. Now is the time to fight, but not to kill. We are here to show you a new way of combat. We know of a new contest, a new battlefield. Watch and learn. Observez et apprenez.'

The two men threw their black coats to the ground, marched away from the Land Rover and took up a position midway between both camps. Freya stood behind them, waiting to take part in the new game they had taught her.

One of the men let a round object fall to the ground, it bounced and he trapped it under his boot. The warriors on both sides were impassive, wondering what was about to happen. Then the two men began kicking the ball to each other while Freya ran between them. She ran to one man and then to the other. She seemed to be following the ball in vain trying to get it. They played the ball higher and it went over Freya's head. The men headed the ball over her, then they began running and passing it to each other along the ground. With one mighty effort, Freya lunged and came down with her feet on the ball. It was a perfect tackle; she got the ball and knocked the man over. Freya tumbled, rose to her feet and found she had the ball to herself. She stood there with one foot on it, panting heavily, while the tall man got to his feet. *That was amazing!* Freya broke into a huge relieved smile.

Both Normans and the Saxons suddenly erupted into a broadside of spontaneous cheering. They crashed their swords against their shields and hoisted their banners high. Drums began to thump out a steady beat. *Boom, boom – boom – boom. Boom, boom – boom – boom.* Freya turned to each side and waved. As the celebration began to wane, one of the men, wiping the sweat from his brow, raised his voice.

'This is the new battle – the new way to fight. You will challenge each other in this new way. In this warfare no life will be lost. You need no weapon, except the ability and strength God has given you. It requires skill and tactics to outwit the enemy. Those who work together will win. Freya will come and choose ten good men from England and ten good men from Gaul to take up the challenge.' He turned to Freya, a tiny and vulnerable figure amongst so many mighty men, 'This is your moment.'

Freya composed herself then crossed the gulf and one by one picked out the strong men of her choosing, looking deep into their eyes as she did so. They dropped their weapons and came forward to face those whom they'd previously wanted to destroy.

And so it started. Freya stood between them and threw the ball high into the air, retreating quickly. It fell and bounced off a mound before twenty ferocious men piled in; there came mayhem and a crunching of limbs. Bodies fell, men were pushed, expletives uttered and punches thrown. But then, from out of the scrum, the ball fell loose and a Norman soldier chased it down and stopped it with his boot. He gave a mighty kick sending the ball to a team mate waving forty yards away. It was the first pass ever made in a competitive game of football. Chanting rose from both sides.

This was just the beginning.

'Freya, our job here is done. It's time for us to go. You have done well.'

Both Normans and Saxons were too engrossed in the contest to see the outsiders leave. The Land Rover climbed the incline as far as the edge of the forest; the camouflage dissolving it against the backdrop of trees. They turned the off-roader around to get one last look – but it wasn't the football that caught their attention – it was something else entirely.

'What the shit is that?'

Freya watched the tall man point towards something gleaming and hanging motionless in the sky. Its brightness cast a glow across the surrounding fields.

'Fuck knows!'

She frowned. *How strange they seem to speak. Not even Uncle Wulfgrim says such things.*

Freya followed their line of sight to where both men were looking. She squinted and held her pale hand over her eyes to shield the glare.

'The sun has sent a messenger,' she gasped.

'Quick,' one of the men yelled. 'Get the recording gear – this is what we came for!'

'We've gotta leave you baby.' The man with the long hair helped Freya from the Land Rover. He laid his hand on her slender shoulder as Hengist bounded out.

The two men looked to the sky and watched in amazement as the apparition descended.

'Oh my God! How could anyone have guessed?'

'Yeah, now we know,' the other replied. 'End of story.'

'Nah, this is where it begins.'

Seconds later Freya watched the four-by-four lurch away over the uneven ground until it disappeared around the curve of the hill.

She had only one thing on her mind. Without a moment's thought Freya raced to her secret place with Hengist by her side. There she could watch the battle unfold. She came to the opening, and hauling herself onto the ancient stone dolmen, stood up to see.

Suddenly she was engulfed with a light. Freya felt bathed in a pure white iridescence but it did not harm her vision. She blinked and the instant Freya opened her eyes she found she was surrounded.

Men? No not men, she thought, *how could they be so tall.* Freya was mesmerised by their dark blue eyes and the serenity of their persona. They shone and their countenance was glorious. Their bright raiment fell in folds to the earth below. Their hair was golden-brown and covered their broad shoulders. No imperfection could be found in their faces. In their presence, Freya felt no fear. The one whose gaze was fixed upon the young girl carried something in his hands. He spoke with words so gentle and yet with such power that it seemed to Freya she heard his voice inside her head.

'Freya you have shown great courage and passed the test. You have much more to offer. Your valour will again be tested. I have brought you this trophy which you have seen before. Take it to the King. It will be a treasure to be kept secret. But you Freya have a greater calling and in time you will be an envoy to one who is yet to come.'

He held the object out in front of her and she took it from his hands. Freya glanced down at the black ball she was holding and when she looked up into the darkened air she found she was all alone.

1

Was this the moment that would make history?

The orange football nestled on the lush Wembley turf. A brief shower had left the pitch glistening like fine dew on a spring morning. From all around came the rising clamour of angry voices and the thunder of hammering feet. If it were at all possible, the vast throng watching would play their part in preventing defeat.

Franz Beckenbauer took several paces back, placed his hands on his hips and looked to the sky for inspiration. The only person now able to prevent a German victory was the man standing on the goal-line. The sun shone down upon the yellow shirt of goalkeeper Gordon Banks. His eyes scrutinised every move the penalty taker made, seeking any clue that might betray which way the shot would be played. Looking on, the England players stood helpless outside the goal area. The multitude around the terraces began to jeer and stamp and wave in a bid to confuse Franz Beckenbauer's train of thought.

Referee Pierluigi Collina's whistle sounded sharp and echoed round the hallowed stadium. The German captain took a deep breath and avoided eye contact with the goalkeeper. He leant forward and lowering his sight to the ball began running towards it. There was a thud as the leather of his boot met the ball and instantly deformed it. A tuft of grass rose into the air and began to float on the breeze, tumbling over gently. All sound vanished. It seemed as if time stood still, the ball motionless, frozen in space. The world watched; faces impassive all around. It took an age but was over in a flash. The shot was hard and low to the goalkeeper's left. Gordon Banks had guessed correctly and was already in flight. The ball travelled a mere twelve yards or slightly more allowing for trigonometry. He was now horizontal, his arm extended, his sinews stretched. All it needed was one deft touch. In that split second the goalkeeper got something on the speeding ball. The faintest fingertip had changed its path and maybe defeat had been avoided.

The ball hit the post and rebounded. The crowd erupted into a crescendo of noise as Gordon Banks stood to his feet, a defiant arm raised aloft as if to spur on his players. On the edge of the penalty area, Bobby Moore was the first to react.

'And here's Moore,' said the commentator. 'He turns and pokes the ball forward to Stanley Matthews. Beckenbauer's distraught – he's holding his head in his hands. Matthews sidesteps the oncoming Rudi Voller. Now the German defence, so often rock-solid and organised is out of place and streaming back. Matthews has found David Beckham out on the left touchline. This final's not over yet. It seems there's still all to play for in the last minute of extra time.

'Beckham bends a long, raking ball, fifty, sixty yards, switching play and it falls pin-point to the feet of Gary Lineker. The Tottenham man controls the ball dead and drives forward down this right side. He passes two defenders and goes to the goal-line and swings in a stunning cross to the edge of the German area. And here comes Alex Bell. He catches it full on the volley. What a shot! He's buried it in the roof of the net. The keeper didn't have a chance. What a strike! It must be all over now. Bell is England's hero. The young man's being mobbed by players and fans alike – he couldn't have hoped for a better England debut. And there's the final whistle. What a finish and what an end to a fantastic game in the stadium where dreams come true…'

The strident peal of a distant bell wrenched Alex from his fantasy. He blinked and let out an audible sigh.

Still wanting to be on the pitch, Alex spat with disgust at being so rudely taken from somewhere he'd rather be. Leaning over the wall he watched his string of spittle glint in the sunlight and spinning on a long downward spiral until finally becoming immersed in the inky swell of the River Thames. His body fluid had been lost just like the thoughts inside his head. He reached into his jacket pocket for his medication. Shaking the container, he realised with a sinking feeling that the tub was empty.

'Bollocks!' Hearing the sound of his own voice focused his mind on reality. Turning round he squinted towards Big Ben, the distinctive edifice rising in the distance. 'Quarter to. Shit!' He dropped the pill bottle into a nearby bin and started walking smartly away from the river.

Flicking his dark, lank hair from his eyes he took a torn paper from the pocket of his denim jacket. The advert from the Yellow Pages showed a place in a tiny back-road he wanted to find which was hidden away in side streets behind tall buildings. Even though the advert was somewhat modest, he was drawn by its strange name: *Time After Time*.

Minutes later he was standing in a cul-de-sac just a stone's throw from the Houses of Parliament and there he found the watch repairers.

The place looked even stranger than he'd imagined. Underneath the name it explained mysteriously: *Experts in Horology*. For a moment Alex had second thoughts about going inside as he was not sure of the meaning of the word *horology*. The connotations did not sound good.

Nearby a man dressed in a long, dark trench-coat stood propped against a lamp-post. His matted hair fell to his shoulders. Tucked under an arm he clutched a bundle of magazines.

'*Big Issue, Big Issue*,' he muttered in a gravelly voice as Alex passed him by.

'Yeah, okay, gimme a copy.' Finding his wallet he handed over a note. 'Keep it,' he said, 'keep the change.'

'Thanks mate.' His voice was flat.

Alex took it, wondering what the seller was doing in such a quiet street, 'Shouldn't you be near a tube station or somewhere? You won't get many takers here!'

'That's okay mate, I'm in no rush. Unlike you, I've got all the time there is. Have a nice day.' He grinned showing stained teeth.

Alex raised his eyebrows then turned to push his way into the shop through the heavy oak door which bore the name: *Harry Hunter esquire.* A tiny bell tinkled as the door opened and shuddered on its old hinges. The place was compact, but all around, in cabinets and on shelves, were hundreds of clocks, watches and the odd barometer. The air seemed to throb with their incessant syncopated ticking. There were scores of different faces all staring at him. Alex looked around and went over to inspect a tall grandfather clock. He tapped the glass face. *This is hardly John Lewis*, he thought, and he said, 'This stuff should be in the British Museum.'

'Can I help you Sir?' came a strident voice.

A tall man wearing a white shirt and pinstriped waistcoat had suddenly appeared behind the counter surprising Alex.

'Er, yeah – sorry, didn't see you there,' Alex spun round.

His first impression was that he was looking at a character from the pages of a Dickens story. The man's complexion was pale and his straw-like hair fell to a starched collar. With a long thin finger, the man scratched his chin.

And yet there was a spark of wisdom in his eyes, Alex thought, maybe someone who possessed more knowledge than ordinary. And perhaps his lean frame belied some hidden strength which was not first obvious.

'Sir?'

Alex coughed, 'It's my Rolex – it's stopped. Can you fix it? It was my Grandpa's.'

He placed the watch with pride onto the counter. It meant a lot to him, as did his grandfather. The horologist peered like an owl in his gold-rimmed glasses.

'Shouldn't be a problem Sir. You can pick it up in a few days.' He made an entry in a hefty ledger on the desk. 'It's *Mr Bell*, I believe?'

'Er, yeah that's right,' Alex said looking down at his shoes. His TV show was in its second successful series but he still got embarrassed when someone recognised him.

The man darted him a look over his glasses before whipping them off. 'I watch your show when I can. I like those old flash-backs best. I do go back a long way you know.' The man's eyes sparkled; he seemed to come to life. 'Arsenal's my team. I was there in '71 when Charlie George scored against Liverpool. You know the game?'

'Yeah, I heard it was a great final.'

'He just cracked it in and fell down flat like a domino; there were just eight minutes to go. We played in yellow that day.' The man's eyes glazed for a second as he retraced the years.

Alex nodded and switched into presenter mode, 'Yeah, well if you watch the show this week, we've a stonking game for you – and I'm talking dead famous! It's not one I enjoy watching myself. In fact I wish it'd never been played. Can't say more for now.'

Alex gave the man one of the charming smiles he usually reserved for favours – or girls – where he felt his dimples lining his cheeks.

'Walls have ears, as they say!'

'Mine have faces!' The horologist glanced at the clocks all around and Alex grinned. 'Okay Mr Bell, I'll look out for you this week.'

'Yep, well, see you soon.' Alex turned to go and almost reached the door.

'Um, Mr Bell – I've just remembered.'

Alex thought the man was about to launch into a long speech of another game he'd seen in the distant past. Instead the watch repairer placed a small object on the counter.

'I wondered if this was for you – being so well known, and that.'

'What do you mean?'

'I believe this has been left for you.'

'*Me*?' Alex frowned.

'I came across it out the back – only last week; forgotten all about it. You are Alex Bell of Fulham, aren't you?'

'Yes, what is it?'

'It looks like someone's been expecting you.'

Alex went over and gently picked it up, as if it might explode if he shook it. It was a scratched tobacco tin with a note held on by an elastic band. He read the scribbled inscription written in pencil.

Urgent! This is for Alex Bell of Fulham who will come to get his Rolex repaired.

Alex read it again and still it made no sense. 'Who left it?'

'Can't say. As I said, it turned up when I was tidying a lot of old stuff – papers, junk and things.'

Alex turned it over but found no clue to its origin.

'I'm quite glad I can get rid of it at last,' he spoke with a wry smile; his blue eyes staring hawk-like at his customer.

Alex wasn't listening; confused thoughts were racing through his head.

'As far as I remember it was here in the early days when I started, and I've been here…what…well it must be almost twenty-nine years now. Doesn't time fly when..?'

'What, *twenty-nine years*! You're joking me. I wasn't even born then!'

Before Alex could say anything more, the syncopated ticking began to change and then suddenly every clock in the shop began to chime together. It was a cacophony of sound.

Alex looked round in surprise. 'What's the time?'

'It's midday precisely, Mr Bell.'

'Look, I've gotta shoot – I'll be back next week.' And he left in a hurry, shaking the door on its hinges.

Outside, the boom of Big Ben filled the grey sky as Alex made his way to the main road. He pursed his lips and breathed out slowly, then pressing the tiny pads into his ears he turned up the volume on his iPod. He'd played *The Dark Side of the Moon* by Pink Floyd a thousand times but had never grown tired of hearing it. His Dad used to play the album at fall blast when Alex was a boy and he had loved it ever since. How appropriate, he thought, when the track *Time* was randomly selected and began to play.

'Ticking away the moments that make up a dull day
You fritter and waste the hours in an offhand way
Kicking around on a piece of ground in your home town
Waiting for someone or something to show you the way
...'

Seeing that the man in the trench-coat had gone, Alex tossed the Big Issue into a waste bin and started running towards the main road.

Two minutes later he was sitting on the back seat of a black cab and heading along Grosvenor Road.

The tin rattled when he shook it. For a while Alex thought about the absurd notion of why he should be holding such a strange thing with an inscription addressed to him. He could think of no rational reason. Gingerly he slipped the paper out and eased off the elastic band; it was perished and snapped easily.

Old Holborn it read in gold letters on the blue lid. It was the brand his grandfather used to smoke and the smell of his pipe would waft everywhere. He would light up on special occasions like Christmas or when his team Fulham Football Club had won. *That didn't happen very often*, Alex remembered with a smile.

He prised open the lid and the tobacco smell instantly brought back the memory of Saturday afternoon tea at Grandpa Bell's house and those long walks in the park. The grass had seemed to stretch forever in all directions. Looking up he would often see huge billowing clouds filling the sky with soaring turrets, sailing ships and mighty dragons.

Then upon the meadows of Wimbledon Common his beloved Gramps would race him to the tall oaks that stood around the fields. They would end up gasping for air and laughing until their sides hurt. They were some of the best days Alex could recall from his troubled past.

And there were those frosty nights when his toes would become numb from the cold and his grandfather would march

Alex into his garden to show him the stars. At a young age Alex could name many constellations and identify a handful of stars. He loved their strange names, such as Cassiopeia, Bellatrix, Orion, Sirius and Betelgeuse, and he marvelled to see the pale smudge of the Milky Way span the black winter night. His grandfather knew so much.

But once Alex let him down.

He remembered the day he'd made a catapult, hewn from a tree in the woods. He had fired many stones at tin cans lined up on a wall but one shot had been badly aimed and, much to his shame and embarrassment, it smashed straight through his grandfather's prized greenhouse. He was only seven at the time and he never did admit that it was his pebble that had gone astray. That afternoon he said nothing but kept his head down in Grandpa Bell's front room as the football results were read out on Grandstand.

The guilt inside was deep seated, and even now after all these years the very thought of Alex's inability to apologise brought a flush to his face. Alex regretted that he would never be able to look his grandfather in the eye and say sorry.

He cleared his throat and concentrated on the task at hand. Inside the tin he found two objects. One was a silver coin which he recognised as a half-crown, money his beloved Gramps would have used. The other was a stopwatch. It was an old analogue type made of chrome and glass. The white face was divided into 60 seconds with a smaller inner circle for counting up to one hour. A steel loop held a black cord for hanging round a person's neck. It was smooth and cool in his hand and Alex thought it had a pleasing weight. He clicked the button with his thumb and the second hand started moving. As if he couldn't quite believe what he was holding, he re-read the scrawled writing.

Urgent! This is for Alex Bell of Fulham who will come to get his Rolex repaired.

Alex stared vacantly out of the taxi window and was worried: *What can be so bloody urgent after all these years?*

2

Alex looked up as his taxi swept by the giant hoarding beside the main road. It proudly displayed the faces of the two presenters riding high in the television wars. Alex grinned wryly. Until last year no one had heard of Alex Bell and Billy Gunn, but now, in World Cup year, they were household names. Audience ratings had soared as their show became compulsive viewing and a number one download. A heady mixture of cheeky gossip from its quirkily handsome co-presenters together with their individual take on classic football matches had the male and female population turning on in droves. The paparazzi lay in wait at almost every venue. Only last week they had hosted the MTV Awards at the O2 Arena and the week before Billy had been mobbed by a mass of screaming girls when he opened a sports store in Manchester.

As the taxi pulled in to the studio forecourt, Alex realised he was late. There was only an hour to go before the recording in front of a live audience. He could see Ella Jones, the Assistant Producer waiting in the entrance lobby. Her arms were crossed with annoyance and the worry lines on her forehead revealed her anxiety. Alex slammed the taxi door.

'Where the hell've you been? We've been calling all morning!'

'Yeah, sorry, I left my phone at home.'

'Lizzie's waiting to go over the schedule. She's frantic.'

'No change there then! Has David turned up?'

'Yep, he's rehearsed already. He's cool.'

'Let's go then.'

Alex followed Ella along the tight corridors turning left and right and then up some stairs. The speed at which she walked betrayed her frustration; her stilettos were clicking like a metronome.

'Come on Ella, relax. I'm pretty good at this you know.' Alex, looking at her slim, agile figure, wondered if he should try his luck once more and invite her back to his place later. *I just need to pick the right moment*, he thought. *Maybe over some Shiraz.*

Ella walked and talked, 'There's this German doctor booked as the guest expert, he's rigged up some plasma screens and computers and stuff. Not exactly cool but I think it'll be one up on Sky. You'll need to get your head round that.' Ella looked over her shoulder at him, brushing back her long blond hair and pushed open some double doors. '...And we've got Jamie Valentine,' she smiled in anticipation of meeting football's current sex symbol. Alex sighed.

They barged into the production room attached to the studio where people were sitting drinking coffee round a large table.

'Sod you Alex; you're cutting it bloody fine!' Billy Gunn stood up from the spread of programme notes in front of him. 'I thought I was gonna have to do it on my own!' Billy rolled his eyes before winking and slapped Alex on the back in matey fashion. They laughed.

'Sorry to spoil your moment and good afternoon to you too, Billy-boy.'

Alex looked around for a coffee which Ella handed to him; black, no sugar, just the way he liked it.

'Listen up everyone.' Lizzie Lennox, the Producer, cut in waving a chewed Bic Biro. 'This week we're going out in our regular slot on Friday night. But Sky's moved their show, *We'll Fight Them on the Pitches,* up against us. We've got ourselves a face-off.'

'Bring it on,' Alex butted in with a sense of sarcasm.

'Let's get it right first time. Got that?' Lizzie cast a piercing stare at Alex and he felt her emerald eyes burning into his.

'Okay, what've we got?' he said trying to appear calm, but inside he felt a twinge of panic coming on.

Lizzie, tucking some stray red hair behind her ear, shuffled the papers on the table and picked up her running order.

'Right, we're starting with a look at some of the lighter moments from this season's football. We'll show our reports of Telford Bentley's brawl at Heathrow followed by Errol Solomon and Stanton Brown's drinking bash in Newcastle which led to that naked streak across the Tyne Bridge. And, it seems Rio Patel and Juan Sebastian Eduardo Ricario have swapped girls, so we've dug up some stuff on that before it hits the tabloids.

'Then we bring in our German guest, Dr Schneider who'll provide technical expertise and analysis when we look back at this week's classic game. If he gets boring, we'll just wind it up and go to Millie's interview with the Liverpool boys.'

'Five minutes to rehearsal ...' a voice on the intercom interrupted them.

'Okay, you guys get to make-up now and talk about the script and your ad libs, then we'll go from the top. I'll speak to you both on talkback.' Lizzie scooped up her papers from the table and, with the briefest glare at Alex, flashed out through the door.

'It's cool Alex,' Billy's eyes twinkled at him, 'You know she'll love you when it's all over, she always does.'

Sitting back on the hard leather couch on set, Alex listened with closed eyes to the theme tune playing out on the studio's foldbacks. He smiled. As a History of Rock and Pop Music graduate, who'd had minor success with his student band *Savage Romance,* he'd long contemplated writing a theme song specifically for the show. He often meddled with tunes and poetry and had written a few lines in the style of the English poet, William Blake, who'd become known posthumously as lyricist for the anthem, *Jerusalem.* When, on the off chance, he'd asked his new friend David Gilmour to arrange it into a musical composition, Alex was surprised when he actually agreed. The guitarist had even suggested that a stadium-sized football choir at Wembley be used for the chorus. But his delight was short-lived. After releasing the song as a single it went to number two in the charts and was beaten to top spot by heavy metal band, *Nux Vomica*, with their rendition of *Land of Hope and Glory*. Despite this, Lizzie Lennox had maintained it was still appropriate to play as a song to open the show. In any case, she was adamant that their alternate Titles of *We Invented Football* and *Turf Wars* would have brought down the ratings. So the song seemed to fit.

'Thirty seconds to recording, thirty seconds,' Sarah, the script supervisor, spoke loud and clear into Alex's ear.

He glanced sideways and gave a thumbs-up to Billy. The Floor Manager, Barry, was telling the audience to sit back and enjoy the show.

'Twenty seconds to recording, twenty.'

Billy took his position, and after checking his microphone transmitter pack was securely in his jeans pocket, did a little dance to the delight of the audience.

'Seven, six, five, four...'

Alex and Billy grinned at each other like naughty school boys. As they heard Sarah say *two*, they flipped up two fingers to the camera in a reverse V-sign. The audience laughed out loud as did the cameramen.

'And cue Titles.'

The opening sequence came up on screens around the studio. It was part live action, part animated images merging together football sequences of knights and crusaders wielding glinting swords. The rock anthem began and the vocals came in...

'Welcome to the show, we'd like to let you know
Tonight there will unfold, a wonder to behold
Not before in history, has there been such a victory
When he who is without age, will take the centre stage
So welcome to the show, welcome to the show.

At the end of the day, when all is said and done
At the end of the day, when battle has been won
At the end of the day, when victory is ours
We'll cry: En-ger-land, En-ger-land
Beneath the Wembley towers...'

The young presenters were ready and standing in the centre of Studio One. Billy stood swaying proudly to the music in his white football shirt with England's crest of three lions and Alex wore the team's second colours, his favourite red shirt. As the applause from the audience rose, Billy heard a voice in his earpiece, 'Cue Billy!' The autocue began scrolling.

'Welcome to *At The End Of The Day* – the show that scores more often than a cabinet minister in a brothel. Alex.'

'Yes that's right Billy, and it's not just the Government that's making all the headlines. In the show tonight, our intrepid reporter, Millie Rivers, gets her kit off: She'll be in the bath with Liverpool boys Damon Vincent and Freddie Queen. We'll be looking back to 1966...'

'...Can we ever forget it?' cut in Billy.

'We're taking a look at the Finals this summer, and top scorer Jamie Valentine is live on our couch with his girlfriend and pop diva, Lola Corolla. I bet she enjoys lying back and thinking of England!'

Barry, the floor manager, who was standing on the edge of the set, raised his hands and motioned clapping and the audience erupted into spontaneous cheering.

'Whatever happened to Posh and Becks?' Billy added when the applause faded. 'But first off tonight we take a look back at the funnier side of this season with some of the year's more memorable tunes. This is *Kiss Me Quick, Kiss Me Slow* from the new girl band: *Suzy Cute and the Cunning Stunts.*'

The music came up as the football videotape started. It was time to shift to the other side of the set. Cameras moved on their pedestals, lights were balanced as the boys found their spot near the plasma screen set-up. They sat on the couch and watched the end of the film play out. Billy laughed on cue.

'Yeah, what did happen to assistant referee Wendy Carmichael when she disappeared down the tunnel after that Celtic game? Guess we'll never know. Alex.'

'Okay, it's flashback time. And we're flashing back to the Swinging Sixties and that infamous day on the 30th July 1966. This was the day when England, wearing red shirts, lined up in the World Cup final to face the old enemy, West Germany. It was destined to be the greatest day in the nation's history. Billy.'

As images from the final played on the plasma screen, the vision-mixer intercut between the boys in the studio and the football montage.

'Why-oh-why did England wear red that day? Wrong choice if you ask me! But this was the final where it was Banks versus Beckenbauer, Stiles versus Schnellinger and Hurst versus Haller. Even HRH Queen Elizabeth was there in neutral yellow. The Germans were one up after twelve minutes courtesy of Helmut Haller before Geoff Hurst squared it six minutes later. This was turning out to be *the* classic World Cup final of all time. In the second half, Geoff's West Ham teammate, Martin Peters, put England into a 2-1 lead and it stayed that way until almost full-time. That's when Jack Charlton nobbled a German and gave away a dodgy free-kick just outside the area. From that spot-kick Wolfgang Weber scrambled a dramatic last-second equaliser.'

'Don't you hate it when that happens?' Alex added.

'Yeah, the Jerrys went mad. England sank in despair, and the National Grid ground to a halt when everyone went off to brew tea right across the country. Alex.'

'England manger, Alf Ramsey rallied his troops and extra time was just as tense. But then, enter a Russian linesman named Tofik Bakhramov. Kenneth Wolstenholme takes up the commentary.'

'Run VT,' Alex and Billy heard in their ears. A soft focus black and white film appeared on the monitors.

'Two goals each', explains BBC commentator Wolstenholme with expectancy. 'There's twenty minutes of the game left.'

German goalkeeper Tilkowski lofts a high ball and clears down field. The towering English defender Jack Charlton is first to the bounce and heads forward. The ball is collected by Nobby Stiles in the centre of the pitch and he plays a clever pass to Alan Ball on the right wing.

'Here's Ball running himself daft.'

The red headed winger gets to the goal-line before a German defender can challenge and he whips in a dangerous low cross to the edge of the six-yard area.

'And now Hurst, can he do it?'

The England centre forward swings his right foot and smashes the ball against the cross-bar like a hammer blow. It rebounds down behind the goalkeeper and bounces out.

'Yes. No. No, the linesman says *No*!'

Players in red shirts and white shirts surround the Swiss referee Gottfried Dienst who is talking to his linesman and trying to find a common language. They resort to hand signals and finally decide. The referee turns and shakes his head.

'No, it's not a goal. No goal,' exclaims Kenneth Wolstenholme as Geoff Hurst can't believe it.

The film freezes on a close up of a haggard Bobby Moore.

'Well that was it,' continued Billy, 'the goal that never was. Alex.'

'Had that gone in, Geoff Hurst would've been knighted.'

'Yeah, and look what happened to Alf Ramsey?' Billy gave a passive stare.

'So, as we all know, England lost 4-2, with goals coming later from a Franz Beckenbauer penalty and then Helmut Haller picking up his second in the dying seconds.'

Alex stopped for dramatic effect, swallowed and looked out to the audience and then beseechingly into the camera. 'I don't know about you Billy but I'd give anything to go back and change that result!'

Billy nodded in agreement, 'Oh yes!'

From the audience an excited girl called out, 'Can I come with you?'

Alex grinned, 'Yeah, just leave your number...Well our studio expert tonight is Dr Ralf Schneider from the Fraunhofer

Institute in Nuremberg. He *claims* to have conclusive proof of what really happened to Geoff Hurst's shot. It's a question that's been a hot debate for many decades. So, Dr Schneider, has the mystery been solved?'

'Good evening Alex, good evening Billy. It's good to be on your show.' His Teutonic accent was evident and surprisingly powerful emerging from his slight frame. He adjusted his tie and undid the button on his tweed jacket, pursing his lips and looking round in the manner of one who knows they're being watched. 'Yes, I think that after all these years, it's safe to say we now know definitively if Geoff Hurst's shot was a goal or not. And I must say this is something which Germany would like to know just as much as England.'

'Okay Dr Schneider, don't keep us in suspense. What's the answer?'

'Well Alex, this is what we did. I think you're aware of our technique; it's something we used to analyse the JFK assassination. In our investigation we collected as many different photos of the actual moment the ball hit the ground. These were from newspaper archives, television, film and also a good number of photos taken by fans in the stadium. We found hundreds of new photos on the Internet. Knowing precisely where they were taken, we built a virtual Wembley and fed each picture into a computer program and so condensed the images into a 3D rendition. Here look.'

He tapped a few keys on the laptop in front of him. A line drawing of Wembley Stadium, complete with twin towers, was projected onto the large plasma screen in the studio. The stadium began to rotate and a scattering of dots started to appear one by one in the image. Alex and Billy looked on open-mouthed.

'Each data point you see in the stadium is a place from where a photo or cine film was taken. After analysing each picture using false-colour, all the digitised images were combined like a seamless collage. We can now zoom in and look closer. As you can see, it's possible to fly around Wembley.

'To make the effect more realistic, we've added the positions of each player, referee and linesmen, and also the lighting conditions, shadows and original colours. We've even been able to reconstruct a good likeness of every person watching. Can you see the Queen? I think it looks more realistic than the film you've just shown.'

Alex felt the hairs on the back of his neck stand up, his hands were clammy. He wished his Grandfather and Dad could be in the audience. They'd argued this point many times over dinner. But now they were both dead and Alex would never have a chance to go to Wembley with either of them. How he longed to see his grandfather. For a moment his mind wandered. Then Alex realised where he was and his professionalism brought him sharply back into focus.

Billy nudged Alex and caught his eye checking he was all right, Alex nodded and they both leaned towards the screen in suspense.

Dr Schneider's voice rose and fell as he pointed out aspects of the stadium.

'Now look as we get closer to the goal area, we can move around the players and view the ball from any angle. Here's Hurst – here's Tilkowski. Now we're right above the goal-line looking down. The goalkeeper is leaning back and falling over. Let's go closer...closer. And there you can see for yourself, a quarter of the ball is on the line. And here's a view from underneath as well. *The ball did not cross the line.* There you have it.'

Lizzie Lennox's voice was quick into Alex's ear, 'Ask him if the study is biased. He's German don't forget.'

Alex turned to the wiry figure of Dr Schneider, perching proudly on the sofa. 'Well I don't think that's what we wanted to hear,' Alex felt his throat tighten with disappointment, he coughed to loosen it. 'So the Russian linesman was right all along. But you could be making this all up just so you can kill-off sport's greatest mystery?'

Dr Schneider smiled insipidly; his watery eyes looked out to the audience. 'Okay, the study was undertaken in Nuremberg where the programming was done. But we also had a team from Durham University who helped with some of the imaging techniques. So there's also English involvement, and I'm sure Professor Jim Wilkinson and the guys at Durham will confirm there has been no conspiracy.'

Alex felt suddenly empty.

'So, after all these years, the truth is out,' Billy said, wondering if this really was the news they wanted to break on their show and whether it would boost the viewing figures. He stood up and walked towards the front row, the camera backing away as he moved. 'Let's see what our studio audience thinks. Are there any questions for Dr Schneider? Yes, that man in the second row with the Sunderland shirt.'

The cameras panned and zoomed in for a close-up as a microphone lowered above him. 'I think he's talking crap!'

The big man sitting next to him agreed and began chanting. 'Yeah – England, England …'

Within seconds, most of the audience were raising their voices in a discordant melee.

'Alright,' shouted Alex using his hands to hush the audience. 'This isn't some cheap Channel 5 show. Let's try someone else. Yeah, that ugly bloke up there, next to the girl in the skimpy Barca top.'

The man leant forward and surprised the audience with his American accent. His delivery was slow and articulate.

'Alex, you said that given the chance, you'd go back and change the result of the World Cup. What would you do? How would you go about it?'

Alex ran his hands through his dark mop of hair. 'What kind of question is that? What do you Yanks know about proper football anyway?' He grimaced. 'Well let's see…I think I'd bribe the Russian linesman. Yeah, I'd say to him before the game, "If you see any dodgy rebounds landing on the goal-line, just say the ball went in and you'll be granted asylum and end up in a nice little prefab in Bognor. No questions asked." Anyway, what the heck, at the end of the day, it's just a game.'

'Okay let's move on now,' Billy interrupted Alex. Lizzie Lennox had just been in his ear saying it was time to wrap up the interview, 'I expect the linesman regretted his decision after that, considering what happened to him. A cosy prefab in Bognor sounds much the better option. Anyway, we'd like to thank Dr Ralf Schneider for finally showing the world that we were truly stuffed in '66. But there were better times ahead, and next week we'll be looking at England's 5-1 win over Germany in Munich in 2001. Pay-back time at last – and we'll also be profiling the veteran TV commentator, Brian Moore, who ironically died the same day. Alex.'

'Still to come, we've got Jamie and Lola on the couch – and Lola will be showing off her new line of *LaBathE* underwear...'

There were a handful of men in the audience who gave a cheer and a whistle.

'That stands for *Lay Back and think of England*,' Billy added with a boyish smirk.

Alex looked straight into the camera, 'But first – playing a track from his new album *Ghosts In The Stadium*, will you welcome, our friend and Pink Floyd guitar hero, the legendary, Mr David Gilmour.'

3

The Pub that stood at the end of the tiny street drew Alex and Billy towards it with a forlorn air. A high brick wall hemmed the cobbles and seemed to guide any wayward stragglers straight to the front door. They had literally stumbled upon The Paper Moon one night after they'd been out on a drinking spree following a successful show. It was tucked away and overlooked but only minutes from some of London's most fashionable streets. The unassuming green door had a leaded window etched with grime and a large tarnished brass letterbox through which no letters had fallen for many years. Alex yanked the handle and they went inside. A familiar yeasty aroma filled the saloon. Alex found the smell comforting, like the smoky, oily richness he remembered that pervaded his grandfather's shed. It was a safe place.

The floor was wooden and the lounge drab. An empty fireplace with a cast-iron surround was to one side at the foot of a smoke-stained chimney breast. On the opposite wall stood a silent jukebox; a radio played quietly by the bar. Several dark wooden tables were spread around the longue. In one corner a man sat drinking a pint and reading a paper; a wide brimmed hat lay next to his glass.

'Usual boys?' said the barman behind the counter, and with a crackle he tuned the radio to a sports channel.

'Yeah, set 'em up Jack,' Alex crossed over to take their regular stools. 'Looks like we got a crowd in tonight!' He glanced over at the man reading in the corner.

'How'd the shoot go?'

'Great! I'm even looking forward to seeing it go out. David Gilmour's got to be the best guitarist ever, well, apart from Hendrix and Brian May and a few others. Audience were a bit crazy.'

'There you go boys.' The barman placed two dripping pints on the counter.

'Cheers Jack, this is the best part of the day.' Billy took the glasses and sat down.

Ever since they had discovered *The Moon*, as they referred to it, they'd made the place their own. It wasn't unusual to visit the pub several times a week and always after a show. The walls were festooned with framed photographs of football teams from different eras. On display were the Royal Arsenal football club of 1888 and the FA Cup winners of the same year, Preston North End. There were drawings showing scenes depicting the origins of football: scores of men, like mobs in a street, kicking a stuffed bladder through some squalid medieval market place, with no regard for equal teams or an offside rule. There were many more pictures of teams and scenes from modern day. Alex had even donated a photo of himself with his old school football team.

Hanging resplendent above the bar was a large flag with the cross of St George, patron saint of England and, above that, stretching across the ceiling like the inside of a fisherman's hut, was a net from a goal. But it was no ordinary net. When the original Wembley Stadium had been razed to the ground many artefacts had been sold off. Alex would have liked one of the twin towers but he was lucky enough to make a successful bid for the net into which many famous players had scored.

The boys downed their pints in one and sighed contentedly as they slapped their glasses back onto the counter.

'So, how'd you think it went?' Alex turned to Billy.

'Tell you what, that Millie's a right little tease. I wouldn't mind getting my Speedos on for her...'

'...Oh yeah! Or off!'

41

'I reckon she should interview us in the bath with a big bottle of bubbly. How hard would that be?'

Alex giggled, relieved that another cracking show was on tape. 'Nice idea. We'll have to run it by Lizzie – when she's not pulling her hair out.'

'What d'ya think of that German bloke?'

'I dunno,' Alex shook his head, 'I wasn't impressed; it looked like one big simulation to me.'

'Yeah, he could've just faked the whole bloody lot. I might've believed him though, if he'd said that Geoff Hurst really scored.'

'Still it was one hell of a computer game,' Alex looked up to Jack, 'Line us up two more of the Shepherd Neame and let's have some of them pork scratchings. Cheers mate.'

'Alright boys, coming up.'

Billy sank his chin into the palm of his hand, 'Do you fancy dropping into Stringfellow's later? We haven't hit that place for a while.'

'Sounds good to me Billy-boy, it was a right scream last time. Remember Zoe and Fatima?'

'Oh yeah!' Billy winked.

'Pete gave us a bottle of that Dom Perignon. Let's get a tune on; it's a bit dead in here.'

He pushed back his stool with a screech and sauntered over to the jukebox. The vintage Seeburg was a splash of colour in the gloomy pub which stood out in stark contrast to the football memorabilia all around. Alex ran his eyes down the selection and picked a track. Being loyal customers, Jack had allowed Alex and Billy to add some of their own music to the collection. Predictably, Alex chose a Pink Floyd track; it was all he ever listened to these days.

The distinctive sound of a cash register crashed and chattered as the intro began. As Alex and Billy started to sing, the man in the corner gave a sideways glance and shifted his position with a rustle of his newspaper. Jack knew when it was time to take cover out the back.

'Money, get away
Get a good job with more pay

And you're okay
Money, it's a gas
Grab the cash with both hands
And make a stash
New car, caviar
Four star day dream
Think I'll buy me a football team...'

'Talking of which,' Alex said, 'what do you make of this?' He slapped a coin on the table and Billy picked it up.

'This is old money,' Billy said, turning the coin over in his fingers.'

'It's pre-decimal,' Alex replied. 'Look, *1966.*'

'Still looks new.'

'It's a half-crown – that's two and six in old money – or twelve and a half pence.'

'Blimey, you know your stuff.'

'Grandpa used to show me his old coins. There were 240 pence in a pound, so eight of these made a quid.'

'Thank God for *MasterCard*. It must've been like carrying a pocket full of shrapnel around. Where'd you get it?'

'Someone gave it to me.'

'How many beers would that've bought in '66?'

Without warning a deep voice interrupted them.

'You could've bought yourself a pint each and still have change for scratchings.'

Alex and Billy turned in surprise. It was the man behind the paper who had spoken. His voice had a cutting edge that was vaguely familiar. He crumpled the Evening Standard on the table and standing up walked over to Alex and Billy.

He towered over them as he approached. He wore an ill-fitting grey suit, under which was a black shirt open at the collar; his head was shaved and he had several days of stubble. His eyes were intensely dark and, as he stared down at them, it seemed he didn't blink.

'Gentlemen,' he paused, 'we meet again.'

The lads looked blankly at each other.

'Uh, yeah,' stammered Alex, 'I can't say I remember you. But if it's about my Tax Return – I'm filing it online – *tonight*.'

'Warwick Vane,' he said flatly as he pulled a stool over and sat with his arms folded. 'Let me remind you Alex. We met not so long ago and I asked you a question but you didn't give me a straight answer. So let me ask you again, under, um, less restricting circumstances.'

'Fire away,' Alex responded, and all the time thinking: *Who is this jerk? Where have I heard that accent before?*

'Gentlemen, you may not dream of living in a prefab in Bognor but you do dream of re-living a famous soccer game.' He was silent for a second looking at each of them in turn with his deep, dark, unblinking eyes, waiting for his comment to sink in.

Alex couldn't place his face. *Bognor* sounded familiar? So did the Chicago accent.

'So my friends, just how would you change the result of that final at Wembley, given half a chance and, maybe, half-a-crown?'

Billy gulped on his beer and Alex flinched.

'It's *you*! In the audience – that was a shit question.'

'Well Alex, that shit question still stands. And if you're in any way interested in changing the result of the game, well, perhaps this ugly bloke can help you in some way.'

'What're you talking about?' Billy scoffed.

'It doesn't have to stay 4-2 to West Germany forever. If you really wanted – you could change it!'

'Crap,' retorted Alex, 'have you had too much of Jack's beer?'

'On the contrary, my head is very clear, and so, I think, is my question. If I were to offer you a way of changing the result of England's biggest ever game, would you take it?'

'I don't get what you're trying to say. Are we to re-write every newspaper and scrub every film that's ever been made?'

'No, it's much easier than that Alex. All you have to do is return to the scene in question, and with a bit of invention, you can change history. Or perhaps it would be more diplomatic to say, *correct it.*'

'Oh yeah, you and H G Wells! Or is this some new blockbuster from Steven bloody Spielberg?' Alex was beginning to find the American obnoxious.

'Haven't you heard about *time-slips*, my friends? They happen everywhere.'

As Alex stared at Warwick Vane, he was reminded of a leathery mafia type from the movies. His lizard eyes were becoming more irritating every second. But Alex decided to play along just a little longer.

'*Time-slips*! Okay, humour me. Tell me all about time-slips.'

Warwick Vane looked down into his beer and took a short breath; his nostrils flared.

'Gentlemen, football is the beautiful game we know. The rules are simple, the objective is clear; the sides are balanced. The game has developed and evolved over hundreds of years. Eleven competitors must pit their skill against another team. The intention is to move a spherical object of defined proportion, composition and mass in such a way as to out-wit and out-manoeuvre the opposition and attempt to place that sphere into a specified target. The other team must attempt to prevent this happening while at the same time trying to place the same sphere into an identical orifice...'

'...*Goal*,' interrupted Alex. 'You mean *goal*...and *ball*.' And Alex thought, *God this bloke's a prat!*

'Exactly. And Newtonian laws of motion apply in this situation. The strategy is intriguing. The simplicity is poetic. The result is unpredictable – but always within a controlled frame of reference. The game owes more to chance and probability than any formulated plan. Football, as we know it, has thrilled billions for over a hundred years. It is a common language.'

Alex took another sip and wished he had not come into The Moon. Jack was wiping down the tables at the far end of the room while occasionally glancing towards the three men, suspicious of his new customer.

'On the other hand,' Vane went on, 'the universe in which we live may appear predictable; ticking like a clock, but it conceals a place full of surprises. We exist in a strange world where nothing is what it seems and nothing is certain anymore. You could walk out of this door and an infinite number of possibilities could come your way. We're finding rules that change, nature that can hide, and goalposts that can move. We're in a world described by mathematics – and the realm of quantum mechanics applies.

'Look at your pint. All your beer is in the glass. But in a universe ruled by quantum mechanics there is a probability of finding some of your beer outside the glass. And I don't mean to say you've spilt it!'

'There's also quite a lot inside me,' Alex snapped, 'which I find is a very natural realm for beer. Look – all this is very entertaining Mr Vane and makes for a good pub chat but what's the bloody point?'

The American was unflustered. 'Alex, we live in two worlds. The ordinary, everyday world we see around us and also a shadow world just out of sight. But sometimes these two worlds collide.

'Stories are rife of people stumbling upon strange out-of-place places which shouldn't be there. Or unusual atmospheric conditions which seem to cause time to change or time to be lost.'

Warwick Vane noisily gulped his beer and wiped his mouth clumsily.

'Boys, let me tell you this: Four English tourists were driving through France when they found a place in Montelimar for an overnight stay. The hotel seemed a bit old fashioned, almost like a working museum, they said. The staff were dressed in clothes which seemed from another age, and the local gendarme they spoke to didn't know about the local motorway. In the morning they went on their way. On their return journey, try as they might, they couldn't find the hotel – it just wasn't there.

'On June 1st 1974, Lesley Brennan was watching a movie on TV around midday. The programme was rudely interrupted by a newsflash about an explosion at the nearby *Nypro* manufacturing plant in Lincolnshire. Lesley's friends Janice and Peter East swung by soon after and she told them about the disaster. But later, on the evening news, the explosion was said to have happened at 5pm. Lesley couldn't believe they got it so wrong. The next day all the papers and TV ran the story. Twenty-eight people had been killed when the plant had blown-up at 4:53pm. It happened five hours after Lesley and her friends had heard. Explain that time shift!'

'How do you remember all this stuff?' asked Billy who was following everything the American was saying. Alex was more distant; a sceptical frown creased his face.

Vane didn't blink, 'It's in my best interest.

'In '96, a security guard was watching the monitors one night in Florida when he saw a factory worker outside become engulfed in a strange glow. The cameras showed the man disappearing. There one minute, the next, gone. A search couldn't find him anywhere. Then two hours later, a flash was seen again and they found him collapsed on the ground. All caught on CCTV. Now where did he go?'

'You tell me?' stammered Billy.

Warwick Vane gave a rare smile. Billy was now hanging on his every word.

'Two children, Angela and Bernard, were walking on a hillside near Manchester in 1942. They met two men in what looked like bright clothing. The men spoke of many things that would happen to the kids and they explained they'd come from far away. The kids drifted into sleep but on waking they walked home to find they'd been gone, not for the two hours they'd thought, but for more than a day. They didn't even see the night come and go.

'On the Chilean hills in 1977, an army exercise was underway when some lights appeared one morning. Corporal Armando Valdes went to investigate thinking it was a simulated attack. As he closed in on the lights he just vanished; his platoon can vouch for that. But then just minutes later he walked in from behind them; he was dazed, confused and disorientated. Later they found his watch had moved on *five* days. He was also sporting several days of designer beard. And there's more…I could go on.'

'Must you?' Alex muttered under his breath. 'Surely these are just urban myths told in pubs the world over!'

'Gentlemen,' Warwick Vane continued, unblinking, 'these are just some of the hundreds of time violations on record. I could carry on until you become convinced, but I return to my original offer. We've learnt more – so much more. We've found a way to overcome the barriers of time, but I'll say no more for now. If you really want to take a ride, there's a ticket waiting for you.'

Billy glanced at Alex with wide eyes; he looked like he was starting to believe. Alex gave a shrug; he was not convinced. His immediate thought was for another pint.

'Mr Vane, I'm beginning to find this rather boring and tedious and full of crap and all I want is a beer.' Alex banged his glass hard onto the table. 'If it's some show you're looking for to present your absurd theories, you'd better look elsewhere! We don't do science fiction.'

Vane rose with a scrape of his stool and towered over them.

'Think about this – just how long is the present – the here and now? It lasts no time at all; well, give or take *Planck-time*. There's only the past and who knows, maybe the future. Think about it – but don't take all day. Perhaps there's a ring of truth in that old adage: *no time like the present*.' He stopped and without blinking held the gaze of the young TV presenters. 'Even soccer players can go outside the pitch to keep the ball in play!

'We'll talk again.'

The tall American placed the wide-brimmed hat securely on his head and, walking to the door, slammed it behind him.

Alex looked at Billy. 'The guy's a mental case; he hasn't got a clue. Anyone knows what *plankton* is. I got an A-star in biology!'

'The bloke's stoned,' Billy added. 'That's the biggest load of garbage I've heard.' Having been drawn into Warwick Vane's stories Billy now sided with his friend.

'You looked like you were starting to believe him!'

As Billy began to protest, Alex fixed him a serious stare.

'I don't know what he's on Billy, but it won't be our show. I'm having a whisky, d'ya want one?'

'Nah, not for me, I've gotta go and get changed,' he said, pulling on his track-suit top. 'Alright, see you outside Stringy's – 'bout ten?'

'Sure thing mate, I'll be there…barring a timewarp.' Alex grinned.

Billy left a note on the counter, gave Jack a nod and walked out of the pub.

Alex sat brooding. There was something deep down playing on his mind but he couldn't put a finger on it. The appearance of Warwick Vane had unnerved him. To see him twice in one day was twice too many as far as he was concerned. *It's just not hanging together, why should he want to gate-crash our show?* His train of thought drifted.

The shiny half-crown lay there on the table beside his glass. He picked it up and spun it round on the table watching it rotate. He could see both sides of the coin superimposed. *Can I see two worlds at the same time?* Gravity finally slowed its spin and just before it fell flat, Alex slapped his hand over the coin with a smack.

'Heads,' he said and with a swig of his whisky, he began mumbling more of the song he was singing earlier with Billy.

'Money, get back
I'm alright Jack
Keep your hands off of my stack
Money, it's a hit
But don't give me that do goody good bullshit…'

His voice trailed off as his eyes were drawn to the photographs on the sepia wall. He homed in on one picture and standing up walked over towards it. He stared at the image as if trying to remember some forgotten detail. There he was. On the front row of the Under-15s school football team: Alex the left-wing back.

The day flooded back. The sun was already high in the sky and there was a palpable sense of anticipation and the sweet smell of grass cuttings. His grandfather had just mown the lawn. Summer had come early.

'Get in the car Alex.'

I wish Dad was here, he thought. *He'd be well proud.*

Alex had spent most of the morning polishing his boots and thinking about the match. Butterflies were fluttering in his stomach. He picked up his bag, slung it onto the back seat and got into his grandfather's blue Ford Focus. It was going to be a great day, he thought, when he would run onto the pitch to play in the West London Schools' Final. Abby Hart was going to be there.

As the team warmed up in the penalty area, passing the ball, joking, swearing, being abusive and casting nervous glances at the other team, Alex caught sight of her. She stood beside the touchline with some of her girlfriends, her dark glossy hair falling over slim shoulders. His heart leapt.

It was a beautiful day in early May when the game got underway. Parents were standing next to local dignitaries and newspaper reporters but, more than anything, it was Abby looking on that caused Alex to run and play for every ball, every tackle, every header, every last shot. He'd seen her earlier in the day and told her he wanted to give her his medal, like a knight offering the lady his favour.

The game was close and tense and those watching cheered and jeered and heckled the referee. There were near misses and good goalkeeping but, late into the second half, Alex sent a low pass into the penalty area and team captain Ross Beaumont was onto it. Just as he was about to shoot, a huge defender brought him down and he writhed in agony. The referee blew; it was a clear penalty. Ross, the regular dead-ball specialist was badly hurt and he limped off the pitch for treatment.

'You'll have to take it Alex.' He winced in pain.

Alex placed the ball on the whitewashed penalty spot. He could feel his heart pounding inside his chest. He sized-up the goalkeeper, a lanky teenager in a dazzling orange shirt. His long limbs seemed to fill the goal like a spider on a cobweb, agile and ready to pounce. Then the referee blew his whistle.

His eyes were fixed on the ball, but as he ran towards it, Alex's thoughts fleetingly found an image of Abby. It just entered his mind without warning. He saw her brown eyes and olive skin and became acutely aware that she was watching nearby. He struck the ball sweetly with his left foot and it flew like a guided missile. But the tall goalkeeper was equal to it and was down in a flash and his desperate lunge deflected the shot away for a corner. It was a brilliant save and his teammates rewarded him with high-fives and whoops of delight.

Alex collapsed on the ground in a heap. All he could see was Abby's angelic face. He had let her down. He covered his head to block out the cheers from the other team; his face buried in the grass, trying to let its intoxicating aroma overwhelm his disappointment.

The vacant face in the photograph did not show the pain that the boy felt that day. Alex stood there and remembered it as if it were yesterday. He glanced down nervously at the striated scar on the palm of his hand and began rubbing it as if to bring him some comfort.

Alex recalled the words his grandfather had said to him after the match as he sniffled in the arms of his hero: 'It's not what you do in life Alex; it's what you make of it.' Grandpa Bell had hugged him and held him until much of the dismay had faded. It had been a pivotal moment in his life.

Suddenly the phone on the wall was ringing like a pneumatic drill. Alex took a sharp intake of breath and ran his hands through his lank hair. He felt like he'd been stunned from a dream.

'Jack, phone...Jack.'

Alex looked around. The barman wasn't behind the counter and he found himself alone in the pub. There was something strange about the air in the room. It didn't feel right. It was darker and the jukebox seemed to be glowing brighter. Still it rang. He walked over to the phone and snatched up the old handset.

'Yes.' The line was silent apart from some background hiss. 'Hello?'

'Alex, it's me, Billy.'

'Billy, what is it?'

'Um, dunno really.' His voice was tense, thin and just audible.

'What time is it? Are you at Stringy's?'

'No...no, forget Stringy's. Listen something's come up.'

'What?'

There was an awkward silence.

'Come on Billy, what's going on?'

'It's... um...urgent!'

'What do you mean *urgent*? Where are you?'

'Alex, listen. They'll be round for you. Just do as they say.'

'Billy don't piss around. What're you talking about?' He took a nervous look at the deserted lounge. 'What time is it anyway?'

'It's gone eleven ...' Billy's voice was torn away and the line went dead.

'Billy ... *Billy*.' No answer. He slammed the phone down. 'Eleven! What do you mean *eleven*? Jack, where the hell are you?'

The only sound he heard came from the off-station radio on the bar. He looked up at the high windows. It was pitch black outside.

Alex felt inside his jacket pocket and pulled out a white plastic tub he'd picked up from his locker at the studio. His hands shook as he ripped off the ring-pull tab and popped in a couple of tablets. The Zydis formulation dissolved as soon as the caplets hit his tongue. He felt no better.

This is mental, how can it be eleven?

A hiss of white noise sounded like a rush of tinnitus coming from the radio. He tuned the dial on the Roberts wireless and found an acoustic guitar playing gently.

The pub door opened and Alex spun round. A tall man, smartly dressed, stood framed in the doorway. His long black hair was tied back in a ponytail and strangely he wore dark glasses at this late hour. Alex raised his eyebrows at him.

'Mr Bell, you're expecting us. Mr Gunn has spoken to you.'

'Who the hell are you? What do you want?'

'All will be explained in great detail. As Mr Gunn said, *it's urgent.*'

'*Urgent*!' repeated Alex. 'Why's everything so bloody urgent all of a sudden?'

Alex, get under control, he told himself. *Deep breaths.*

'The car's outside Mr Bell.' The chauffeur spoke tersely and left without saying more.

Alex looked again for Jack, and hoping the medication would soon start working, began to teeter slowly towards the door. *This is crazy, but at least I might get a lift home.*

He stepped out through the pub entrance and into the cold night air of the dark side of The Moon.

4

Raindrops ran like tiny rivers down the window and fanned into streaks as the limousine surged forward. Alex Bell peered out. He saw only distorted images streaming by like the confused thoughts inside his head. *What's happening to me?* Blurred and bleeding lights from passing bars, street lamps and traffic lights morphed together in a dizzying prism of colour, fusing like the ever-changing patterns inside a kaleidoscope. The dreamscape only seemed enhanced by the alcohol in his bloodstream and a twinge of nausea in his stomach.

'We've been worried about you Alex.'

He turned to look at the attractive woman sitting opposite. The ambient glow of the Daimler's plush interior gave a halo effect round her lean brown body. When she crossed her strong legs and placed her hands in her lap, Alex could see how well she wore the navy Armani suit. Her hair was darker than his, raven black and her voice soft with no trace of accent.

Alex looked into her deep green eyes and he realised that although he had never met this woman before, the circumstances seemed strangely familiar. He was reminded of a cameo scene from some old film; but he couldn't place the movie.

'We feel the time has come to act now.'

'What do you mean?' asked Alex. He had no idea what she was talking about.

'You're being followed.'

'By who?'

'We're not certain.'

'Are you the police?'

'No.'

Alex looked down in frustration and squeezed his forehead. *Why am I being driven through London in some luxury car?* The alcohol blazing through his brain did nothing to clarify his thoughts, or help his headache.

'All will be explained soon enough Alex. Trust me.'

'I don't even know who you are.' He tried to guess her age, thirty, forty? He couldn't tell.

'Victoria Trevelyan.' Her voice was refined; she had the air of a professional business woman. 'I want to help you Alex.'

'I don't need help.'

'You will do.' She held his gaze. 'Have you been aware of anyone watching you?'

'Can't say I have.'

'Have any strangers tried to get in touch with you?'

'Nope.' It was a quick answer. Then he remembered what had happened a month ago when he'd arrived home after covering a story in the Stade de France in Paris. He'd pushed the key into the front door on the stroke of midnight. Thinking about drinking a chilled beer from his fridge, he'd let his bag fall to the floor. But the moment he began walking up the stairs, something felt very wrong.

'What the ...' he'd trodden on something in the dark, almost tripping over. When he flicked on the light he saw his favourite sports books were strewn across the landing. 'What's this all about?'

'I had a break in,' Alex revealed to Victoria Trevelyan. 'A few weeks ago,'

'Yes, you called your sister, and then Billy, but they knew nothing.'

'That's right. How do you ...'

'We know.'

'Nothing was taken – as far as I could tell – not even my Fender Strat signed by David Gilmour. It was still hanging on the wall in the front room.'

'You may just have been unlucky; perhaps someone doing drugs – or looking for them. But there could have been more to it.'

Alex looked bleakly through the rain-smeared window. He blew out slowly through pursed lips and shook his head. He couldn't even place the part of London they were driving through. *Docklands*, he thought, although he could see no sign of the skyscraper, Canary Wharf, a landmark visible for miles around.

What's going on? Why had the pills not kicked in? Too many questions.

Just as he'd decided to thank this Victoria for the ride and ask to be dropped home, he felt the car make a sudden turn and descend a steep incline. In front he saw a high brick wall blocking the way; it was covered with elaborate graffiti. As they approached, the entire section began to slide sideways until it retracted out of sight. The gloomy skyline became darker and then disappeared altogether as the car continued down the ramp and drove underground. Looking beyond the chauffeur, Alex could make out a long concrete tunnel stretching ahead in the glare of the car's headlights.

'Welcome to Trinity, Alex.'

5

The concrete tunnel was featureless. All Alex could make out was a monotonous grey wall passing by on either side. He lifted his wrist up to the light, but then remembered he didn't have his watch on or his mobile phone. He felt helpless without either. It was impossible to tell how long they'd been travelling. Amber lights suddenly flickered overhead. The interior of the car became golden and Victoria Trevelyan smiled at Alex, her volcanic eyes flashing. To his embarrassment, Alex flushed like a schoolboy and tore his gaze away. He was not prepared to be entrapped by her deadly lava.

'What's Trinity?' he snapped, turning to look out the rear window.

The tunnel's perspective closed towards a vanishing point that seemed a long distance behind. *When we stop, I'll do a runner. But where to?*

'You'll find out soon enough Alex.' Victoria spoke softly. 'Here we are.' Her green eyes smouldered with a look that Alex found sexually intimidating.

The car swung from the tunnel into what resembled a massive underground aircraft hangar. A huge gate descended behind the car like a portcullis, sealing them in. Everything was dazzling white.

'Let's go,' Victoria sounded business-like.

Alex opened the door and stepped out frowning as he looked around. His first impression was that the clinical surroundings seemed to be matched by the strange odours of disinfectant and organic solvents. *The loading bay of a hospital?*

He noticed the rubberised marks of tyre tread on the white floor showing that the Daimler had already used this place as a turning circle. He slammed the car door and the boom reverberated.

'Follow me Alex.' Victoria led him to a short flight of steps; her heels clicking loudly on the concrete. He hadn't realised how tall she was and couldn't help but notice how tightly her skirt hugged her shapely thighs. She reminded him of an athlete from Jamaica he'd once interviewed.

They reached a walkway that ran along one side. In the far corner a door glided sideways as they approached. The corridor beyond was less glaring, it felt warmer and Alex heard a muted hum. A man, observing their approach, sat in yellow overalls on an electric vehicle like a golf buggy.

'Hop on Alex, this ride won't be quite so far.'

They climbed up and sat side by side behind the man in yellow and the cart pulled away without a sound.

The corridor stretched ahead. On either side were large rectangular windows, some had blinds that were closed. Alex thought they could be laboratories as he saw people dressed in yellow overalls moving around. Some rooms were filled with electronic equipment; others were empty. In one unit he saw a group of workers piecing together what appeared to be a large metal object on a long bench. It was composed of many silver-grey fragments of differing shape and size. They were trying to put it together like a large jigsaw puzzle. In another bay, a team seemed to be examining a body on an operating table. One or two people were distracted and looked out into the corridor. As the buggy passed by, Alex squinted to look closer but the blinds quickly blinked shut concealing everything inside.

'What's going on here?'

'Trinity is a research organisation, Alex, with fingers in many pies. Privately funded...'

'I've never heard of it.'

'I'm not surprised. That's because it doesn't officially exist.'

Alex nodded his head and winked. 'Oh yeah! Just like the Ark of the Covenant.'

'Now that's another story altogether.'

'... And that UFO incident at Roswell.'

'Steady on Alex, you can't believe everything you read on the internet. We're talking about reality here. Let's take the elevator.'

They had been riding on the electric cart for a few minutes when the driver came to a stop and Victoria stepped onto the polished floor. Under the lights her navy suit had a glossy sheen which drew Alex's attention as she moved with an elegant stride.

'Come on Alex, we're going down.'

'*Down*! How low can we go?' It was a deep-seated phobia that came back to him.

Alex had a fear of enclosed spaces ever since he'd fallen down a disused well-shaft playing with friends. He was five. Thankfully his grandfather and a long ladder came to the rescue after someone had raised the alarm. Only his pride had been hurt, but he had never forgotten it. Since then he'd always taken the stairs.

The elevator was lined with mirrors on all sides, including the floor and ceiling. Alex felt he was at the centre of a virtual universe. Rows of tiny pinpoint lights added to the impression that they were standing inside a thousand cubes. Everywhere he looked he saw himself and Victoria stretching away in all directions towards infinity. It was a Cartesian illusion that began to give him vertigo the more he stared. His stomach jumped as he felt an impulsive jolt when the lift moved. His eyes were tired, his skin clammy. Alex just managed to resist holding on to Victoria's arm to avoid losing his balance. A moment later he sensed the elevator slow and the door slid open to reveal another corridor that was reassuringly solid and stationary.

He let out a sigh and coughed with sarcastic relief, 'Wow, Disney rides too!'

They walked into another spotless corridor identical to the one in which they had just been but with a notable exception. Spanning almost the entire length of one wall, Alex saw what he first took to be a continuous cartoon, like those in a child's comic. But then he realised what it was.

'I know this,' he said, waving a finger in the air. 'It's that tapestry. The French one.'

'The *Bayeux* Tapestry,' clarified Victoria. 'This is a copy of course. The original's in the Musée de la Tapisserie in Bayeux. As you can see it runs almost the length of a football pitch: 230 feet long and twenty inches high.'

She continued in the manner of a tour guide, 'It shows 72 scenes which tell the story of how William of Normandy defeated the Saxon King, Harold II of England. And it's not here just to decorate the corridor.'

'You know a lot about this stuff.'

'I should do, it's one of my pet projects,' she said looking over to Alex as they walked along. 'This is like an early documentary. It gives the whole account in chronological order but it's this scene over here that interests me most.'

Alex looked fleetingly at the colourful images as he passed by. There were many inscriptions in Latin but he had no idea what they meant. He followed Victoria until they reached a section of the tapestry that was being examined by two young women.

'Look at this Alex,' she said, pointing her manicured fingers over a section.

He saw what looked like someone on a throne being attended by a servant.

'I'm guessing,' he said, 'that's the king as it says *Harold* right above him.'

'Inspired deduction,' replied Victoria, 'you'll make a historian yet.'

Alex saw that to the monarch's left were a group of men observing the sky. Next to the inscription *Istimirant Stella* was a strange object.

'Halley's Comet,' said Victoria, seeing what he was looking at. 'Or that's what history would have us believe.

Traditionally, comets are said to be harbingers of bad tidings, bringing catastrophes of biblical proportions. This apparition did not disappoint. The year was 1066 when the Normans, led by William, invaded the south of England. They were met by Harold in a place called Battle.'

'It had the right name. Shame it wasn't *Middle Wallop* – we might've won!'

'*Battle* wasn't the name at the time. The invasion happened on open land just north of Hastings. Every year enthusiasts re-enact it. A great day out and very interesting; I've seen it myself – and they throw in falconry, beer, and pigs on spits just for good measure. Now, Harold had brought with him, by comparison, a poorly equipped army. As it turned out, it was a rout. William had horses and bowmen that could launch a volley right into the heart of the English army. Harold caught one in the eye, and the rest as they say is ...'

'...History,' finished Alex.

'Well actually it was *his story*,' Victoria pointed a finger at King William. 'But it's not just the invasion that interests me. It's the comet.' She tapped the strange image in the sky.

'Why?'

'It was the English astronomer, Edmond Halley, a friend of Sir Isaac Newton, who gave his name to this long distance traveller. He worked out that the comets seen in 1531 and 1607 were one and the same; as was the comet he'd seen in 1682. It was just on a celestial merry-go-round, swinging by the sun like a boomerang and then heading back into space to lay dormant in the far reaches of the solar system. In other words, it was returning every 76 years – give or take a year. He speculated that it would again be seen in 1759. Although Halley died before that, his prediction turned out to be spectacularly true. So in his honour, they named the wanderer after him when it duly arrived back in the skies that very year.'

She looked again at the mural spread along the wall. 'But there's one little problem.'

'What's that?' Alex was intrigued.

'Is this image in the Bayeux Tapestry *really* Halley's Comet?'

'What d'you mean?'

'Halley's Comet was last seen in 1986 – and I remember looking at it from my own backyard through a pair of binoculars. It wasn't very impressive, just a fuzzy smudge that hung around for a few weeks. So from 1986, if you count back 76 years to 1910 then 1834 and so on, the nearest date to 1066 would be 1074. That's eight years out. Good sightings of the comet were also recorded in 66 AD and 240 BC. But counting forward in cycles of 76 years you come to 1061. Again, not very close.'

She paused, allowing Alex to digest what she had said; then she carried on. 'So what apparition *was* seen in the sky in the year of the French invasion?'

'I haven't got a clue.'

'Good answer! We're not entirely sure either. And that's what we're working on.' She sighed and turned away from the tapestry. 'Time to go Alex, there are some people I want you to meet.'

As they walked along a pristine corridor, Alex was confused as to why he was here in a place he never knew existed and which seemed to sprawl for miles below London. They turned a corner to reveal a brightly-lit area that opened up into a huge atrium. A fountain spouted in the centre, trickling water over rounded rocks. There was a piazza with terracotta tiles surrounded by white tables and colourful parasols where people were milling around talking and eating salads and pastries and drinking fruit cocktails. Alex looked around in disbelief. Victoria took his arm and led him across the tiled precinct, over to a circular table beside some plants and a large overhanging palm. A man sat in one corner strumming a Spanish guitar.

'It may be gone midnight Alex but we've still got a skeleton crew working in Trinity.'

Some men at a table turned round as they approached.

'I believe you've already met these gentlemen.' She waved her hand in the direction of the group seated at the table. 'This is Warwick Vane, Dr Ralf Schneider and, of course, you know Billy.'

6

Alex needed a large cappuccino and a cinnamon bagel filled with cream cheese and smoked salmon before he attempted to make any sense of what was happening. He devoured it like a ravenous wolf. Pork scratchings aside, it was hours since he'd last eaten anything wholesome.

'As you can see Alex, I said we'd get to talk again.' Warwick Vane itched his stubbled chin and stared with unblinking eyes.

'Let's hope you make more sense this time,' he replied wiping his mouth. Alex found his gangster accent infuriating. His regard for the unshaven American had not wavered since their last exchange in The Moon. He remembered all too clearly the absurd stories with which Vane had tried to convince him how time itself could move, bend and slow down. *What does this jerk want now? And that German academic, Schneider, for that matter?* His mind was sharper now that the alcohol had been metabolised.

'Perhaps this time Alex, you'll give me a little more attention.'

'Well gentlemen,' interrupted Victoria with authority and wanting to avoid a confrontation in the atrium, 'I'd like to get you guys into a slightly more appropriate forum. We've got a few things to talk about and Ralf has a demo that I think you'll find very interesting. There's more to Trinity than comets and cappuccinos Alex.'

The plain yellow door gave no clue about what lay beyond. A modest sign above it seemed to hint at the extent of research being conducted within Trinity: *Area 66*.

'Looks like some place, eh?' Billy said to Alex in a hushed voice, nervously twitching his freckled nose.

'Yeah, like a weird James Bond set or something.'

'Who knows, we might even run into Q!'

'No guesses who's M then,' Alex said glancing towards Victoria who was tapping in a security code on the panel beside the door. 'So what's the big deal; what's going on Billy?'

Billy shook his head vehemently to impress Alex that he really didn't know any more than him. 'I dunno. They've kept me in the dark. Schneider mentioned earlier that he wanted to take us to a footy game.'

'I can live with that!'

'Yeah, but this game's in the old Wembley stadium.'

Alex looked confused. 'Blimey!'

'In you go guys.' Victoria beckoned with a wave of her long fingers.

Alex had expected to see something spectacular behind the yellow door. Instead they walked into what appeared to be an ordinary boardroom. There was a large elliptical oak table surrounded by twelve leather chairs neatly spaced; the lighting was sombre.

'Sit down please,' invited Victoria. 'Warwick you have the floor.'

'Thanks.' He stood up and threw his grey jacket onto the back of a chair; his black shirt was just as creased. Rolling up his sleeves he scratched his chin with a chewed fingernail and cleared his throat.

'Alex and Billy, it was good to talk to you in The Moon yesterday. However, our conversation was too damn brief. There were other things I had to tell you, so hopefully I've now got your full attention.'

Alex began to switch off.

Warwick Vane picked up a remote control and, aiming it towards the wall behind him, gave it a shake like a wand. An image of earth seen from space came into view. Swirling clouds, blue oceans and coloured lands could be seen framed against a starless backdrop.

'I want to talk about a spaceship – and this is no exotic craft allegedly crashed in some desert with the loss of alien crew and all evidence. This is one where we have actual proof of its existence. It carries many beings and we've seen them. It's travelled through space; it's travelled through time. It's a most extraordinary and wonderful vehicle. This unique transport system carries seven billion passengers. They are you and me and the entire human race. I'm talking about spaceship earth.'

He gestured towards the gibbous planet filling the wall like a stained-glass window in a bible-black surround.

'It's a time-machine. The passing of time on this ark slows by one second every three weeks and by fifteen seconds each year. Because of its movement through space, in four years the earth and all its teeming inhabitants will have lost one minute of time. Time-travel is happening. That's a fact. And this is what I want to talk to you about.'

Alex shifted uncomfortably and rolled his eyes. A feeling like jet-lag drained his body, and the thought of another one of Vane's lectures left him cold. All he wanted to do was crawl into bed and sleep for twelve hours. It was only the slug of caffeine which was keeping him going at the moment. Billy, however, looked seriously interested. Warwick Vane continued as his Chicago accent cut through the boardroom.

Here we go! Alex sensed what was coming.

'On August 15, 1943, at the height of World War II, a remarkable experiment took place. It was to change the way scientists would view the universe forever. It was called *Project Rainbow*.'

He aimed the remote control and a grainy black and white photograph of a small battleship appeared behind him.

'The USS Eldridge was sailing into Delaware Bay on the east coast of the United States; on board were a full crew. Unbeknown to that crew, a secret wartime project was being conducted using the Eldridge. One of the leading scientists involved with Rainbow was an elderly Nikola Tesla, the American pioneer of electric power fields. I don't suppose you've heard of him. But working behind the scenes was the most famous scientist of all, *Albert Einstein.*'

Alex and Billy looked at each other in recognition of his name.

'Special military operations were under the command of John Von Neumann. They were looking into the effect of electromagnetic fields. Absurd as it sounds they wanted to see if they could make a warship *disappear*. It was to be the ultimate camouflage – invisible to the naked eye and also radar. But, as it turned out, things didn't go to plan. In fact, it was a disaster.

'On that morning the generators were powered up. As the intensity of the electric field increased, sailors spoke of their hair standing on end as well as a mild discomfort. But things got worse. They reported noise and vibration; their vision began to blur and the metal walls became transparent and were said to look like red-coloured gelatine. Others said they could actually put their hands through the walls; they lacked any kind of substance. And then the ship vanished.

'Nothing more of the Eldridge was seen again in Delaware Bay. Then twenty-four hours later the destroyer materialises off Norfolk, Virginia, 150 miles south. It was clear that something had gone badly wrong. One hundred and twenty men were missing, forty were dead, many embedded in the metal of the ship. Only twenty-one survived.'

'Sh... you're starting to scare me!' cut in Billy.

'All of this is true and documented. There are numerous books written and a host of sites on the internet. But take some of that stuff with a pinch of salt. There are hundreds of head-cases who want to cash in on the action, each with their own crack-pot theories.

'The military claim no such thing happened of course. They have a more mundane explanation for what went on. Even in recent years the US Navy has dismissed the whole affair saying it was just a routine investigation into degaussing the ship against mines and torpedoes. They say that events have been exaggerated through Chinese whispers and false information.'

Alex sat up suddenly. The caffeine seemed to pump his heart a little faster. 'Trust the Chinese to get involved! Come on Warwick, where's this going?'

'Give me a bit longer Alex. I'm just setting the scene. As I said, this was only the beginning of Rainbow. What happened next was mind-blowing.

'Al Bielek and his brother Duncan were working below deck in the control room of the Eldridge that day. For some reason they were shielded from the electromagnetic forces and not physically affected to the same degree as the men on deck. When the machinery in the control room began arcing they went up top. That's when they saw the chaos. They freaked out. Their first thought was to jump over board. And when they did, they didn't fall in the sea. Instead, they landed on dry land, inside a military camp. Montauk Base on Long Island, New York, to be exact. The strange thing was – they'd been expected.

'They were met by service personnel, one of which they thought they recognised, but they couldn't be sure at first. It was actually John Von Neumann. Yeah, the commander – but he looked very different. He was older, much older than when they'd seen him an hour before. In fact, he was forty years older!

'The truth is, Al and Duncan Bielek were in a military base in *1983*. How Von Neumann knew when and where they would turn up is not known.

'They saw things they'd never seen before: they watched colour TV; they learnt that the Germans had been defeated and they discovered that men had walked on the moon.

'It transpired that in Montauk an initiative called *Phoenix* was underway. A project had actually been set up in readiness for the Bielek brothers to arrive. Once they'd touched down, so to speak, the Bieleks were to get debriefed and then sent straight back – back forty years using a device Montauk had developed. It's rumoured that this machine had been designed by people who had knowledge beyond anything currently available at that time. Where did *they* come from? But that's just conjecture.

'In any case, back they went. Their task was to destroy the equipment on the Eldridge which was causing the technical problems. This they did. They duly arrived back and smashed the crap to smithereens.'

The picture of the USS Eldridge again appeared on the screen.

'On deck, they discovered that their brother was among the casualties. Yeah, there were three brothers on board; they used to do that sort of thing then. Like others, he was stuck fast in the metal of the ship's wall – and he was dying. This was too much for Duncan to cope with and he jumped overboard. He's never been found. He could have gone anywhere – or more likely – *anywhen*!'

Warwick Vane paused and the image of the destroyer faded from the wall. He looked over to Alex and Billy.

'If you want to know more about Rainbow you can read Al Beilek's account. Here's his book.'

Warwick Vane slung a paperback onto the polished surface of the long table. It went spinning across the oak veneer. Alex snapped it up and read the cover.

'*The Philadelphia Experiment*. What's this all about?'

'Gentlemen, I'm telling you this just to let you know that time travel is not only possible – it has happened. The US and British governments won't admit it but the evidence is out there.'

He stared at them without blinking then placed the remote control back on the table to show he'd finished.

Alex butted in, 'What's all this garbage got to do with us? We're just TV presenters!'

Victoria spoke, 'It will be to your advantage to listen to what Trinity has to offer. You will find out soon. Thank you Warwick.'

Alex became pacified when Victoria Trevelyan looked at him with her searching green eyes. He felt spellbound by her presence.

She went on, 'I want to leave aside the concept of *time* for the moment. I suspect that Ralf is going to tell us something that will be far more to your liking. But first of all we need to move next door.' She rose gracefully and walking across the room opened a door. 'This way.'

As they went in they were amazed at what they found.

'This is more like it!' Billy said with a wry smile.

7

They stood inside a large circular room which had no windows. The air-con was set low and Alex felt an immediate chill. The ceiling was domed and cathedral-like. Dull ambient lighting cast a yellow glow on the plain walls, but what drew Alex's attention straightaway was the array of twenty-four footballs evenly spaced around the perimeter of the room. Each one sat on a transparent column and was illuminated like museum exhibits. In the half-light they seemed to float in mid-air.

Alex and Billy gave each other an appreciative glance. They had shared a passion for football ever since a chance meeting at a summer sports camp both aged fourteen. Then for a while their lives had drifted apart only to be reunited when they were chosen to front their popular football show. It seemed like destiny and they had become almost like brothers. Their telepathic chemistry in front of the cameras was now legendary.

'The history of football,' proclaimed Victoria Trevelyan. 'Here we have hard evidence of the key instrument at the heart of the beautiful game.'

They followed her into the room where they saw a raised dais in the centre. Victoria led them up three steps and they stood on the circular platform. The only other object in the chamber was a small touch-screen on an oval desk. When Victoria tapped it the lighting dimmed even lower leaving the balls glowing all around them.

Alex looked at each one in turn as they hovered about five metres away. Some he recognised; some he'd never seen before.

'Over the centuries the shape hasn't changed very much but the dimensions, weight and construction have evolved.'

She touched the screen again. The lighting on every football was lowered except for one.

'This ball is the gold standard in the world at the moment. I'm sure you recognise the livery. In a season it will be out of fashion and replaced with a new design, equally merchandisable. It conforms to regulations that were established in the last century. So, for a size 5 football the circumference must be 27 to 28 inches and the weight 14 to 16 ounces. I'm talking imperial measurements here, in keeping with the country where the specifications were established – *England* of course. Likewise, the dimensions of a football pitch are still described using the old British system of *yards*.'

Victoria gave the touch-pad a gentle prod.

'Going right back in time, here you can see a pig's bladder which would have been inflated by the powerful lungs of a strong man. It's been knotted like a balloon. This ball dates back to the seventeenth century and would have been used by the mob football teams of the day, although team should be used loosely. The sides would compete against each other and run riot through streets and towns. More people would join as the contest went on, possibly hundreds playing on each side. There were no rules and no boundaries and probably no goals either. The bladder you're looking at was found in central London.

'This next ball demonstrates the advances made in the second half of the nineteenth century. A bladder composed of India rubber was inflated with a pump. It was contained inside an outer skin of leather panels sewn together. It was the first truly-round ball.'

As Victoria summarised each ball, Alex listened intently as if he were to be tested later. The hairs on the back of his neck were alert as he followed her lecture on the Lilywhite number 5; a ball which had been used in the inaugural game between Sheffield and London in 1866 after the rules had been drawn up in the Freemasons' Arms in Covent Garden. Alex new the area well. Then there was the Adidas ball called *Telstar*, designed by Richard Buckminster Fuller.

'The design was crafted on good science,' Victoria explained. 'Synthetic chemists have been able to create complex carbon based molecules using this shape. They called it *buckminsterfullerene.*'

'That's a mouthful!' said Billy.

She switched the lighting to yet another ball which began to glow with a pale fluorescence.

'In recent years the number of panels hasn't changed – until this radical new concept. It represents the state-of-the-art in terms of football technology. It has no seams and it's made from a synthetic fabric which resembles leather. It's called the *Spherica* and comes with *SmartTrack* software installed as standard; the most geometrically accurate and aerodynamic ball ever manufactured. Elite soccer players will be able to perform tricks with this ball which almost defy gravity.'

'Hold up,' said Alex, feeling confused, 'I don't remember this one.'

Billy shook his sandy head in agreement.

Alex stepped down from the dais and went over to look more closely. The surface of the ball sparkled with a holographic sheen. He squeezed it and concentric pressure rings with rainbow chiaroscuro colours formed around his fingertips. It was a perfect sphere with no seams or panels that Alex could make out. He could feel that the surface had a stippled texture.

'I've never seen this ball before,' he said, looking back to Victoria. She nodded sagely.

'You will Alex. In a few years it will be used all round the world and the way soccer will be played will change forever.'

'Hey Alex, we could beat Sky with a feature on all this stuff.'

'Yeah, but how we gonna get all these balls out?'

'One thing's for certain,' Victoria said sharply, 'these exhibits are going nowhere. They're unique and much sought after – and the *Spherica* is a secret, details of it must not leave this room.'

'Where did you get it?' asked Billy. 'You can't buy these on eBay!'

'That's classified. However we may have something we *can* lend you. But more of that later. I'd like to show you one last ball. This was the one that started everything.'

She touched the keypad and a black orb became illuminated on its stand.

'This ball is the oldest. It contains a rubberised bladder like those used in footballs more recently. As you can see, it can still be inflated to a reasonable pressure. The panels are geometrically exquisite. If you look close you'll see they are made from circles filled in with curved triangles. The sections fit perfectly and are held together with staples made of gold. The panels are not made of leather, as you'd think; instead they are composed of a polymeric material more like the *Spherica*. The nature of this material is still to be identified. Carbon dating measurements have shown that this object is likely to originate from the mid-eleventh century.

'That, as you know Alex, pins it down to one of my favourite eras: the Norman invasion of Britain. There are records that show some form of primitive soccer was introduced into England around the time of William of Normandy.

'We've also recovered tiny pollen grains that were embedded in the seams between the panels and these have been identified as varieties indigenous to southern England.

'But the existence of this object is a mystery. Because of the nature of its design, it puts it way beyond any technology available a thousand years ago. For that reason it can truly be classified as an *oopart*.'

'A *what*?' asked Alex, raising his eyebrows.

'Oopart – *out of place artefact* – something that shouldn't be there. Gentlemen, this unusual specimen is very likely the genesis of all footballs. It was the very first.'

'Cool!' exclaimed Billy realising the full impact of what he was looking at.

'I'll give you a thousand pounds for it,' Alex said hopefully. When Victoria gave him a curt look and did not reply, he upped his offer. 'Alright, ten thousand!'

'It's not for sale at any price,' Victoria was emphatic. 'This little treasure will never be seen by the general public. It's the Holy Grail of the football world.'

Alex and Billy clutched each other's arms in disbelief and studied the ball as if they would never see it again.

'Too bad,' said Alex eventually. 'It should be on display somewhere, you know, the British Museum, or our show. Where was it found?'

'It was unearthed in a vault beneath one of this country's most impregnable places: the Tower of London.'

Billy was bubbling over with excitement 'Wow, just think, King Willy could've bent this little baby Beckham-like round four men in chain-mail. It doesn't get any better than that!'

Alex nodded, 'Yeah we've gotta upgrade the opening Titles now, Billy. Scrap that Lionheart stuff. Let's have Willy doing a bender outside the Tower – and some hooded geezer lopping the head off a German or Scot. No, not a Scot, we could lose our audience up north – make it a Frenchie.'

'But William came from France.'

'Ah yeah, whatever! Look, I've got to take a leak – all this talk about bladders! That coffee's gone right through me.' He turned to Warwick Vane. 'Where's the gents?'

Alex suddenly felt he needed a break from Trinity. He could think of many other things he'd rather be doing.

As the boys left, Victoria made a sideways glance and began talking in hushed tones. Her eyes sharpened. 'They suspect nothing.'

'Sie sind verbrauchbar.' Schneider replied.

A minute later Alex and Billy were alone and standing next to each other by the urinals. Alex let out a slow sigh and blew the limp hair from his eyes.

'God Billy, it's totally weird. I'm just not sure what to think about all this Trinity crap. That Rainbow nonsense was a load of garbage – you know, disappearing ships and stuff –

but Victoria can tell it straight when it comes to football. We gotta find some way to get that Genesis ball. We'd be like Indiana Jones of the soccer world.' Alex's mind was racing ahead.

'Look,' replied Billy, 'you've seen the balls, I've seen the balls. All we have to do is make copies and run an item on the history of the game. Who needs the originals? We can get pollen nerds in and all sorts of people, even Mr Bucky. We can make out we've found football cave paintings in Brazil.'

'Good shout mate. The papers make it up, so why can't we. We'll be the best footy show ever. I really hate that Lance Bradford on World Cup Countdown.'

They were quiet for a moment as they finished with a shake, then Billy spoke.

'Scary thing happened on the way.'

'What's that?'

'I'd just left The Moon, right, so I thought I'd get some sarnies at Sandra's, 'cos I knew I'd be hungry later. As I went round the corner by The George, all these girls spotted me, you know, they wanted me to sign their tops and stuff.'

'Don't sound that scary!'

'No, that's not it. I signed their things and they cleared off. But then right in front of me was this big guy, ugly bugger he was, with some nasty facial hair. He just stared at me like he wanted to look through my brain. And he said to me, "We know what you're up to – stay out of it," or something like that. I thought he was talking about going to Stringy's. You know, perhaps Pete had a job on, or something. And this bloke was holding a guitar case. He could've had a gun in there!'

'What d'ya do?'

'I got the hell out of there. I hammered it down some side street then passed that Eureka club we went to. I was gonna cut across the green when a black car screeched up in front of me and a door flew open. I thought I was gonna be shot.'

Billy had gone pale in the re-telling of his story. 'It was Warwick Vane. "Get yer butt in", he said.'

Alex nodded his head. 'Yeah, it was the same for me but without the ugly bugger. What's going on?'

'It means we're caught up in some dodgy mess. Who are these people anyway?'

'Yeah the sooner we get out of here the better.'

Their exchange was suddenly interrupted by a noise from the corridor outside. They heard a bump, some heavy feet running and then shouting.

'What the f...?' exclaimed Alex who was immediately distracted. Until then it had been virtually silent inside Trinity.

The noise grew louder and they heard other voices, a shout and more feet running.

'I'm gonna look,' Alex said and he gingerly stepped onto the urinal.

Standing up straight he managed to prise open the latch on the frosted window. Billy joined him on the next urinal and they peered through the gap.

First of all, they could see only the marble floor in the corridor outside, although they could still hear some sort of commotion going on. Then, as the rumpus grew, they saw feet appearing in their narrow field of view. Some wore yellow overalls; others had leather boots. Men were shouting.

'Get them in.'

'Move 'em.'

'Don't let them go.'

Then Alex and Billy heard other voices.

'Le roi vient.'

'Il surmontera.'

'Le sang fonctionnera com des fleuves au-dessus de l'Angleterre.'

Alex whispered, 'Is that French?'

'Sounds like weird French to me.'

Then they saw a man wearing boots kicking out at someone in yellow. A huge kafuffle began as five or six men in overalls descended in a heap on two others in leather garb and brought them down with a thud onto the polished floor. Alex and Billy saw what appeared to be two men dressed like warriors. They had heavy fabric trousers tucked into their boots. Their jackets were made of dark leather over which they wore a corselet of fine chain mail. On their heads they had dull, bronze-coloured helmets. One fell off and rolled along the floor revealing his long brown hair. His skin was olive, his eyes dark, almost black.

'Il y aura de vengeance,' he was shouting, as if his life depended on it.

After struggling for a few minutes the two warriors were over-powered as reinforcements from Trinity's yellow overall brigade arrived. As the two foreigners were quelled and led away, they were still uttering spirited cries of resistance.

Then it became quiet.

'What the hell was that all about?'

Billy wrinkled his freckled nose. 'Search me. Perhaps they were practising crowd control for the next Millwall game.' He laughed nervously.

'Did you catch anything they said?'

'Nope, I dropped French. They looked old-fashioned; perhaps they were from one of those re-enactment societies?'

'Yeah, Victoria mentioned them earlier! Come on, I suppose we'd better get back before we're missed. Keep an eye out for an escape route.' Alex hopped off the urinal and landed on the tiles.

Billy was slower getting down and the cistern flushed automatically drenching his feet. 'Shit!'

'One way to clean your trainers!' Alex smiled for the first time since arriving in Trinity. 'I use a bidet.'

As they arrived back in the circular room, Billy walked in shiftily, self-conscious of the tide rising up his jeans. Dr Ralf Schneider was standing on the raised platform while Victoria Trevelyan and Warwick Vane stood discussing something heatedly nearby.

'Come up here boys,' he called out. 'There's something I must show you. Last time we met I demonstrated how we were able to reconstruct a 3D rendition of Geoff's much disputed no-goal. Those data were gathered when I worked with the techies at Nuremberg. Things have moved on since I came here to Trinity. I'd like to show you something in a little more detail using *NovoGen* software. Let's go to a game.'

He touched the tiny screen on the table. The ambient lighting in the circular room was reduced to a residual glow. It reminded Alex of a school trip he'd once been on when his Science class were taken to the London Planetarium. He'd been struck by the way the auditorium magically changed and he found himself looking up to a perfectly clear night sky, peppered with thousands of stars. Alex watched Schneider touch a number of menus on the luminous screen. The circular room filled with light and colour in a complete 360-degree panorama and the place was instantly transformed into the most recognisable of all famous sporting amphitheatres.

'Behold, Wembley Stadium.'

8

As soon as he heard the roar of the crowd Alex was there.

He lifted his head and closed his eyes for a second, remembering, breathing deeply. The senses flooded back: the terraces vibrated; the shout of many voices; the drift of smoke; the verdant pastures of Wembley. A memory released.

They had been chanting *En-gland, En-gland* at the first international match he'd ever attended. It was during the Euro tournament in 1996; England was the host nation. *Three Lions On A Shirt* was the anthem, sung with pride all over the country. Much was expected. None more so than when the home team lined up to play Holland – a team full of flair and invention. Alex sang with his father in the stands behind David Seaman's goal. No one could have predicted how the passion from the terraces would spill onto the pitch and ignite one of England's bravest stands. On their day, Holland could beat any team and here they stood on the same turf as the nation that invented football. England wore white – Holland their unique orange. It would be a game full of incident, full of drama, full of goals. Before the game, no punter could have realised how decisive the victory was to be. When Paul Gascoigne and Teddy Sheringham combined with Alan Shearer to score the stunning third goal, Alex was ecstatic. It got even better when the fourth went in. They became known as Sheringham and Shearer, the SAS. They dared to win.

Alex had flung his puny arms aloft and let out a scream of delight. It would rank as one of England's most memorable goals – and it was the 18th June – his birthday.

But then, Alex remembered, in the semi-final, England met Germany. Thirty years had passed since that terrible game on the same battlefield. Would this be a day for revenge? It was one goal each after extra time and it had come to penalties. It went to sudden death; the first team to miss would lose. Then up stepped Gareth Southgate in those drab grey colours they wore that day. Europe watched as the central defender ran forward to take his spot-kick. Oliver Kahn got two strong hands on the ball and parried it away. England were out.

'No, not again!' Alex realised he'd spoken out loud.

Ralf Schneider killed the sound and the atmosphere was broken. Billy coughed and looked around, Alex sighed deeply. They both felt drained by their memories.

The computer scientist began talking, 'That was just for starters. Now, here we are, it's the 30th July 1966. When I showed you this footage last time, I proved that Geoff Hurst's shot did not cross the goal-line, ending the debate which has raged for decades. This time I have a far more powerful tool to explore Wembley. Have a look at the definition. You can see every face in the stadium.'

Billy let out a whistle when he saw the detail of the image.

Ralf Schneider tilted the view up to the vast roof revealing the famous twin towers and then back down to an almost capacity crowd.

'This is half-an-hour before kick-off. There's a timer projected on the wall to give us a reference. It shows T-minus 29 minutes 29 seconds and counting. You can see people talking, some are walking around, and most are singing and chanting. I'll show you what this program can do.'

Alex itched his head and the nerves in his legs began to pulsate. He saw that Schneider wore what seemed to be thimbles on his fingertips. He began stroking his fingers across on the table then he held up his hand and pointed.

'Here we go,' said the German.

The view shrank as the image launched skyward like a rocket. Almost instantly they saw the entire Wembley

Stadium spread out below. People were bustling along Wembley Way, the main concourse into the stadium. Then their birds-eye view started to plummet below the roof towards the grass and began to level off and head towards an exit above the stands. The view took them over the heads of fans and suddenly descended into the darker passage way underneath the terraces. The high ceiling slanted like a vast cavern. Thousands were jostling towards the gates to get into the stadium. Then they raced through an entrance and were back on the pitch. The timer showed there were just moments to kick-off. Half-an-hour had elapsed in thirty seconds. The players were warming up: England in red; West Germany in white. The image closed in on one football player. His eyes were blue; his wavy hair blond, his stature impressive; a born leader. He had all the characteristics that would have made him an icon in the German master race of decades past. It could be no one else. The face of Bobby Moore filled the wall of the circular room. The picture froze, leaving his image there in front of them.

'Wow,' said Alex softly. 'Some ride! Grand Theft Auto doesn't even come close.' He felt exhausted just by watching.

'The best is yet to come Alex. Would you like to see the game?'

'You mean the *worst*! We all know what happened. Don't rub it in for God's sake.'

'Okay Alex, to save you suffering, I'll just select two key moments.'

He aimed a thimble. The giant mural-like image of England's legendary captain vanished and was replaced by a scene from the match. The clock showed that a little more than 118 minutes had elapsed. Extra time was underway and there were only two minutes left to play.

'I don't want to watch,' Alex said screwing up his face. 'I know what happens. Jackie Charlton was sent off for that stupid head-butt on Overath, and then Nobby Stiles brings down Weber to give away a penalty. It's not what should've happened. It was the wrong bloody script.'

'It's 3-2 with about 90 seconds left on the clock. I'm going to bring up Kenneth Wolstenholme's commentary.'

Within the large image a small grainy black and white picture was inserted. This was the original BBC coverage which had been broadcast live all round the world. The action began and the vintage commentary started.

'So there are just seconds left of this World Championship. Is there enough time for England to pull it back? Here's Banks. He rolls the ball to captain Bobby Moore, if anyone can inspire the team, surely it must be him. He strokes the ball forward and finds Martin Peters who rides a tackle from Uwe Seeler. Peters finds Roger Hunt on the right wing. The Wembley turf is breaking up now. And here's Hunt, he twists his way past Schnellinger. He sees Alan Ball, but Hurst is screaming for the ball on the edge of the area. Hunt has found him. This is Hurst, is this England's chance to snatch a last minute equaliser? The whole of Wembley is roaring him on. He goes past Weber, only the goalkeeper to beat. And he's smashed it against the post. Oh, no! Tilkowski collects. Was that England's final throw? Referee Dienst waves play on, and he looks at his watch. The goalkeeper finds Beckenbauer. Now what can he do? He's on the half-way line. Now England are short at the back; it's three against two. They're missing Jack Charlton in the middle. Beckenbauer has played it into the area – and here comes Haller. He's on his own, only Banks to beat. And he does. The Germans go mad. They think it's all over – it is now. The referee blows for full-time. West Germany have won by four goals to two and are the new world champions. And there are people on the pitch.'

'I don't want to see anymore,' Alex said wincing. 'It's too painful, this is worse than water boarding.'

Schneider paused the picture, leaving Franz Beckenbauer embracing Helmut Haller who was holding his fist high above his head.

'Pain can be healed Alex,' Victoria seized her chance. 'Warwick has already explained to you that it's not the end of the story. We know a way to tweak the conclusion. You've said on record that this is the one result you would most like to change. I know that Alex, that's why you are here. We want to help you.'

'Just cut the crap and explain.' Alex levelled a stern glare towards Victoria.

'You've seen that Trinity is no tin-pot organisation. We have at our disposal, the knowledge and resources that most multinationals only dream of – that's if they knew about us. Gentlemen, we have more than that.'

Victoria smiled, her green eyes flashing as she walked towards Alex and Billy.

'We have a *machine*. A machine that's been kept secret for half a century. And as Warwick said, there are two tickets going if you want to take a ride. Let me convince you.'

A black and white photograph appeared on the wall.

'This is the story of a brilliant scientist called Benjamin Janus, born in Israel, grew up in Poland. Just before the outbreak of the World War II, when he was fifteen, his family emigrated to New York to start a new life. Janus went on to Princeton University to study for an MS in mathematics and then a PhD in theoretical physics. His talent and ideas were discovered when he was lecturing on quantum tunnelling and he was invited to join the Rainbow team. He worked on the project for almost five years until it was disbanded following the disaster of the Eldridge. He left Philadelphia and came to Britain where he worked for the Ministry of Defence. After two years he went into hiding and was not heard of for some time. We know that during those years he'd been working on a machine that could actually disrupt the flow of time. Warwick.'

Before the tall unshaven American could say anything, Alex cut in.

'You're not gonna tell us about black holes. It always comes down to black holes!'

'Don't give me that black hole crap,' Vane snapped. 'Even Carl Sagan said you don't need them to circumvent time. I've given you enough evidence already. We are all time travellers on the earth. Ben Janus found a way to harness time travel without the need for speed. In fact, you don't even have to reach 88 miles an hour.'

Billy grinned in agreement and gave a stage whisper across to Alex, 'Remember, that was in *Back To The Future?* You know, in a DeLorean.'

Alex shot Billy a silent warning.

'That's right,' went on Warwick Vane. 'And here in England we have a machine. And there's no flux-capacitor in sight.'

'To be precise,' added Victoria, 'it's here in Trinity.'

'*Trinity*!' Alex was taken back.

'Yes, Benjamin Janus finished building the machine in the mid-Sixties. He wasn't entirely sure what would happen when he fired it up. But when he did, it formed a bridge that linked two opposite poles. And we've tested it.'

'*And*?'

'And – we'll show you what happened. Ralf – demo.'

A dark amorphous mass was projected onto the wall. A fuzzy light could be seen, but nothing recognisable. Victoria carried on.

'This was our experiment. We placed a beehive inside the machine containing a considerable colony. Ten of the bees had micro cameras attached to their bodies, so we could track where they'd been. As you know worker bees are able to fly many miles and navigate back to their hive. So the swarm were let loose. I don't think they found a great deal of pollen but they did find something which interested us very much. They flew out and then they flew back again.'

The grey mass began to fluctuate. Some colour appeared but it was still not possible to make anything out. Then a grainy image appeared. It was set at an angle but the object was unmistakable. There was no doubt about what it could be.

'This photo represents our *one small step*,' Victoria said with a smile that signified a breakthrough. 'This red double-decker bus was just the beginning. You can make out the number on the front: *twenty-one*. We believe this was taken close to London Bridge. Oh, and no bees were harmed in this experiment.

'We were encouraged by this sortie and planned something more elaborate. Have a look.'

Alex and Billy turned and looked towards the screen. First of all they saw nothing. Then they saw *themselves*.

'What's this?' asked Alex.

'We can see you through a *TabCam*.' Victoria continued, 'Watch.'

As they studied their own image on the screen the viewing angle began to change. It was as if the camera was seeing them from above and then from behind and then from the front again.

'How's it done?' asked Alex, gazing into thin air.

'Look there,' said Billy, pointing.

Alex followed the line of his finger and saw a tiny silver ball, like a marble, floating in the room above their heads. Then it moved in a circle around them. Alex wondered at the advanced engineering that must have gone into its design.

'It's state of the art,' said Victoria. 'What MI6 would do to get their hands on one of these. The nano-technology beats anything they've got. It contains a camera and a propulsion system. As you can see it's virtually invisible. We put one in the machine and this is what we used it for.' She ran her hands over her hips as if to smooth creases from her skirt which were not there.

The image on the wall changed from a close up of Billy to something which took Alex's breath away. The view showed a scene in a busy London street. They saw old cars in lines of traffic. People were walking along; men in bowler hats carrying umbrellas; women in short coats and mini-skirts.

'It's Oxford Street,' said Victoria. 'We can program the *TabCam* and it will follow any route using coordinates.'

The street scene changed and they saw the roads of London from an elevation of about 100 metres. Alex was amazed at the lack of tall buildings. Looking down they could see some familiar sights: Big Ben and the Houses of Parliament, The Mall, St James's Park and Buckingham Palace, and then travelling west something that made Alex gasp. First of all they saw a Union flag fluttering in the breeze.

Then as the *TabCam* continued its flight, the most striking and well known of all stadia came into view, and with it, the famous twin towers.

'*Wembley*!' Alex couldn't believe it. He was now absorbed by the story he was hearing.

'Wembley in *1966*,' clarified Victoria.

Dr Ralf Schneider lifted his thimble and paused the flight of the *TabCam*. The aerial view of England's prestigious stadium remained frozen before them.

'Alex and Billy,' said Victoria, as the two TV presenters were coming to terms with what they were looking at, 'you've said how much you would like to change the result of the game between England and West Germany. We have the technology and we have a game plan. Yes you'll be our first human pilots. But there's another reason, Alex, why you especially, will want to change the result. Ralf show them.'

Alex gave Victoria a stunned look.

As they had seen in the computer simulation, the camera began to dive towards the green turf and levelled off a few metres above the pitch and veered away. Now the *TabCam* moved horizontally and Alex could see that Wembley was full of people. Banners were being waved and fans were chanting. The camera continued travelling and closed in on two members of the crowd: a tall, dark haired man with a young boy at his side reading a programme. The man was savouring the atmosphere in anticipation.

Alex was shocked. 'It's my *Grandpa*, and that must be my *Dad*!'

He became quiet as he watched the scene unfold. *This is impossible*, he thought.

'Is this true Alex?' Billy couldn't believe it either. 'You look like your Granddad.'

'Yeah, they were there.' Alex recalled a conversation he'd once overheard between his Dad and grandfather. 'Something happened. Grandpa never spoke about it. And of course Dad...' His voice trailed away and he turned to Victoria standing in the room watching his reaction. 'Look, explain what's going on,' confusion was etched all over his face. 'This'd better be good.'

Victoria walked over to one of the balls perched on a stand.

'I didn't tell you about this one before, but I need to now.'

The ball she held in her dark hands was orange. It had eighteen leather sections grouped into a pattern of three parallel panels, of which there were six. The middle panel of each was itself divided into three, so in all, there were thirty strips of leather sewn together. She bounced it on the floor and threw it to Alex.

'There were a number of stories kicking around about this ball, so to speak. In 2001 this World Cup football was on display at Waterloo Station.'

Instantly something stirred within Alex.

As Victoria spoke, a veil was lifted and a memory from many years earlier fell into place.

There had been a kiss with Abby Hart. It came back to him in a flash and his heart leapt.

9

Above the platform, the hands on the four faces of the famous clock advanced in synchronised motion by one minute every sixty seconds. At precisely seventeen minutes past five o'clock in the evening, the Eurostar from Paris glided into the station humming like a giant vacuum cleaner. Inside the coaches, faces peered through misted windows to see their journey had come to an end.

Rain lashed down from leaden skies. The concourse seethed with the haphazard weavings of commuters on their homeward journeys. Waterloo Station echoed with the boom of announcements while travel information flickered and changed on display screens overhead. A row of faces looked up impassively trying to find their departure. For those who had just missed a train, time seemed to slow, and for those anxious to make a connection, time was racing. Others took refuge in crowded station shops or wandered round sipping hot drinks from polystyrene cups. Scores chatted on mobile phones while others sent text messages telling how late they would be.

Alex Bell put his arm round Abby Hart and kissed her.

'Back to school tomorrow,' he felt resigned but wasn't concerned. 'I still haven't done my graphics coursework. Mr McLean can have it next week. Who cares if I get a detention?'

'Thanks for spoiling the moment,' Abby replied looking into his dark eyes. Then a smile spread across her face and she pulled Alex closer and kissed him on the cheek. 'Let's get going,' she whispered.

Alex unfolded a crumpled Underground map.

'Right, we need to take this grey line to Westminster. What line's that?'

'Jubilee.'

'Yep, then the District back to Putney. Should be home in time for the snooker.'

Abby looked appalled. '*What*!'

'Only joking,' Alex grinned and stroking her long dark hair, kissed her on the lips. 'What's the rush? Let's find a KFC or something.'

He slipped his fingers into the back pocket of Abby's jeans and they began walking across the platform.

Close to a stall selling calendars stood a glass cabinet that contained an artefact from another century. Those passing by took little notice, but Alex saw it and out of curiosity guided Abby over to look.

'What is it?' she asked.

'Some old football!' He looked at the inscription. 'It's the one used in that final.'

'Why's it orange?'

'They used to play with heavy balls like this; head one of these on a wet morning and you'd know all about it.'

Abby quickly lost interest. 'Look, I just want to get a bottle of water and a *Heat* magazine; I'll be right back.' She turned and headed for WH Smith.

Alex wondered why this ball should be on show at Waterloo Station; it seemed strangely out of place. But as he studied it, the station suddenly plunged into darkness. In surprise he swivelled round, 'What's going on…?'

All that could be seen were lights from train windows standing at the platforms and the pale glow from mobile phones. Alex looked for Abby. Then a Tannoy message blasted a distorted announcement across the station: 'Ladies and gentlemen please be patient as we rectify the power failure.'

Several minutes passed. First the emergency circuits cut in casting a light so dim it was difficult to read a newspaper, then after what seemed an age, the main lights sputtered into life to muted cheers from some bystanders. Alex scanned the platform but there was still no sign of Abby amongst the crowd standing on the concourse. *Where is she?* he thought and bit his lip.

He turned again to look at the display case holding the exhibit and for a moment thought the ball had moved on its plinth. A few metres away, commuters were already walking through the space where the stall selling calendars had been only minutes earlier.

His thoughts were interrupted when someone placed a hand on his neck. Alex spun round and Abby kissed him gently. He closed his eyes and Waterloo Station disappeared.

Sod the graphics. It can wait.

10

He had been there. Trinity were so close and he did not know it.

'Alex, the ball you are holding is the key to how the match result can be changed. Trinity was able to make a substitution and take away the original, and so add another unique item to its collection. Ralf, please elucidate.'

The German cleared his throat and turned to look at their guests.

'The pivotal moment in '66 happened when Geoff Hurst's shot hit the crossbar, rebounded onto the pitch, and then out.'

He tapped the touchpad.

'I've memorised the time: ninety-nine minutes and fourteen seconds'

The image on the screen changed to show the instant during the game when the ball landed on the goal-line.

'It's universally agreed to be *the* most controversial sporting moment of all time. This is the sequence which must be changed. It's this crucial event that must be given a different outcome. Shortly after this chance in extra time, West Germany scored, and so went on to win. We've got to change this exact moment so that there is a goal and not a rebound.'

'C'mon how can that happen?' Alex protested. 'That's impossible!'

'It's quite simple. You have the answer in your hands.'

Alex looked at the ball, tossed it a few inches into the air and said, '*I do*?'

'Yah, as Victoria said, we need to use the actual ball used in the final. Then we must weigh it precisely.'

'Why do you want to know its weight?' asked Billy.

'Because the ball was too light by a few milligrams. What we have done is to increase its weight by a fraction.'

'What's the point of that?'

'Simply this Alex – if Geoff Hurst were to kick the ball with the same force, according to Newton's laws of motion, it would take a different trajectory and hit the crossbar further in on the underside and fall down beyond the goal-line.'

'3-2,' added Victoria. 'As you may know, that dreaded crossbar is on display in the museum at Wembley Stadium.'

Alex and Billy were silent for a second.

'Oh brilliant!' Alex said sarcastically. 'So all we've got to do is swap the match ball with this one.'

'Got it in one.'

The boys looked at each other with baffled expressions.

'Just how are we gonna to do that?' Billy screwed up his face.

'That's the easy part,' replied Ralf. 'Have a look at what happened at the end of full-time.'

The dying moments of the second half came up on the wall. Ralf Schneider projected the large synthesised image together with the black and white coverage from the BBC.

'I know this; it's the equaliser,' Alex said, 'where they make it 2-2. We were just a minute away from winning and becoming world champions. There goes Weber scrambling it passed Gordon Banks. Shit!'

'This is what I want you to see.'

Seconds later England line up and take the centre-kick to restart the game.

'And there goes the whistle for the end of ninety minutes. So you can see how near England were to the World Championships. But now they have another thirty minutes.'

The disappointment in commentator Kenneth Wolstenholme's voice was evident.

The England players hang their heads and the ball runs loose. In frustration at coming so close to winning, Nobby

Stiles' body language reflects the expletives he utters. He mouths something then runs up and strikes the ball on the half-way line. It sails past Tilkowski's goal and beyond into the open area behind.

'Look,' said Ralf Schneider, 'the TV coverage shows the ball disappearing off screen, but the synth image on the widescreen shows exactly where the ball ends up. Remember, there was only one match ball in the 1966 final, unlike today where many are used. So the ball which has just disappeared to the perimeter of the stadium is the one that must be recovered before extra time begins. This is the perfect opportunity to make a swap. Right now there's confusion and excitement all-round the stadium. All eyes are on the players in the centre circle. This is the only chance. This is *your* moment. You've just got to be in the right place at the right time.'

'Hold on,' said Alex throwing up a hand; he had a blank look. 'There's something that don't smell right here. Just supposing we agree to such a ridiculous idea, what's in all this for you? You being a German and that.'

Victoria stepped forward, her manicured fingers raised with the grace of a ballerina.

'Alex, there are a number of reasons why we can help each other. First of all boys, you get your wish to rewrite the books and allow England to rightly win on merit. You would have done your duty for your country. And just think about what you could bring back and present on your show. You'll have first-hand knowledge of what actually went on in England's finest hour.'

'Hey, she's got a point there,' Alex whispered to Billy, remembering the pain that Grandpa Bell always showed whenever the Final was mentioned.

'Yeah, we could get Bobby Moore's autograph; they're more valuable when someone's dead.'

'Better still, we could get him to sign his biography. He'd love to read it.'

'Now hold on guys, who's going to believe that Bobby Moore signed a book that was published after he died?'

'Good thinking Batman!'

'Also,' went on Victoria realising she was beginning to convince the boys, 'Trinity gets to fully prove the success of the machine. Our trials with the bees and the *TabCam* have already shown that it works. All we need now are a couple of adventurers – no experience necessary. Oh, by the way, *TabCam* stands for *There And Back Camera* – so the ride comes with a return ticket. The big bonus is that the Swinging Sixties were voted the best decade of the twentieth century. So you could live it for one day.'

She paused for effect.

'There's also one minor diplomatic incident we'd like to correct ourselves. Strangely enough it's tied up with your own reason for going. It concerns the Russian linesman. You're aware of what happened to him. As you know the English fans blamed Tofik Bakhramov for not convincing the referee that the ball had crossed the line. We now know he was right – but that's not what a group of passionate fans thought. He was the only one who could have influenced the ref's decision. His death was unfortunate and sparked off a chain of events which had far reaching effects. Little is known of the repercussions that followed.

'There were a number of tit-for-tat reprisals which became more than a little embarrassing for some of the major governments. Following Bakhramov's death, the Soviets hit back with the disappearance of Sam Donaldson, England's FIFA representative. Two weeks later, Valery Granatkin, the Soviet representative at FIFA failed to return from a soccer symposium in Yugoslavia. There were no drunken English supporters this time. Then things sadly escalated. We believe the Soviet's next intended target was Hugh Cavan, the FIFA rep for Northern Ireland. Unfortunately for everyone, they got the wrong man.'

'What happened then?' asked Alex who was now following everything Victoria was saying. It was a complete revelation to him.

'Joe McGuire's body was found in a hotel in Rome, where it must be said, Cavan was also staying at the time. Big mistake.'

'Why?'

Joe McGuire was the FIFA delegate for the *United States*.'

'*Ouch*!' Billy drew a hiss of breath in through his clenched teeth.

'A Cold War loomed.'

'Yeah, big mistake,' echoed Alex.

'Then things started to go crazy. A U2 spy plane was shot down somewhere over the Bering Sea. When it became public, the US claimed it was in neutral airspace. The Soviets said it was over Siberia. Then an Aeroflot transporter plane went missing over the Balkans. Even the deaths of Apollo astronauts, Grissom, White and Chaffee in January '67, and the apparent re-entry failure that caused the death of cosmonaut Vladimir Komarov in the same year, have been linked with the conspiracy.

'So you can see, making a correction to that judgement by the linesman Bakhramov seems only prudent for all parties concerned. Maybe that's the least we could do. The governments of Britain, the United States and the former Soviet Union will be able to look back as if nothing had happened.

'Oh, by the way, don't let anyone mislead you, Tofik Bakhramov wasn't Russian – he came from *Azerbaijan*.'

Victoria looked at Alex and Billy who both had vacant expressions. 'Voila! Air-brushed from history.' She smiled.

'I see what you mean,' said Alex, lying. 'I think!'

'And last of all,' went on Victoria, 'it's a very good time to go now. We've already said that the machine is a bridge spanning two sides that are decades apart. That bridge is like the vortex of a tornado. At the end where the twister touches down, there's some movement on the ground. It's like that with the machine. It may be that a traveller could arrive spot on, then again, it might be a few weeks either side. But, the telemetry we're receiving shows just how rigid the link is behaving. It's rock stable. It's now or never. We can get you there to within a day or so.'

'Talk about hard sell,' Billy turned to Alex, 'she could flog cellulite to a supermodel!'

Before they could say anything else, even if they understood it, Victoria spoke again.

'Warwick, bring in the stuff. Gentlemen, you're dressed almost perfectly. Even your England football shirts will do nicely, and so will your Levis. Alex, your Nike trainers are going to look way out of place – but I think we'll get away with it. There's no point in turning up and looking like aliens have landed. Billy's hair could be a touch longer. Don't forget The Beatles are the biggest thing ever. Still it's the Sixties and just about anything goes.

'Thanks Warwick. Right, these bags contain everything you'll need, including money and your Wembley ID.'

'Wow, you've thought of everything,' exclaimed Billy, looking at the blue holdalls and thinking he was about to go on holiday.

Alex felt events were moving too quickly. 'There's something that don't seem to hang together. We're supposed to be ball-boys, right? Look at us, we're way too old. We'll stick out like a couple of clowns!'

'Alex, at the 1966 final, all the ball-boys were in their early twenties, some were over six feet tall.'

'Oh, okay.' Alex conceded the point. 'It still feels like you're press-ganging us into something we don't want to do. What gives you the right...?' He didn't finish.

A shrill noise suddenly filled the room.

Victoria was first to speak, 'Security alert. What is it Ralf?'

He hit the touch screen and up came a view of a long anonymous corridor. In the distance people could be seen running towards the camera; there were twenty, maybe thirty men. Alex and Billy watched, wondering what was happening. Still the siren screamed. As the group approached they could be seen dressed in dark breastplates, chain mail and helmets. They didn't look happy.

'Nice welcoming party,' Alex said.

'Yeah, the frogs are out,' Billy added.

The mob ran on and went under the view of the camera. At the far end appeared another group dressed in yellow overalls; they carried batons and stun guns.

'We've got a breach. Where are they?'

But before Ralf Schneider could reply there came a rumble outside the room.

'They're close. Warwick, back door.' Victoria pointed a finger.

The tall man from Chicago snatched up the bags and Schneider operated a sliding door.

'This way boys,' Vane called in a way they couldn't refuse; his eyes glared, wide and piercing.

There was no hesitation. They ran into a dark, airless void that felt cool and musty. An array of lights flickered on illuminating a long tunnel stretching away before them.

'Follow me. Quick.'

For the first time Alex detected a trace of anxiety in the American's voice.

With a grinding sound, the door closed behind them. Then, from somewhere deep inside Trinity there came a shuddering explosion.

11

The dull lighting gave little help to show the way. Alex blinked and could see diffuse images etched on his retina like fuzzy photographs. They were the fading impressions of the lights he'd left behind inside Trinity.

As they made their way through the tunnel, pieces of grit crunched under their trainers and echoed on the hard brick walls. The tunnel was dank, and a putrid smell hung in the foul air that reminded Alex of an open sewer. They passed cracks in the brickwork from which trickled rancid water; a green slime of mossy lichen sprawled over the walls. One by one they splashed through a puddle that was seeping across the concrete floor.

Alex spotted black rats scurrying along beside him. Their tails looked like thick rope and their long whiskers twitched erratically. One evil looking creature with a swollen tumour on its body looked up at Alex giving him a fright. Then quickly they disappeared into an unseen fracture and were gone.

'Ugh! Wait for me,' he gulped and picked up the pace to catch the other two who were haring along in front. He thought he heard running water and then he saw a dark fissure in the brick wall. Alex peered through. He gripped a rusty railing which flaked off in his hand. He caught sight of ripples down below, but the rising stench that filled his nostrils gripped his throat and made him gag. Warwick Vane turned to see Alex staring through the gap into the darkness beyond.

'Old Victorian waterways. They go on for hundreds of miles below London. There's a labyrinth down here. Most haven't been used for a century or more. During the war they were opened up to run information from the Cabinet War Room to strategic sites in the Capital. You get lost in here, you'll never get out.'

Warwick Vane's voice seemed loud and harsh and carried with added sibilance down the length of the arched passage. Alex held his arms out sideways; he found he could touch the grimy walls on either side. As he did, the entrance of a black tunnel branched off to his right and was gone as he walked on with an urgent stride. Just for a moment he wondered what monsters lurked in this subterranean world. *I don't want to hang around to find out*, he thought.

Up ahead he saw Billy and Vane had stopped. Then he saw the tall man, and then Billy, were both squeezing through a narrow opening. Alex followed them and discovered they had emerged into a wider, brighter tunnel. It was warmer and drier and the air smelt fresher than the cesspit they'd left behind. Alex saw that he was now standing inside a passageway of the London Underground – the subway system beneath the Capital.

'Okay guys,' said Vane, 'this is where I leave you. We'll be in touch. The platform's down there. I need to get back to Trinity.'

He dropped the bags on the floor with a reverberant clatter and with one final look disappeared back through the narrow gap in the wall.

'Hey, wait!' Billy shouted, looking into the void where he heard Vane's footsteps echoing. Then he turned to Alex, 'He was keen to get rid of us.'

'Let him go, I'm just glad we're out of that place. They've obviously got some domestic problem to sort out.' Alex sighed, 'Did you see those rats back there? They had bubonic plague or something.' He picked up his bag and slung it over his shoulder. 'C'mon, let's get the tube – should be home in an hour.'

The wooden escalator wasn't moving. *Typical*, thought Alex. They lugged their bags down a long flight of steps. At the bottom, a white tiled walkway tarnished with the excrement of years curved around and led them onto an empty platform. A train was already waiting.

'Hey, that's handy,' said Billy with a triumphant smile. 'How often does that happen?'

'Yeah, but what's the station? We should've asked Vane.'

Alex found the answer on the wall.

'*Moorgate* – can't say I know this platform.'

The tube train with a drab red livery stood with its doors open. There were two carriages and Alex and Billy jumped into the rear coach.

'Boy these trains don't get any better, do they? Look at the state of this thing.'

'Yeah, I've seen better toilets!' Billy added.

Trailing along the length of the carriage was a bundle of multi-coloured cable. It snaked under seats and Alex saw that it rose up next to the door and into an open panel in the curved ceiling. A misty vapour seeped from a crack in the wooden floor and drifted along the carriage beneath the seats.

'What's it being repaired or something?'

'What a heap!' Billy kicked the cable and there came an audible fizzing noise.

A dull grey brushed metal cabinet stood where some seats had been removed. The size of an upright fridge-freezer, it had numerous flashing push buttons and a flat-screen built in. There was a heavy electric smell hanging in the air. It reminded Alex of the ozone made from the blue arcing on the bumper cars he used to ride at seaside funfairs.

Curiously he pressed one of the square buttons. It changed from red to yellow and the flat-screen lit up and began scrolling through various menus.

'Shit!' Alex walked away.

They waited a few minutes but the train didn't move.

'Oh, c'mon,' exclaimed Billy. 'Let's go!' He thumped on a window in frustration.

Alex stood up impatiently and looked out of the open door. There was no one around; no sound to be heard, not even a display screen giving travel information. *Nothing*, Alex thought. *Not even a rat.*

'Is this the Circle Line?' he muttered to himself, 'or the Hammersmith? I don't recognise it.'

He stepped back inside the carriage and went over to his friend. He found him slumped over his bag, his eyes shut.

'Well done Billy-boy, think I'll join you. Wake me up when we get there.'

He pulled out his iPod and pressed the foam pads into his ears. In his confused state, Alex couldn't quite determine how long it had been since he'd last slept. He sat down and curled into a dishevelled heap next to a smeared window. His mind began to drift as the music welled up and engulfed him. Closing his eyes, he let out a deep sigh as the emotions of the last few hours evaporated. He felt comfortably numb as if he'd lost all feeling in his weary limbs. The last thing he was aware of were the doors closing gently and the train beginning to move, like a ship silently slipping anchor.

The grimy white tiles on the wall outside seemed to shimmer and blur and vanish into a visage of forgetfulness. There was no sense of movement, just a darkness that overcame everything. Not even the raw power of Pink Floyd inside his head could stop him from falling into a state where his faculties slowed to the point of unconsciousness. It had been a long day.

Outside, the slanting walls began to blaze with the reflection of brilliant colours that flickered and flashed and cast strident fiery images around the tunnel.

12

Alex dreamed he was looking down at his tiny footprints in the damp sand. He saw the wandering trail he'd left behind. Straightaway he knew that the marks showed where he had been – like a record of his past life.

The smell of salt and seaweed wafted on a breeze and high above came the desperate cry of a seagull. Suddenly a wave came rushing in and covered the tracks and flowed in a cool surge around his ankles. He laughed. When the water had receded, his footprints had vanished like a distant memory and he couldn't tell where he had been.

Beside his feet he found a shell of pastel colours thrust upon the shore by the force of the tide. He picked it up and touched its jagged surface, then he slipped his fingers inside and felt how smooth it was. Not knowing why, he pressed the shell to his ear and was amazed to hear the sound of the sea inside. His eyes became wide with wonder.

The little boy looked over to see his mother sitting on a tartan blanket and cradling Lily in her arms. His father had just climbed the steep path that led to the car park above the cliff. Alex knew he would be back soon with a picnic.

It was then that Alex caught sight of someone standing alone on the dry sand in the shadows of a deep cleft. How tall she was, Alex thought, he had never seen anyone like her before.

'Mummy,' he called, and pointed his tiny finger.

His mother looked over and smiled, 'Be careful,' she said, 'the waves come in quickly.'

Alex watched the person for some time while pretending to idle himself with the shell he had found. The stranger's eyes were deepest turquoise, like the ebbing sea that broke along the shore, and her flaxen hair cascaded in ringlets over her shoulders. The folds of her dress appeared to mesmerise like a mirage in the sunlight, and her face seemed to radiate joy. Alex wasn't worried unduly by the presence of this woman, but he thought it odd that his mother was unaware of her standing so nearby.

In the end, Alex turned to look at the vast ocean; it was the biggest and most beautiful thing he had ever seen in the three years of his life. He had become captivated by the incessant flow of the restless waves.

Alex toddled down towards the edge where the waves came lapping and saw something that excited him.

'*Fish*,' he shouted. 'Little fish!' He stood there entranced.

Dropping the shell he stepped into the sea. The golden fish darted and lured him further. He watched its flight, glancing this way and that, just below the crystal surface and soon he found the sea had risen above his waist.

'Come back Alex,' was the last thing he heard his mother say. There was a gasp of panic in her voice.

In the next moment he lost his balance as the sea-floor deepened steeply and a strong wave came crashing over him and drew him down.

It was a weird sensation. He had not known it before. He had never been in a place so strange, where no air could be breathed, and unseen forces tugged him back and forth, and sounds were dull and muffled. Then he saw the golden fish, only inches from his grasp. It hovered there for just a second and then with a flick of its tail disappeared from sight. Alex found himself alone. Drifting aimlessly he looked up to see the cloudless sky.

A face distorted by refraction appeared above the waves. He recognised her dark eyes and saw how haunted they were. Then a brightness like the sun filled the sky beyond, and he heard a mighty rushing wind that frothed the ocean and a potent force came and lifted him from the sea.

In a heartbeat, Alex found himself looking down at the wide blue circle of the earth below.

13

Alex was jolted rudely from his short sleep. Billy was shaking his shoulders.

'What? What do you want?'

'Wake up.'

'What's going on?' Alex felt stiff and wished he was still dreaming.

'We've stopped.'

'Are we there?'

'No – don't think so.'

'What do you mean *no*?'

'I mean – *no* we haven't gone anywhere.'

'What're you talking about?' Alex opened his eyes.

'We're still in Moorgate.'

Alex stood up, yawned and went to the open door.

Billy joined him. 'See what I mean?'

'What the hell's going on? This isn't the same station.'

'It says *Moorgate* – look.'

'That's a different sign.'

'How can we leave Moorgate and end up in Moorgate?'

'Maybe we've been shunted into a different siding or something. I dunno, maybe we've just gone round the Circle Line. That's it. We've gone all the way round and stopped where we started.'

Billy wasn't convinced and his blank stare showed it.

Alex stepped onto the platform and began walking along beside the train. He could see no other passengers in either carriage.

'There's your answer,' he said shouting back.

'What's that?'

'No driver! The train's going nowhere.'

'What do we do now?'

Alex looked around. He saw an exit and stairs leading up from the platform.

'Let's get a bus – or a taxi – whatever we see first.'

'Good thinking.'

Alex began to climb the soiled stairs and looked at the washed-out adverts plastered on the walls.

'Here you go mate.'

'What?'

'Yer bag.'

'What did we take these for anyway?'

'I dunno. They might have some useful footy stuff in them.'

'Look! Since when was *Oxo* and *Cocoa* big business?' Alex gestured towards some adverts peeling on the subway.

'Search me – I just want chips with a big saveloy. Failing that we'll hit the first Indian.'

They went on and eventually came to a wide walkway that levelled off and continued for a few hundred yards. Suddenly they heard a deep booming noise that sent a rumble through the tunnel. Then they heard another and it carried on every ten seconds or so.

'Shit, what's that?'

'Don't know, but I think it's a good idea to get out of here.' Billy had concern etched all over his face.

They walked a little further and sensed the air becoming fresher. Their pace had automatically quickened after hearing the deep banging noise. Alex felt he was being hit in the stomach by a heavyweight boxer every time the boom sounded. With each thud, cement powder could be seen flaking off between the bricks and falling to the floor in a dusty cloud.

This isn't good, he thought.

'Look, an exit,' Billy said with obvious relief.

They walked to the opening and squinted out in the glare of daylight.

'It's a building site,' exclaimed Alex shading his eyes and feeling that something was wrong.

Dumper trucks were splashing through muddy water. A tall crane was hoisting a girder high overhead and a giant hammer was driving a metal pile into the ground causing the thumping sound they'd heard.

'Hey you, what d'you think you're doing of?'

'We've been spotted. Watch out, here comes the foreman. What an ugly pillock he is!'

A huge man in a waterproof jacket began walking in their direction. He wore black Wellington boots caked in mud. As he approached he ran a fat hand across his cropped hair and put his safety helmet on.

'What you bloody up to down there? You could get yourselves bloody killed.'

'We were just, um, just...' stammered Alex. 'We were just...'

'...We were just giving it a final check,' added Billy. 'It's all fine, just go ahead. All clear!' He gave a thumbs-up sign and a wide grin.

'And make sure that perimeter fence is secure,' Alex said pointing. 'We don't want no vagrants or wild animals getting in and injuring themselves, would we now?'

'Right,' said Billy. 'We're off for an urgent meeting with our project manager at Canary Wharf, and she don't like lateness, so we gotta go ASAP.'

Before the foreman could say anything else, they began zigzagging between girders, trucks and heaps of hard-core to find their way out. The big workman took off his hard hat and scratched his spiky red hair.

'Blimey, what's the world coming to? We've got safety inspectors straight out of school! And who's ever heard of Canary Wharf? What – they importing wild fowl these days?' He stood there for a moment and spat into a puddle. 'Alright Ted, back it up.'

A large truck began reversing as the foreman waved his hand.

'Keep it coming. Hold it there – okay let it go.'

The rear of the truck lifted and a flap opened releasing tons of hard-core and billows of dust. Like an avalanche it thundered into the entrance where Alex and Billy had been standing two minutes earlier.

The lads picked their way through the building site and found themselves beside a busy road.

'You seeing what I'm seeing?' Billy couldn't quite believe it.

'I think so! Where the hell are we?'

The road where they were standing was a sea of traffic going nowhere. But what disturbed them most were the cars they saw tailing back in both directions. After what seemed a long and awkward few seconds, Billy was the first to speak.

'This has got to be some kind of vintage car pageant, or something.'

'God knows!' Alex let out a sigh. 'D'you know what? I've hated Vane ever since we met him, but maybe there's more to the old bastard than I first thought.'

'Yeah, and that tube-train didn't feel right the moment we got on it.'

14

Across the high-street Billy was waving a newspaper. Above the traffic Alex couldn't make out what he was saying. Car horns sounded sporadically and the tantalising aroma from a nearby restaurant drifted along the thoroughfare.

'*What*?' shouted Alex. 'What is it?'

'It's really happening,' Billy said as he dodged between lines of cars and dumped his bag next to Alex. 'Look at this.'

'I thought the Express was a *tabloid*. It's massive!'

'...No – *the headline*.'

'*England Expects*,' Alex read. 'Alf Ramsey and the England team are today preparing for their greatest game of all time. Tomorrow at 3 o'clock they will line up against West Germany in the World Cup final in London's Wembley Stadium. Bobby Moore will captain the side who start as favourites to receive the Jules Rimet trophy from Her Majesty Queen Elizabeth.' Alex stopped and flattened out the paper. 'It's dated: *Friday, July 29th, 1966*.' He took a deep breath. 'You know what this means?' He looked at Billy with a pained expression.

'What?'

'It means we're up to our necks in one big pile of shite!'

Neither spoke for almost a minute. Alex read again the front page, then lowering the broadsheet he scanned the length of Oxford Street.

'We've actually landed right where we wanted. Vane was right after all, you know, all that quantum crap and stuff about time-slips.'

'What we gonna do now?' A queasy feeling began to grow inside Billy.

They were silent for another minute as the truth began to sink in.

'We need to think about this,' Alex said finally. 'Let's get a cup of tea – don't suppose we can get anything stronger at this time of the day.'

The view from the tea shop on the corner of New Bond Street looked out onto a high-street that was strangely familiar to Alex, yet so different.

On the other side of the road stood the entrance to Debenhams – a place he'd walked past many times. Alex couldn't believe what he was seeing through the window of the tea house. He lost count of the number of bright coloured Austin Minis. Some had chequered roofs, some were decked in Union Jacks, and one was covered in purple felt. There were also expensive cars; a Rolls Royce Silver Shadow and an Aston Martin DB3. Two E-type Jaguars came crawling by. One had an open top; the second was flanked by a group of Morris Minors which seemed well represented on the London streets; most of which were grey or green. He saw other cars which were not known to him: Imp, Zephyr, Corsair, Humber and Zodiac.

A pale cream Isetta bubble car pulled up just outside. The wide curving front door opened revealing a tiny cock-pit inside. A man dressed smartly in a powder-blue suit and bright yellow chiffon tie sat behind the steering wheel. He beckoned and a tall girl with long blond hair emerged from a shop. She wore a white top with a bright red Stewart tartan mini-skirt and knee-length white patent leather boots. With poise she stepped nimbly into the car beside him and squeezed her long legs inside as the front of the bubble came down closing them in. The car barged its way back into the traffic like a dodgem at the fair ground.

'Wow! This is a dream,' Alex said under his breath. 'It's like some bloody Terence Stamp movie. You know, Modesty Blaise or something!'

'Never heard of it.' Billy was emptying his bag all over the table. He tipped it up and the contents fell out knocking the cruet onto the floor and spilling a spiral of salt over the Axminster carpet.

'Shit. That's bad luck! What's all this stuff we got in here?'

'A retro track suit,' Alex was disappointed. 'It's not even Adidas!'

'No not *retro*, this is the real thing.'

Spread over the table was a two piece plain grey jogging suit made by Saxonclad with elasticated cuffs and ankles. The jacket had a zip-up front. There were also some black Umbro trainers, and a map of London, circa mid-Sixties. Under the tracksuit they found a copy of the match programme.

'At least we won't have to buy one of these,' Alex flicked through the pages. 'It only cost two-and-six.'

'What's this?' Billy snatched up a small card attached to a cord. He turned it over and saw a photograph of himself. 'It's a pass to Wembley. We really are going to be ball-boys. Where was this taken?'

'Hey, good one of you,' Alex said looking at the ID. 'Dunno, probably somewhere in Trinity.'

Alex unzipped his own bag. 'And this Billy-boy is why we're here. Our secret weapon!'

For a moment Alex was reminded that somewhere inside Wembley Stadium would be his grandfather. *Will I find him? Why did he never talk about the final?* He felt a sense of unease.

Billy whistled and picked it up. It looked far from new, bearing the impressions of scuffs and scratches on its leather panels.

'Looks like Vane's been having a kick-about,' Alex said.

'I doubt it somehow; he's a Yank. He wouldn't have a clue.'

Alex took the ball and ran his fingers round it. He sniffed the leather and detected the unmistakable trace of dubbin. 'Can we change history with this Slazenger baby?' he mused.

'You bet we can.' He looked at his friend and felt excited. 'Billy we need a plan.'

'What sort of plan?'

'We've gotta get ourselves to Wembley.' Their purpose was suddenly becoming clear.

'Let's hope Trinity have worked this out,' Billy added. 'We can be like Frodo and Sam taking the magic ring to Mount Doom. You know, it could be our quest!'

'Yeah right Billy, I think you're getting carried away. We're talking reality here. Just let me know when you see Gandalf riding into the sunset on Shadowfax.'

A waitress sidled over to their table. Her blond hair was wrapped neatly in a tight bun and she wore a soft pink trouser suit.

'Would you boys like anything else?' She flipped open a little pad.

'Yeah,' Alex hesitated, 'can I have a cheese and pickle sandwich and another tea, thanks. Billy?'

'Same for me – and some of that chocolate cake,' he prodded the picture on the menu. 'And the bill. Ta.'

'Nice watch,' she said, seeing Billy's expensive Seiko.

He looked down at his digital. 'Yeah, it's um, it's just a cheap copy I picked up in Bangkok,' he said lying.

'It ain't got no hands.'

'No, they don't use hands in Thailand. These are Oriental numbers.'

'Oh.' She glanced at the objects strewn across the table. 'Looks like you boys are getting ready for the big game. I guess we're all going to be glued to the telly tomorrow.' She gave them a wry smile and walked off.

'Yeah, but some of us will be getting a better view than sitting round some old black and white TV,' Alex watched her strut away. 'You're in there mate.'

'Not my type; she's from Romford. I can't stand chavs!'

They left the tea house and discovered the pale sunshine had been replaced by a light drizzle.

Alex found a gent's hairdresser, Dal's Barbers, tucked away in a road just off Oxford Street. He had agreed to meet up in a record store that Billy pointed out close to Selfridges.

The place was empty apart from the barber who was idling his time with a crossword. A dark wooden radio with a brown cloth grill and two large Bakelite dials was playing quietly. The man was short, middle aged and had a large stomach distending over a black leather belt. He scratched the stubble on his chin and ran his chubby hands over his bald, shiny pate.

'Step right up lad, we're not exactly busy right now.' His voice was deep and seemed to resonate in the tiny shop. 'I'm stuck on six-across. Any ideas?'

'What is it?' Alex felt put on the spot.

'*Lifts a chopper whichever way round it goes*. Five letters.'

'Sounds a bit cryptic. Um, that'd be *Rotor*. See it's a palindrome – whichever way round it goes. It's the same forwards and backwards.'

'Hey kid, you're good.' He pencilled it in.

Alex put his bag down on a plastic chair and peeled off his denim jacket.

The barber looked at Alex's football shirt. 'How'd you know England are playing in red? They've only just said it on the wireless.'

'Lucky guess really. It's my favourite shirt.'

'We've got to be lucky tomorrow, you know. Them Germans are good. They say Beckenbauer's the best midfielder in the world.'

'Yeah, but Bobby Moore's better – nothing fazes him. We beat 'em before – didn't we?'

'Too right lad. Okay, now what can I do you for?'

'Um, give me a John Lennon,' Alex stammered, staring at his reflection in the mirror, not sure what he was asking for.

'Good choice mate. Them Beatles ain't that bad you know. Some people hate their bloody noise, but I say they ain't all bad – though Lennon's just come out and said the Beatles are more popular than Jesus. He could be right, but

114

when did he last walk across the Mersey? My niece went to see them the other month – she screamed so much she pissed her knickers!'

He picked up an aluminium comb and began waving a pair of scissors around snapping them in the air as if rehearsing, then he began snipping away.

'I dunno why we're in red,' the barber said, 'it should be them who should change. It's us what's playing at home.'

'Yeah, I've always said that was a stupid choice.'

'So you did know we'd be in red?'

'Um, what I mean is – why should the home team change their kit? They should play in their own colours. Maybe their white shirts are still in the wash.' Alex winced for saying something so ridiculous. He pretended to chuckle.

At that moment the door opened with a clatter and Alex caught sight of a man in the mirror walk over and sit in the corner. He picked up a well-thumbed Playboy magazine from a pile and began turning the pages.

'So what's been England's best game?' the barber asked as he trimmed Alex's fringe.

'Let's see...we started off with a nil-nil against Uruguay and we're getting better. Bobby Charlton had a fantastic game against Portugal in the semi – and Nobby had a blinder marking out Eusebio. He's been the star of the tournament.' Alex was racking his brains for as much detail as he could recall. 'And that game against the Argie-bargies was a bit scary. Rattin got sent off; he's a nasty piece of work. They were a bunch of animals. It was like the Falklands all over again...'

'*Falklands*?'

'Oh, I must have been thinking of another game!'

'Right,' said the barber, and reaching for the razor went to work on Alex's neck. 'So what's the score gonna be?'

'Dunno really. It could go either way. The Germans always score. They beat Hungary in the semi...'

'*Russia*.'

'Oh yeah. I think it'll go to extra time and England'll sneak it through Geoff Hurst. But don't put money on it.'

'I hope you're right mate.' He held up a mirror behind Alex. 'There you go mate, how's that?'

'Yeah, good – I'll be singing *Lucy In The Sky* tonight.'

The barber gave Alex a confused look. 'That'll be a shilling.' He loosened the cape and whisked it away with the bravado of a matador in a bullring.

'Thanks a lot.' Alex dug into his pocket. 'There you go – and have one of these big boys.' He gave the barber an extra penny.

'Thanks guv.'

Alex picked up his bag and jacket and went to leave.

'You're not from here, are you?'

'Um, no,' Alex said, wondering if the barber had seen through his pretence. 'I come and go. Mainly round the M25.'

'I knew it. You talk different.'

Alex opened the door but the barber hadn't finished.

'You heard about Hurst?'

'What?'

'It was on the wireless just now. He's pulled something in training and might not start. It could be Jimmy Greaves up front.'

'Blimey,' exclaimed Alex. 'That puts the kibosh on things. See ya,' and he left, slamming the door behind him.

'Right, next' the barber said turning round.

But the room was empty.

'Where the hell did he go?'

Alex flicked through the Cup Final programme as he made his way back to Oxford Street. His mind was in turmoil. He noticed his fingers had started to tremble and his breathing had become erratic. It was a feeling he had not known for many years. When he was young he had been prone to panic attacks.

But if Geoff Hurst doesn't play, what will happen? He thought for a second about the futility of their task if the England striker did not appear on the pitch when the teams line up to play. *Was some ironic twist about to be dealt?* Beads of sweat rolled down his forehead. He brushed them away with the striated scar on his hand.

A sudden gust came rushing along the street flapping the pages of Alex's programme and dissolving his anguished thoughts.

'A *cyclone*! Shit. Come on Alex, no more tricks.' He spoke out loud and could not calm a rising dormant phobia.

A distant memory of when he was a boy returned from the recesses of his mind. He had seen her before. He raked clumsily inside his jacket for his tablets. *Surely not here? Why now?*

He passed a bright red telephone booth and sensed a pair of eyes following him. When he turned he saw a woman open the kiosk door and step onto the pavement. As her searching eyes held him he felt a stab of terror.

She stood tall, athletic, clad in a black leather cat-suit and knee length boots. Her long hair was jet and her eyes of amber flame seared like laser beams. Her skin, the colour of ebony, was perfect in every way. When she spoke her voice was smooth and deep and powerful, and Alex saw the whiteness of her vampire-like canines and fear took hold of him.

'As you can see Alex, your mind can overcome time itself.'

'Go away Siren.'

'You brought me here Alex.'

'No, not now – go away from me. I thought you'd be gone forever.'

'I knew you as a boy – and I know your future.'

'You know nothing.'

'I know everything about you.'

'Fuck off! Go back to Finisterre. You're just an illusion.' He found he had clenched his fists and was beginning to shake uncontrollably.

'Can an illusion do this Alex?'

She flexed a long whip and raising it above her head brought it swiftly down onto the grey stone pavement. It cracked like thunder and orange sparks flashed and danced from the slender tip. Alex's heart began to pound as he watched Siren somersault backwards and with one leap spring

117

to the roof of the kiosk with the agility of a panther. She stood there glaring down at him with eyes of fire.

'I will always be with you, you know that.'

He threw a handful of tablets onto his tongue and they dissolved quickly.

She raised the whip and brought it down hissing as it sliced through the air. The end flayed faster than sound and the sonic crack caught Alex on the shin. Pain flooded through his body and a rush of adrenalin caused the transfixed man to turn and flee.

'You can run Alex, but I will be inside your head forever!'

He didn't look back. Rounding a corner he almost collided with a dozen boys riding coloured Lambrettas that buzzed like a swarm of wasps. He weaved between them and one teenager fell off tumbling across the road.

'Hey, watch it!' someone yelled.

Alex caught sight of a large open door just off the side-street. *Mods and Cyclones won't find me there*, he thought. He dived through without thinking, and then losing his balance, went sprawling across the floor inside. Seconds later he was coughing and wheezing on the worn stone tiles of an old church. The contents of his bag spilled out and the football went rolling along the length of the aisle towards the altar. A choir was singing in the chancel; they were dressed in burgundy robes and held hymn sheets. Several boys turned to see Alex face down beside the wooden pews.

A feeling of dizziness came over him as he hauled himself up. Alex ran a hand through his hair, breathed a sigh, and was instantly drawn to the west window where a huge stained-glass rose above the altar. He saw the kind face of a shepherd looking down at him. His eyes were deepest blue, like the ocean, Alex thought. And as he looked into those eyes the blueness seemed to widen and Alex found himself gazing out to a distant horizon where sea met sky. All around he saw golden sand. Then there came the sound of rhythmic beating, like giant wings, and when Alex looked up a mighty wind fell upon him and a great darkness quenched the canopy of sky.

The vision caused Alex to drop to his knees. He felt damp grass under his hands; rutted, uneven and earthy. A shout went up: '*The king is coming,*' and in the half-light Alex saw men with banners and smoke and horses, and a hail of arrows like a swift shadow cut through the air with a scream. He staggered a few steps and smelt the coppery stench of blood. *Where am I?* He panicked. Then he heard drums like the tide crashing against a cliff, and when he turned, there were men clad in leather and armour, all running as if playing out some bizarre game.

He rubbed his eyes in disbelief. Then towards him, through the height of battle, Alex saw the form of a small girl; her tousled hair trailed in the wind. She was a portrait of innocence amid a scene of chaos. In her hands she carried a dark object. When she spoke, her voice was tender, but it filled the air around him: '*I'm coming for you Alex.*'

His senses were released and the sound vanished. There came a sudden stillness and all Alex heard was the gentle harmony of choristers singing, and all he saw were the deep blue eyes of the shepherd looking down.

> '*...Be there at our sleeping and give us, we pray*
> *Your peace in our hearts Lord, at the end of the day.*'

15

Billy had spent twenty minutes leafing through hundreds of record sleeves. They seemed enormous as each one flopped over when he looked at their covers. *How do people carry these things? They weigh a ton.* Some bands he'd heard of: The Beatles, The Rolling Stones, The Kinks, The Who. Other artists he didn't know: Georgie Fame, The Seekers, Jackie Trent, Spencer Davies, Dusty Springfield, Manfred Mann. The list was endless.

While he'd been there, the theme tune of England's football team had been playing non-stop. Billy began singing along with Lonnie Donegan. A poster on the wall displayed the mascot as a scruffy lion sporting a Union Jack waist-coat. It was *World Cup Willie…*

'Willie, Willie…World Cup Willie…
He's tough as a lion and never will give up
That's why Willie is favourite for the cup
Willie, Willie…World Cup Willie…'

After a while he began changing the lyrics.

'That's why Billy is favourite for the cup, Billy, Billy…'

'What a wicked smell!' came a voice from behind him.

Billy jumped. 'Alex, what the hell…'

'iPods don't even come close?' Alex was sniffing the black vinyl of a Dave Clark Five album. 'What have we been missing all these years?'

The medication had targeted regions of his brain and cyclones and visions had been banished. A smile spread across his face. 'Hey look, *Tom Jones*,' Alex pointed to a photo on the wall. And who's that rock chick?'

'*Lulu* – she was on our show last year.'

'Wow, she goes back a long way – Lizzie loved her. What've you found?'

'This song's England's World Cup theme tune.'

'It's crap – flipping Willie – they should've banned it!'

'Guess what's number one right now?'

'Don't have a clue – *The Beatles*?'

'Nope. *Chris Farlowe And The Thunderbirds* with their song *Out Of Time*.'

'Hey – it could've been written for us!'

'Yeah. Here look what I got.' Billy dug into his bag and pulled out a golden object that looked like an angel. 'Nice piece of bling, eh?'

Alex grabbed the replica of the Jules Rimet World Cup trophy. 'Cool.'

'Solid gold plastic,' Billy said, 'cost a couple of quid in Carnaby Street.'

Alex tapped it and turned it over. 'Made in China. It'll look good in The Moon.'

'Yeah, if we get back!' Billy stuffed it back in his bag. 'Nice hair by the way; now you look like a proper 60s boy.'

'Thanks mate. Let's go, there's no point in buying any of this stuff, you can't exactly play these fossils. I want to check out Selfridges and pick up some of that Old Spice – you know, that splash-on James Bond uses.'

16

'D'you knows who I had in the back of my cab the other day?' The taxi driver squinted into his rear-view mirror at the three passengers sitting behind him. His attempt to make small talk fell on deaf ears.

No one said a thing; their faces blank, staring. The driver had seen many passengers in his cab, but these men made him feel nervous each time he shot a glance in their direction. The two beside the doors were heavily built and wore black suits. The man in the middle was tall and lean with blond wavy hair and a dark moustache. He sat hunched; his hands clasped awkwardly around his knees.

'Alright, I'll tell you,' he said after no response was forthcoming. 'It was that woman what got caught up with that spy scandal a few years ago.'

He flashed a look to see their reaction. Nothing.

'You know, *Christine Keeler*. She passed on secrets to them bleedin' Ruskies. What was his name, Ivanov something – or something Ivanov. Anyways, he worked for the Soviet embassy. By all accounts she was knocking off some bloke who had inside knowledge. *Stephen Ward*. Remember him? He did his self in. So something must have been going on. I reckon it was a bleedin' Soviet plot to bring down the British government. God knows how many times they've tried.'

The driver checked his mirror and got the same steely stare.

'Now, John Profumo, he got caught with his trousers down, and he was a bloody Tory minister at the time. Who can you trust these days! So when it all came out, so to speak, he had to go of course. Ain't surprising really, 'cause he was Secretary of State. You know one of them big knobs. At least that's what Christine Keeler said. So, Profumo resigns, Ward tops his self and Ivanov gets shipped back to Moscow. And he's not heard of again. Bleedin' farce I'd say. There's got to be more to it than that. I reckon the bloody Russians want to invade England.

'And I had Christine Keeler in the back of my cab, and d'you knows what I wanted to ask her?'

His mirror showed the man with the dark moustache sitting uneasily between the two heavyweights. Their gaze was vacant; their eyes intimidating. No one spoke.

'Alright, never mind. If you look to your left you can see the Tower of London.'

Their heads turned together and they peered through the window.

'Now the Tower of London was built by William the Conqueror of France nine-hundred years ago. Since 1066 England has never fallen to any other invader. Not the Frogs, the Krauts, the Ruskies or the Japs. Not that the Japs have ever tried. Come to think of it, it's only the Frogs and Krauts what have had a go. Oh, apart from them Spanish – and Franny Drake sorted them out good and proper. Off Plymouth as a matter of fact – but that's another story.'

The driver smoothed back his receding hair with fingers plump like chipolatas. He relished every minute of his job. Every day brought something different.

'So where was it next? Buck House and then a bit of shopping. Don't you just love London? Never a dull moment. Did I tell you there's a big game on tomorrow? 'Cause I can tell you don't come from these parts. We're up against them bleedin' Krauts again. It could be World War III out there tomorrow. I don't suppose you're that interested, coming from abroad and that. I guess you just want to look around. You'll find London'll grind to a stop. My advice is keep away from Wembley. Go check out a bar in Covent Garden and keep well away.'

The reflection in his mirror showed three impassive faces.

Thirty minutes later the black cab pulled up in a bustling high-street. Georgy Makarov paid the fair and Anatoly Petrova swung open the door above the curb and knocked over a pedestrian.

Alex Bell went sprawling across the pavement; his bag thudding into Billy Gunn.

'Watch out,' Alex screamed, looking up at the huge man dressed in black; his massive bulk eclipsed the sky.

'Uh, comrade, excuse.' His voice was deep and thick with an accent inherited from the extremities of Siberia. He held out a strong hand and pulled Alex to his feet with one jolt. 'Excuse,' he repeated.

The two other men got out of the taxi. One slammed the door and they headed with intent towards the entrance of Selfridges. They had nothing so lavish back in their homeland. Alex and Billy watched them go in.

'Bloody typical,' Billy was saying. 'They come over here and think they own the bloody place.'

Alex continued to stare. 'Do you know...Do you know who that was?'

'No idea. Why should I?'

'It was that Russian bloke – the *linesman* – no he's from *Azerbaijan*.'

'Who *Tofik*?' replied Billy not believing him. 'You sure?'

'Yeah, we saw him in Trinity – yesterday?'

'No it's decades away now – but you're right – we did see him, Schneider put him up on the screen.'

'Yeah, he had blond hair and a black 'tach.' Alex's mind was racing. 'This could be our chance to get ahead of tomorrow's game.'

'What're you talking about?'

'Come on let's find him. Quick, dig out that Wembley programme, I've got an idea.'

Billy wasn't warming to the plan, whatever that may be, but he reluctantly followed Alex into Selfridges.

It wasn't difficult hunting down two massive men in dark suits and a tall, lean man with blond hair and a black moustache. They were loitering around the lingerie section.

'Looks like Tofik's old lady could do with some excitement in the bedroom department,' Billy commented.

'Or his mistress!'

'How can we be sure it's him?'

'We can't. Look, if I go up behind him and call his name, he'll turn round. If it's not him – he won't. That's the theory.'

'It's a long shot.' Billy knew it wouldn't work.

Idly perusing at the underwear, they sidled over to where the three were standing. The tall man with the dark moustache was examining a lacy bodice. Alex went as close as he dared. A number of shoppers were passing through the aisle and he hid behind them for temporary cover. The men were talking in muffled tones using a language Alex couldn't make out.

'Mr Bakhramov,' Alex said in a timid voice, testing out his idea. There was no response. He tried a little louder, 'Mr Bakhramov.' Still the tall man carried on running his fingers over a cream coloured camisole. This time Alex shouted and Billy looked away with embarrassment: '*Tofik.*'

One of the large minders turned and scowled at Alex, his Mongolian features were creased across his face.

'Go. You go,' he said in a heavy accent.

Then the tall man turned to see what was happening.

'Mr Bakhramov,' persisted Alex, thrusting the programme towards him, 'can I have your autograph and a quick word. It's urgent.'

'Погворнте русского?' the linesman replied.

For a moment Alex delayed as a train of thought suddenly entered his head. Maybe it was because the man had actually spoken to him, albeit something Alex couldn't understand, or maybe it was because he'd already been told about something being *urgent*. He couldn't quite work it out. But he went on, waving his hands frantically in the hope that it would help with what he was saying.

'Tomorrow...World Cup. Geoff Hurst kicks – ball falls on line. Goal. Give goal. Yes. *Geoff Hurst – ball – goal*!'

They stood facing each other, and for a few seconds there was an awkward silence. 'I think Mrs Bakhramov would like these French knickers,' Alex added with a smirk.

'Idiot,' one of the accomplices said and steered the tall man away into the depths of Selfridges. The man with the moustache stared back at them with a confused look as he was harried away. Then he was gone; swallowed up amongst the hoard of busy shoppers.

'It *was* him Billy.' Alex was certain. 'I think I may have got a subliminal message through.'

17

Alex and Billy strolled along Oxford Street as if it were just another day out in London.

Almost every store displayed posters of the England team. Red, white and blue scarves and rosettes festooned shop fronts. Banners with *Come on Boys* and *England for the Cup* were in abundance, as were photographs of Captain Bobby Moore and the World Cup mascot.

'It's Willie!' cried Billy on passing one shop. '...*He's tough as a lion, and never will give up, that's why Willie is favourite for the cup...*'

'Knock it off Billy. Don't forget you're a ball-boy. You won't be singing tomorrow.'

They were near Carnaby Street and close to the stores Biba and Lady Jane when Alex heard a busker playing a road-worn acoustic guitar. He stood there propped against a lamppost outside the men's fashion shop Barron John. He wore a dark grey trench-coat and a maroon beret. His guitar case lay open by his feet containing a heap of coins. Business had been good. As they approached, Alex pulled out a silver six-pence from his pocket and tossed it in.

'Thanks mate,' the guitarist said, shifting chords from G to E-minor.

'Nice song.'

Moments later Alex found he was humming the tune. 'Have you heard that song before?'

'Nope.' Billy was more intent on looking at the London road map he'd found in his bag. 'Why don't we head up here to the Telecom Tower,' he said. 'I think you can go up to a viewing gallery. It was the original London Eye. Hey look it says here: the *PO Tower*. This map's old! And look, there it is, up that street,' he pointed. 'Right where it should be.'

Reaching 580 feet above the surrounding buildings stood the iconic pencil-like structure built in the mid-Sixties.

'Let's check it out then. What else we got to do?' We've seen just about all there is in London.'

'Yeah, but not *this* London!' Alex added with a grin.

They walked north along Tottenham Court Road. Alex still had the busker's tune spinning round inside his head. *What is that song?* He felt infuriated at not being able to identify it. *I just can't get it out – I've heard it before.*

A few minutes later, shielding their eyes, they stared up at the Post Office Tower rising above them towards the cloudy sky. The column was built of grey concrete and blue glass and near the top were aerials and communication dishes and higher still the bulge of the revolving restaurant with its observation gallery. It had been hailed an architectural wonder when it was opened to the public just two months ago. The design was quite literally a revolutionary landmark on the London skyline, as instantly recognised as St Paul's Cathedral, Big Ben and Tower Bridge.

They approached the entrance and walked up the wide steps. Standing at the top were two security officers wearing drab navy blue suits. One of them came over.

'Excuse me gentlemen, you can't go up today; there's a private function going on. Only those involved in tomorrow's World Cup can attend.'

'What sort of function is it?' Alex was keen to know.

'They got guests from show-biz up there. Footballers, entertainment, that sort of thing – a real good bash I've heard. You boys had better be moving on, sorry.'

Alex and Billy exchanged a look.

'Is this good enough?' Alex produced his Wembley ID, knowing he had nothing to lose.

The guard inspected it and flashed it towards his colleague.

'Ball-boys, eh? The lifts are right over there.' He pointed.

'That's four-bob you've saved.' The other guard called out: 'Enjoy the show.'

Alex and Billy didn't hesitate. They leapt up the wide steps that led to the elevator. The logo above them displayed the name of the viewing gallery in red and blue lettering: *Topofthetower*. Seconds later they were inside.

'What a result! This could be working out better than we planned,' Billy said.

'Too right mate; who wants to walk the streets when there's a show to go to...'

'And food...'

'Yeah, these passes are better than American Express!' Alex hung the ID round his neck.

The elevators were called *Express Lifts* for a good reason. In-keeping with the Tower's futuristic design, they could reach the viewing gallery on the thirty-fourth floor in forty seconds. No other building in the country could boast such a rate of climb. The doors closed and their increased weight signalled that they had begun to ascend. For a second, Alex recalled the pang of vertigo he'd experienced deep inside Trinity.

His moment of anxiety seemed to jolt the annoying tune to return and haunt him. And then he realised where he'd heard it. In fact, he'd heard it countless times, but never from a busker on a London street – and certainly never from a musician in 1966.

'Billy,' Alex said grabbing his friend's arm, 'that tune – I know what it is – but it's impossible!'

'What d'you mean?'

The floor levels were counting up on a mechanical display screen: 26, 27, 28...

Alex began to sing: '*We're just two lost souls swimming in a fish bowl, year after year...*'

'What *Floyd*?'

'*...Running over the same old ground. What have we found? The same old fears. Wish you were here...*'

'That's an old song.'

'Yeah, but Roger Waters didn't write it until, um, '75. That's what, nine years' time!'

32, 33, 34… The lift door slid open letting in a rush of colour.

Alex and Billy gawped. The place was filled with chatter and laughter and people.

George Best, the famous football player, had his arm round a girl with long blond hair and he was whispering into the ear of another.

18

Above a short flight of steps, and framed by an arched stone entrance, stood a young woman dressed in a blue trouser suit; her wavy blond hair caught in the breeze that flowed through the London road. On her lapel she wore a gold brooch that glinted in the late morning sunlight. She looked down to her party of guests standing along the pavement and began to address them with a fluent patter she had used before.

'Please select the appropriate translation on your *BabelComs* and I'll go on.' She paused for a second. 'Well here we are in Long Acre and as you can see we're right outside The Freemasons' Arms just two minutes from Covent Garden. Although the outside of the building hasn't changed much over the past few hundred years, one thing has, and that's the name. Originally it was called The Freemasons' Tavern which dated back to the seventeenth century. Before this four storey building was erected there used to be a far older meeting place which would have been frequented by influential people from high society. Nell Gwyn would have sung here, Samuel Pepys may have written his diary here, and scientists like Isaac Newton and Edmond Halley would have drunk a pint or two. Even Charles II could have refreshed himself as London burned.'

Her guests listened and occasionally nodded to each other as if picking up on some interesting nugget about the history of the City.

'Then moving on, in the 1860s, the rules of football were first discussed and written down by a group who wanted to regulate tighter control over a game which more resembled rugby rather than soccer. Before that, the game was played in the streets by large mobs who used no rules whatsoever. It was here then, that the laws of the game were born. So let's go inside.'

The party trooped up the steps and entered through the heavy black door. The hostess held the door and pointed the way to the lounge.

'Ah, Mr Sinyavsky,' she looked down towards the pavement, 'these steps are not Zimmer-frame friendly. Let me give you a hand.'

When the guide walked into the bar, her party were already busy studying the menu on the small wooden tables and glancing around at the drab décor. One grey-haired lady had bought a postcard of London showing Trafalgar Square. She started writing, although she knew for certain it would not be sent. Using the old cliché she had begun with: *Wish you were here...*

The Rep walked into the centre of the lounge and turned to speak.

'Perhaps not the prettiest of London pubs,' she said, waving a slender hand in the air, 'but nonetheless it has its own place in history. Although not obvious, if you look over there you'll see a manuscript bearing the original fourteen rules. Among the pioneers at the time were graduates from Cambridge University who wanted to make the distinction between rugby and football. In those days it wasn't clear at all because running with the ball in football was allowed. So in this public house, representatives of several London teams including Blackheath, The War Office, Crusaders and No Names of Kilburn met to thrash out the rules, and Mr Ebenezer Cobb Morley proposed the formation of the FA.

'The laws became known as the Cambridge Rules and they were agreed on Monday, 26th October 1863. One member once famously said: "Football is a gentleman's game played by hooligans, and rugby is a hooligan's game played by gentlemen." Maybe he was right. Even in the modern game there are many thugs playing in the English league!

'If you read the rules, you'll find there were no need for throw-ins, crossbars or even goalkeepers. And strangely enough, there was no clause for equal numbers of players – but – they did have the foresight to include an off-side rule. I think you'll agree the Beautiful Game has come a long way since then.

'Yes, and you can also see there are the obligatory photos of some of the famous captains like Jimmy Armfield, Billy Wright and Johnny Haynes – and there's England manager Walter Winterbottom with Queen Elizabeth. And right there, on the plaque, it reads: *The Football Association founded here.*

'So, ladies and gentlemen, I hope you enjoy your lunch, which of course will be typical of this era. You certainly won't find a gluten-free diet.

'It just leaves me to remind you that tomorrow will be our visit to the game at Wembley Stadium. Please can I ask you to assemble promptly after breakfast. Don't forget to bring your *iCams*, *ePochs*, *holophones* and other *rKive* devices. I'm sure you'll want to catch all those historic moments – whatever happens.

'Once again, have a great day, and thank you for travelling with *Quantum Tours.*'

19

Alex and Billy were suddenly engulfed by scores of guests dressed in bright and garish clothing. In comparison, George Best looked positively conservative in a white suit and purple shirt. His two acquaintances were far more informal. Both had the briefest of miniskirts and wore stilettos that made them stand taller than the famous Manchester United football player. They were giggling and sipping Martini from fluted glasses. One of the girls popped an olive into George's mouth and then gently pressed the tip of her long, false fingernail into the dimple on his chin. She laughed.

A waiter came by balancing a silver tray on one hand. As he scooted by, Alex and Billy grabbed a glass each, then they forced their way in amongst the guests. Alex drank his straightaway and took another as he passed a waitress. He had no idea what he was drinking. *Anything cold and alcoholic*, he thought.

A vivid whirlpool of emerald and violet wriggled and pulsed across an expanse of wall, in time with thumping music. Large posters had been erected showing photos of England's games during the World Cup tournament. One famous shot Alex had seen before was taken after the whistle in the semi-final. It showed Alf Ramsey stopping George Cohen from swapping his shirt with an Argentine player. The manager had branded the South Americans as *animals* when their captain, Antonio Rattin, refused to leave the field after being sent off.

Hanging from the ceiling were a festive display of Union flags and banners displaying *Come on England*. Alex was thankful that World Cup Willie was nowhere to be seen. Nearby, a group of celebrities were having their photographs taken and Alex recognised former England skipper Billy Wright with his wife Babs and heavyweight boxer Henry Cooper. Flashlights were popping and people were shaking hands and grinning broadly.

'Hey, the original Posh and Becks!'

'This is better than any gig we got back home,' added Billy who had started to move in time with the music.

'Yeah, I feel a Sixties party coming on when we get back.'

'What if we don't get back?'

'Sod it – who cares? We got a final to watch. Look, I want to see the view from up here.'

They pushed their way towards one of the large windows that spanned the revolving restaurant. As they weaved between the crowd, they picked up snippets of random conversation.

'...Harold Wilson; look at what happened in '63...'

'...The Hollies are just fab darling...'

'...Caviar's damn good, hey, get us another sherbet Gerry...'

'...Maybe Bobby Charlton, maybe Jimmy Greaves. Who knows..?'

'There, over there,' Alex said, pointing.

'Hold on, it's not easy humping this bag and carrying a glass...'

'Just drink it.'

'...Barbara Windsor – you don't get many of them to the pound ...'

'...So I said to Ringo, "Why *Yellow Submarine*?" and he said. "Well I was bound to get a go one day..."'

'...*Paper knickers* – it's true Penny, they're the latest thing. Wear them once then throw them away...'

'...Thank God for Pickles; we'd be right up the creek...'

'…Look I backed Arkle in the Gold Cup – so I say put your money on the Germans…'

'…It's the ninth time I've seen the Sound of Music…'

'…I think that's Mary Quant over there, and who's that with her – is that Jean Shrimpton..?'

'What's that song Billy? You seem to know all these old ones.'

'Um, it's the Dave Clark Five – *Glad All Over*…'

'Wow, you know your stuff!'

Billy joined in, '…*I'm feeling, boom, boom, glad all over, yes, I'm-a, boom, boom, glad all over, baby I'm, boom, boom, glad all over, so glad you're mi-i-i-i-ine*…'

'Okay Billy, dump your gear down here. Let's have a look.'

The window offered a wonderful panorama of west London with the sun a blaze of vermilion low in the sky. Alex scanned the darkening horizon; how different the skyline looked, he thought.

'Look, right there,' he sounded excited.

Billy squinted and followed his gaze.

'The Twin Towers. What a sight!' It had been many years since Alex had seen the old Wembley Stadium. 'Just like St Paul's Cathedral, only twice as good!'

'That's where our journey ends.'

'Nope, that's where it starts Billy-boy.'

Alex leant forward and pressed the palms of his hands on the window and stared longingly at the famous sporting theatre in the distance. He found it hard to believe that it had really come to this. Only a day ago he and Billy had walked into The Moon and found Warwick Vane waiting for them. How bizarre, Alex thought, that the meeting with some unkempt American telling stories about time-slips was now decades hence. *Are we to grow old and never again do another show*? His train of thought was suddenly snatched away by a voice booming over the PA.

'Ladies and gentlemen…'

Alex turned to see a man in a black tuxedo bathed in a spotlight and standing on a platform.

'I hope you're all enjoying the evening. We're all here to wish Bobby Moore and the boys great success and we're sure that this time tomorrow there will be an even bigger party...'

There were shouts and cheers and one loud voice let out, 'Come on England.'

'...So, to get the party off to a flying start, will you welcome someone I know you'll enjoy watching. You won't have seen anything like this before – she's sensational; she rules – she is – *Miss Britannia* ...'

The lights were killed, and there, silhouetted on the stage was the slim figure of a young woman. Her lithe body had fine curves outlined perfectly by a huge luminous clock face, in front of which she stood motionless. Her back was to the audience and Alex realised to his surprise that she wore nothing apart from a pair of briefs and high-heels. There was a sharp wolf-whistle. Then all at once there came a flash of light and a crash of sound.

A sudden vortex of synthesized music like a surging spiral began spinning inside Alex's head. He tried to remember where he had heard it before. It turned out to be the distinctive theme tune from the cult BBC series: *Doctor Who*. Created by the Radiophonic Workshop, it was one of the most enduring pieces of television music. During countless episodes, young children had taken refuge behind front room sofas the moment the theme tune had erupted from the opening Titles.

And there, surrounded by this sound stood a woman with her arms crossed and fingers clasped over her slender shoulders. Her dark hair hung in waves down her back. The second hand on the large clock began ticking backwards from twelve, and as it moved anticlockwise a most extraordinary thing happened.

Britannia flung her arms in the air and from nowhere a bra strap attached itself, the clasp fastening across her naked back. Where it had come from, no one could tell. She swivelled to face the audience and did a high kick; her stiletto reached above her head. As she brought her foot back to the floor she wore a tight navy blue skirt cut just above the knee. Next she performed a pirouette and suddenly she was wearing a matching jacket. She gyrated her hips in time with the pulsing music and when she flayed her long black hair it magically wrapped neatly on top of her head. For the first time Alex saw her attractive face and her dark eyes. The clock showed the reverse striptease had taken exactly sixty seconds. The audience began to cheer and clap and many men were whistling, but Britannia had a further surprise.

Slowly she began to rise above the stage. Alex was astonished. Even though it was dark he could see no means of support. She began to move in a smooth arc, sweeping effortlessly a few feet above the audience. Eventually she came to rest over the backward ticking timepiece. Britannia lowered herself into an opening and Alex saw that the clock wasn't flat but had depth to it. Defying gravity she floated gently down and pointing her fingers towards the ceiling, slipped inside and disappeared from sight.

At that very second a woman emerged from the crowd and began to climb the stairs to the stage. She wore a white mini-skirt and white knee length boots; her dark hair hung over her shoulders. As she reached the clock she spun round and raised her hands in the air and struck a pose. Wearing a Union Jack top was *Britannia*.

The boys looked at each other in amazement.

'Wow, she rocks,' Alex said.

'Yeah, I've got a boner,' added Billy.

When they looked again, she was gone.

The audience applauded loudly until they were interrupted by the compere.

'...Ladies and gentlemen – the breath-taking Britannia...'

'Let's get another drink Billy-boy. I need a shot of something after that.'

Alex snatched another cocktail as a tray went by. The lack of food and the rapid injection of alcohol were conspiring to make Alex feel light-headed.

'That bloke over there in the pink chiffon,' Alex said waving his glass around, 'I've seen him before...'

'That's *David Bowie*.'

'You're right – it's a young Bowie. A few years and Ziggy Stardust will...' Alex stopped because it wasn't Billy who had spoken.

Standing beside them was a man in a tweed jacket. His mop of hair was a mess and he wore heavy black-rimmed glasses.

'Who the heck's *Ziggy Stardust*?' The words whistled through the gap between his teeth.

'Um, just a friend.'

'Dick Miller...Daily Sketch.' He thrust out a hand and Alex shook it automatically.

'I'm just moving around and sniffing out a story. So how'd you guys get in?' He flipped open a notepad.

'Same way as everyone else,' Alex said, 'we were invited. D'you think we gate crashed?'

'Cause we're ball-boys,' cut in Billy, 'for the game.'

'What tomorrow?'

'Yeah, we'll be there – right by the pitch.'

'Wow, that's really interesting.' He licked the lead on a stubby pencil and scribbled something down.

'Let's get this straight – so you're gonna be running around fetching the ball?'

'Got it in one. The clue's right there Dickie-boy.'

'Well you're gonna get a helluva view.'

'Yeah, we're gonna see it all – extra time, the lot. We'll even see when the ball lands on the line.' The alcohol was starting to loosen his tongue and play tricks with his thinking.

Billy tugged Alex's arm. He felt his friend was saying more than he should.

'What's that?' said Miller.

'We'll be able to see it all,' Billy intervened, 'even when we score.'

'Are we gonna score then?'

'Yeah, I'd say Hurst'll get a couple.'

'And a dodgy one,' Alex added.

Billy turned and gave Alex a stare. 'Shut up,' he whispered through gritted teeth.

'Who did you guys say you were?'

'Alan Ball and Ziggy Stardust!'

Suddenly there was a flash from the reporter's camera and a blast of light imprinted a fading ghost on their eyesight.

Alex and Billy blinked instinctively and when their vision returned they were thankful to find that Dick Miller was nowhere to be seen. The speakers blared again.

'...And so ladies and gentlemen, will you put your hands together for a new band on the scene. John Lennon has said they could be the next Beatles. Will you welcome these boys from London; they are ... *The Pink Floyd*.'

20

Alex's jaw fell open and he spilt his drink down his England football shirt. Standing there in front of him and illuminated in spectral colours was the original line-up who, in a few years, were to become world famous.

Roger Waters was tuning his Rickenbacker bass; Richard Wright stooped over his Hammond organ; Nick Mason sat ready behind his Premier drum kit, and there in the centre, wearing a psychedelic shirt, was the inspiration behind the band. Syd Barrett was fiddling with the controls on his Fender Telecaster. He ran his hand through his long curly hair and looked over to the band. Mounted high on each side stood a stack of Vox speakers. There came a sudden shrill noise rising like a rocket and then the drums began to pound a steady rhythm.

'I know this,' Alex said. '*See Emily Play,*' he shouted and punched a fist into the air like someone who'd just seen their team score.

Then Syd Barrett stepped up to the microphone to sing as a squeal of feedback whistled uncontrollably.

'Emily tries but misunderstands
She's often inclined to borrow
Somebody's dream 'til tomorrow
There is no other day, let's try it another way
You'll lose your mind and play, free games for May
See Emily play...'

'Billy, we're actually seeing Floyd in one of their first gigs. I've never seen Syd before.' Alex was in rapture.

'Where's Dave Gilmour?'

'He doesn't feature for another year or so. Then of course they chuck Syd out. They just didn't pick him up one day – and that was it – goodbye to a genius.'

'Why'd they do that?'

'Good question. Syd began to lose it big time. There're only so many prima donnas you can have in a band full of inflated egos. Sometimes they wouldn't talk to each other for years. It was a miracle they got back together for that *Live8* gig. Who was it? Bob Geldof must have thrown in some humungous sweeteners. The rest as they say is…'

'…The *future*.'

'Yeah, right.'

The song finished to muted applause and was immediately followed with a driving guitar rhythm played by Syd Barrett, with Nick Mason striking heavily on drums.

'Oh yeah – *Astronomy Domine*,' Alex seemed delirious.

'*Astronomy what*?'

'*Domine* – it was Floyd's first real adventure into psychedelia. These boys were doing this before The Beatles, Hendrix and Zeppelin. But then they were probably on something when they wrote this stuff.'

There was a deluge of colour which vibrated spontaneously to the rhythm. Fractal patterns fell on Syd Barrett's face as he began to sing.

'*Lime and limpid green, a second scene*
A fight between the blue you once knew, floating down
The sound resounds around the waters underground
Jupiter and Saturn, Oberon, Miranda and Titania
Neptune, Titan, stars can frighten…'

As Alex watched, flashes of white light began to explode in all directions. Bolts seemed to leap from their guitars and drums. Syd stamped his boot and there came another flash.

'Hey, I didn't know they were using lasers this early.'

'What you talking about?'

'It's just going everywhere,' Alex shouted and threw his hands around. 'All over the place.'

'I don't know what you're mean. What lasers?' Billy couldn't see what he was talking about.

'This is just so good.'

'I've seen better.'

'Yeah, but not in the Sixties.'

'True.' Billy thought Alex must be over-reacting on watching the original line-up of his favourite band play live.

Syd Barrett broke into a guitar solo which screamed a sonic avalanche. Many guests moved away in disgust. They had never before heard such radical improvisations. The song finished with the band chanting.

'Lime and limpid green, the sounds surround
The icy waters underground.'

Alex whooped with delight and clapped with more enthusiasm than anyone else. Most were not impressed and someone shouted: 'Where's *The Stones*?'

Darkness descended and when the lights came up The Pink Floyd were out of sight.

'I've gotta meet these guys,' Alex said. 'It might be my only chance. I'll be back. Perhaps if I warn Syd to stay off the mushrooms…'

'Alex, don't cock this up. We're just ball-boys…'

Billy had a feeling that Alex was somehow not himself. He put it down to his friend's excitement.

As he watched Alex push his way through the crowd, Billy felt a gentle tap on his shoulder. When he turned round he was surprised to see who was standing next to him.

Alex found Syd Barrett putting his guitar away into a shoddy black hard-case. He was stooping on the floor surrounded by yards of tangled cable, a large tape machine and a battered effects box.

'Hey man – fab gig!' Alex adlibbed, hoping his colloquial turn of phrase matched the lingo of Sixties London.

The band's front-man looked up but didn't recognise who had spoken and went on clipping his guitar case together.

'We've done better,' he said flatly.

'Thought you might've done *Interstellar Overdrive*.'

The last latch on the case clicked shut and the guitarist momentarily stopped, then standing to his full height, faced Alex.

'You heard *Overdrive*?'

'Well, kind of.' For a moment Alex wondered if he'd said the right thing.

'I can count on one hand those who've heard Overdrive. We're only just working on it.' The musician squinted.

Syd Barrett stood a little taller than Alex. The lighting picked out his frizzy hair and his intense dark eyes. Alex realised they were both about the same age.

'Um, I've talked to people who've, um, heard you rehearsing. Yeah, you know, Dave.'

'*Dave*?'

'David Gilmour.'

'You know Dave?'

'Yeah. Well, I've met him a couple of times at the *UFO Club*.' Alex had a copy of Nick Mason's biography: *Inside Out – A Personal History Of Pink Floyd*. In it he'd read that the Underground Freak Out Club was the venue where the band had performed and where they had met David Gilmour.

'He's a good bloke, Dave. Useful. He's got some nice licks,' Syd Barrett added.

'You should stick around with Dave. You never know, he might fit in.'

'Maybe.'

Alex looked round and saw Roger Waters talking to Nick Mason. *I can't believe this is happening; I'm actually talking to Syd Barrett.*

The drummer was dismantling his kit. As he was shifting the snare, the high-hat toppled and crashed to the floor. The sound caused Alex to see sparks fly in all directions.

'Wow, you guys can do some crazy stuff.'

'We're getting there,' Syd said; his eyelids heavy, his stare vacant.

Alex dug into his bag. 'Look, I don't suppose I should be doing this, but there's something I think you should hear. Stick these in your ears.'

'What is it?'

'It's an iPod – but that doesn't matter – have a listen. You may want to run it by Roger. I think he'll find it very interesting. This stuff beats Sergeant Pepper's any day!'

'Sergeant who?' Syd Barrett pressed the tiny pads into his ears.

'Never mind – you'll find out next year. Look it's been like, far-out talking to you. Can you stick your name on my World Cup programme?'

'Yeah sure thing. There you go mate.'

'Thanks. And can I suggest that you drop the prefix *The* from your band's name. *Pink Floyd* sounds much more cool. Trust me!'

The guitarist looked at him. 'Pink Floyd, eh?' His eyes seemed empty.

'Yeah,' Alex said with a grin. He slapped him on the shoulder and left. It was the last time he saw Syd Barrett, and it was the first time that the guitarist had heard The Dark Side of the Moon.

Alex threaded his way into the crowd and then looked back. He saw the eccentric musician staring trance-like as he listened. With one hand he held a small pad in his ear; with the other he turned the iPod over, admiring its sleek simplicity.

When Alex found Billy he was talking with a young woman. As he approached she turned round. It was Britannia.

'Hello Alex, Billy's been telling me all about you.' Her voice was soft and precise, a London accent with a hint of somewhere else. Luscious dark hair hung over her bare shoulders and her intense stare drew Alex towards her.

'Has he? That's Billy for you, always out to impress the girls.'

'Now Alex, I hear you've got something a bit special with you.' Britannia gestured as Alex held his rucksack tightly. 'In your bag I believe.'

He was taken aback. *What does she know?* Alex sent Billy a steely look. 'It's supposed to be a secret,' Alex hissed through clenched teeth.

'You know – the *programme*. I was telling Britannia how we ran into Tofik.'

'Oh yeah,' Alex dropped his guard and relaxed. 'I just got Syd Barrett's.'

'Well, you're getting quite a collection,' she smiled, 'who will it be next: *Bobby Moore*?'

'I wish. Autographs are worth more when someone's…'

'…*Dead*?' interrupted Britannia.

'Um, yeah, I guess so.'

Billy broke the awkward silence. 'Britannia was about to explain how she did it.'

'Did what?'

'Her act; you know, how she did all that backwards stuff.'

Both boys looked at the young woman with interest. Just a few minutes ago they had experienced a rush of testosterone which had electrified their senses producing all manner of biochemical reactions.

She brushed away dark hair from her shoulder with a flick of her fingers. 'It's just science,' she said. 'There's no secret – magic and science – it's all the same.'

'What about that flying stunt?' asked Alex, 'I couldn't see any strings.'

'Science again – and a bit of illusion.' Her eyes twinkled.

'Science was never that interesting when I was at school,' Alex said.

'Perhaps you went to the wrong school.'

'Yeah, I should've gone to *Hogwarts*!'

'As that famous scientist, Arthur C Clarke once said: "*Any sufficiently advanced technology is indistinguishable from magic.*"'

'Yeah, and his film, *2001*, was crap. No one understood it.' Just for a moment Alex wondered if the novel had been published in 1966. *Would anyone know*? He thought. He plucked another drink from a passing salver and took a slurp. 'So what celebs we got here tonight, apart from you and Floyd?'

'I'm not sure I can be compared to such A-listers, but let's see.' She looked around. 'I saw Twiggy and Justin de

Villeneuve earlier. Over there by the bar, that's Cathy McGowan talking to Crispian St Peters. She presents *Ready Steady Go*. And someone mentioned that Ray Davies was here, but I haven't seen him.'

'What the Kinks bloke?' Billy said.

'Yeah him.'

'He's a dedicated follower of fashion,' Billy added quoting a line from his song.

'Apparently he's wearing purple flairs and a gold waistcoat.'

'Shouldn't be hard to spot then.'

'And the Tory MP, Norman St John Stevas was seen sniffing round some mystery blond.'

'No change there then – it'll be all over the tabloids tomorrow,' Alex added with sarcasm.

'No change indeed – it might even make the *broadsheets*.' She held his gaze. 'So Alex, why are you here?'

He looked into her dark, searching eyes and realised that the liberal quantity of alcohol coursing through his veins was starting to cloud his thinking. His mind was slowing and his vision began to spin.

'Boy, you cut to the chase Brit. We're just a couple of ordinary guys out to fulfil a dream.'

'And what is your dream Alex?'

'I expect Billy's already told you. We've got this gig tomorrow and we're gonna be keeping the final going.'

'Yes Billy did mention it. And just how was it you got such a lucrative deal?'

'We, um, volunteered.'

'…Yeah, we like to do a bit a charity work,' Billy put in.

'And like, we were in the right place at the right time.'

Britannia paused and gave them both a scrutinising look. 'If you ask me, I think you boys are in hot water.'

'What do you mean?' Alex was sharp. 'I'd say it was *tepid*.'

'I mean there's more to what you're saying.'

'Nope, that's it. We're just a couple of local boys about to make good.'

'Maybe, but at what cost? I sense there's more to it than that.'

'Come on Brit, what're you trying to say?' Alex was becoming more irate as the alcohol was taking hold.

'I think you boys are in some kind of trouble.'

'Well we're not.' Alex was emphatic. He brushed his hands through his hair and tried to focus on the attractive woman standing in front of him. He found her stunning but the more he spoke to her the more he disliked her probing questions.

'Anyway, what's it to you?'

'I know about you Alex – more than you think.'

'You're talking crap? There's no one here who knows anything about me.'

'No there isn't, is there, *Alex James Bell*?' She was assertive but softly spoken.

'So what! Anyone can read my tag.' He waved his ID at Britannia and Billy snatched it up.

'But it doesn't give your second name.'

'What!'

'*James* is a family name. You were named after your mother.'

'Is that true?' Billy asked.

'Yeah, but…Have you set me up Billy?'

'I've said nothing.'

It took several seconds for the revelation to sink in. *How could she know*? Alex shot a look to Billy and back to Britannia. Suddenly he felt a wave of nausea rising inside him. *How could she possibly know*?

'I gotta go to the gents,' he stammered.

Almost in a panic he barged his way between the hordes of guests and bounced off Diana Dors. He dropped the glass and it shattered on the parquet floor. His steps became erratic and the guests milling around only hindered his escape. As he looked at the faces he passed he was shocked to see that some had eyes that seemed to bleed with emerald or yellow or a deep crimson colour. Beads of sweat began to trickle down his brow and his pulse began to race.

When he burst into the refuge of the gentlemen's rest room he was alone. He found he was breathing heavily as he staggered over to a basin and stared at his own reflection in the mirror. His bag fell to the tiled floor and the sound reverberated. Filling a sink with cold water he splashed handfuls over his face and then immersed his head in the basin. His skin seemed to be on fire. The relief was wonderful. He held his breath for as long as he could and then came up gasping for air. 'How could she have known?' He stood there looking at his distorted face in the mirror.

His eyes stared back at him; vacant, confused, lost. *This is all Vane's fault. I wish he'd never been in The Moon. Timeslips suck!*

He pulled the plug and watched the water spiral down. *That's bloody weird*, he thought, as gravity twisted the water. *It's spinning the wrong way.*

Suddenly a toilet door flew open with a crash. Alex spun round and couldn't believe what he saw. Dressed in a black uniform, was a dwarf. On his jacket were two rows of brass buttons. His head was bald and he stood no taller than three feet. In one hand he held a rifle with a fixed bayonet. Alex realised he was running straight towards him.

'Aargh!' the dwarf cried. His voice was surprisingly loud. He held his rifle pointing forward as if he were leaping from a trench on some battlefield. But just as he got to within a few strides of Alex he plunged the bayonet into the holdall on the floor. The long knife made a tearing noise as it pierced the canvas. Then sprinting with short strides, his tiny legs carried him out of the rest room with the sound of his boots smacking on the tiled-floor. As fast as he had appeared he was gone, all in the space of a few seconds. Alex stood there transfixed and pinned to the basin which was starting to overflow.

'Hey!' Alex scooped up his bag and barged open the door. For a moment he stopped because what he saw was not what he expected. The door behind him flapped back and forth on heavy hinges and the bright light filtered through until the door closed. The thumping bass music from the party disappeared. There was silence. It was cold and dark. He took a step and his trainers scrunched grit underfoot. Large flagstones stretched away in front of him. He found himself in a narrow passage with high stone walls on either side. Somewhere up ahead he heard footsteps fading away.

'Come back you little shit.'

Without thinking he followed the sound. *What is this*, he thought, *some kind of service shaft*?

A little further on, Alex found that the passage began to curve and as it did he tripped on something hard. He stumbled and found he'd reached a flight of steps. Looking up he saw stairs climbing above like a keep in a castle. A glowing torch flickered on the wall. He could still hear footsteps somewhere above. The staircase spiralled steeply and he soon found he was breathing hard. *What am I doing*? *Where is this*? he thought. *I must be near the top of the tower by now.*

At that moment there came a sound that caused Alex to freeze where he stood. It was a deep and ghastly scream that sent a shudder through the stale air. It came from a narrow slit, like an archer's window, in the brickwork above him. With muscles quivering he found a purchase and raised himself up to look. For a split second, in the dark, he caught sight of a figure – an outline of a man. Then he heard a shout.

'It is done! The beast is slain.'

Alex's grip loosened and he fell onto a floor covered in thick carpet. There were voices. He thought he could hear Billy. His fingernails clutched at the dots and shapes in the weave. All around were patterns that Alex found confusing. They mutated into ants. Marching ants, countless in number surrounded him and spread like leprosy over his arm. The lines of insects began to twist and contort and writhe and hiss, and they became a brood of vipers that squirmed and stank like the gush of sulphurous vomit. Then as the apparition dissolved he lost all sense of being.

21

It was black.

As black as anything could be, and yet it was blacker still. Alex could see nothing, not even his hands in front of his face.

There was no sound. No breath of wind.

Only the faintest of heart beats pulsing within him. The silence was suffocating; like being wrapped inside rolls of sumptuous eiderdown.

Some way off, Alex couldn't tell how far, he saw a tiny violet light. A smudge that shifted and moved like a fire-fly trapped in a glass jar. At first he thought his mind had conjured a ghost, but the light did not diminish or disappear. He tried to touch it but was only able to blot it out with his hand. For the first time he could make out the tip of one finger. Then the colour deepened becoming indigo and then blue and green and finally a deep burgundy. The glimmer spread into a circle and encompassed Alex like an equator and the redness intensified. Bisecting the ring, with the likeness of fire, grew a brilliant red cross that hung before him. At last he could make out his own form. As the light brightened he saw his bare feet resting on soft ground. Stooping, he snatched away at a clump on which he stood. The smell in his palm evoked a distant memory. It was damp, like sweet dew on a spring morning. The tuft of grass in his hand smelt wonderful.

The lawn on which he stood was perfect. A verdant carpet stretched away all around him. And there beside him he saw a white circle. Kneeling down he touched the ashen spot. The material on the grass was dry and powdery and stuck to his skin. Brushing his fingers, a fine cloud of talcum fell gently to the ground and became lost among the blades.

A sound like trumpets erupted sending a fanfare, so thunderous, that the anthem could be seen and felt. The air shook with vibrant energy and swift pressure waves caused Alex to lose his balance, like a surging tide racing past him onto a beach where tsunami crash.

After a while the overture decayed like reverberations receding into the depths of a cavern and as the last trace of sound fell silent the air felt calm as if a storm had blown away. The cadence left an emptiness all around; only the fiery cross burned brightly. And then, not far away, stood a shadowy figure outlined by brilliance. It was a knight dressed in armour. He clasped a shield close to him and held a sword above his head. A helmet covered his face and a searing light came from within his visor. Beside him stood a wondrous animal; a white horse champing at the bit and stamping on the ground. On its head was a golden mask protecting it from the slings and arrows of battle. Embedded in the ground stood a mast bearing his colours; one flag showed a red cross, the other bore three lions. The emblems wavered in the lifting breeze and a veiled mist began to drift. The knight stood in front of a huge mound. Alex saw armoured scales and realised it was some mighty beast. Then he saw a pool of black liquid seeping from a fatal wound in the neck of the slain dragon.

The champion stepped forward and his breastplate fell to the ground revealing a crimson tunic. He plunged his sword into the ground, and removing his helmet, placed it on the hilt. His panoply fell away showing the true colours of the captain. On his tunic he wore three lions. His blond hair caught the wind; his blue eyes fixed on Alex. He stood there arrayed in regal splendour. It was *Bobby Moore*.

'Come forward Alex.' His voice was strong and cutting, with an edge that sliced through the air.

Awe overcame him as he approached the one he revered.

'Alex, it's good that you are here. I need your help. Soon we will take to the field for our country. We stand on the verge of greatness but there is a battle yet to be won. The eyes of the world will be watching.

'This country has a heritage which we must never let go. Not since the Battle of Hastings, nine-hundred years ago, has this land known defeat. But the spirit of this nation has not been conquered and tomorrow that spirit will once again be tested. Our resolve is steadfast and sure.

'You know what must be done. Do not waver from what lies ahead. We will face this contest together, Alex, you and I. As sure as the sun will rise tomorrow, so will our place in history be.'

The ball-boy looked up to the captain of his country.

'I don't think I can do it. I am only human.'

'No Alex, this is your time and tomorrow will be your day.'

'How can I be sure that we will win?'

'Look for the sign Alex, according to the prophecy.'

'What sign?'

'One will divide our last defeat and bring victory.'

'I don't understand.'

'You will know it when you see it Alex. That one is coming.'

As Alex was puzzling over the mystery there came a flash of white light overhead. Like a magnesium firework it lit the ground where they were standing. Then there came another flash followed by another and then another. Alex looked to the sky, shielding his eyes from the glare. Flares like shooting stars came sailing by. First there were just a few and then the number increased until the whole zenith was ablaze with an intense whiteness.

The Earth is spinning, Alex thought, *so fast that the universe is passing. A thousand years in one second*!

The ground glowed deepest emerald. Then it became clear where he had been standing. The perfect lawn on which he stood bore markings he knew. He saw that the white circle he had touched was the centre-spot of the most famous of football pitches. All around, and silhouette against the brilliance of the sky, was a battlefield where Alex had been when just a boy. It was a theatre of dreams.

Wembley Stadium stood like a lofty mountain range; its twin peaks towered high above him. Alex fell to his knees as his vision became obscured by a galaxy of stars.

Then there was nothing to see except the incessant flow of never ending light.

22

The whiteness separated into a spectrum of light which brought with it an explosion of sound that squeezed the tympanum inside Alex's ears.

First of all it made no sense but after a while he could pick out disfigured faces shimmering like an oasis in a desert and distorted voices gurgling like echoes underwater. During fleeting moments he caught fragments of speech. He could tell Billy and Britannia lurked somewhere in the mix.

'…Get him to the lift,' a female voice was saying.

'…What's happened – what's wrong with him?'

It became dark and the gush of sound disappeared and gave way to a low pitched drone.

'…He's tripping!'

'…How?'

'…Maybe his drink's been spiked.'

The droning stopped and Alex felt strong hands hauling him. Bright lights came and went in a dizzy dance and he thought he could make out the sound of traffic screaming by. As he felt himself crumple into a foetal position, there came an overwhelming smell of plastic and for a while he knew nothing else as he fell into a restless sleep.

He was being rocked back and forth and sensed a feeling of motion. Light filtered down from somewhere above and a memory came to him. In a flash of hindsight he recalled a journey through unknown streets until he had reached Trinity in the depths of London. Then instantly that memory was lost.

He thought he could hear Billy talking but he couldn't make out what he was saying. Then everything juddered and all movement ceased. For a moment Alex was aware that he was lying down and the only sound he could hear was his own laboured breathing. He lay there for several minutes not daring to stir; his eyes moving, searching for some clue but seeing nothing. It took an age and a great effort of will, but finally Alex raised himself and sat up. He was gripping something tightly and discovered it was the passenger seat of a small car. He had been hunched up on the backseat next to his bag.

He was alone. It was a Mini, he was sure of it; nothing else could be this small. Yes, he saw the badge on the steering wheel. He rubbed an arc across a misted window and wondered where Billy was. It was night. All he could make out were some amorphous shapes, perhaps trees, and a distant haze, maybe a glow from the city.

Then Alex caught sight of tiny yellow lights dancing in the dark. No, he saw them reflected in the wing mirror; they were behind him. He twisted awkwardly and squinting through the rear window saw a mass of lights; darting, flashing and flitting haphazardly like a swarm of luminous locusts.

'What the devil...' he gasped. 'They know I'm here.'

There came a multitude, a legion, and they flashed and hovered in the most lurid of green and red and yellow colours that hurt to look at. And Alex realised that each light roved in pairs. *Eyes*, he thought, *thousands of eyes looking for me.*

Then a deep pounding started like the rhythmic sound of fervent fans stamping in the stadium. Nervously he felt for the striated scar on the palm of his hand and began caressing it with his thumb; it did not help to calm his fears. Each thump sent a shockwave. *Boom, kaboom; boom, kaboom; boom, kaboom.* And then the chanting started. Slow at first, but then the tempo quickened. *Zigga zagga, zigga zagga, zigga zagga.* As the eyes swarmed and surrounded the car, the intensity of the chant increased. *Zigga zagga, zigga zagga, oi, oi, oi. Zigga zagga, zigga zagga, oi, oi, oi. Zigga zagga, zigga zagga, oi, oi, oi.* And it went on until Alex could bear it no longer.

Gnarled fists began to pummel the car and there appeared the grotesque shapes of black figures leaning against the windows. *Demons*, he screamed, *demons have come to get me.* One dark shadow forced its way through the mob; its eyes bleeding a crimson glare. It stood there for a moment then with one jolt wrenched the door open. Brightness flooded in causing Alex to shield his eyes.

'You're okay – thank God,' it was Billy's voice.

Alex lay there panting; beads of sweat trickled down his face. He was wedged in the foot-well clutching the bag as if his life depended on it.

'I'm fine,' he stuttered, 'there's nothing wrong with me – I've just got a headache.'

'We thought you were gone.' Billy breathed a sigh of relief. 'You gave us some fright.'

'Look, I'm okay – I could do with a drink. Thanks for scaring off those bloody eyes.'

'What eyes…?'

'Don't matter, give me a hand, I'm stuck.'

Outside, Alex stretched, leant against the car and breathed the morning air. The Mini gleamed red in the sunshine; on the roof was a Union Jack.

'Nice car.' He looked around and saw traffic some way off and shops and neat terraced cottages, but rising high was a huge structure blotting out half the skyline. 'Where the hell are we?'

'Don't you know it?'

'Can't say I do.'

'You've been here before. It's *your* team!'

Alex looked again at the imposing grey building with open terraces and rickety turnstiles.

'*Stamford Bridge*,' he was baffled. 'Bloody hell – blue is the colour, football is the game…' He started to sing.

'Look there's The Shed,' Billy said pointing to a ramshackle corrugated roof over a terrace. 'Don't look much, does it?'

'You're right, the famous Shed,' and he began singing, 'Chelsea...Chelsea...from Stamford Bridge to Wem-ber-ley; we'll keep the blue flag flying high...' He stopped and looked around, 'Boy this place is a crap-hole. Thank God for Roman Abramovich!'

'Well you seem better – last night I thought you were dead.'

'A few hours' sleep did the trick.'

'You mean *trip*. Brit thinks your drink was spiked.'

'Where is she anyway?'

'She'll be back later. She lives near here, in the suitably named *Britannia Road* just off Fulham Road.'

'Wow, the Bridge is right in her backyard. She could watch every game.'

'Why'd she wanna see a rubbish team like this?' Billy Gunn had always been a Gunner and followed his team Arsenal in north London. 'Who plays here these days anyway?'

Alex frowned, 'That'd be, let's see, Peter Bonetti and Bobby Tambling. I think it's too early for Ossie and Chopper.'

Billy thought for a second, 'There's something about Brit.'

'What do you mean?'

'Dunno really – it's just a feeling. She seems to know too much. How could she know your Mum's maiden name?'

'Yeah, that's scary.' The conversation at the party came back to Alex.

'At least she gave you a bed for the night – well, backseat.'

'Why'd she park here?'

'No space outside her flat. Look we got a bit of time to kill, let's have a kick-about.'

'What here?'

'Yeah, in there,' Billy aimed a thumb over his shoulder.

'On the pitch?'

'There's a way in.'

'Come on then – I've always wanted to play for Chelsea.'

An excited smile spread over his face. He scooped up his bag and pulling out a bottle of water, downed the lot.

'That's better – let's go.' Then Alex let out a cry, '*It's gone!* We've failed. That bloody dwarf!'

'What you talking about Alex? What's gone? What dwarf?'

'The *ball*. It's not in my bag!'

'I've got it.'

'Where?'

'In there.' He pointed to the ramshackle stadium.

'Billy, what're you up to? Don't blow our cover. We cock this up, we cock up history!'

Alex followed Billy to an open gate and they walked over a wide terrace beside the Shed End then down steps between blue painted railings. There were no seats in sight, just a wide open space of hard unforgiving concrete covered in dirt.

'Look over there.' Billy shot out an index finger.

Across half the ground were two teams getting ready for a game. They had dumped bags down to mark out goals, and there on the pitch, Alex saw the orange ball.

'I found them earlier, when you were sleeping it off. They're going to Wembley. That lot over there are Germans. You up for this?'

One of the English boys looked up, 'Come on we're starting.'

Alex felt a sudden thrill as he stepped onto the pitch. Deep down he wished he could have played in stadia like this, but presenting a TV show about the game was the next best thing.

A tall boy, almost twenty, came over to meet them; he walked with an air of arrogance.

'Alright fellas, I'm Phil. We got Woodsy over there and that bloke with the red hair is Jones. Actually he's from Swansea but he's got a good left peg, so he's in. The big bloke in goal is Dobbo, he plays rugger – but he's good with his hands. We got a couple of other guys sitting over there by the dugouts, but they're useless. Where'd you wanna play?'

'I'll go up front,' Alex said.

'Defence,' added Billy.

'Good stuff,' said Phil. 'Let's beat the crap out of them Krauts.'

The Germans looked huge. They stood there, lanky and blond, each with a rash of acne. Most were taller than Phil Carpenter. They began bellowing to one another as if to engender some team spirit that would give them the edge. Each wore a white West German football shirt. Manfred Grimm came over and spoke to them.

'Your shirts are all different – you play in skins.'

Phil didn't argue, 'Okay,' and he turned to the team, 'alright, get 'em off. They can have kick-off.'

Seconds later both teams lined up; the ball was under Michael Riesenger's foot. Then he knocked it gently to Manfred Grimm who simply stopped it for the on-rushing Gunter Huber who gave the ball such a punt in his black Adidas Santiago boots that it seemed to whistle as it flew. The ball sailed fully thirty yards between Brian Woods and Alex, above Phil Carpenter, and soared past Steve Dobson in goal who was tightening the belt on his trousers. One-nil. The Germans leapt in the air and whooped with delight.

'Are we playing head-height? Alex asked.

'No head-height – no off-sides,' yelled Manfred Grimm.

'Come on Tommy,' taunted Gunter Huber. 'Come and get us!'

'Right Jerry – this means war.' Brian Woods levelled a glare at Gunter Huber. 'Dobbo, roll it out.'

Billy Gunn received the pass from the goalkeeper and knocked it to Brian Woods. Straightaway Michael Reisinger was on him and felled him with one scything tackle. Woods hit the ground hard, rolled over and found himself looking up at Reisinger haring off towards Steve Dobson's goal. Billy watched the six-foot youth bearing down on him like a charging bull on the streets of Pamplona. He wondered if he should tackle him or get out of the way. Reisinger got to within a few feet when he heard Manfred Grimm calling out.

'Bandits at nine o'clock.'

But it was too late. Gareth Jones intercepted Reisinger like an Exocet missile. The German went sprawling and ended up writhing on the grass clutching his thigh. The Welshman tumbled and fell on top of Michael Reisinger.

Billy Gunn calmly collected the loose ball and threaded it forward to Phil Carpenter who turned, carried it twenty yards and found Alex Bell moving swiftly down the left side. Alex took one touch and sent the ball to the feet of Brian Woods who jinked round Klaus Mohler and sent Jürgen Schmidt the wrong way. One-all.

'Jerry your defences are breeched,' Woods mocked defiantly, and he waggled an accusing finger at Manfred Grimm. 'You may be bigger and uglier, but we have stealth.'

Phil Carpenter turned to his team, clapped his hands and shouted, 'Okay chaps, this is D-day, let's give 'em flak.'

After that the game settled down into a more orderly fashion and flowed back and forth with more football and less dogfight. It was while the game was going on that Alex was able to snatch a quick word with Billy.

'I've just remembered…'

'What?'

'Right here. Chelsea's first goalkeeper…'

'Yeah…'

'He was like twenty stone, right…*Fatty Foulke*…'

'So…'

'Thing was…hold on…'

The ball came to Alex and he smashed a speculative pass up towards Phil and Brian who were both waving their arms.

'…Thing was, they made him look even bigger by sticking two small ball-boys behind the goal.'

'So what?'

'They were the first ball-boys ever. How about that? Kind of ironic really. Here we are – we could be just as important as them.'

'How'd you know that stuff?'

'I went on the stadium tour.'

'Hey, who's that lot up there?' Billy gestured.

Alex looked up towards the Shed End. Ten, maybe a dozen people were standing on the terrace watching. Some were talking; one or two were pointing.

'What do they want?'

'God knows.'

The next voice the boys heard was Steve Dobson's.

'Behind you!'

Alex and Billy turned to see Manfred Grimm bearing down on them silently like a U-boat in the North Sea. They had almost no time to react. Out of desperation Billy swung wildly at the German's feet. Grimm went spinning into a cartwheel and both players crashed onto the grass. In an effort to clear the ball, Alex took a swipe and tried to thump it out of danger. It was a powerful strike but it only went a few yards before colliding with the head of Gunter Huber who was following through. The ball flew high into the air and looped into the stand. It bounced on the concrete and was caught by one of the onlookers.

The players stared up waiting for them to return it. Instead they held onto the ball and began passing it to each other; some were taking photographs.

'Hey,' Alex shouted, 'throw it.'

He was just about to clamber onto the terrace and retrieve it himself when the ball came bouncing back. Alex gave them a stare and one of the group had the audacity to take his photograph using a gadget he couldn't recognise. Angrily he turned and pumped the ball back onto the pitch, then spun round to the group and stuck up a middle finger.

The Germans had a free-kick at the point where Billy had up-ended Manfred Grimm. They took it short and they took it quickly. Gunter Huber laid it off and Michael Risinger fired home between the bags. The low drive found its way under the despairing Dobson who was at full stretch. It was six-five to the Germans.

Alex was furious. Not only had he almost lost the ball to a group of overzealous interlopers but the Germans had taken the free-kick before he was back on the pitch.

'Dobbo,' he called, raising a hand.

The goalkeeper rolled it out to him. Slowly at first he began to dribble the ball, then he picked up the pace. The Germans were back-tracking and shouting to each other to mark up. Then Alex laid it sideways to Billy and went on a run towards goal. Billy held it for a moment and then sent a long ball which bisected the German defence and found Alex who was sneaking in round the back. It was a perfect pass. Alex trapped it and went passed Heinz Henning in one sweeping move. He was just yards from the goal. His annoyance was still welling up as he smashed the ball beyond the transfixed Jürgen Schmidt. At the same time he followed in and floored the goalkeeper leaving him swearing in a stream of German. Six-six.

'That's how Geoff Hurst's gonna do it.'

In frustration, Heinz Henning belted the ball away. '*Englische scheiße!*'

Then quickly the game came to an end when a voice boomed, 'Hey you!'

For a moment Alex thought that one of the German boys was objecting to his questionable follow-through on Jürgen Schmidt. But it wasn't a German accent.

'Clear off. You shouldn't be here.'

A grounds-man with a face like thunder, wearing grey overalls and brandishing a garden fork was approaching them from across the pitch. The boys stood for a moment and then one by one they began scrambling their bags and jackets together for a quick exit.

'Let's go Billy,' Alex called. 'Grab the ball.'

It was while Billy was retrieving the ball from near the dug-out that Alex found he was suddenly confronted by two attractive teenage girls. They had been with the group he had seen on the terrace. He looked at them in surprise. They wore bright garish clothing and both had a band of mask-like purple mascara around their eyes.

'Whoa. Nice make-up!'

'We love you,' one girl said. 'Can I have your autograph and put your fingerprint on my *qPid*.' She held a small device in her hand.

'Yeah, I wanna photo with you?' the other said. 'So I can upload it on *SpaceBook*.'

'Sure.' Alex felt as if he were back home outside the studio. He took her black marker and scribbled into a notebook, adding a kiss as he always did if they were female. 'There you go ladies.' He smiled as they posed each side and took a few intimate selfies.

'Thanks,' Alex said, not knowing what a *qPid* was.

He pressed his fingertip onto the girl's device. It glowed pink and an electronic voice said, 'New lover added to harem. He is sensitive, mysterious and extrovert. A typical Gemini with Cancerian traits. He must let the past go if he is to fulfil his dreams.'

'Wow, I've got his DNA!' She was ecstatic.

'Mm, interesting,' Alex mused, looking warily at the tiny gizmo she held.

One of the girls began unfolding a newspaper.

'No, don't let him see it.'

'He must know.'

They both began to wrestle with the paper.

'We must give it to him.'

'No.'

It tore, and a strip fell onto the grass. They quickly turned and began to head out of the stadium, one looked back.

'I love you Alex. Don't go.' Then as they slipped across the terrace she called back, 'I've been here before!'

Alex looked down at the torn page. The banner read: *Sunday Telegraph*. He picked it up.

'What does she mean, *I've been here before*?' He read, 'July 31st 1966…but that's…*tomorrow*!'

The paper was ripped and only the top section of the front page was left. The main headline read: *Health Minister's Dilemma*, and under that: *Premier Returns to Deeper Crisis*.

'What the hell's this all about?'

But then Alex found on the right hand side a smaller headline that said: *Win Snatched in Extra Time*. There was a dark photograph that showed the Jules Rimet trophy being held aloft against the backdrop of Wembley Stadium, but Alex couldn't tell who was holding it. Below the headline was another which read starkly: *Final Marred by Death of Ball Boy*. The rest was torn away. His hands began to shake as it dawned upon him what this could mean. Alex's thoughts were interrupted.

'There you go mate.' It was Billy. He bounced the ball and then stuffed it into the bag. 'Let's get out of here before the old bloke sticks his fork up my arse. Hey you okay Alex?' Billy could see that his friend's face looked drained.

Alex swallowed, 'Um, yeah, I'm just feeling knackered.' He thrust the paper into his back pocket. 'Them Krauts were well good.'

They made their way over the drab concrete and out through the side gate behind the Shed. It was quiet; only a trickle of traffic could be seen moving along Fulham Road. They saw Britannia's red Mini parked beside a row of cottages just outside the ground; the Union flag on the roof glinted in the morning sunshine. Standing next to the car was a woman dressed in a black uniform.

'Shit, we've got a ticket!' gasped Alex. 'Bloody traffic warden!'

'Yeah, and it's not even our car. What we gonna do?'

The woman turned round and they breathed a sigh of relief. It was Britannia.

'There you are boys – I've been waiting for you,' her voice sounded calm as she watched them approaching. 'I'm glad you seem better Alex.'

They eyed her up and down. She looked immaculate in a tight fitting uniform.

'Is this another one of your quick change…?'

'…I know what you're thinking Alex. No, I've got a day job. Actually, both you and I have the same appointment.'

'What's that then?'

'I'm going to Wembley as well. As you can see, I'm a member of St John Ambulance. Well, a volunteer.'

'*What*?'

'Yeah, I'm a trained medic. I once performed a tracheotomy at the Notting Hill Carnival. And that's not easy when you're being blasted by five thousand watts of Bob Marley...'

The boys looked at each other in disbelief.

'...So you might see me pitch-side when you're running the line.' She smiled.

'You're actually going to be at Wembley?' Alex didn't believe her.

'That's right. So what I suggest guys, is that you take my Mini. It's going to be heaving on public transport. I'm sure you know the way.'

'The *Mini*!' Alex hesitated, glancing at the car and then back to Britannia. 'And how're you gonna get there?'

'*Ambulance*, of course! And here it comes now.'

A large white vehicle turned in off the main road and came towards them. Britannia flung the keys and Billy instinctively snatched them out of the air.

'Don't forget about the choke.'

'Um, yeah, I watched you – that little pull-out knob thing.'

The ambulance rumbled up beside them and the rear doors flew open.

'Hop up Brit,' someone called.

She pulled herself onto the step and stood facing them framed in the doorway. Her uniform hugged her slim figure.

'Look out for me,' she said, 'and don't tell anyone you're going to Wembley.'

'Why?' Alex asked trying to raise his voice above the growling engine.

'Say no more than you have to. You're in a bit of trouble, and you know it.'

'What...what?' screamed Alex. 'What trouble?' And then the memory of their exchange in the Post Office Tower came back to him. 'How d'you know my Mum's name?'

The engine was revving and most of what Britannia said was lost in the noise.

'...I know about you Alex – more than you think...'

The ambulance pulled away with Britannia still hanging out.

'...And I know about *Trinity*.'

She slammed the door as the ambulance began to accelerate, belching a cloud of black diesel exhaust as it picked up speed.

Billy turned to Alex – he looked confused, 'Did she say *Bob Marley*?'

23

Close to the cemetery and joining Fulham Palace Road was Atalanta Street. It was within shouting distance of Craven Cottage overlooking the Thames, home to Fulham Football Club. Alex knew it well. He had lived there for almost twenty years. He remembered the times he had spent hunting ghosts amongst the lichen clad tombstones, and the cold spring days when his parents would march him down to the river each year to watch the Boat Race. His father would stand in a pub garden drinking beer while Alex would run along the towpath until his lungs almost burst trying to beat the crews of Oxford and Cambridge as they raced from Putney to Mortlake.

On dark Sunday evenings he would listen to the Shipping Forecast on the radio. And always as he listened there came a draft that seemed to howl from under the dining room door. It would rise and fall like the sound of some distant banshee. And he would shake and shiver with fear. The timbre of the man's haunting voice petrified him, and he understood none of what was said. He could only imagine the terrible fate that befell the wayward mariners lost in the storm-tossed sea.

So much had happened there.

Alex could recall countless days that shaped his life and the memories that would never leave him. As a teenager he developed what appeared to be a natural gift for writing. Teachers often said he had ability beyond his years for creating and describing the most abstract of ideas and inventing the most believable characters. Others said he was a loner who would take himself off to the trees beyond the football fields until he was found by staff out looking for him. He was said to have special needs, but his parents had other ideas. Yes, he liked his own company for hours on end, but he had a wonderful imagination. Or so they thought. But over the years, an underlying medical condition had been clouding Alex's emotional state of being.

He had come second in a national writing competition. His story, *Fractals Of The Mind*, was about Jessica, a young girl who becomes lost in her uncle's attic and discovers a golden box full of stars. It was a great shock to his parents when Alex decided to attend Canterbury Christ Church to study the history of rock music with a view to becoming a journalist. They had hoped he would write the next novel to follow *Harry Potter*.

After university he would return to Atalanta Street for almost two years, but when he was twenty-three he moved into a shared apartment close to the Thames. Not long after that, he was offered a research role with London based *Working Title Films*. Just over a year later, through a lucky break, he would be fronting the popular football show: *At the End of the Day*.

But it was his first home that harboured a secret. It was something he would never share with anyone.

Instead of driving directly to Wembley, Alex persuaded Billy to make a detour. Following Alex's frantic hand movements and random instructions Billy found himself driving Britannia's Mini along fashionable King's Road. They saw boutiques, antique shops, smart tenements and people dressed in clothes which seemed to have been designed in fabrics reflecting all the colours of the rainbow. The Thames was out of sight but Billy sensed they were following a course broadly parallel to the city's river. Although the Mini was small, there were many other makes of car of similar size. The traffic seemed to abound with the likes of Hillman Imp, Morris Minor and Ford Prefect, then a luxurious Bentley or Jaguar would flash by in the other direction.

'I hope this thing's got air bags,' Billy said as he came to a stop at a pelican crossing. The lights blinked amber and he followed on behind a motorbike and sidecar.

'There's more to Brit than we know,' Alex suddenly said.

'Yeah, maybe more than we can guess.'

'It's still bugging me…how she knew about my Mum?'

'…Yeah, and Bob Marley…'

'…And Trinity. And that begs the question…'

'What?'

'Does she know about Vane and their time experiments and stuff? I'm not liking this the more I think about it.'

'Well you can ask her yourself when you see her at Wembley.'

'Yeah and the ambulance thing…it just don't add up. We get tricked into taking a ride back to '66, then up pops Wonder Woman who seems to know all about me. Would you trust her Billy?'

'Did you say *trust* or *lust*? There's something I'd like to…'

'…Turn right here. See those allotments, the Thames is just over there, and you might catch a glimpse of the Fulham ground up these roads. Okay, right here…now pull up over there.'

The journey from Stamford Bridge had taken just a few minutes. Billy parked the car by a pavement, cranked on the handbrake and they got out.

'Wow, this is just like a time-warp,' Alex said. He immediately regretted saying it because the thought of Warwick Vane and his time-slips came to mind. He was thankful that Billy interrupted his train of thought.

'While you have a butchers, I'm just going down to that corner shop – I fancy some chocolate. Be right back.'

Alex stood there for several minutes recounting the days, and then he walked a few steps and placed his hand on a wrought iron gate. It rattled on its hinges with that familiar sound he had heard a thousand times. It was a gentle jangle that signalled indoors that someone was coming. Immediately he felt himself crouching behind the obscured glass in the hallway and peeking through at the distorted shapes that approached the front door.

The house looked just as it did when he had lived there. Maybe the door was a different colour, maybe the shrubs had yet to grow and fill the garden. Never-the-less, it was home. Alex mentally totted up the years it would be before his parents would arrive – perhaps a decade – then another ten before he would be kicking a ball in the street, much to the annoyance of Mrs Ferminger across the road. But it still remained unmistakably home. He rattled the gate again to remind himself.

The crazy-paved path led to a red door. On either side were windows rising from the ground to the overhanging porch above the entrance. They had a bubbled texture like a grape pattern in the glass. Alex remembered squinting through the glass and seeing grotesque and misshapen people walking by. Visitors like the dustmen on Thursdays and the milkman coming to the door would take on ugly refracted shapes as they approached. They were to become some of the strange denizens that would invade Alex's world. He would give them names: Cromarty, Viking, Biscay, Finisterre. They would often appear from a deepening depression or an anticyclone.

His concentration was snapped by two girls playing with a radio in a car parked behind him. The windows had been wound down and they were tuning the large plastic dial and scanning through the channels. He heard noise and hisses and snatches of music and then a radio station. It was a catalyst and a distant memory came flooding back. A disc jockey spoke.

'...And now a request from Rebecca Bell and husband George of Fulham. They'd like a song for their son Alex who goes to big school today. So Alex, this is just to let you know your Mum and Dad are thinking about you – and don't believe all the stories you hear. No big lout from 5C is gonna flush your head down the toilet. Well not on the first day anyway. This is *Another Brick in the Wall...*'

'We don't need no education
We don't need no thought control

No dark sarcasm in the classroom
Teachers leave them kids alone…'

'Mrs Bell, Dr Raja will see you now.'

Rebecca Bell pushed open the panelled door and led Alex in holding his hand. The man behind the desk removed his half-moon glasses and looked up.

'Ah Alex, Mrs Bell, come in; take a seat.' His Punjabi accent was heavy and difficult to follow.

The room was gloomy and the sweet pungency of ether hung in the air. There was a tiny cracked window high up in one corner; it was stained brown and looked out onto a dark brick wall. Dr Raja sat beneath an Anglepoise lamp which he tilted to illuminate the papers on his desk. The harsh light cast a shadow across his face and Alex could see the man staring at him through the glare. He blinked, smoothed his grey moustache and then ran his fingers over his dark skin and his receding hairline. Reaching over to a tray piled high with documents; he lifted some papers onto the desk. He opened a buff envelope. Alex saw a glint of light catch the gold cufflinks on Dr Raja's sleeve. *Like a star in space*, he thought.

The psychiatrist exhaled a long sigh. 'So Alex, how are you?'

The young boy was fiddling with a plastic Star Wars figure; his mother gave him a nudge.

He hesitated, 'Um, I'm feeling good.'

'Just remind me Alex; how old are you?'

'Ten.'

'Yes, and let's see, it was six months ago when you came to see me. What have you been doing with yourself?'

Alex puckered his lips and wiped his finger under his nose.

'Football. Writing…' his voice faded.

'*Writing*! Tell me what you write about Alex?'

'Um, usually I write about football and battles.'

'*Battles*?'

'War.'

'What happens in these battles?'

'Fighting. People die. And there are people who watch.'

172

'People watch the war?'

'Yes.'

'Who are these people?'

'They are *Watchers.*'

'Why are they there?'

'They watch.' Alex lost interest and gazed around the walls of Dr Raja's dark surgery.

'Now you've painted some pictures. Here they are.'

He went to another desk and scooped up a collection of crinkled papers splashed with colour.

'Do you remember these paintings Alex?'

'Yes.'

'Tell me about them.'

'They're battles.'

'What's this picture about?'

Alex's memory switched on. 'This is when William the Conqueror invaded England. These are Norman archers from Brittany and these are Saxons, and that is King Harold. The Saxon lines are made up of housecarls and fyrds.'

'And what is this group doing in the middle?'

'Playing football.'

'Playing football in a battle?'

'Yes.'

'Tell me about *this* painting.' Dr Raja placed another of Alex's pictures on the desk.

'It's a battle.'

'Is it a real battle?'

'Yes. These are British and these are Germans.' Alex waved his tiny fingers over the colour and Rebecca Bell leant forward to look closer.

'Tell me more Alex, when did this happen?'

'1914.'

'The First World War?'

'It's Christmas. The war stopped for one day and they played football on the battlefield: *No Man's Land.*'

'Who are these here?' he pointed a long spidery finger.

'They are Watchers. I call them the *Horamungus.*'

'The *who*?

'The Ho-ra-mun-gus,' he exaggerated the name. 'They see what's happening.'

'Who are the Horamungus Alex?'

'They come and go.'

'Where do they come from and where do they go?'

'They come to see the day; then they go back.'

'Back to where?'

'Where they came.'

'And where is that?'

'It's hard to say. Faraway.'

'And what are these lights?'

'They are like stars – *sky people*.'

Dr Raja tapped the picture with his finger nail. 'Why are these sky people here?'

'They come from above. Shadows.'

'*Shadows*?'

'There are Shadows of day and Shadows of night. Light and dark.'

'And where do they come from?'

'Out of sight. Nearby. Don't know.'

'That's interesting Alex. Is there anything else you can tell me?'

'Germany won 3-2.'

He stopped and rubbed his nose again and looked at Dr Raja.

'Sometimes I see them.'

'Who do you see Alex?'

'Shadows. They come to me.' The boy looked up to the psychiatrist; his dark eyes wide and staring.

As if he'd heard enough, Dr Raja tidied up the paintings and set them to one side.

'Alex you've been very helpful, thank you. Now if you could just wait outside with Mrs McConnell, I'd like to talk to your mum for a moment.'

Alex walked into the reception and the door closed behind Rebecca Bell. Dr Raja picked up a grey tortoise shell fountain pen and began twirling it between his fingers.

'Mrs Bell, I believe the experiences that Alex is exhibiting are due to stimuli coming from within him and have nothing to do with the external world. It's nothing new. Some children live in an imaginary world. This can be a result of cognitive processes manifesting in many ways. Pathways in the brain can release chemicals that cause smell and sounds and hallucinations that can be as real as anything we experience around us. Imagined characters take on a true presence and become part of some children's world.'

'Is this a long term illness?' asked Rebecca, 'will it get worse?' The thought that there could be something wrong with Alex's brain was beginning to cause her some distress.

'*Illness* has strong overtones Mrs Bell and can be misleading.' He removed the cap on his pen and began doodling on the blotter covering his desk. 'As for *long term*, I've known children of Alex's age to be completely free of any visual hallucinations by their early teens. I don't think there's any need to be unduly worried. Shadows, Watchers, Horamungus – they will go away.

'So this is what I plan to do. There's a new antipsychotic drug, *valamotrigine,* which has been successful in recent paediatric clinical trials. It's shown great benefit in the treatment of Asperger's and related conditions with virtually no side-effects to speak of. I'd like to prescribe this medication for Alex and see how he responds over the next few months. If there's a significant decline in Alex's state of mind, then we'll have him straight back in. How does that sound Mrs Bell?'

That was the extent of Alex's memory. He could recall no more.

The gate rattled on its hinges and he found himself looking down at a small boy standing on the garden path. He was dressed in a white football shirt and blue jeans and had dirty trainers on his feet. The boy idly kicked a ball across the garden and it became wedged beneath a rose bush. His hair was dark and his eyes were wide.

'You know who she is, don't you?' the boy said slowly.

'*Britannia*? I'm not sure,' Alex rattled the gate as he spoke. 'Maybe I do. I don't know'

'She's left handed like you. You saw her writing.'

'How does she know Mum's name?'

'Why d'you think?'

'She knows us.'

'Yeah, but how did she find out?'

'Dunno – she surfed the Net.'

'You know that can't be right.'

'Yeah, the Net weren't around then.'

Alex looked into the boy's eyes. There seemed to be a hidden sadness there. In his hand he clutched a large shell. It was beige and cream and had a rough crustaceous exterior; inside it was shiny, smooth and pink with flecks of maroon. He held it to his ear and his eyes seemed to widen.

'I hear a voice,' he whispered, 'and the sea splashing on the beach.'

'It's just an illusion. It's not real.'

'Someone's speaking. They need help. If I could only hear what they say.'

'No. Listen to your heart not your senses.'

'Someone needs help.'

'Let me help *you*.' Alex stared for a moment at the boy. 'If there comes a time when you're called to take a penalty,' he stopped and the gate rattled once more, 'hit it low to the left. Don't think about going right. That's all I can tell you…Abby will be there.'

The boy looked up. 'You know who Brit is, don't you? Deep down you know.'

'She knows about Trinity.'

'She's been there.'

'So where has she come from?'

'You know Alex.'

'I've got this paper,' he pulled out the torn Sunday Telegraph from his pocket.

'Yes, worrying, isn't it.'

'Who were those people on the terrace?'

'We know, don't we?'

'They were Watchers.'

'Yes, the Horamungus.'

'They are here.'

'Yes.'

'What do they want?'

'He's coming.'

'Who?'

'Billy.'

'*Billy*?' His train of thought evaporated and the boy vanished.

'Yeah, I'm here mate.'

Alex rattled the gate and swung round to see his friend standing next to him.

'You okay Alex, you sound tense? Do you want some Bourneville or one of these Jamboree bags?

'No I'm fine. This is where I lived. That's my bedroom up there.'

'I got a bottle of Tizer. Do you remember this stuff?'

'Um, yeah.' Alex wasn't listening.

'What's that you got?'

He glanced down and realised he was still clutching the torn page from the Sunday Telegraph. He shoved it back into his jeans and felt his heart rate begin to quicken.

'It's nothing. Let's go.'

As they got back into the Mini, Alex bit his lip and wondered if he had just one day to live.

24

Ralf Schneider flexed his *e-glove* and logged on.

The screen on the laptop melted into an image showing three people sitting round a table. They were seen from above; one was tapping a keypad. Schneider's screen displayed a hand reaching up; it grew bigger and grabbed at the air. He gently captured the tiny device hovering overhead and nestled it down into a tray with five others. They looked like six miniature eggs in a box.

'These *eye-Bots* are an improvement on the *TabCams* we used during trials of the machine. They're smaller, faster and have greater resolution. Have a look.' The German began shaping circles on the Formica table using his meshed glove.

Up came a scene of a vast crowd with excited faces staring, thousands chanting and Union flags waving.

'These are images we received from the default timeline...'

'...Is that the current timeline?' cut in Vane, his voice harsh.

'Yes they're equivalent. There's a greater than ninety-nine percent probability this is our slice.'

'It's the one percent that gives me the creeps.' Vane shot the German a stare.

Schneider panned through a swathe in the Wembley stands and zoomed high up to a position just below the overhanging roof. A number of people could be seen standing behind the last tier of supporters.

'It's a bit dark, and we might be able to clean it up, but it's this group here I want you to look at.' He touched the screen with his white glove.

'Who are they?' asked Victoria Trevelyan. 'They don't look like football fans. Not a rosette between them.'

'We don't know. They've not been catalogued.'

'Have they been missed from the metadata?'

'We've got visual coverage of the entire stadium – but we've not seen them before.'

Vane said, 'So what you saying Ralf? I thought we had the whole damn 97k mapped.'

Schneider looked up; his forehead creased with furrows. 'They may not have been there in '66.'

'*What*? Look we know who sold burgers, ball-boys, bog cleaners, every bum on seats. Are you saying there are some we missed?'

'There could be ten, maybe twelve.'

Victoria leant forward. '*Transients*?'

'It's possible. We're gonna send in another eye to get a better look.'

Vane drew a breath through clenched teeth. '*Transients* – shit, why's it gotta be Transients? That's another frigging interjection. This could screw things up big time…Transbos suck!'

'Let's not get distracted,' Victoria reassured in a calm voice. 'It's a situation we'll have to monitor. They may just be personnel we've missed. Let's get back to the game in hand. Where's our target Ralf?'

'I'll come to that in a moment,' he looked at the clock on his laptop. 'I think we're just about to get a visit.'

'So they're here then?' Victoria glanced up. 'Right on cue.'

'The surveillance is good.'

The door opened and two men walked in and sat at a table in the corner and ordered tea.

Behind Ralf Schneider a boy turned round and peered over the high plastic sofa-seats.

'That's a wicked telly mate. Can you get *Doctor Who* on it?'

'Clear off kid.' Vane glared at the spotty boy and he sank down beside his mother.

One of the young men in the corner heard the commotion and stood up sensing something familiar about the voice he'd heard. He froze. His mouth opened but no words came out. It was Victoria Trevelyan who was first to speak.

'Ah Alex, Billy, it's good to see you again. Come and join us.'

Alex's expression was one of disbelief. His face visibly paled. 'What're you doing here?' For a moment he thought he was back in the bowels of Trinity. He held eye contact briefly with Warwick Vane. He had taken an instant dislike to him the moment he'd seen him in the TV studio.

'We've been expecting you.'

'*Us?*'

'Yes,' said Victoria. 'Brunch is on us.'

Alex and Billy sidled over, watched by the spotty boy on the next table. 'Kevin it's rude to stare,' his mother scolded.

'How did you get here?' Alex asked.

'Same way as you.' Ralf Schneider drew a line on the table with his glove.

'You used us as guinea pigs, didn't you? You only sent us down the tube to find out it was safe.' Billy was seething.

'No we were perfectly happy with the performance of the machine,' added the German, 'we knew it would work. There was just a tiny question over the timing that we were, um…'

'…Testing,' finished Victoria.

'That's right,' confirmed Schneider. 'Now tell me boys, this will help us next time – what was the precise time you emerged? Give or take a few minutes.'

Alex looked at Billy. 'Dunno, we fell asleep. What do you think Billy? It was well after midday.'

His friend nodded in agreement. 'We heard Big Ben when we were waiting for the bus?'

'Yeah, it was three o'clock, so we must've landed about an hour before that.'

'What day?'

'Yesterday.' Alex wondered where the conversation was going.

'Friday. Excellent, the link is stable.' Schneider described more movement on the table and tilted the screen round to Vane. 'We did think you might arrive to see the Uruguay game three weeks ago...'

'Nice, we could've seen all the World Cup,' Billy added with a smile.

Alex was sharp, 'What about you? Did you give *yourself* a debrief?'

'We need all the data we can get,' Vane said.

'...We trusted the telemetry, which was good, and so was the dead reckoning. How you say it: *right on the button*,' added the German.

'Yeah, and had you got it wrong, I reckon we would've arrived dead!' Billy was being sarcastic but Ralf Schneider didn't see the funny side. 'Why you here anyway? Checking up on us?'

'Gentlemen,' it was Victoria, her voice calm and unhurried, 'we thought, why should you have all the action? We'd like to see the game as well, considering all the research that's gone into this little project. And we can watch you do your stuff.'

'I don't believe that for a minute,' Alex retorted.

'It's true.' Her green eyes smouldered and Alex felt intimidated. 'As you know Trinity is especially interested in the Cold War tit-for-tat events that affected the super powers following the death of the linesman Tofik Bakhramov. We want to oversee that history is air-brushed diplomatically.'

'Why can't you just let it go? After all it's in the past.'

'Not yet it isn't! Events like this might one day be used as a political excuse to tread on the toes of another government. Who knows what could happen?'

'You're hardly guardian angels,' said Alex.

'No, but we're the next best thing.' Victoria smiled and a feeling of anger began to well-up inside Alex.

'So what do you think about time-slips guys?' It was Warwick Vane.

He was wearing a long black coat and had several days of dirty stubble. As far as Alex was concerned it was the wrong thing to say. And he pounced.

'Sod you Vane; I'd rather be in The Moon having a pint.'

'Alright Alex, I was only asking.' He held up his hands as if to say *enough* and stared at the boys without blinking.

Alex gave Warwick Vane a dark look. *The bloke's a pillock*, he thought. *Why are they really here?*

'You had some kind of riot going on in Trinity,' Billy remembered. 'What was that all about?'

'It was just a minor skirmish,' Victoria said, 'they were brought under control.'

'Who were they?'

'They were...under observation.'

'They spoke French.'

'They *were* French.'

'Why were they there?'

'It was just research. Nothing sinister.'

'They were dressed like soldiers.'

'Play acting,' put in Vane, 'it was pretence. You know, like a reality show. We were looking at various psychological situations.'

'You got up to some weird stuff down there,' Alex said. 'It didn't seem legal if you ask me.'

'Don't worry Alex,' Victoria assured, 'no one got hurt. Now tell me, what have you been doing since you arrived in London?'

A waitress hurried over with tea and plates of steaming English breakfast. Alex was famished and smothered everything with ketchup squeezed from a large red plastic tomato. He suddenly felt better and began to describe how he'd met Syd Barrett and Pink Floyd at the party in the Post Office Tower. Victoria seemed intrigued by Britannia's performance.

'How do you think she did it?' she asked.

'Not sure,' Alex replied. 'A bit of science – a bit of magic. That's what she said.'

'Yeah and we had a kick-about in Stamford Bridge,' Billy said. 'Against the Krauts.'

As Ralf Schneider scowled at Billy, Alex let his fork clatter onto the floor. He used the distraction as a cue.

'Come on Billy we've got a game to watch.' Alex was itching to get away from their overbearing company and tedious questioning.

They picked up their bags and turned to go. The spotty boy on the table next to them shouted in a squeaky voice, 'I've seen you on the telly.'

Alex spun round to look at him.

'You're Doctor Who's assistant, aren't you?'

'I'm just a time-traveller!' He winked and left the café with Billy in tow.

'There, I knew it Mum.'

Victoria sipped her tea. 'Where were we Ralf?' Trinity's Controller wanted to get back to business.

The image specialist waved a gloved hand like the conductor in an orchestra.

'I'll pin-point our target later. There's something unusual I need to show you.'

The panorama on the screen tilted and moved skyward above the domed towers. They saw a bright light. Schneider increased the magnification until it filled the screen. It was yellow and silver with deeper golden hues that flamed and shimmered like a mirage.

'What is it?' asked Victoria. 'It doesn't look like the sun.'

'The sun's way off screen.'

'Is it reflection from passing aircraft?'

'No chance. The Heathrow flight path is six miles south. We think it's close to the stadium and maybe several metres in diameter. It was in view for a few seconds. It just came and went. We were lucky to catch it.'

'D'you have any idea?'

'None. The equipment was working normally. All data streams were being received as expected.' He moved his hand. 'See what happens when I filter out the glare.'

He waved his hand and the background became black and the object changed into a flickering cross that pulsed erratically on the laptop like an abstract screensaver.

'*Holy shit*!' exclaimed Warwick Vane, leaning forward. 'I've seen archives of UFOs like this. There was a spate of them all over Devon in the Sixties with reports of police chasing these things down country lanes. Maybe it was more widespread than first thought. That is one big anomaly.'

'Does it pose a risk?' asked Victoria.

'I doubt it – but who can say – we're working at the edge of reason here.'

'Where nothing is certain anymore,' added Vane, his eyes frozen.

'We'll just have to keep a close watch on this situation. We don't want to be tripped up by the unexpected.' Victoria paused, 'Which leads us to another surprise. Alex hinted that *she* is here. There can be only one person he was talking about.'

Warwick Vane scratched his greying stubble and cleared his throat, 'She must be taken out.' They all looked at each other for a moment.

'No,' insisted Victoria, 'she's more useful in circulation. She knows so much, and that will help us.'

Ralf Schneider slapped down his laptop impatiently; his eyes narrowed, 'Wir schrauben die kleinen scheiße wenn die zeit kommt!'

25

'Could do with *SatNav!*' Billy's face was etched with concentration. 'Get that map out we got from Trinity.' As he left Hammersmith Broadway, Billy aimed Britannia's Mini in the direction of Shepherd's Bush along the A219 towards White City. His knowledge of London's road network lay several decades in the future.

'Yeah, and seat belts. Look at those fans on the way already.' Alex saw a group of England supporters dressed in red, white and blue and carrying a flag. One had a rattle which he swivelled above his head. It made a racket as the wooden ratchet crackled along the street like a machine gun. 'It don't seem right, not having seat belts in here. We'd fly right through the windscreen in a crash.'

'This windscreen's so small you'd get stuck half-way out.'

'True,' agreed Alex and he began raking through the glove compartment. 'There's something not right about Trinity,' he mused. 'First we get taken to their place which turns out to be a secret base, you know, like some James Bond set. Then we get fired down the tube and end up here. Then they turn up to spoil the party. It's just not hanging together. What do they want?'

'Maybe they're here to take us back. We don't know how to drive that damn machine.'

Alex was quiet. 'I hadn't thought of that.' After a moment he added, 'We could always go to my grandparents in Wimbledon. That'll scare them. "Hello, you don't know me –

I'm Alex your grandson." I could beat me Dad up! What's this stuff?'

He unfolded a crumpled paper.

'You heard of *Quantum Tours* Billy?'

'Nope.'

'Says something about embarkation times, whatever they are, and a visit programme to the World Cup.' Alex shrugged.

'Like a holiday itinerary?'

'Guess so. It's for someone called *BeBe*.'

'Where do we go here?' Billy slowed as they came to a crossroads.

Alex squinted. 'Um, straight on, I think. We want Hangar Lane.'

Billy dropped down a gear and zipped across the traffic lights. 'I think we're lost.'

'We're not lost. We've just got to work out where we are. Trust me – I've been here before. Once. I think.'

'Yeah, and which century was that?'

'Just keep going, we should pick up the North Circular.'

'Was that built in '66?'

Alex read the paper again, 'Dad used to call Mum *BeBe*.'

'Isn't your mum *Rebecca*?'

'*Becky*.' He shoved the paper back into the glove box and slammed it shut. 'There you go Billy-boy!' Alex sounded excited. He remembered as a teenager seeing the new Wembley Stadium for the first time just after sunset one evening. He had been walking with friends along the south bank of the Thames opposite Fulham football ground. The magnificent arch was illuminated like a golden rainbow that seemed to span the horizon. When the stadium had first been flood-lit, pilots taking off from Birmingham had reported seeing a bright light in the south of England. As they approached London they discovered it was Wembley. *It really is the best stadium in the world*, Alex remembered thinking. But the sight he now saw evoked far more emotion.

'Right there Billy,' he pointed, '*The Twin Towers*.'

'Mount Doom!'

'Yeah, follow them towers.'

There was a sudden jolt and the car lurched.

'Shit, we've got a flat!' Billy screwed his face up.

The car limped with an awkward gait and he pulled over. Billy was still cursing under his breath as the lads got out to inspect the damage. The near-side rear tyre was squashed to the tarmac.

'What we gonna do?' Alex was desperate; his mind was already racing ahead to the kick-off at 3 o'clock. 'We'll never get there now!' He looked to the overcast sky and ran his hands through his dark hair.

Billy was calmer. 'Let's see if Brit's got a spare.'

He started poking around inside the Mini's tiny boot. Alex stood behind him and tried to think of other ways to get to Wembley. Suddenly he saw the whole thing falling apart. He wiped his forehead and found his skin felt clammy. *What is Plan B?* He realised he didn't have one.

A bright red double-decker bus pulled up next to him blocking out half the sky. He tried to see if it was going anywhere near the stadium. On the side in gold letters Alex read *London Transport*. He thought it strange that the windows were mirrored. He found his own reflection staring back at him and saw how flustered he felt.

At the rear, a concertina door slid open and as the bus drove slowly by he suddenly felt strong arms haul him inside. The last thing he saw as his vision blurred was Billy with his head still buried in the boot of Brit's Mini.

'What the f...'

Alex took a sharp intake of breath and couldn't quite believe where he'd ended up.

He found himself looking, not at rows of seats as he'd expected, but an open area that reached to a high ceiling. Alex quickly forgot about Billy or even that he was standing inside a London bus. Beneath his feet he sensed a faint tremor and felt the bus moving. The place was full of colour and light and he felt there was something strangely familiar about what he saw.

'Hiya Alex.'

An attractive girl with alluring eyes spoke with an accent Alex couldn't place. She wore a gold spandex body suit under a transparent plastic tabard. On her chest she had an Andy Warhol screen print of Marilyn Monroe. Her blue platform heels were at least eight inches tall and she towered over Alex.

'What's going on?' He glared at her as if she were the reason for him being here.

'*Time TV*,' she replied with an infectious smile. 'We're running a broadcast about *you* Alex.'

He was shocked. 'What do you know about *me*?'

'It's a kind of docudrama. We're following you all the way to Wembley. We want to see if you succeed or fail.'

Alex was caught by surprise. He tried to form some words but found he couldn't speak. *It was a secret.* 'What the hell do you mean?' he gasped.

'We know just about everything.' She flashed her teeth, 'except the outcome of course.'

Alex studied her for a moment. He thought her accent sounded American although she looked vaguely Japanese.

'There are megabucks riding on you Alex.' Her eyes widened with excitement.

She waved a hand and Alex became aware of an audience surrounding him; maybe twenty or so on each side. They wore outlandish clothing and all seemed to be staring at him. He realised this must be impossible.

'It's like a Tardis in here.'

'In a way it is Alex. You could say this is a time machine.'

'A *time*...' His voice faded.

'You'd better believe it baby.' The girl moved across the floor and walked through the image of those watching. 'They're just a projection Alex, like a hologram.'

Some of those in the audience waved and called out. 'Way to go Alex,' and 'Good luck.' Someone else yelled: 'I've got a thousand big ones on you to fail mate.' They laughed.

Alex spun round to face the young woman in the gold outfit. 'They're not here,' she said. 'In fact, they're far away.

Over the horizon. I won't bore you with the details Alex but you're seeing them through a wormhole…'

A wormhole he thought, *where have I heard that before?*

'Even in your time, such an idea was thought possible. Electromagnetic signals can pass through this link. It connects the future and the past.'

'*The future*,' Alex was dumfounded, this had to be some elaborate joke. He began to feel light-headed.

'We're going live in thirty.' A disembodied voice invaded the space all around. The presenter took up a central position and several technicians moved equipment across the floor. Alex saw behind her two large flat screens.

She saw what he was looking at. 'This one shows live feed from Wembley, and the other one…' she stopped for a moment, then up came a picture. Alex was stunned. 'This one,' she said, 'will play highlights from your very own show: *At the End of the Day.*'

There he was with Billy. They were talking to Jamie Valentine and Lola Corolla on the couch. Then there was a clip of Millie Rivers drinking champagne in a Jacuzzi with two Liverpool football strikers. He remembered it as if it were yesterday. In effect it was. Alex's jaw dropped. Then some electronic music welled up and a deep voiceover began.

'This broadcast is brought to you by our *WormLight* connect using the magic of *TimeShare* technology in association with *Virgin Continuum*. And here's your host…Miss Ali Zane.'

The audience all around clapped and cheered, lighting moved and focussed on Ali as a plasma wall erupted into colour.

'Today, Time TV brings you *Back to Reality*, the only reality show that takes you back. And we're here in the original Wembley Stadium. It's 11:17 local time Saturday, July 30, 1966. We'll be following the events of your chosen time-star, Alex Bell, live as they happen.'

The downloaded image of the audience from the other end of the wormhole filled the bus. They cheered again.

Ali Zane carried on. 'In just a few hours we should have several new billionaires.' This announcement was greeted with a huge cheer from the audience many decades in the future, but whose images were displayed all around.

Alex scanned the studio. He saw that one of the plasmas showed the West German team leaving their hotel and boarding a coach. Manager Helmut Schoen and Captain Uwe Seeler were waving as they climbed the steps. The other screen had a close up of David Gilmour playing an extended guitar solo from his track: *Ghosts In The Stadium*. Alex thought that the retro technology was in stark contrast to the holographic projection that filled the studio.

It's just a bus! He couldn't believe it.

Ali Zane had taken up a position in the centre of the studio. The camera zoomed into her round face showing her royal blue bob and sparkling turquoise mascara mask that surrounded her intense eyes. Her lips were glossy and fluorescent red.

'Welcome to the show, as Alex would say. There are just 3 hours 43 minutes to kick-off at Wembley. And here are the latest stats which have been crunched from an eco-registered voting population of 13.47 mega entries using *DarkGlass* matrix-modelling: 29% say that Alex won't actually reach Wembley. 91% think that the goal will not be given, and a massive 73% say *Yes* to the question: *Will Alex die in the process*? It doesn't look good for Alex Bell and Billy Gunn.

'Just remember, in the future it's already happened. The past is not so certain!'

Alex was standing beside the host. His face showed his confusion as he held out upturned hands as if to say: *What's going on*?

'Now, let's have a question for Alex.'

'At the end of the day, what do you want to happen?' someone in the audience shouted.

Alex was suddenly put on the spot and he floundered for an answer. 'We're just going to watch the final,' he said at last, stalling for time and trying desperately to think of something more entertaining to say.

'What's your role at the final? There must be more to it than you wanting to be a ball-boy.'

'I can't go into detail. You'll have to wait and see.' His confidence in front of an audience was returning and he started to play along with the game. 'Between us, me and Billy know exactly what to do.'

'What you gonna do then?'

'That's one that Billy knows!'

The audience laughed. Then sporadic voices came fast, one after the other.

'We know about Abby Hart…'

'If you don't go through with your plan we'll give you a cure for your sister's pulmonary hypertension.'

'What!' Alex exclaimed, turning round to see who had spoken.

'And your Dad…'

'What? What about my Dad?'

'One at a time.' Ali Zane interrupted raising her slender hand.

But then her voice was smothered by a sudden noise and a flash of light. A pressure wave punched Alex in the stomach and for a second he reeled. In the next moment two figures quickly appeared from where the door had been blown away. The audience looked on in horror; some screamed. Watching more than a century in the future they could give no help.

Ali Zane was on the floor; the blast had knocked her off her jacked-up heels. Two men clad in grey boiler suits came towards Alex at speed. One wore a mask with a caricature of Ronald Reagan; the other had the green face of Shrek.

'No one move,' yelled Reagan.

Shrek had a fire-arm levelled at Ali Zane on the floor. 'Do as we say and no one gets it.'

Ronald Reagan twisted Alex's arm behind him and forced it up his back. He winced in pain. They dragged him towards the entrance where a third person was standing – a woman. She had the face of Margaret Thatcher.

Alex was struggling, 'Hey! Fuck off.'

'This way,' Mrs Thatcher said, and pulled him onto the pavement outside.

Alex saw traffic passing and a park nearby. There was no sign of Billy.

Ali Zane had been dazed but she regained her composure. The gate-crashing imposters had not been interested in her. Flicking her blue hair back into place Ali stood to her feet and called out: 'Get live feed of this. Follow what happens. *Everything*. Who are those shits?'

Behind the bus was a black Porsche Cayenne. It had huge alloy wheels, darkened windows and the paintwork gleamed in the daylight.

What's a Porsche doing here? Alex couldn't work it out.

Behind the wheel sat a man wearing Ray-Ban sun glasses. He was revving the V8 engine and nervously chewing gum.

Alex kicked and struggled; he didn't want to go quietly. *Where's Billy?*

They bundled him towards the four-by-four. Margaret Thatcher had the rear door open ready.

'What the fuck do you want?' Alex blurted out.

'The result must stand Alex.' Reagan had a German accent. 'If England wins, a future syndicate will lose more than a billion dollars. That can't happen.'

Alex wriggled free and tore off his mask. The man had a wide pock-marked face. Alex had never seen him before.

Shrek pressed the gun against Alex's head and cocked the trigger.

'There will be those who will seek you out – and they will deal with you Mr Bell.'

Alex looked into the eyes behind the green mask. The thought that he was a hunted man filled him with dread.

'The Nazi Party still lives Alex.' The man with the pock-marked face spoke again; there was an overpowering smell of garlic on his breath. 'And our time will come.' He pulled Alex closer by screwing up his football shirt. 'You can't play God with what has already been.'

'But the game hasn't happened yet!' Alex was defiant.

'Fuck you.'

A surge of adrenalin was suddenly released inside Alex and without thinking he aimed a fist at Reagan's nose. The man recoiled and staggered backwards. Alex was just as surprised as the German. It had been a knee-jerk reaction, albeit with his fist.

Then there came a deep rumble followed by a searing scream that cut the air. All four turned to see a man and a woman some fifty metres away. It sounded like a jet fighter taking off.

They covered their ears and Alex felt as if his brain had become numb. His eyesight smeared. He tried to focus and saw a blond woman holding something. Next to her was a tall man in a suit. The air around them seemed to distort like a heat haze near fire.

One of the men shouted something but Alex couldn't hear what he said. All sound had become dulled. As they began to pile into the Porsche, Alex took his chance. He kicked out at Shrek then turned and ran into the park like a sprinter out of the blocks. He was afraid to look round thinking that one of the terrorists could be close. His vision was misting as he tried to make out who the woman was in the pale blue suit or the tall man with her.

He began to lose consciousness as every step became more uncertain and more laboured. Moments later he crashed head-long into a park bench and was out for the count.

26

Alex liked nothing more than hiding himself away in Grandpa Bell's dusty potting shed.

It had a smell all of its own. There was a narcotic mix of creosote, *Swarfega*, turpentine, *Araldite* and antifreeze. Alex thought the odours all blended together to form an aromatic potpourri like no other. Scores of drippy paint pots reached to the roof on rickety shelves that looked as if they would fall at any moment. Amongst an assortment of random objects amassed over the years, Alex found some treasures stashed away in a draw that had become wedged tight. He prised it open with a chisel and saw countless screws, ball bearings, wax candles, a magnet, a compass and all sorts of rusty tools that Grandpa would have used.

By accident he stumbled on a small steam engine hidden away behind wooden boxes at the back of the shed. When Alex polished it with a rag he found it was made of shiny yellow brass with bearings that moved smoothly. He filled the engine with water and when he lit a wick underneath using a jar of methylated spirit, it began to boil. The steam powered a single wheel that began to spin on an axle. Steam hissed from the chimney. Alex thought it made a wonderful rhythmic chugging sound as the wheel turned with increasing speed.

Grandpa's shed was one of his favourite places. As he grew up, his hide-away provided many journeys of discovery and endless adventures into the unknown.

Then one day after school Alex came to see his Grandfather and went straight into the shed. He had met a girl.

She was different to any other he had ever seen. Alex had spotted her in the playground and wondered why he had not seen her before. Perhaps she had just arrived in Fulham. Her name was Abby Hart from 10 Windsor. She had glorious dark hair and eyes that seemed to mesmerise. While Alex was kicking a ball around with his class-mates he managed to bump into her. It was clumsy and contrived, but it worked like a dream.

'Sorry,' Alex apologised.

'That's alright.' She looked at him and brushed hair from her eyes.

'Um, haven't seen you before. Are you new?'

'Yes, just moved in.'

The conversation wasn't riveting, but it was a start.

Alex met Abby again the next day and walked her home. She had never heard of Pink Floyd, but she could be forgiven for that. A few days later Alex was holding her hand. And then he kissed her. *Wow, this is amazing!*

Alex thought about Abby as he sat on the floor of Grandpa's shed. Using a screwdriver he scratched her name into the square leg of a sturdy wooden workbench. Around her name he etched a heart as neatly as he could.

It was about this time in Alex's life that the hauntings began to fade. No longer did Cyclones pester or Shadows lurk nearby. Maybe it was due to the adolescent teenager finding someone new in his life who mattered more than anything else. For a while Alex felt a sense of peace.

'There, *Abby Hart*,' he said out loud.

Without warning the shed door was flung open with surprising force. It was Grandpa Bell. His face looked strained; his eyes were red-raw. Alex knew straightaway that something was wrong.

'Come here Alex. Your Mum's just phoned from the hospital. There's been a terrible accident. Your Dad's...' He faltered and cleared his throat. 'Your Dad's been killed in a car crash...'

The words cut through him like a knife. It was a stab of pain like Alex had never known before.

'No Grandpa. No!'

He fell into his Grandfather's long arms and sobbed without stopping.

27

'No...No...No!' Alex was thrashing wildly on the grass. Billy managed to haul him into a sitting position and he calmed down.

'What's going on?' Billy was anxious seeing his friend in distress. Not for the first time.

Alex looked around. His head felt fuzzy but he was unharmed. 'You don't want to know.' He let out a long sigh and looked at Billy. 'How's the car?'

'Sorted.'

'Let's get going then. We've got a game to see.'

The park looked quiet as they went to find Brit's Mini. Alex saw no terrorists in masks or the woman in blue with the tall man. Neither was there any sign of a red bus with mirrored windows. Alex was relieved.

He felt inside his denim jacket and pulled out a small white tub.

'Do you need those pills?' Billy asked.

'Yeah, they keep the nightmares away.'

It seemed all of London's traffic had converged and snarled to a halt as they came to the tight streets of Wembley. A deluge of supporters, English and German were ambling along singing, shouting, chanting and taunting each other. It was all good natured. A far cry from some stand-offs Alex had seen at football matches he'd been to.

It took an age as Billy edged ever closer to the stadium. They saw scores of police waving the traffic on. Then finally, a host of parking attendants in white coats appeared and began sending cars and coaches into the giant concrete car park that surrounded the complex.

Then in front of them, Alex and Billy saw the massive stadium filling the sky-line. It stood there like some huge ark; its ponderous presence a testimony to the history of battles it had staged.

'Look at that Billy. It's been worth it just to get this far.'

Billy wrenched on the hand brake and stared. 'Think I'm gonna piss myself.' He looked nervous. 'We've never done anything like this.'

'Come on mate, we can do this. If we can go live to millions each week…'

'Yeah, but that's different.' Billy looked up to the Union flag flying high over one of the white domes. 'We could be about to change everything. And if we do…' his voice trailed off.

'Yeah Billy, what?'

'It makes you wonder what kind of world we'll go back to. This could change everything!'

'There's no time for second thoughts. We got some business to do. Let's go Frodo.' He slapped Billy on the back. Alex was also feeling apprehensive but he didn't want to show it.

The air outside was a comfortable temperature but up above heavy clouds threatened rain. The boys swung their bags over their shoulders and moved towards the fans spilling along Wembley Way. Alex noticed straightaway that only he and Billy were wearing England shirts. He suddenly felt out of place and buttoned his denim jacket.

They'd only taken a few steps when a large black Bentley pulled up silently beside them. Alex didn't see it. He turned and found himself suddenly sprawled over its shiny bonnet. Apart from his pride, he had not been hurt.

'Hey watch where you're going,' he yelled at the chauffeur. Bending down he looked in through the window. What he saw inside took him by surprise. Sitting in the car was the match referee Gottfried Dienst with his two linesmen, Tofik Bakhramov and Dr Karol Galba. They had made their way through central London from the Kensington Close Hotel. All three were dressed in smart navy blue FIFA regulation suits. They sat inside the Bentley staring impassively. The car carried on and the next moment Alex found himself gazing through the window into the eyes of Tofik Bakhramov. *Yeah, you'd better watch yourself; I'll be seeing you later.*

'Poor bloke, I wonder if he knows what's coming to him.'

Billy said, 'If all goes to plan he'll be reffing after this.'

'Yeah, or taking early retirement in some prefab in Bognor.'

They moved on and saw stalls with food and people in white coats selling match programmes and rosettes.

'Hotdogs,' Billy grinned. 'What a great smell!'

'What's that bloke selling there – *programmes*?' Alex asked as they shuffled along amid the tide of supporters.

'Looks like the *Big Issue*.'

Alex studied the man but was swept along by the crowd. The surge took them towards the large concrete stairs that led up to one of the entrances. He grabbed a railing and climbed the steps.

'Did they have the Big Issue in the Sixties?' Alex couldn't see the man who had been swallowed up amongst the thousands.

'Dunno I've never read it. Look we've gotta get in so we can get changed.'

'I think I've seen him before.' Alex was still scouring the faces when he heard Billy explaining to an official that they were ball-boys and needed to get ready. They flashed their ID badges then cranked the turnstile and were through.

'How easy was that? Billy said. A smile spread across his face and he forgot about the fears he'd had earlier.

Although there were a mass of supporters outside, by contrast the stadium was almost empty. Grounds-men were making last minute touches so that Wembley was ready to be seen on televisions across the world. The BBC were going through final checks with camera angles and microphone levels. It would be the Corporation's broadcast that would allow the world to watch history in the making. In a seat overlooking the pitch, match commentator Kenneth Wolstenholme was running over some notes he had prepared the night before.

'This is fantastic,' Alex said as they bounded down the terrace steps towards the pitch like children let loose in a sweet shop. On the field the massed bands of Her Majesty's Royal Marines rehearsed one last march.

A light shower began to fall as they walked across the cinder perimeter and onto the lush turf. Alex's heart was pounding with excitement as he stood on the Wembley grass for the first time.

'That's one small step for man – one giant leap for...'

'...*England*. Come on Alex we need to get our stuff on.'

High above, and invisible amid the fine rain, there darted an artefact crafted by technology from another age.

A tiny eye.

28

They emerged from the tunnel. Heroes ready to do battle. On home soil, the English wore scarlet with the invader in white. Onto the battlefield they came amidst a crescendo of sound. The ambitions of nations would be examined during the course of one day. From his commentary position, Kenneth Wolstenholme spoke to the world; his voice was clear, distinguished, exact.

'This is the day we've all been waiting for: the final of the eighth World Cup competition between England, the host nation, and West Germany...'

From one end of the stadium the teams trooped out in two lines. Rain had fallen during the afternoon and a drizzle hung in the air as the players entered the theatre of dreams.

'...With Bobby Moore of England, Cohen, Ball, Banks, Wilson, Charlton – Bobby Charlton – Peters, Stiles, and Jackie Charlton bringing up the rear. And West Germany, captained by Uwe Seeler, who twelve years ago, made his debut on this very ground for West Germany when he was eighteen. At that time West Germany were world champions having won the World Cup in 1954. They were fourth in 1958. England have never before got past the quarter final stage.'

The teams filed onto the rain soaked grass. High above, the scoreboard waited to display the first goal. They jogged in parallel behind the match officials towards the centre of the pitch. Leading the way was referee Gottfried Dienst flanked by his linesmen, Karol Galba and Tofik Bakhramov; they wore their familiar black kit. It would be many years before the officials would break with tradition.

All around voices sang, banners waved and feet stamped on concrete terracing. Above the two towers, huge flags unfurled in the summer breeze and stood out proudly over the famous Grade II listed building.

'And before the play begins, those rival supporters are having a chanting, shouting and singing match with each other,' said Kenneth Wolstenholme.

The three men in charge took their position on the half-way line with England moving into place next to Galba and West Germany beside Bakhramov. They stood in line facing the Royal Box. Alf Ramsey had chosen his first-eleven. There could be no substitutes. If a man were to go off injured, no other player could take his place. The manager had kept faith with the side that beat Argentina in the quarter final and Portugal in the semi. There would be no start for Jimmy Greaves as Geoff Hurst would again spearhead the attack.

'England have two brothers in the World Cup final team just as West Germany had in 1954 when Fritz and Ottmar Walter played. Her Majesty arrives in the royal box. Behind her, His Royal Highness Prince Philip the Duke of Edinburgh. Harold Wilson, the Prime Minister on the extreme left, and Lord Harewood the President of the Football Association.'

The band struck up and *God Save The Queen* rang out around the stadium. Standing among a sea of grey, the Queen in yellow could be seen above the thirty-nine steps that countless teams had climbed to receive their trophies. The ranks of English supporters sang and their voices rose together in mutual patriotic fervour. As the anthem came to an end, cheers erupted spontaneously across the terraces. The German national anthem *Das Lied Der Deutschen* followed sung by a more modest contingent but with no less passion.

'Thousands of German supporters salute their team as the band of Her Majesty's Royal Marines, Portsmouth Group, leave the arena and any moment now the World Cup final will begin.'

In his commentary position opposite the Royal Box, Kenneth Wolstenholme turned to his colleague Wally Barnes sitting beside him. The men exchanged a brief nod and Wally held up his crossed fingers. 'Good luck,' he said.

In the centre circle below, watched by referee Dienst, the two generals, Bobby Moore and Uwe Seeler shook hands and swapped pennants. Between the official's boots sat the orange ball upon the limed spot.

'Bobby Moore, captain of England – the usual exchange of banners – the toss-up which could be vital,' the commentator added.

Dienst spoke both English and German, but Moore pointed to the silver coin in the referee's hand. The official flicked it into the air and it landed on the Wembley turf. The England skipper bent down and found his choice was good. The referee blew a shrill whistle to signal that the game was about to begin. The sound carried around the stadium and mixed with the applause and cheers that rose in expectation from the 96, 924 watching from the stands.

'Blast!' Alex let out a cry in frustration.

'What is it?'

'*The time*! I need to know the time.' He looked back at Billy as they stood beside the pitch. 'So we know when the goals go in.'

'What about up there?' Billy pointed towards the huge Radio Times scoreboard and got a surprise. 'Doesn't Wembley have a clock? Use my watch then.'

'No, I need to know the splits between each goal. Wait a minute.'

He knelt down and opening his bag began to rummage inside. Seconds later he held a tobacco tin in his hand.

'What's that? D'you want a roll-up?'

'No. Someone gave it to me.'

He dug his nails into the lid and it popped open.

'That's handy,' Billy said looking at the stopwatch Alex was holding by the black cord.

'Yeah, just the job. Now we can work out when the goals go in.'

He hung it round his neck. Just before putting the tin back into the bag he took out the half-crown and tossed it into the air.

'Heads we win.' He caught the coin and shoved it into the pocket in his grey jogging bottoms.

Kenneth Wolstenholme spoke to the world: 'The England team in unfamiliar dark shirts have never been beaten in a football match by West Germany. The rain has stopped; the excitement is intense. The ground in many places is soft...'

Referee Dienst blew his whistle to start the game and Wolfgang Weber fired a long pass towards Helmut Haller on the right wing but it was over hit and went straight into touch for an England throw.

'...But the 1966 World Cup is underway.'

'Lift-off!' Alex pressed the button on the stopwatch. He looked at Billy, 'Helmut Haller will score in twelve minutes.'

Alex and Billy saw on the far side that Ray Wilson had made a pass to Bobby Moore. The captain returned it short to Wilson who threaded it forward to Martin Peters on the left wing. Peters dropped the ball inside to Bobby Charlton who laid it off for Nobby Stiles who was moving through the centre of the German half. Stiles struck the ball with his right foot and the shot cannoned off the German defence and away from danger.

'There's Beckenbauer; this elegant midfield player,' Wolstenholme said.

The number four would become known as *Der Kaiser* and he would pioneer the World Cup finals in a united Germany in forty years' time.

The German passing broke down and the ball was collected by Bobby Moore in the centre circle. He gave it a prod forward and Geoff Hurst laid it off for Martin Peters who shot. It was blocked and deflected high in a looping arc. Peters attempted to strike the rebound but the shot went tamely wide, watched by Hans Tilkowski wearing black in the German goal. The referee signalled a goal-kick.

'Looks like home advantage,' Billy said.

'Yeah, I remember this. It won't last.' Alex checked the watch. 'Let's move down behind Banks's goal. We're not official ball-boys and I don't want anyone to see us.'

'What d'you mean, there's a hundred thousand here? How can we *not* be seen?'

'I'm still trying to get over the idea that we shouldn't be here.'

'I haven't,' Billy said, forgetting the fear he'd felt outside the stadium. 'Look at that great bit of play by Bobby Moore. He's better than Tony Adams.'

Alex dropped his bag onto the loose cinders twenty yards behind the goal. 'Base camp! Let's do it here; it'll be quieter than along the sides. Haller should be sticking it in pretty soon.'

'Why don't we tell Gordon to watch out for Haller's shot?'

'No. No, we can't interfere with the game. Not yet anyway. Who knows what'll happen? We might change it before we have to change it! If you see what I mean.'

They looked over to see Schnellinger taking a throw to a defender in his goal area.

'Schulz – tremendous sweeper in the German defence,' said Kenneth Wolstenholme. He played a long, speculative ball towards the English eighteen-yard line and it was headed away by Bobby Moore. 'Emmerich,' the forward struck the ball low into England's penalty area. 'Oh a chance.' Siggy Held dragged his shot wide with his left foot and Gordon Banks was relieved to watch the ball go out for a goal-kick.

'A chance fell to Held. Incidentally, if this competition is not to become the most defensive-minded, seven goals have got to be produced in this final. That would give the same average goals per game as 1962.'

Alex glanced along the pitch and counted at least six ball-boys dressed in grey track suits like him. He and Billy were the only two behind Gordon Banks' goal. There would come a time, he knew it, when he would have to retrieve a wide shot. Maybe the cameras would be on him. At some point in extra time, he would play a significant part and the whole world would be witness. He shuddered.

Bobby Charlton was taking a throw-in on the far side just below the Royal Box. He stood next to a ball-boy who was several inches taller than the England forward. Alan Ball collected the throw and played it back to Charlton who saw an opportunity and in turn laid a pass into the middle of the German half.

'Out comes Stiles. Good thinking Stiles,' added Kenneth Wolstenholme. He played it forward to the edge of the German area. 'Hunt.' Wolfgang Weber intercepted and struck it away. 'Strong German defence. They're quick to come and cover. Haller to Seeler who's got Held on his left. Five men covering Banks. Back to Emmerich.'

The German number eleven thrashed wildly and the ball flew off at an angle and was more a threat to the corner flag than the goal. The English supporters let out a chorus of ironic cheers.

'That was the wrong foot for Mr Emmerich – top scorer in Germany last season.'

Alex checked his stopwatch, 'Only five minutes gone. This is taking forever!'

There came a cauldron of noise from the multitude which seemed to spread and heave and echo like the movement of an ocean. One section of German fans began chanting: 'Uwe...Uwe...Uwe.' The Germanic accolade filled the air; 'Oovay...Oovay...Oovay...' a tribute to their leader: Captain Uwe Seeler. The sound carried around the terraces like some ancient war cry.

I'm in a volcano, Alex thought. He suddenly felt dizzy. *It's gonna blow...this is Mount Doom all over again... I can't do this.* 'I'm gonna bottle-it Billy.' He let out a gasp and in anger kicked the bag beside his feet. He felt the ball inside. 'I'm gonna screw this up big time.'

'Bull-shit! This is what you wanted. This is why you're here. If *we* don't do it, then it won't get done.'

'Who says we've gotta do this?'

'Look, we got here, didn't we?'

206

'So...?'

'So...I dunno, maybe we've been allowed to. Maybe someone, somewhere, wants this to happen. I don't mean Vane.'

'Who then?'

'God knows...I dunno. Yeah, maybe even him! Perhaps we're all given one wish and this is ours.'

A sudden roar from the fans ended their conversation. England were breaking from midfield.

'Bobby Charlton to Hunt, and Hurst moving up. And so to Stiles again – and in goes Hunt. Charlton – Bobby Charlton – Hurst...Cohen...' Kenneth Wolstenholme described the move.

A cluster of players tangled around the German goal-line and two collided falling to the ground.

'...And the goalkeeper, flat-out injured. And Alan Ball gives away a free kick pushing Tilkowski. Obviously a bang in the face. Probably saying to himself, "Well I heard Mohammed Ali – Cassius Clay – was here, but I didn't think he was on the field."'

Alex looked at his stopwatch. 'Ten minutes gone. Here comes Haller. This is it Billy,' Alex pointed towards the German goal at the far end. 'Look, Peters has put that shot wide. From the goal-kick they bring it forward and Wilson takes out Seeler on the half-way line.'

The Germans jeered and whistled as their captain was brought down.

'See, it's panning out just like it should. This game's sticking to the plot alright. Here we go, Seeler plays it to Haller. I've seen this a hundred times. Haller gives it back then it goes to Schnellinger who plays it left to Held. It's coming our way Billy. Haller's already moved to the edge of the area.'

Alex looked again at his stopwatch. 'Yep, twelve minutes. This is it – Held's let it fly. Now watch Ray Wilson cock it up.'

'Schnellinger now to Held, number ten,' said Wolstenholme. 'Oh Wilson gives it to Haller.'

The German striker sent a low right foot shot past Gordon Banks and into the left side of the goal. The net rippled.

'A goal! West Germany have scored. Twelve minutes have gone and Helmut Haller has put West Germany in the lead.'

The German fans erupted into a wild frenzy and flags of black, red and yellow were waved around Wembley.

'There he goes,' shouted Billy, drowned by the sound of the German supporters, 'on that poncy celebration he always did.'

'Banks never got a chance. I think it was deflected off Moore's foot. Did you see that Billy?'

'That was Ray Wilson's fault. He should've cleared it.'

'Yeah, and we would've won.'

Maybe it was that low moment in Ray Wilson's life that would haunt the full back for the rest of his career because he would eventually leave football to become an undertaker.

'And if English hearts have now slumped,' added Kenneth Wolstenholme, 'let me tell them that this is the fourth World Cup final I've seen, and in the previous three, the team that scored first…*lost*.'

Referee Dienst blew his whistle and England kicked off from the centre spot.

Alex turned to Billy and held up the stopwatch. 'We've got six minutes before Geoff Hurst gets the equaliser.'

'Shame we got no time to place a bet,' Billy added with a smirk.

'Right, let's work this out. At the end of full-time, Nobby Stiles is gonna belt it and it'll land somewhere over there.' Alex pointed towards the edge of the cinder semi-circle behind the goal. 'We've gotta be ready. It's the only time Wembley won't be watching.'

'Yeah, and out of TV shot as well.'

'So when I give you a shout, "*Here it comes*", get our little Slazenger baby ready. I grab the match ball and you can get the replica back to the Ref. Sound good?'

'Piece of piss, as my Dad used to say! Actually it's the real match ball.'

'Yeah, I'm having trouble getting my head round that. How can there be *two*?'

'...The German supporters making all the noise at the moment,' said Wolstenholme, as Bobby Charlton collected a long punt from goalkeeper Hans Tilkowski. Charlton guided it gently with his left foot to his captain advancing along the left wing. 'Now Moore will pick up the attack...'

'This is it Billy,' Alex checked his stopwatch. 'Bobby Moore gets fouled and we score from the kick.' Both boys stared across the pitch to the far side where play was going on. The referee blew his whistle.

'...And brought down by Overath.'

Bobby Moore yelled and with quick thinking took the free kick as the German defence backed away. He fired a long cross deep into the penalty area where Geoff Hurst was standing unmarked. The tall number ten rose to head the ball with perfect timing and it shot beyond Hans Tilkowski stranded on his goal-line.

'In it goes! It's the equaliser,' the BBC commentator couldn't hide his delight.

Hurst celebrated in front of a line of photographers. Wembley erupted into sound and relief was audibly lifted from the ranks of English supporters. Wally Barnes sitting next to Kenneth Wolstenholme took up the commentary.

'A brilliant piece of football there by Bobby Moore. He looked up and saw that the Germans had momentarily gone flat across the penalty area and he flighted it across to his home club player who must always be looking for this type of cross. A great Bobby Moore improvisation and it's put England back on level terms now.'

In the spontaneity of the moment Alex and Billy found themselves leaping and hugging each other.

'England...England...' Alex began shouting. He turned to see someone standing next to him. She had her arms aloft in celebration. It was Britannia. She smiled and came over to him and embraced him. For several seconds she held him; wisps of her dark hair brushed across his face. Alex put his arms around her and could feel her slim body inside her black uniform. In that moment, he didn't care that he hardly knew her.

'I need to talk to you Alex. It's urgent.' She spoke into his ear and her eyes strayed as she glanced over his shoulder towards the multitudes spanning the terraces. 'It's Trinity. They're not here to watch you. They've come for someone. You're just a smoke-screen Alex.'

'What're you talking about Brit?' He looked into her eyes. But all he could think was that there was something strangely familiar about her. For a split second there came a flash from his deep memory and he thought he knew her. Then just as quick, his recall evaporated and was gone.

She let go of him and spoke to both ball-boys. 'You'd better listen good, 'cause the future might never be the same again!'

29

'Ladies and gentlemen, Quantum Tours welcomes you to Wembley Stadium.'

The courier's calm voice was picked up by a tiny piezo microphone concealed under her hairline. The dozen guests could hear her perfectly with their in-ear receivers, even amid the noise of the World Cup final. She turned and looked across the football pitch from their vantage point high in the stands.

'For some of you this may be your first visit with us, and I know that there are those here specially to relive again this unique sporting event. We hope you enjoy the experience. As you can see, and hear, the passion for the game has not diminished over the years.'

She spoke to a couple standing beside her. 'It's always good to have you back again Mr and Mrs Nakamura.' The courier was polite as she noticed they were decked with copious recording devices.

'Oh yes,' Kaito Nakamura replied, 'we wouldn't miss another trip to '66. It's become our favourite vacation.'

Seconds later he re-played to Mrs Nakamura the conversation he'd just had with their attractive hostess.

Daisy smiled. 'You never know what will happen next,' she said.

'かもしれないが、なかなか今日はされます!'   the courier replied with fluent ease and waved a hand in the direction of the pitch.

'Yes, maybe,' said Daisy Nakamura.

Turning to her guests the courier re-activated her tiny microphone, 'You will notice straightaway that the fabled Twin Towers have become somewhat overstated in literature and electronic archives. We were led to believe that their elegance could rival the splendour of the Taj Mahal before it was destroyed during the Indian Uprising. Sadly that's far from the truth. They look tired and in need of a makeover. They stand just a quarter the height of the arch which adorned the second stadium at the turn of the 21st Century. And that arch itself was dwarfed twenty-three years later by the *Halo*. Even so, this art deco architecture is a proud statement of the British Empire which dates from the 1920s. In 1948, after the Second World War, Wembley was host to the Olympic Games and for some seventy years it was the most revered of all stadia on earth. After all, it was home to the country that invented football.

'All around, you can see the rudimentary nature of the terracing. There is very little seating, so you'll have to stand for the duration of the game. I can only apologise Mr Sinyavsky. If you're having difficulty negotiating the steep terrace with your jet-Zimmer, let me know and I'll make some alternative arrangements.'

The Russian nodded showing he understood.

'Let me take this opportunity to point out some of the more significant A-listers here today. If you divert your optics over there, just above the centre of the pitch, you will see Her Majesty Queen Elizabeth, dressed in a delicate shade of lemon. As you can tell she seems to be enjoying the occasion. If you tune to *LipSync* you will be able to hear what she is saying. And just to the right of the Queen, and back one row, you can pick out Princess Michael of Kent dressed in a rather tasteful pale blue suit.' The courier pointed and some of her party aimed their trinoculars.

'But more relevant to this event, you can make out the two figures below us, standing there behind Gordon Banks' goal. The ball-boys in grey are Alex Bell and Billy Gunn.'

Her party of guests strained and twisted to see where she was looking. Some even gasped.

'I wonder what their contribution will be to this game,' she added.

'Yah, it is them', one of the party said lowering his *digizoom*. His accent was Teutonic.

30

A sudden brightness came over the stadium as Kenneth Wolstenholme delivered his commentary that would become iconic.

'We're getting everything this afternoon – the sun has now come out!'

The Germans were breaking from defence as Uwe Seeler fired a long ball forward from the centre circle. It flew over the heads of the English back line towards the German front man.

'Oh offside; Haller.'

Gordon Banks retrieved the ball and tossed it to Bobby Moore who took the spot-kick to restart play. It came to Nobby Stiles who drove a long pass beyond his own front line. The ball was a waste and the Germans countered again down the right flank.

'Now you can see how the Germans are playing – with Beckenbauer going forward to add to the attack.'

The move came to nothing and Bobby Moore received a short throw from Gordon Banks who had picked up the loose ball.

'Now Moore; comes Stiles...' but the midfielder is robbed by Siggy Held who finds the German goal scorer on the half-way line.

'...Now Haller...now Beckenbauer moving forward again. This is Emmerich; there's Beckenbauer approaching him. This is Held...'

Almost within touching distance of the corner flag, the ball is centred from the left wing.

'Emmerich going over the middle...Seeler.'

The German forward jumped and his height took him above Bobby Moore. It was a battle between two gladiators that would be contested during the game. On this occasion the man in white came out on top but he headed wide and the ball was shepherded out by George Cohen on the six-yard line. The referee waved for a goal-kick as the ball ran behind onto the cinders. Groans and cheers echoed around Wembley.

Behind the goal, Britannia was talking to the ball-boys. 'It's Trinity. I haven't found them yet, but they're in the stadium somewhere.'

'Hold on Brit,' cut in Alex. 'Here comes the ball.'

He sprinted the short distance on the crunchy cinders as the ball rolled towards him. Picking it up he lobbed the ball into the hands of Gordon Banks who was standing on the Wembley turf.

'There you go Gordon.'

'Thanks,' the England number one said and turned and placed the ball on the pitch. The goalkeeper's career would last another six years only to be cut short when he would lose an eye in a car accident.

Wow, I gave Gordon Banks the ball. I'm actually part of the World Cup. I've been seen by the world. There's no going back now.

Alex was suddenly gripped by a sense of panic and excitement.

As he walked to his position behind the goal, he sniffed his hands and detected the unmistakable smell of dubbin. The thought struck him that Trinity may have increased the weight of their ball by imbibing the leather with a liberal smearing of dubbin. *Trinity*, he thought, *Trinity*.

'Trinity,' Alex blurted out when he reached Britannia, 'what the do you know about Trinity?'

She rested her slender fingers on Alex's shoulder as if to reassure him.

'Quite a lot! They're not here just to help you with your secret ambition. They have a hidden agenda. They're here for something completely different.'

'What're they here for then?' Alex was flummoxed by her knowledge of some future organisation. Maybe Trinity existed in the Sixties, he thought.

'Not *what* Alex, but *who*!'

'What do you mean?' he said sharply.

'Benjamin Janus.'

'*Benjamin Janus*. That rings a bell!'

'Yeah, that Trevelyan woman told us about him,' Billy added. 'Remember?'

'They may have told you something, but perhaps not the whole story.'

Britannia's voice could just be made out amid the Wembley noise that surrounded them. 'It gets a bit deep – but here goes.' She took a breath.

'In the Sixties, Britain, the US and the Soviet Union got caught up in a bitter Cold War triangle that lasted years. People died or were bribed or defected or changed their names, or their gender or went missing. Some came and went from the highest of government positions. Behind the space-race there was a star-war going on. Many have said that the moon landings were faked in some giant hangar in New Mexico. It's not true. When Neil and Buzz stepped onto the Sea of Tranquillity, the Soviets actually had a craft parked in lunar orbit having tracked the Eagle all the way. Thankfully it was never used. Had those men not come back, then the superpowers may well have nuked us all several times over...'

'Why you telling us this Brit? Right here at the World Cup final...'

'I'm coming to that. Some astronauts *did* disappear...'

'Yeah we heard.'

'...And so did many other important people. What Trinity may not have told you was that an RAF Wessex helicopter went down in the North Sea eighteen months after Bakhramov was bludgeoned to death. Yes, that bloke over there with the yellow flag.'

'So what's the big deal with the chopper?'

'On board was Ben Janus. He's the genius behind the machine. Haven't you worked it out yet Alex? Janus is here and Trinity want to snatch him before he ends up in a condemned Wessex. Right now he's working on some advanced machine that can go anywhere. Trinity want that technology. It would give them the power to change just about anything they wanted. Have you got the drift?'

'Yes, but...,' Alex hesitated. 'If we sort the result of this match, then Tofik makes the right choice and doesn't get scratched-out. And so...um...Ben Janus doesn't end up in the sea. Right?'

For a moment Alex wondered if he'd just let slip the purpose of why he and Billy were masquerading as ball-boys.

'Maybe Trinity thinks you're gonna screw up.'

Alex and Billy were stunned. They had not planned on failing. After several seconds Billy was first to speak.

'Okay Brit, you'd better answer this good. How'd you know all this stuff?'

'Yeah, and how'd you know why *we're* here?' Alex added, and the thought struck him, how could she know about the moon landings or the death of Tofik Bakhramov? They were someway in the future! More worrying thought Alex; it seemed she knew the reason why they were at Wembley.

There was a deafening roar from the Wembley multitude.

Gordon Banks dived full stretch and pushed away a fizzing shot from a German midfielder.

'Overath. Oh a fine save.' Kenneth Wolstenholme sounded as stunned as the fans.

The ball had been parried out of the six-yard box and another white-shirted player was there to stab at the ball.

'Emmerich.'

Banks caught the second shot full in the stomach. It was becoming a barrage. The goalkeeper got to his feet and threw the ball out to Bobby Charlton.

'Well done Gordon Banks; the hero of England,' Kenneth Wolstenholme remarked.

Bobby Charlton, his distinctive thin hair trailing in the breeze, played the ball out to the left-wing on the half-way line.

'Wilson....you can see Charlton, number nine in the dark shirt. Look for Beckenbauer. There's Beckenbauer shadowing him everywhere. Beckenbauer is number four in white.'

The ball was carried by the English midfield across the width of the pitch and reached George Cohen on the opposite flank. He made a thirty-yard pass towards his number twenty-one close to the corner flag. The English attacker sent the German defender spinning as he tried to reach the pass.

'And Hunt pushing or elbowing. Free kick to West Germany.'

Gottfried Dienst blew straightaway and indicated a tug on the defender.

Alex checked his stopwatch. Half-time was looming.

'Five minutes Billy.' He called over to his friend who had wandered off towards Gordon Banks' goal.

Alex scanned the mighty bowl of Wembley Stadium and picked out excited faces in the crowd. It was history in the making and through a series of unlikely events he had become part of it. He knew that somewhere amongst the multitude were Grandpa Bell and his Dad.

I don't suppose I'll ever get to see them, he thought. *Why did Grandpa never talk about this amazing day? Something so bad must have happened.*

Britannia adjusted her starchy uniform and looked Alex square in the eyes. What she said next left him in a state of shock.

31

'Hey, half-time's nearly up,' commented a lady from New York. She was watching from high in the Wembley stands and recording live feed on her *rKive*. 'This soccer match is turning out to be one helluva game. I'm gonna recommend to the Academy that all new graduates upcoming to the Cosmos should study these World Cup series. There's so much to learn from these retro tactics. Who's that attractive woman down there with Gunn and Bell? I think I've seen her before.'

The Quantum Tours' courier turned to speak to the American. 'That girl in the uniform is a member of St John. But I think, as the game develops we may find that she becomes far more integral to the event.

'Maybe you have seen her before Juno.'

32

'I used to work for Trinity,' Britannia said to Alex.

'*Trinity...you*?' he didn't believe her. 'What did you do there?'

'Well...' she paused, 'I was part of a team looking at key historic events. We found things that the world doesn't know about. Talk about conspiracy! There's a mass of evidence to show that hundreds of famous incidents have been tampered with...'

'...*Tampered*?'

'...*Changed*... by people who shouldn't have been there – people who may have come from the future.'

'You're having me on.'

'*You're* here, aren't you?'

Alex could say nothing, for he realised he was in a time and place where he had no reason to be.

'Alright, give me an example.'

'There's a multitude. Okay, *1066* – the Battle of Hastings...'

'What about it? What happened?'

'We don't know for sure, but the battle came to a stop sometime in the afternoon. Something happened which shouldn't have. An object came out of the sky and changed the course of the battle. It was no wandering star, that's for sure. Halley's comet was hanging around Saturn at the time.'

'You've gotta be joking!'

'Am I laughing? Anyway that's not the only reason I worked for Trinity.' She paused as a ripple of noise spread around the stadium. 'I was there to see what Trinity were up to.'

'So you're not a magician then?'

'I do that for fun.'

'St John's..?'

'A disguise. My background's in the regulation of time and motion. I've got a PhD in temporal synchronicity dysfunction.'

'*Temporal...what*? This is mental.' Alex thought she was starting to sound like Warwick Vane.

'Did they tell you what *Trinity* stands for?'

'No we only got to see a few old balls and some froggy soldiers.'

'You may have seen it written somewhere as T-R-I-N-I$_4$-T$_2$-Y: *Time Research Into Nexus Inventions for Travelling to Yesterday.*'

'Blimey that's a mouthful. What does *Nexus* mean?'

'It's a link or bond, or the bridge that the machine joined between two separate times. The machine formed a connection to the future when it was fired up in '66. For Trinity, it's become a way back to yesterday. And if Victoria Trevelyan gets hold of Ben Janus, he'll be a way of reaching tomorrow.'

'How'd you mean?'

'Once they get him back, they'll want him to point the machine the other way and travel forwards. They could screw up the future for all of us. Going back and changing the past is one thing, but meddling with the future is like playing roulette with our destinies...'

The crowd exploded once more and Alex turned to see that Gordon Banks had just made a flying save to stop Uwe Seeler scoring from long range. The England goalkeeper had tipped a rifled shot round the post and the ball was being collected by a ball-boy on the far side. The Germans were beginning to pummel the English. It was turning into a blitzkrieg. A corner was being taken short and Helmut Haller collected the pass on the edge of the penalty area. He jinked past Geoff Hurst and fired a high centre straight over the crossbar just missing the rank of photographers behind the goal.

'Here it comes Billy – your turn this time.' Alex screamed to his friend who was standing ten yards away.

'I've got it,' Billy shouted, and he tossed it to Gordon Banks who was keen to get on with the game.

Alex gave him a thumbs-up. 'Nice one mate.' He glanced at his stopwatch. 'Billy, we're into time-added-on. Gotta be just a minute left at the most.' He turned back to Britannia. 'So how did you get here – when you were working for Trinity?'

'I left Trinity ages ago. I didn't use the machine you did.'

'How then?'

'There are others.'

'What, *machines*?'

'Yes. There are some which have been kept hidden.'

'*Hidden*?'

'Secret.'

'Okay, so tell me Brit – why're you *really* here?' It was a question which had begun to burn inside him, and he needed to know.

'Well Alex,' she looked oddly coy for a moment, 'to make sure…to make sure nothing happens to *you*.'

'*Me*! He thumped his chest. 'Do you know why we're here?'

'Yes. I know everything.'

Gottfried Dienst blew his whistle to end the first-half.

All over England, kettles were switched on and tea began brewing as the National Grid experienced the biggest power surge in British history.

33

The massed bands of Her Majesties Royal Marines trooped out from the tunnel playing the World Cup March. They stepped in time to the boom of the bass drum that reverberated like a pounding cannon around the stadium. The company rounded the goal and marched onto the pitch having no regard for the players or officials leaving for half-time. Gaps in the terraces opened up as thousands disappeared into the belly of Wembley in search of food, drink and the 361 toilets.

'I'm gonna look around,' Billy called over to Alex.

'We got fifteen minutes. Make sure you're back. And don't do anything stupid.'

'You know me!'

'Yeah, that's what I'm worried about.'

Billy smirked and wandered off.

'Hey, did you see this Brit?' He flicked open the Cup Final programme. 'Look at this timetable: kick-off, 3:00pm; half-time, 3:45, and get this, presentation of the Jules Rimet cup, *4:40*. That's a bit premature; I'm expecting extra time.'

She levelled her smouldering eyes at him. 'Who knows Alex, maybe it will be decided at the end of ninety minutes.'

'Do you know something I don't?' Alex gave her an anxious look.

'No – but in a world of uncertainty, anything can happen. And usually does.'

34

'Where the hell's Billy gone?' said a voice high up in the stands. 'He just disappeared down the players' tunnel.'

'Perhaps he wants a piss,' Warwick Vane spoke dead-pan to Ralf Schneider. 'Don't worry; just keep an eye on our target. I'm watching Britannia. At this rate we could buy one and get one free!'

Schneider flipped open the tiny palmtop and flashed it towards Vane. 'There, perfect close up of Janus, and look, Victoria's right behind him.'

The dark skinned woman, immaculately dressed, looked strangely out of place amongst the English supporters. But no one noticed. All eyes were on the game.

The image they looked at came from the invisible *eye-bot* hovering above them.

'We could send an *eye* to follow Billy,' Schneider said.

'No need, he's only here to soak in the atmosphere. We'll wait for Victoria's signal and then we'll move.'

They looked twenty yards below and saw the Controller of Trinity put her finger to one ear and on turning round gave them a curt nod. Right in front of her stood Benjamin Janus who was talking with a physics colleague from the University of Oxford. Victoria could tell that their conversation was more about space-time than half-time. She was excited by the prospect of getting the genius of time-travel on board. The possibilities for Trinity would be endless.

35

Alex checked his stopwatch.

'Twelve minutes before they come out. Then we'll get England kicking towards us – should get a good view of Martin Peters' goal. This marching music's starting to do my head in.' He turned to the young woman standing next to him and saw how intensely dark her eyes were. 'Does football interest you Brit?'

'I love it. My Dad used to take me to watch Fulham when I was a teenager.'

'Tell me Brit, how do you know my Mum?'

She looked at Alex and decided to tell him a little more. 'Like you, I'm from the future.'

'I thought so. I keep thinking I've seen you somewhere. Have you worked in Studio 6?'

'No Alex. Although I know about your Mum, I don't actually know her.' She thought for a moment, 'I met her once, but I was too young to remember.'

'Do you know her from stuff you found in Trinity then?'

'No, I worked in Trinity purely for observational reasons.' She paused and her eyes drifted around the stadium that engulfed them as if looking for something. 'Alex you'd better believe me when I tell you this…'

'What?'

She held his stare with hers. 'I'm from *2066*.'

'*Twenty…You're what*?' He looked at her as if he'd misheard, or she was joking.

'Yes,' she said. 'A hundred years from now.'

36

Billy had followed the players into the tunnel. No one had tried to stop him, so he carried on walking along a shabby corridor beneath the stadium. The breeze-block walls were painted grey, and from the ceiling hung fluorescent tubes grimy with age. High above came a deep reverberation of the many thousand spectators moving around on the concrete floors. Far from being the jewel in the football crown, it seemed to Billy that the world's greatest stadium was more like the labyrinth of a wartime bunker he had once visited on a school trip. Dust scuffed under his feet and the smell of polish pervaded the stifled air. He heard feet approaching and turning saw three men appear round a corner.

'It's a good game,' Gottfried Dienst was saying in English. 'It is flowing well. Let us keep the game open.'

Tofik Bakhramov looked at the referee and nodded in agreement. He had understood nothing.

Dienst went on, 'In the second-half I will continue to run the diagonal. Can I ask you both to stay on the same sides? No change. Okay?'

The two linesmen looked at Dienst.

'Yah,' said Karol Galba.

Tofik Bakhramov, the official from Azerbaijan had a blank face but replied, 'Okay.'

As they passed Billy, just for a second Gottfried Dienst rested his hand on the ball boy's shoulder as if to thank him for his help during the game. Then they were gone.

This is amazing, Billy thought. *We'll have to get some of these guys on the show when we're back. Who's still around? Martin Peters?*

'Hey, you lost boy?'

A voice called out from along the corridor. A man was standing there wearing a navy blazer with an embroidered crest on his breast pocket. He had a ruddy complexion as if he'd drunk some alcoholic beverage during the first half.

'Um, no. I'm just, um, getting the oranges. In case the game goes to extra time.'

'Oh, righteo.' The man in the blazer stroked his wide moustache. 'You may want to find the cafeteria. Down there I think,' he pointed. 'You're wasting your time though lad – England'll win it easy. Charlton to get a couple I'd say.'

'Yeah, right, thanks.'

The man strode away with a military gait.

Outside, the Royal Marines began another march. The sound penetrated deep into Wembley. Billy rounded a corner and almost walked into someone standing by a door. He wore a brown workshop coat and a cloth cap.

'Sorry,' said Billy, 'I was…'

'That's alright sonny. Is it a good game?' His voice was gruff, as if he smoked a packet a day.

'Um, yes. It's everything I thought it would be.'

'I heard two goals go in.'

'It's pretty much even. The Germans could've gone ahead but Banksy made a great save.' Billy weighed up the man. He was middle aged and overweight. His brown workshop coat was held together with one button and a safety pin. He seemed rooted to the spot. 'Haven't you been watching?'

'No, I've got to be here. I've been told.'

'Don't you have a ticket?'

'I'm guarding this door.'

'What's in there?'

'I'm not supposed to tell. It's a secret. But honest Bob knows that you can keep a secret too – being a ball-boy and that.'

'Yeah, that's right Bob.'

227

'Have a guess what's inside.'

'I don't have a clue. I dunno…*commentators*.'

'Nope, try again.'

'*Oranges*…for extra time.'

'Nope.'

'Oh, um, *England*…the team.'

'Nope.' Bob looked pleased that Billy could not guess. 'I've got a very important job. Usually I set up the nets or put the flags on the corner posts, but not today. One more guess.' He seemed desperate to share the secret with someone.

He's not the brightest light on the Christmas tree, Billy thought. '*The Queen*,' he said.

'Wrong again.'

'What's in there then?' Billy was now keen to find out.

Bob shot a glance both ways, then he looked Billy straight in the eye. 'Don't tell. It's the actual *World Cup*.'

'*What*?' exclaimed Billy.

'Yeah, the Rules Jimet.'

'…*Jules Rimet*.'

'Same difference. Actually, there's two – the real World Cup and a copy – in case the proper one got lost I s'pose.' Bob grinned and a smile froze on his wide face.

Billy thought for a moment, and it took him a few seconds to reply, but when he did, he said: 'Can I see? I've got one. You can buy them in Carnaby Street.'

37

Alex stared at Britannia in total disbelief. 'You don't come from where I do then?'

'Nowhere near – well, same place – different time.'

It took a while for Alex to grasp the idea that this attractive young woman standing in front of him was from a time many decades after his own. *That's impossible* he thought.

'Alright Brit, tell me, who's king in 2066? Who won the FA cup? Who's been nuked...?'

'Alex...' she held up a hand, 'I can't give that sort of information. It's against my constitution. In any case, you could use it for your own gain and you'd become like Trinity, having power to change the world. Sorry.'

'What bloody constitution you talking about?'

'*Temporal regs.*'

'*Regs?*'

'Regulations – the rules governing time movement. This'll be the only thing I'm going to let you into about the future. The World Parliament passed regulations controlling time movement...'

'...There's a World Parliament?'

'Sort of, it's a spin-off from the UN.'

'Is it in New York?'

'No, Europe – *Rome*. Look, I can't say too much.'

'Is Europe big in 2066? What about China?' There was so much he wanted to ask.

'Alex, do you want to hear this?' She gave him a stare and he backed off.

'Yeah, go on.'

'This is how it breaks down: Observers may only look from a distance of non-interference.'

'What's an *Observer*?'

'Just that – someone who circumvents a time zone and observes; a benevolent agent who looks and doesn't touch. Just like you.'

'What if I touch something?'

'I'm coming to that. It depends on the degree of interference. At no time must any contact be made in the retrograde timeline. This may cause the propagation of a parallel timeline which may deviate irreversibly from the default timeline.

'Premeditated changes to a retrograde timeline will result in irreversible deviation leading to a permanent alteration to that timeline.

'Change to a retrograde timeline will result in the propagation of a tangential parallel timeline which will give rise to significant alternate events.

'More recently, well more recently where I come from, the governing body decided there was a more fundamental principle that had been overlooked. So they added the *zeroth law of temporal dynamics*. This says that the mere presence of an Observer or Changer, in the retrograde timeline is likely to alter that timeline.'

She stopped and waited for it to sink in. 'Well, what do you think?'

'Brit, you're full of shit!'

Alex let out a sigh as if trying to come to terms with what she had said. He kicked the bag beside his feet because he understood none of it. Except that he was an Observer, or was he a Changer?

'Does that mean I could change things just by being here?'

'Yes, very likely.'

'Well I've got nothing to lose then.' He was thinking about what he had to do.

'Alex, I've got something that'll interest you.'

'Does it come with long words?'

'No, you just have to look at it.'

'Bring it on.'

She produced a shiny silver rectangle from her shoulder bag, about the size of a credit card.

'Look at this,' she said, and moved it in a slow circle around him. 'It's just recorded your image. Put it in your pocket.'

'Are you going to do some magic?'

'Sort of. It will seem like magic to you, but it's nothing more than technology that's yet to hit the streets. Now put this visor on.' She unravelled a coiled transparent strip which shaped into an arc. 'Wear this like a pair of shades.'

The narrow band held in place over his eyes.

'Wow!' I see *Wembley*. But not this Wembley.'

'It's a future Wembley,' Britannia said wearing her own visor.

'Now I see you!' He turned his head. 'I see everything. It's like we're both there.'

'These are head-up displays, but several generations on. They're called *SpEx – Spatial Explorer*. They download *SenseSurround* to give this 360 display. I can see you and you can see me and we can both go to a game together. At the moment the stadium's empty, but I can select a virtual crowd.'

As Alex looked he could see the arena was filling with people and he could hear noise and feel the atmosphere. Britannia moved towards him and held his hand. They stood together amidst the visage of a future Wembley which resembled the second stadium Alex new well. They had become avatars in an imaginary world; facsimiles of themselves having the ability to interact with computer simulation. He looked up.

'This is so cool. Hey, there's a double arch.'

'Yes, the Wembley you know, designed by Norman Foster got a new look in '23. The second arch is a hollow tube through which they beam coloured light. It was erected to celebrate one hundred years after the very first game. Do you remember your history?'

'Um, yeah: The *White Horse* final. Bolton beat West Ham.'

'It's called the *Centenary Arch* but it got dubbed the *Halo*.'

'...*Billy*!'

'Billy? He'll be back soon.'

'No, the white horse was called *Billy*.'

'I didn't know that. Anyway, you can link in thousands wearing *SpEx*, and it's as if they'd all be there, even if you're standing in some desert. The fans you can see are synthesised, but you could invite as many friends as you want and watch your favourite game together.'

'Amazing! Here come the teams.'

A roar from the virtual Wembley came up as the sound was transmitted through the contacts pressing gently above Alex's ears. Flares and fireworks erupted and lit the terraces, and high above, the translucent arch was filled with colour. A crimson bow adorned the stadium. Onto the pitch ran the teams.

'Hey, Man United and Newcastle!'

'Yep, they're still big.'

'They've got no sponsors on their shirts.'

'Advertising has been banned.'

'How are the clubs funded then?'

'All top flight teams have been taken over by billionaires. There's no need to pump money in from sponsorship. Quite the reverse, many clubs support charities and new businesses.'

'Is that a *woman* in goal for Man U?'

'*Zhang Li Po*. She's over two metres and seems to defy gravity with her acrobatics.'

'What's the world coming to? Scientists will be searching for the football gene next.'

'Funny you should say that...Oh and the game has changed from what you know. For one thing, there's no offside anymore.'

'No way!'

The game kicked-off as one of the three referees blew her *whistle*. At least that hasn't changed Alex noted. A woman with a deep contralto voice began to commentate.

'Newcastle take the centre having dumped out Blackpool, 5-4, in the semi. Stanley Vegas fires a well good ball out left to Dick Wallaby, the first Aborigine to play in the English league. And, shit, he's taken out by Man U's line-backer, Abdul O'Malley. Referee, India Nduku, indicates a direct-free and, feckme, I'd say O'Malley's lucky not to get an amber caution in the first minute. Here comes Newcastle's Van Daemon looking to punish the champion's quarter line with one of his anti-grav benders. Zhang's hollering at her defence to tag each Newky player as they strafe inside the pen-zone...'

For a moment, what Alex heard did not fit with what he was seeing. Then he realised that there were two games juxtaposed. He removed the *SpEx* and a future final was replaced by one from the past. The commentary was in stark contrast.

'And Bobby Moore leads out England for the start of the second half. There's Charlton, Bobby Charlton, in the dark shirt. What can he do for his country? Schnellinger and Seeler in white – and here is referee Gottfried Dienst with his linesmen.'

Wembley was filling up again as the volume rose inside the stadium. Rival supporters began chanting. Kenneth Wolstenholme continued to talk as the BBC broadcast live to the nations of the world.

'Where's Billy?' Alex said searching the pitch anxiously.

38

The fifteen minute interval was almost over as the ranks of supporters began filling the terraces once again. High above in the stands near the top, the courier from Quantum Tours noticed that one of her party was missing. A powered Zimmer was standing unattended nearby.

'Juno, have you seen Mr Sinyavsky? He doesn't seem to be here.'

'Well Ma'am, he was standing right here just a moment…there he goes now,' she pointed below.

The courier turned to see the Russian leaping down the steps between the terracing. He seemed to be in a hurry.

39

The cheaply painted door to the changing room crashed open and out came the England team. Their boots clattered on the pitted lino.

'Let's go boys.' Captain Bobby Moore clapped his hands and led by example. 'We can do this. Give your very, very best. Let's see Alan, Martin and Bobby driving through looking to get it up to Roger and Geoff. Bobby if you see a gap, just let one go.'

Last out of the dressing room were Jack Charlton and Nobby Stiles who were laughing and seemed undaunted by the occasion.

'...So I took him out,' Jack Charlton was saying.

'Yeah,' added Nobby Stiles, 'he went down like a sack of spuds. I thought you'd kicked his balls off!'

'C'mon mate – into battle. We ain't lost for 900 years.'

'Yeah, let's go stuff Jerry.'

Finally, manager Alf Ramsey dressed in a blue tracksuit emerged. He walked with trainer Harold Stephenson. They appeared to be in no hurry to reach pitch-side. Saying nothing they looked resolute as they followed their team out of the tunnel.

Billy had held back and stood there alone in the corridor. The sound of Wembley heaved above him like an irritable bowel from the depths of the earth below. He was surprised to find himself staring into the empty changing room of the England team. Around the corner a door opened and he heard a mix of German voices. Uwe Seeler was shouting something.

Without thinking Billy stepped into the vacant changing room and found it strewn with assorted bags, clothing and towels. The air was heavy with the acrid smell of horse-oil.

40

The sky began to darken like some prophetic warning.

Alex fumbled with his stopwatch and wiped the rain out of his eyes. From the expanse of Wembley Stadium, the home supporters, with renewed faith started chanting: '*England, England, England…*' as Geoff Hurst, Bobby Charlton and Roger Hunt lined up in the centre circle. The referee raised an arm and signalled to his linesmen.

'Torrential rain as England start the second half,' explained Kenneth Wolstenholme. 'May I just remind you that if the scores are level after ninety minutes there is half-an-hour's extra time…'

Gottfried Dienst pierced the air with a sharp whistle and Geoff Hurst laid a pass back to Alan Ball.

'…If they're still level…a replay here on Tuesday night.'

Bobby Moore played a square pass to Ray Wilson on the half-way line. He fired a long, left foot kick that flew to the edge of the German-D. It was headed clear by a defender but only as far as the England number seven.

'Ball…there's Bobby Charlton, can he get that right foot shot in?'

The England inside-right rounded Willi Schulz who stabbed out a foot causing Charlton to tumble in the penalty area. His momentum carried him off the pitch and he almost collided with a line of photographers. The English supporters screamed.

'Penalty!' shouted Alex, turning to Britannia. 'That was a clear penalty. 'Course, it won't be given. It never was.' He turned away in disgust.

Not one of the England players threw their hands into the air or argued with referee Dienst. How times had changed, Alex thought.

'Play on – goal kick,' said Wolstenholme as Bobby Charlton picked himself up and shook hands with Willi Schulz.

'That was a definite penalty Brit – and Schulz should've got a red. Wow, only twenty seconds gone. What a start! Where the heck's Billy?'

Alex scanned the stadium. *Nowhere*!

A sickening feeling began to well up inside him. Then he remembered the torn paper from tomorrow's news describing his untimely death.

Alex began to panic.

41

'Overath gets through a lot of hard work in midfield, this fellow,' the BBC commentator said.

The German number twelve picked up the loose ball outside his penalty area and played a fifteen-yard pass to the right wing before Ray Wilson could claim it. But the reliable captain miscued and the ball ran harmlessly out of play.

'Oh Seeler, I wonder what he was saying to himself?'

The German forward stamped with frustration on the soaked Wembley turf.

Wilson's throw fell to Bobby Moore on the half-way line. His long pass towards the left corner flag was controlled by the English centre forward playing only his third game in the tournament. He was closely shadowed by right back Horst-Dieter Höttges. Geoff Hurst turned inside the defender but the ball ran away only to be collected by Nobby Stiles. The gutsy midfielder looked up and placed a pass out right for Alan Ball, and the youngest Englishman on the pitch floated a high centre into the heart of the German defence.

'Ball – and Cohen coming up in support.'

Unmarked on the penalty spot the England number sixteen rose unchallenged.

'Peters!' Kenneth Wolstenholme's voice registered a trace of excitement, but the header went wide. 'Martin Peters, I think, will be in the England team for a long time to come.'

Billy Gunn was passing behind the goal and ran to collect the ball that had gone wide. For a moment he saw how exactly alike it was to the one they had secreted in their bag. Hans

Tilkowski walked towards him so he lobbed the ball over to the German goalkeeper.

'Hey Billy,' Alex shouted when he saw him. 'Where the hell've you been? The third goal's coming up.' He pointed to the stopwatch hanging round his neck.

'I got held up.'

'Come on then. We can't cock this up when it comes to the switch.'

Britannia stood beside Alex, but her mind was elsewhere. Every few minutes she glanced up and scanned the mass of ecstatic supporters curving round the huge terrace behind them.

What's she looking for, Alex thought. *Does she know something?*

42

'The encryption is based on the Fibonacci sequence: 1, 1, 2, 3, 5, 8, 13...' the Israeli said straining his voice amid the din of Wembley Stadium.

'I know that, but how does an infinite series relate to the universe?' Piers Van Dyke took his eyes off the football to face the physicist standing next to him.

'There is design in everything we see. God has etched his signature on nature itself. Like an artist signing his canvas. For instance, if the earth were a little closer to the sun, we'd fry – a little further away – we'd freeze. We orbit at precisely the right distance for life to be. The ratio of nitrogen and oxygen is just right. If gravity was a little less, we'd lose the atmosphere and all life would perish...'

'We'd be watching a weird football match if gravity was different.'

'We would.' Benjamin Janus took a small black notebook from his pocket and scribbled some notes with a blunt pencil. He looked up and spoke to the Dutchman with the sour face he always wore. 'And why do some sounds on a piano blend together in a pleasing way when others do not? Are our brains conditioned to respond to a certain order of things? And yet...' the scientist held his pencil in the air and jiggled it around. 'And yet, a stable note, say middle C, will sound different if you were moving past it – or if it were moving past you. The sound of a bell on a police car appears higher when it comes towards you and lower when it goes away. But we know the pitch does not change...'

'And that's true for light as well.'

'Correct Piers. Moving light redshifts – and, as you know, it's been used as a yard-stick to measure the size of the universe. Its constancy is a benchmark everywhere. But one elusive question remains: if God created everything in a split second – very much less than one day – did light itself move faster than it does now?'

'What would be the implications of that?' The man from Noordwijk was beginning to lose interest. He was becoming increasingly annoyed that he couldn't concentrate on the game.

'It would mean the universe is younger than it looks. Just like our research Piers, the universe is one big time machine.'

Van Dyke turned back to the football. 'Hey, Bobby Moore's got the ball.'

Benjamin Janus wrote a thought into his notebook; his mind was focused on other things.

'On Monday Piers, we'll reverse the polarity.'

43

The tall England captain wearing number six collected the ball deep in his half and played a long pass through the centre of the pitch. In turn, Geoff Hurst played a quick one-two with Martin Peters but the Germans intercepted and the ball ran loose.

'The ever reliable Schulz,' explained Kenneth Wolstenholme, as the solid defender got to the ball first.

Now it was the turn of the team in white to counter. The ball was swung in-field and the German goal scorer went for it, but Martin Peters was sticking to him like a fly on toffee. The ball bounced and seemed to strike Helmut Haller below his shoulder.

'Handball,' cried Peters, and threw his arms in the air.

The referee was only ten yards away and indicated that it had struck Haller's shirt. He waved play on.

Kenneth Wolstenholme clarified, 'That was the chest, says referee Mr Dienst of Switzerland.'

Bobby Moore was able to regain possession near the corner flag and England looked to build as the captain pumped a long ball into the German half once more. Then spontaneously, as a reaction to the referee's decision, the English supporters began chanting: '*Oh my, what a referee, what a referee, what a referee. Oh my, what a referee – what a referee he is…*'

'Listen to them Billy. At least it's clean! We could teach them a few songs that'll get complaints on the BBC.'

Alex turned to his friend and found he had walked over to a section of supporters and was leading them in the singing. He was waving his arms and conducting.

'Billy, what're you doing?'

'Hey, ball-boy. What's that mean?' One of the supporters called out to Alex.

'Um…take no notice of him. It's a kind of naval term. He used to be in the sea cadets. If you don't like someone, there's a saying about throwing him over board. Or *weighing anchor*.' Alex was making it up.

He grabbed Billy by the arm and pulled him back towards the touchline.

Billy was enthused and seemed caught up by the moment. 'Let's start a Mexican wave!'

'No,' Alex snapped back. 'The Mexican wave hasn't been invented yet! We could cause a time fracture.'

'*A what*? You're talking crap.'

'Yeah, I blame Brit. Look, not only are we on TV, but Trinity are here somewhere. We gotta be careful. Let's go.'

The English fans Billy had been entertaining continued to chant and point in the direction of Gottfried Dienst.

'Referee weigh-anchor…Referee's a wanker…'

44

A conversation between members of Trinity was continuing in the stands many rows from the football and not far from the Quantum Tours party.

Aerial images from an *eye-bot* were being received from pitch-side. The actions of two ball-boys were under close scrutiny.

'See, Alex and Billy are already influencing the course of events,' observed Ralf Schneider. 'We knew this would be dangerous.' He was becoming increasingly nervous. 'They are interacting with the crowd. Their influence is altering the balance of stability to the point where they could trigger a discontinuity. This cannot be allowed to happen.'

Warwick Vane did not reply; he had other concerns on his mind. He ran his finger nails through the stubble on his chin and stared without blinking.

After arriving at Wembley, Trinity's surveillance had shown that there was a party of twelve who had no right to be watching. Their presence was a mystery which was giving the American an unwanted distraction. He hoped they were just benevolent transients; anything more sinister could scupper Trinity's agenda. Some had been identified, but their purpose remained unclear.

'Yes, Branislav Sinyavsky was right,' Ralf Schneider said, 'Alex and Billy must be stopped before things go too far.'

'Where did he go anyway?'

The Russian's powered Zimmer stood discarded on the terrace.

'Looks like a miracle happened!'

'Shit!' Vane spoke in a monotone. 'Contact Victoria. We must move now.'

45

'Here we go Billy. We're coming up to Martin Peters' goal. Seventy-seven minutes.'

Alex held up his stopwatch and the sunlight glinted on its glass face. Just then Alex wondered why he should be holding an old analogue stopwatch. The note from the horology repairers had said it was for him. *How was that possible*? His thoughts were lost as the Germans advanced and the noise of their fans heralded an attack.

They both wheeled round to watch the play at the far end of the stadium. But Alan Ball had made a decisive tackle to prevent a German incursion and he broke down the right flank.

The ball filtered across the pitch changing the angle of attack. It reached the balding striker.

'Bobby Charlton...a great yawning gap down the middle...' The BBC commentator had seen a chance open up for England.

The number nine powered his way into a central position and threaded a pass to the edge of the German area.

'Hunt...here comes Ball.'

The player who started the move sped in from the right side and struck a fierce shot that flashed into the side netting as Hans Tilkowski dived low to his left.

'Corner kick,' Wolstenholme said as Alan Ball retrieved the ball and went over to take it. 'I remember the day before the competition began. Billy Wright was saying that the last twenty minutes would be in England's favour on this pitch. The crowd seem to sense it.'

The players were strewn around the penalty area, but not all the English intruders had been picked up by the Germans. As the supporters' excitement mounted, Alan Ball swung in a right footed corner which fell loose to Geoff Hurst on the edge of the area. He controlled the ball and struck it between two defenders. Horst Höttges stood firm in front of goal. He managed to stretch his foot to block the shot as he was falling. The rebound looped some fifteen feet into the air as three of England's front line advanced. The number sixteen was the first to it and he swung a right foot that connected just yards in front of goal. The net was shaken.

'What a chance. It's a goal...Peters...'

The goal scorer spun round and raced away with his arms in the air. He was immediately flanked by Roger Hunt and Geoff Hurst. The English supporters celebrated with a chorus of noise and much relief. Sitting next to Kenneth Wolstenholme, Wally Barnes spoke calmly from his commentary position.

'And that undoubtedly was a well-taken goal by Peters. He could have blasted it over the top, but he stabbed at it – kept his knee over the ball – and England, 2-1 in the lead now, and deservedly so because they have been piling on the pressure. And what I am convinced is that Bobby Moore will drive them on now for the last twelve minutes...he's really gonna drive them now.'

'There's Martin Peters,' continued Wolstenholme, 'the man who scored the goal which could well win the World Cup for England.'

Alex and Billy leapt into the air and were caught up with the sense of euphoria sweeping around Wembley Stadium.

'This isn't going to last,' Alex said to Britannia.

'Enjoy it while you can,' she replied, and smiled with excitement.

'Let's hope we can enjoy it after extra time.'

Billy had an idea. 'Do you wanna stroll up the other end? I fancy seeing the German goal. We've come a long way. Let's make the most of it.'

'Good thinking. We can find out if it hurts as much in real life as it does on TV. But we've gotta get back here damn quick, 'cause Nobby's big kick comes straight after the restart.'

'Are you boys sure you want to go through with this?' Britannia seemed intent on changing their minds.

'That's why we're here,' Alex was even more certain now that the time to switch the ball was getting closer. 'I haven't crossed some big time zone for nothing. Let's do it.'

They left the cinders and walked past the corner flag just as Alan Ball was hacked down by Horst Höttges twenty yards away. The English supporters were incensed and a howl of whistles filled the air. Ball picked himself up and took the kick. It fell invitingly for Jack Charlton who was bearing down deep into the German penalty area, but Uwe Seeler managed to get a foot in and punted the ball out of danger.

'I don't remember Jackie Charlton ever getting that close to a goal,' Billy said with disbelief.

'He almost made it 3-1.'

'Yeah, game over!'

The two ball-boys and a member of St John Ambulance did not look out of place beside the pitch. All eyes were on the football. They continued their slow walk along the touchline opposite Alf Ramsey who was sitting with his England colleagues. Looking across the pitch they could see him following the game. He appeared impassive and showed no sign of the torment he must be feeling. The English fans began chanting: '*We want three...we want three...*' Then in full cry they switched to a more patriotic song as the Union Jacks and flags of St George began a wave of colour all around.

'Hey, they're singing your song Brit,' Alex observed.

The strains of *Rule Britannia* echoed through the stadium. They passed near to Tofik Bakhramov and a minute later reached the far corner flag. There they sat on the grass next to the line of photographers behind Gordon Banks' goal.

'Perfect,' said Billy. 'How long we got?'

Alex checked his stopwatch. 'Just over three minutes before Weber sticks it in.'

The BBC was broadcasting to some four-hundred million worldwide. In the UK alone, it would become the most watched live broadcast of all time. As the second half drew to a close, it seemed almost certain that England, on home soil, would be crowned victors. The Prime Minister, Harold Wilson, watching from the Royal Box, had predicted a 2-1 win for his country. But, much like a week in politics, he had not foreseen the sensational twists that were about to unfold.

Across the land, traffic stopped, people crowded round sets in television show rooms and holidays were delayed. More tea was brewed and front rooms were filled with friends and families anxiously glued to grainy black and white screens.

It was the voice of Kenneth Wolstenholme that would forever be synonymous with this the most famous of sporting commentaries. 'Thirteen years ago, the Hungarians came and showed that England were no longer masters of football. And in these thirteen years, England has fashioned a team which is on the threshold of being world champions.'

Gordon Banks looked down field and thumped a goal-kick to the half-way line. The flight of the ball was halted by some desperate German intervention and the play was forced back deep into the England defence by a succession of headers. Referee Gottfried Dienst saw the signals from his linesmen that time was up. Around the oval of the stadium, many thousands of English spectators were whistling impatiently for the end to come. The ball was lobbed forward towards Uwe Seeler just outside England's penalty area. Jack Charlton rose to head clear. The German captain backed into the defender and Charlton crashed down clumsily onto Seeler and bundled him off the ball. The referee blew, but it wasn't for the end of the game – it was a foul.

'And it's a free-kick to West Germany. One minute to go. Just sixty seconds.' Kenneth Wolstenholme's voice betrayed a slight tremor.

Nobby Stiles began arguing with Dienst, but the referee indicated the point of infringement and waved away the red-shirted players. The defence retreated like a battalion under siege.

'This is it Billy. Crunch time!'

The ball-boys got to their feet for a better view.

Siggy Held and Lothar Emmerich were standing over the ball debating what to do. The referee wasn't happy with England's defence and began pacing the wall back ten yards. Emmerich had already scored a stunning goal against Spain which Franz Beckenbauer would say some years later was the best he had ever seen.

'Every Englishman coming back...every German going forward...' said Wolstenholme.

The wall stood ragged and out of shape. Peters, Stiles, Bobby Charlton, Hunt and Hurst presented a barrier that did not look solid.

'Now will the Germans snatch a dramatic equaliser and bring us to extra time?'

Finally satisfied with the wall, the referee stepped away and blew the whistle. The German number eleven drove the ball like an arrow with his left foot.

'Emmerich coming in...'

It flashed by the wall and cannoned into the lunging George Cohen. Alan Ball and Bobby Moore watched helplessly as the bounce fell to Siggy Held who rammed the ball with as much strength as he could find at the end of the game. It skimmed beyond Jack Charlton striking Karl-Heinz Schnellinger on the back. It had become a game of pin-ball.

'And he's...oh, yes he must do...' the BBC commentator stammered.

Then the ball ran loose and trickled agonisingly along the six-yard line. Ray Wilson and Gordon Banks watched it roll in front of a goal-mouth that gaped like a chasm. And then Wolfgang Weber pounced. He struck the ball beyond the outstretched arms of the goalkeeper whose fingers missed by an inch. The net shuddered.

'...They have done! Weber has scored in the last seconds.'

The Germans were ecstatic. Wolfgang Weber leapt into the air and was surrounded by his exultant team-mates. Their supporters went wild with excitement.

'...Thirty seconds from the end and Weber has equalised. What a dramatic end.'

The English fans were stunned into silence. Moments earlier they thought they had won. Even Alex and Billy stood there with an expression of shock, and they had known what was coming. A goal they had seen a hundred times had just been played out in front of them. They looked across the pitch and saw the English forwards lining up to kick-off from the centre.

'Billy!' It suddenly dawned on Alex, 'we've gotta get back. Nobby's gonna blast it!'

Billy snatched up the bag and they sped off along the touchline with Britannia in tow.

'Get the ball out,' Alex screamed.

They were just beyond the half-way line as a whistle signalled England to kick-off then almost immediately there was a second.

'We are now in injury time,' Kenneth Wolstenholme said with finality. '...And there goes the whistle for the end of ninety minutes. You can see how near England were to the World Championship. But now they have another thirty minutes.'

At the sound of the whistle Jack Charlton let the ball roll from his boot. It fell lazily in front of Nobby Stiles who smashed it with all the venom he could muster. It sailed to the other end of the pitch and onto the semi-circle of cinders just as Alex and Billy knew it would.

This was to be the ball-boys' defining moment.

In the terrace high above, the movements of Alex Bell and Billy Gunn, who had no right to be there, had not gone unnoticed. They were being closely monitored using *eye-bot* technology by members of a secret organisation called Trinity. Nearby, delegates with Quantum Tours were recording the events as they happened using equipment from another century. Not far from Wembley Stadium, a future broadcasting Company, Time TV, were taking late bets on the outcome of the game – and the potential death of Alex Bell.

They were still racing as the Slazenger match ball came to rest on the gravel in front of them. For a moment Alex hesitated, looking at it sitting there on the shingle like a prize waiting to be seized. *Should I*, he thought. *This could change everything. We might go back to a different world.* Then without thinking he scooped it up and turned to Billy behind him who was carrying the bag.

'Get it out Billy. C'mon, we've only got…'

Alright…alright, I'm…'

The next moment Alex heard Billy swear.

'What is it Billy?'

'The bloody ball…' He held it up.

'…What?'

'Someone's burst the fucking ball!'

46

Their secret weapon was no longer a secret.

Alex and Billy looked at each other in disbelief not knowing what to do next. Neither said anything for what seemed an age. Alex stood there rooted to the cinders clutching the match ball he had just picked up after Nobby Stiles' long range kick.

'We've blown it' he stammered, looking at the deflated ball Billy was holding. A thousand questions began to run through his mind all at the same time. None of which he could answer. *How will the game finish? What will it be like when we get home? Where's Grandpa? Why?* 'We've cocked it up big time' he said at last, 'and there's nothing we can do about it. Where's Brit gone?'

'No idea,' Billy said, 'she was right here.'

'Gotta get this ball back to Dienst; he'll want to start the game.' With a heavy heart, Alex jogged over to the centre spot while Billy, muttering expletives, stuffed the punctured ball back into his bag.

When Alex reached the half-way line he sensed a distinct shift in the atmosphere inside the stadium. The voices of the English supporters seemed muted, having come so close to a victory only to see it snatched away in the last seconds. The Germans on the other hand were ecstatic. Banners of yellow, red and black festooned the terraces and Teutonic chants filled the air.

Alex found the players sprawled on the grass; some lay on their backs having their aching calves massaged. He watched

Jimmy Greaves, dressed in a designer suit he had bought specially in west London chatting to his teammates. The creative England forward had been injured in the group matches and replaced by Geoff Hurst against Argentina. Alf Ramsey was moving between his players, talking to each one and encouraging them to stand and get ready to play.

'You've beaten them once, then lost it. Now go out there and beat them again.' He pulled Bobby Moore to his feet. 'Look, the Germans are finished. Don't let them see you down. Show them you're still ready to fight.' His voice was calm, steady and well spoken; a far cry from the east London accent that had been erased through months of elocution.

Nobby Stiles rolled down his socks and spat through the gap in his teeth. Slowly the other players hauled themselves up as Bobby Moore rallied his troops.

'C'mon,' he called in a strong voice, 'Let's do this for our country and for those we love. This may be the only chance we'll ever get. Hey, ball-boy, get me some water please.' He looked straight at Alex who turned to see Billy coming up behind him slopping two large jugs. Alex grabbed one and passed it to the captain.

'There you go Bobby.'

'Thanks,' he said.

The English players stood there in darkened jerseys, stained by the sweat of their endeavours. Following the showers it had become a humid day and appropriately the temperature had reached 19°C, 66°F.

Billy saw the desperate expressions on the players' faces as he moved among the team. Nobby Stiles took a jug and emptied it over his head.

As the players began to drift away towards the goals in readiness for extra time, Alex saw that referee Gottfried Dienst was in conversation with his linesmen. He seemed flustered and made animated gestures to Karol Galba and Tofik Bakhramov. Alex realised that the referee had somehow mislaid the coin he needed for the restart.

'*Money...money,*' he heard him say. 'No money!' Dienst simulated a flicking action to demonstrate the toss.

255

Whether or not his coin had slipped out onto the pitch, Alex couldn't tell, but in that moment he suddenly remembered. He reached into his track-suit pocket and pulled out the half-crown.

'Herr Dienst…Herr Dienst,' he said holding out the coin.

At once the anxiety on the referee's face was replaced by an embarrassed grin.

'Thank you ball-boy.' Taking the coin Gottfried Dienst blew his whistle to bring the captains together. It was a signal for a loud eruption that rang around Wembley as Alex and Billy made their way back to the touchline.

From his commentary position, Kenneth Wolstenholme broadcast the start of extra time.

'Off we go. Fifteen minutes each way. Stiles has got his stockings rolled down – Ball has got stockings rolled down. This is a sign that cramp is creeping into the consideration.'

The Germans took the centre as Wolfgang Overath played a short ball forward to Lothar Emmerich who instinctively fired a shot that rebounded off Nobby Stiles and went out for a German throw. Karl-Heinz Schnellinger stepped up and took it, and Lothar Emmerich, who was closely marked by George Cohen, headed it back to the number three who rifled in a cross that was met by Jack Charlton on the six-yard line. In turn he headed the ball to the edge of the penalty area and it ran loose towards the German goal-scorer.

'In comes Haller.'

The forward sliced the shot and it rolled harmlessly into the rank of photographers behind Gordon Banks' goal.

'Never has a World Cup final produced such a finish; first time they've ever had to play extra time in a final.' Kenneth Wolstenholme checked the notes in front of him.

'Something's flippin' odd here Billy!'

'What?'

'I expected England to be playing towards the Radio Times end, over there.'

'But they're not.'

'I can see that! So what's changed?'

'Perhaps Bobby Moore won the toss.'

'No he lost it, we know that…' Alex was silent for a second. 'But maybe he *did* win it.'

'What you saying Alex?'

The penny dropped. 'It was *my* half-crown. That's the difference. It was a fifty-fifty chance. Maybe the toss went the other way.'

'What does that mean?'

'It means…God knows. We'll have to wait and see.'

'How much time?'

'We've got about three minutes before Geoff hits the bar. Then it's up to Tofik.' Alex looked across to the linesman and wondered how important that would be for both of them. *Where's Brit gone?* he wondered.

'Well, I should imagine there are one or two people saying: "What did I do with that stub of my ticket?"' explained Kenneth Wolstenholme to the millions watching the BBC coverage. '"I think I threw it away when I thought England were going to win!" And anybody here today, if it's a replay, they can buy a replay ticket by presenting the stub of their ticket; after that, the tickets are on sale to the general public.'

Nobby Stiles grimaced with fatigue revealing his missing teeth. He picked up a short pass from Bobby Charlton and played a one-touch to George Cohen. The right-back found the industrious Alan Ball on the right flank just yards from where Alex and Billy were making their way along the touchline.

'C'mon Alan,' yelled Billy, 'get it over. Geoff's in the box.'

'Nothing'll come of this,' added Alex.

Alan Ball evaded the close scrutiny from Karl-Heinz Schnellinger and realised that George Cohen had followed him to the corner flag. He let the number three make the cross which flew harmlessly wide behind Hans Tilkowski's goal. It was a lofted shot that would not have looked out of place on a rugby field. And it would be another thirty-seven years before George Cohen would watch his nephew, Ben, win the Rugby World Cup for England.

'That was crap,' Billy threw a hand in the air. 'My Nan could've done better than that!'

'This is it Billy. This is where Hurst cracks it against the bar. Keep an eye on Tofik.'

Billy glanced sideways and saw the Soviet linesman just feet away. He held his flag low and stared hawk-like towards the cluster of players in the penalty area.

'Alex, Billy, there you are.' A voice came from behind them. The ball-boys turned to see Britannia standing there.

'Where've you been Brit?' Alex asked, remembering she had gone missing at the time they found the ball had punctured. *Did she do it*? he thought.

She stood there in her black uniform and a small bag over her shoulder. 'I got called away. A man collapsed. Amazing what a dose of smelling salts can do.'

'You're just in time. This is what we've been waiting for.' Alex was still sceptical about why she had disappeared.

Across the penalty area Willi Schulz was playing a one-two with Hans Tilkowski who pumped a long kick beyond the half-way line.

'Twenty minutes of the game left,' said Kenneth Wolstenholme. If there was any tension in his voice, he did not show it.

Jack Charlton headed down the goalkeeper's high punt and Nobby Stiles collected the ball in the middle of the pitch. Stiles found he had space around him and made a forty yard pass over the head of Karl-Heinz Schnellinger towards the corner flag where Alex and Billy were standing. Even after one hundred minutes of play Alan Ball still had the speed to reach the searching pass.

'Here's Ball, running himself daft,' said the commentator.

The winger took it almost to the goal-line and swung in a cross right footed.

'Watch the line Billy. See where it lands.'

Geoff Hurst was standing close to the penalty spot and saw the cross coming his way. He threw up his foot and cleverly brought the ball down and swivelled in one movement. Schulz and Schnellinger were close, waiting to pounce. Goalkeeper Tilkowski stood rooted to the goal-line just yards away; his cap shielding the sun that now shone down on Wembley. As Hurst fell back he struck the ball and sent it arrowing towards the crossbar.

'Now Hurst, can he do it?' Wolstenholme sensed a chance.

Hans Tilkowski dived, but failed to get a hand on it. The goalkeeper twisted acrobatically to see the ball rebound down behind him. Geoff Hurst and Willi Schulz ended up on the grass while Horst Höttges could only watch by the goalpost. The ball had gained spin by hitting the underside of the bar and when it slammed into the ground it took a big bounce away from the goal. Roger Hunt came racing in and threw his hands in the air as if to celebrate. He was followed by Wolfgang Weber who headed the loose ball over the bar.

'He's done it!' Kenneth Wolstenholme was emphatic.

'Did you see Billy? Was it over?'

'Yeah, um, dunno.'

Alex looked at Tofik Bakhramov who was standing just yards away. He was momentarily static, as if replaying the incident in his mind's eye.

'Was it in Toff?' Alex shouted. He had not been convinced and feared the worst.

Geoff Hurst had pulled himself up; a blank look showed his uncertainty as he turned to the linesman. Referee Dienst was thirty yards away and had not seen where the ball had landed.

'Yes...no, the linesman says "No."' The BBC commentator couldn't tell.

The referee ran over to his official as Wembley waited in muted uproar.

Billy, who had been standing next to Bakhramov, turned to the supporters and began inciting the crowd by shouting: 'Goal...goal...goal!' The fans responded and tried to sway the referee's decision.

'The linesman says "No,"' repeated Kenneth Wolstenholme.

'C'mon Tofik, you saw it go in,' Billy screamed. 'Are you blind?'

At that moment Alex caught sight of a silver streak and wondered if he'd imagined it. He scanned the air above and saw it again, hanging before him just for a second. It was a tiny metal sphere no larger than a marble. Then it vanished.

'An *eye*,' he said under his breath, and instinctively looked for its controllers.

They were close, he knew it, and he realised Trinity wanted to change history just as much as he did.

47

Alex's train of thought was torn from Trinity back to Tofik Bakhramov.

He turned to see the linesman talking to Gottfried Dienst. They were trying to converse with no common language. Both officials were confronted by Roger Hunt, Willi Schulz and Alan Ball. Each player was keen to describe how they had seen it. And surrounding this huddle was the entire Wembley Stadium. Then the linesman waved a hand and the referee blew his whistle and began marching towards the centre circle.

'It's a *goal*. It's a goal!' exclaimed Kenneth Wolstenholme. Unseen in his cramped position, the commentator punched the air with delight and downed a mug of cold tea. '…All the Germans go mad at the referee, and the linesman who can only speak Russian and Turkish. So, England are in the lead again, 3-2. Well, I thought for a moment the linesman had said "*No*". He seemed to be shaking his head.'

A wave of rapture swept around Wembley like a surging tide. Martin Peters sprinted thirty yards to lift his West Ham team-mate off the ground. At the same time, Alex and Billy jumped and screamed and embraced Britannia. In that pivotal moment they had more to celebrate than anyone else in the stadium.

'We've done it! We've bloody gone and done it,' Alex was suddenly hoarse with emotion. 'God knows how!'

In their ecstasy, they became oblivious to what happened next. Even Britannia caught the mood and joined in with the chant that welled-up from the terraces: '*We want four...we want four...we want four...*'

The only thing on Alex's mind was that he had never in any book or internet site or TV broadcast or DVD seen the score-line that was now emblazoned at each end of Wembley Stadium. It was as if the memory Alex had known had been forgotten and rewritten. A shrill whistle brought his reverie to an end, and so too, the first half of extra time.

It took just a minute for the teams to change ends, and in that time, Alex, Billy and Britannia walked to the end where Gordon Banks had now taken up position. The referee signalled to his linesmen the start of the second period of extra time and Alex clicked his stopwatch not knowing what he was now timing.

'Away we go,' declared Kenneth Wolstenholme.

The game started and Franz Beckenbauer played a simple pass to Lothar Emmerich but Jack Charlton intercepted a ball aimed for Siggy Held and it went out of play for a German throw.

Then Britannia became distracted by some commotion going on high in the terrace behind them. It was in a section she had been watching as closely as the game.

'Look up there,' she said.

Half a dozen stewards and two policemen had merged into the fans. There seemed to be a riot going on amongst the supporters.

48

Benjamin Janus was protesting his innocence.

'Some men jumped on me!'

'Well where are they now Sir?' asked PC McPhee in his plumb voice. 'I'm afraid you're causing a bit of a disturbance, so I've got to ask you to come with me to the station.'

'Look it wasn't us. These men attacked me.'

'I'm sorry Sir, all we saw were you two idiots throwing yourselves around like Laurel and Hardy. You'll have to come quietly, 'cause you won't be seeing the rest of the game.'

'But we haven't done anything…'

'You'll have to explain that to Superintendent Gubby, and he don't take fools gladly. If you catch me drift.'

Benjamin Janus and Piers Van Dyke finally came to realise they would not see the end of the match no matter how much of a fight they put up. Janus reluctantly left with the police. As he did, he glanced one way to watch the game and another way to catch sight of the men who had quickly melted into the crowd.

Not far away Ralf Schneider touched his earphone having just received a message from the Controller of Trinity.

In turn, he spoke into a radio, 'Schicken sie in!'

49

The stadium erupted as Siggy Held cut into the penalty area and rifled a shot that flew high and almost reached the lower tiers behind Gordon Banks' goal.

'The West German players at this stage look a little stronger than the England players,' Wally Barnes said. 'But I think this is understandable because they've got to throw everything into attack in the closing minutes of extra time.'

'Eight minutes left. England lead 3-2,' added Kenneth Wolstenholme.

'Hey Billy, we really have changed this game. Look, there's Jack Charlton.'

'Yeah, so what?'

'He wasn't sent off. You know, when he head-butted Overath.'

Billy turned to Alex, 'Shit, you're right. What have we done?'

A chorus rang out around the stadium as the home fans began to sense victory for the second time: *Oh when the reds, go marching in, oh when the reds go marching in. I want to be, in that number, oh when the reds go marching in...*

The showers had cleared and now bright sunshine cast dark shadows across a pitch scarred with divots and tufts from the ravages of battle. The brilliance only served to spotlight the drama being played out in front of millions.

Suddenly a beautiful woman was standing next to Alex and Billy. She had blond hair and was dressed in a smart blue suit. Alex caught sight of a gold brooch glinting on her lapel.

'Bo! I've been looking for you.' Britannia seemed relieved. They gave each other a hug.

The ball-boys stared in surprise.

'They know we're here,' the woman said, her voice was tense. 'They just tried to take Janus, and failed. It'll be us next.'

Britannia replied, 'We have to get these boys out. It'd be a calamity if something happened to them.'

Alex spoke, 'Hey, hold it! Who's she, and what's going on?'

'Alex this is *Bo – Boadicea*.'

Alex frowned and looked at each in turn. 'You've both got bloody weird names!'

'We're sisters,' Britannia said.

'Twins,' added Boadicea.

'Think about it Alex. At the party, how was I able to appear and disappear? Certainly not on my own.'

'*Twins*,' was all Alex could say; he still looked confused. 'But you flew!'

'No I didn't. That was *Bo*. Anyway, it was all down to science. Isaac Newton would've had an orgasm.'

'Look,' said Boadicea, 'Mr Sinyavsky's gone AWOL. I suspect he's got some grudge against Soviet linesmen, and Warwick Vane and Victoria Trevelyan have gone to ground. They'll have this place sealed off by now. They've got back-up, I've seen them.'

'Where's your party?'

'Up there.' Boadicea pointed towards the high stands.

Alex shielded his eyes and squinted in the direction the Rep in her smart blue suit was looking. There was something about what he saw that held his gaze like steel to a magnet. Deep inside, his hippocampus triggered countless connections that excited some of the 100 billion neurons squeezed into his convoluted brain. A multitude of sensory cues allowed one stored memory to come to the fore.

Alex almost stopped breathing as he found himself instantly transported into Dr Raja's dark surgery.

The air was heavy with the sweet odour of ether. Paintings crackled as the psychiatrist studied their meaning. His mind was suddenly drawn to the greyness of a battlefield – a landscape that defied belief. The German troops faced the British across a crater strewn wilderness; the smell of sweat, the sense of fear and the frost upon the ground. There was an uneasy lull over the desolation of *No Man's Land*. Standing nearby, and unseen, were the Horamungus; observers who should not have been witness to the event. They had peculiar names that froze Alex's blood every time he thought about them. They were like ghosts that haunted him. Amongst their number were: Trafalgar, Hebrides, Utsire and German Bight.

'The *Horamungus*...the *Horamungus*,' he said in a whisper that was drowned-out by the collective sound of Wembley Stadium.

'The *who*?' asked Britannia. 'What did you say?'

'The *Horamungus*. I know their like. I've seen them before. They *who are among us*! They shouldn't be here.' His voice trailed off and he stared vacantly as if hypnotised.

'Neither should we,' cut in Billy. 'I don't like the sound of Vane on the loose.'

Britannia turned to her sister. 'Get down to the Thames. We'll meet you there.'

Boadicea nodded and looked up to her party. 'I'll have time to get them later.'

'Brit, there's so much crap going on. Why should we trust you? What does Trinity want?'

She turned to face him. 'Alex there's something I really need to tell you.' And she wondered if this was the right time.

But before she could say anything, Alex heard a familiar voice rise above the sound of singing and he froze.

'Gentlemen, now that your project seems complete, it's payback time.' Warwick Vane stood at the foot of a concrete stairway with his black coat touching the bottom step. Behind him were two other men. 'And Miss Britannia, I'm so pleased to meet you again. I believe we have some unfinished business to settle.'

'We owe you nothing, Vane,' Alex yelled. 'We tested the machine and that was it. You can stick your time-slips up your arse.' He turned to Billy and the twins, 'Let's split.'

50

'This way Alex,' Britannia screamed, and she ran down to one of the exits at pitch level. Billy sprinted across the cinders and Boadicea slipped into one of the terraces and hid herself amongst the supporters.

The walkway inside Wembley Stadium was vast; it had to be to allow one hundred thousand people to move around. But as Alex and Britannia ran along the curving concourse they found it empty. They saw a handful of stewards and some kiosks serving food and drink. There were no supporters. They were all watching the final action as the game came to an uncertain conclusion. The roof heaved high above like a giant stamping on a mountain. Alex remembered the interior of the stadium from the simulation he'd seen in Trinity. He felt part of some complex virtual game and for a second wondered if someone was controlling him. From behind came the sound of others running.

Britannia looked back nervously, 'In here Alex.' She pulled his arm.

'But it's the *Ladies*!'

'Get in quick.'

There were no ladies in sight. Alex found himself gripping a basin and looking at his reflection in the mirror. 'What the heck's going on Brit? We could do with some of your magic now.'

'Alex, I came here for one reason...'

'Oh yeah, what was that, to do a few tricks and dress up in a uniform?'

'No, it's far more important than that. I came for *you*!'

'What you talking about?' Alex's face showed a stunned look.

'Because, Alex...quiet.' She put a finger to her lips. Outside came the heavy feet of men running on the concourse then disappearing past them. 'I came to help you Alex.'

'*What*?'

'I couldn't let anything happen to you. Let's get out of here.'

As Alex followed Britannia he checked his stopwatch. 'There's only a minute left.' As far as he could tell, no other goals had been scored. He caught up with her as the curving concourse straightened out. 'What do you mean: You don't want anything to happen to me?'

She stopped to face him. 'I should've told you before Alex. If something happens to you, then where does that leave me? Let's just say I'm as interested in your wellbeing as you are.'

'You're talking in riddles Brit. Start making sense.'

She had no time to explain. They heard a sound behind them and turning round saw three men approaching at speed. Each wore black and was built like an athlete.

'Get out by the pitch,' Britannia called; there was a quiver in her voice. 'It'll be safer there.'

They sprinted fifty yards and then saw two more men coming towards them. One was Warwick Vane.

'Shit,' cried Alex, 'we gotta go through the tunnel. It leads to the pitch.'

Alex grabbed her hand to go, but as he did, Vane arrived with his black coat flailing and he seized Britannia holding her in an arm lock. She let out a cry of pain.

'You're coming with us Brit,' he rasped. 'There's so much you know that we want.'

Alex spun round and kicked Vane in the shin and then he aimed his trainer at the groin of the man next to him and let fly. It was a good shot and the man fell to the floor rolling in agony. It would be several painful minutes before he could stand. Vane went spinning, and losing his balance, fell backwards onto the concrete.

'Let's go Brit.' For a moment she stood there and looked at him as if rooted to the spot. 'What is it?' Close by he saw Vane getting to his feet.

'Alex…you're my goddamn *grandfather*!'

51

'*What*?' Alex stared at Britannia in disbelief.

'It's true.' She snatched his hand and pulled him out into the glare of the sunlight. His mind was thrown into in a state of shock; thoughts came and went but made no sense.

They ran through the high tunnel and straightaway the Wembley roar exploded like a rocket taking off. Alex caught a glimpse of Alf Ramsey sitting calmly surrounded by his England colleagues who were on their feet with excitement. Perhaps the manager was contemplating that his prediction of England winning the World Cup was about to be realised. Not far away was Helmut Schoen and his squad sitting on the German bench; their faces were etched with more concern. With Britannia running beside him Alex looked over to the far side of the pitch and saw the last moments of football being played out.

Bobby Moore had collected the ball outside his penalty area. Some of the German players were on their knees with exhaustion. England's skipper shot a long pass forward just as referee Gottfried Dienst raised the whistle to his mouth.

'It's all over,' Kenneth Wolstenholme raised his voice. '*No!*'

Alex and Britannia crossed over the side-line and ran onto the pitch in full view of Wembley. Karl-Heinz Schnellinger watched them go by and wondered what was happening. Alex twisted and saw the black figure of Warwick Vane twenty yards behind. They sprinted towards the linesman, Karol Galba. Just then Alex caught a glimpse of something odd above the roof of the stadium. It was a light so bright, he thought the floodlights had come on. *No, it must be the sun.* It was a fleeting silver-yellow light, like a fiery cross that moved and hovered and then was gone.

I'm hallucinating!

Bobby Moore's long pass not only wasted away the last seconds of the match, but the ball looped over the German defence and fell kindly to the feet of Geoff Hurst. He only had goalkeeper Hans Tilkowski in front of him. Wembley would never again know such a time as this.

Kenneth Wolstenholme spoke the final words that were to become immortalised: 'And here comes Hurst. Some people are on the pitch…they think it's all over…'

'Hey Brit,' shouted Alex, 'don't look now, I think we're offside!'

Despite his attempt to make light of a worsening situation, deep inside, Alex was still reeling from what Britannia had just told him. *Surely, it couldn't be true.* And when he turned to look at her beside him, he realised there was something strangely familiar about her. *Maybe I do know her.*

As he tried to take it all in, he suddenly lost his footing and crashed to the Wembley turf.

52

The ground was uneven and soft underfoot. It had rained all day and several times Alex slipped and almost fell as he weaved between the headstones in the cemetery.

Thick mud was caked to the soles of his favourite Puma trainers; like lead weights stopping his feet from moving. The sun had long set and the dark clouds above provided a canopy of blackness through which no star could shine.

Then he saw them.

Three boys dodging between the graves like shifting shapes evaporating into the darkness. Alex gave them names: Dogger, Rockall and Malin. They sneaked and darted and hid behind tombstones. One moment he saw them, the next, he didn't. He crouched behind a rough lichen-covered stone and tried to control his breathing. The faintest noise could betray where he was. Now and then he heard their voices. Sometimes they shouted abuse; sometimes they threw twigs and stones. At school they said they were friends. But they would often laugh and call him names that hurt when he thought about them in the darkness of his bedroom. Just because he saw things they had never seen. He thought about the visions he witnessed and the visitors who would come to him. How could they see things which were invisible? Only he had been allowed.

He knew he was special. He had been chosen.

An autumn gust tugged at the branches of the swaying boughs and a scattering of rusty leaves fell around Alex. A chill wind picked up and hissed through the grass and trees and between the weathered headstones. And the hiss became a whistle, shrill and harsh that pierced the air, and there amidst the screech there came a mournful sound like packs of wolves howling in the darkness all around.

Then spectres, black shadows, shrewd and stealth, slipped unnoticed into the world; the ghostly forms from a realm nearby. Their eyes flickered like red flame and from their nostrils came a foul stench like sulphur. They were the lost phantoms that lurk unseen and move unhindered through the fabric of time and space. Their business was terror and disorder and deception. On this occasion they had come to pester a boy who often came alone to the cemetery. It was there they entered in and moved between the graves.

But there amongst them were those who were greater still.

There came a flash so sudden and so bright that Alex thought there had been an explosion overhead. For a second the land was bathed in a golden light, and in the next it was night again. Alex became aware that the wind had faded and the chill air had warmed, and on looking up he saw a sky filled with stars. The heavens were as clear as any night he could remember. He picked out Cassiopeia, just as his grandfather had shown him, and traced the belt of Orion down to Sirius, sparkling like a sapphire low above the horizon. Overhead shone Jupiter, the greatest of all planets that circled the sun. A silver star went shooting by and for a moment scratched the sky.

'Wow a meteor!' he said aloud and stood up to look.

As far as Alex could tell, the boys were nowhere to be seen. So stepping away from the gravestone he followed a path into a garden in the middle of the cemetery. It took him some time to realise that he could find his way quite easily under a dark sky without a moon. All around there seemed to be a glow. Then gradually the glow increased until there was a brilliance of such intensity that the trees cast long shadows that stretched across the grass. In front of Alex was a crumbling mausoleum, and above the tomb was a living creature that shone with light. She stood more than seven feet tall. Her face was beautiful and her hair fell to her shoulders.

Alex could not describe the depth of blue he saw in those eyes. It reminded him of the azure sea he had seen one summer when he stood beside a golden beach. As she moved her robes shone with an iridescence that shimmered with a spectrum of colour. Alex thought she looked like a mighty warrior, for round her waist hung a long sword and in one hand she held a gleaming helmet. He felt no fear but stood there in a state of wonder.

In splendour, the warrior came and towered over the boy and suddenly Alex was aware that she was surrounded by at least a dozen of these supreme creatures that filled the garden with light.

An angel, he thought. *The Shadows of day have come as I knew they would.* He named her *Helios* because she was like the sun.

'Alex,' the seraph said, her voice was rich and powerful and subtle, and yet its timbre came softly to his ears. 'I bring a message about your life. You must know that there will be times which will be hard. Do not be afraid for I will be near. One day I will come to you again, for you will need me.'

As she spoke, her wings unfurled with such radiant purity and whiteness, and their expanse eclipsed the stars in the umbrella of dark sky above. And to the boy it seemed that the angel's robes sang in harmony as the fabric rustled and he saw colours that glistened in the folds of her garment. But it was her magnificent sword that tempted him. It fell to the ground below from a belt made of woven bdellium. Its length was greater than Alex himself. With burnished gold it shone, tempered in a celestial fire, its double-edge gleaming like a brilliant sunlit ribbon hemming an evening cloud.

Then reaching out, Alex touched the hilt. It was made of transparent diamond and etched upon it was a grip that resembled a lattice weave. And as he touched it, Alex felt a surge like electricity purge his body. Dizziness overcame him, and as he fell to the ground he inhaled the wondrous aroma of the lush damp grass in the garden. Then an intoxicating fragrance filled the air that was like an exotic perfume which lingered long after the glorious light had diminished.

53

As the earth circled the sun at a speed of 66 000 miles per hour, between the years 1066 and 1966, the teeming citizens of this world lost time equivalent to one-sixth of a day.

The earth was a time machine.

And so the prophecy came to be fulfilled. The visible sign of this revelation was about to be realised.

Gottfried Dienst sent a shrill whistle around the Empire Stadium at Wembley bringing to an end the 1966 World Cup final. England had triumphed over West Germany.

The euphoria in the stadium was a reflection of the joy that was being experienced across the country and all the way north to Hadrian's Wall on the border with Scotland. In their ecstasy the English fans celebrated as if it were VE Day all over again. Songs, shouts and flags went up, and some supporters spilled onto the pitch in an outpouring of patriotic fervour. The statistics from the match showed it to be one of the most entertaining games of all time. There had been forty-seven attempts on goal by England to West Germany's thirty-eight.

Alex looked down at his hands and saw the striated scar on his palm was smeared with grass. It was a reminder that he had once touched a Shadow.

He was only down for a few seconds but the fall looked heavy. Hundreds of supporters had seen it happen. One man was concerned enough to run out from the first row close to the corner flag. He had dark hair, an England fan in his thirties who was lean, athletic and quick thinking. He lifted Alex into a sitting position as Britannia stood over them. Anxiety showed on her face. She scanned the pitch and saw that Warwick Vane was nowhere to be seen.

'Thanks,' he said to the supporter. 'I think I hit a crater.' He was woozy and his head felt as if it was spinning.

Alex looked into the dark eyes of the man helping him up. Immediately his thoughts were sifting through the old photographs in the big box his parents used to keep under their bed. His heart leapt as he realised who he was looking at. Suddenly he was alert. It was *him*.

'*Gramps...*' He could say no more because his voice choked.

The stranger looked back with a puzzled expression.

'*Grandpa Bell.*' Alex was certain and a deep emotion began to well up inside him. The impossible had happened. Of all the places he could choose to be with his grandfather, Alex thought, this would be it.

The man said nothing. He couldn't.

'Is Dad here? Alex said. '*George!*'

The man's eyesight strayed to the supporters nearby. There stood a boy aged seven. He looked like a young Alex.

The brief encounter on the Wembley turf lasted only a moment, but it was enough for Alex.

'I did it for you Grandpa.'

And then he remembered that the man he was looking at would lose his life just a week before the launch of *At the End of the Day*. It was a bitter beginning to his new career. His first show was tinged with a sadness he had to hide. But he had carried on in the memory of his hero.

'I did it for you Grandpa,' he repeated, as if he'd not heard.

The man continued to stare at the ball-boy he held in his arms. Alex could not even guess what he must be thinking. Finally he opened his mouth, but no words came.

'It's not what you do in life...' Alex said.

'...It's what you make of it,' Grandpa Bell finished.

As the tall man lifted Alex to his feet, he caught sight of something glinting on his wrist. It was a shiny Rolex with a black leather strap. Now Alex was certain who he was.

They held each other's gaze and said no more. It was a time of union that neither could understand.

During those pivotal seconds, as their lives crossed, Britannia took a device from her pocket and recorded the event for herself. She would always treasure it.

Just then Billy arrived; he couldn't hide his excitement. 'I saw you on the pitch. We did it. We actually won!'

Alex thought about introducing Billy to his grandfather, but under the circumstances he decided to tell him later – or maybe not at all.

'Yeah, nice one mate. Looks like we're done.'

Alex gave Grandpa Bell a hug and looking over to the England players he saw brothers Jack and Bobby Charlton in a similar embrace. He said nothing more but watched the tall athletic man stride back to the terrace and stand beside his young father. It was an image he would remember forever even though Grandpa Bell would never speak about what happened. Like many soldiers who lived through the events of D-Day and never spoke about it, he would remain mute when it came to the World Cup final.

Perhaps something completely different and shocking happened in the other Final, Alex thought. *Or was it because he met me and never came to terms with it*! He would never know.

Britannia was standing beside Billy. She said, 'I've got to get you boys away from here. Trinity will be swarming like flies.'

'How the hell do you know about *Trinity*?' Billy remembered she had warned them not to talk about the secret organisation when she drove away in the ambulance outside Stamford Bridge.

'She used to work for them,' Alex added.

'*What*?'

'It's true. She knows Vane and Victoria and the German bloke.'

'Alright,' Billy said holding up a hand, 'this is more complicated than I thought.' He had other ideas. 'Look, all I want to do is catch a bit of the action.' He pulled out his mobile phone. 'I want some video. I can't wait to get this on *YouTube*!'

With an eager grin Billy held his mobile in the air and started to record history. As he looked around he saw his was the only phone on display. *What a bloody scoop*, he thought.

Alex turned to Britannia and suddenly saw her in a new light. *She's my granddaughter*! As he stared at her with his intense dark eyes, like a mirror, she looked back at him. *My family line has come together on one amazing day*!

His thoughts were quickly broken when a hand slapped him on the shoulder.

'Hey, ball-boy,' someone said with a strong voice.

Alex turned to see the referee, Gottfried Dienst, standing beside him. For a moment he thought he was going to say something about them invading the pitch.

'England win!' Dienst said in his heavy accent. 'You have lucky money.' He tossed the half-crown to Alex. 'Thank you,' the referee said with a smile.

'Um, danke,' Alex replied, and the official jogged away to join his linesmen.

'They're about to get the cup,' Billy said, and held his phone aloft to record the event. 'This'll be something to show your grandchildren.'

'I'm way ahead of you there Billy,' Alex glanced over towards Britannia. Then it suddenly dawned on him that Bo was also his granddaughter.

'One man has not come to the pitch,' spoke Kenneth Wolstenholme from his commentary position, 'Alf Ramsey, the man who schemed all this is still as calm and as cool as ever. He's still standing in the position he's held all match. The reserves are on; there's George Eastham, there's Jimmy Armfield, there's John Connelly – this great moment in English sporting history – as Bobby Moore goes up to collect the World Cup. Alf Ramsey's walking forward to shake his hand; the first sign of emotion from this man who has organised this victory.'

The captain began to climb the thirty-nine steps that led to the Royal Box. He was followed by the goal scorer Geoff Hurst and Bobby Charlton who was wiping tears from his eyes. And so the rest of the team followed: Roger Hunt who had seen the third goal cross the line, and the second man to score, Martin Peters. Then came Jack Charlton, Ray Wilson, Alan Ball, George Cohen, Nobby Stiles, and bringing up the rear in his yellow shirt was goalkeeper Gordon Banks.

As he approached the dignitaries, Bobby Moore wiped his hands on his shorts, and holding out his hand, bowed.

'Her Majesty the Queen,' said BBC commentator Kenneth Wolstenholme, as she presented the Jules Rimet trophy to the captain. 'It's only twelve inches high, it's solid gold and it means England are world champions.'

As Bobby Moore lifted the cup above his head, the English supporters sent up a mighty roar. Across the country, family holidays had been put on hold, excited pedestrians peered into shop windows at tiny black and white pictures, and more tea was brewed in celebration. It was just after 5:20 in the afternoon, forty minutes after the time the match programme showed the game would end.

There had been no foresight for drama.

The massed bands of Her Majesty's Royal Marines struck up the National Anthem of Great Britain as the team descended the flight of steps from the presentation. As they came together on the pitch Geoff Hurst and Ray Wilson hoisted Bobby Moore onto their shoulders and the captain held the golden trophy in the air. It was a photograph that would embellish countless history books. Billy caught it on video. His mind was already racing ahead with ideas of how he could use this unique footage.

The image of Uwe Seeler supported by Helmut Haller and Franz Beckenbauer had been eclipsed and erased forever.

Bobby Moore had only been raised up for a few seconds when he dropped down and began the lap of honour.

Alex turned to Billy. 'Come on let's join them. We've earned this. They couldn't have done it without us. You too Brit.'

A horde of people followed on behind the victors, all wanting to be part of it. There were other footballers who hadn't played, trainers, reporters, photographers, stewards, police, and with them came three people who should not have been there. Billy caught it all on his mobile camera.

Suddenly the ranks of English supporters broke into a song made famous by Liverpool fans: '*We've won the cup, we've won the cup, ee aye addio, we've won the cup.*' Alex and Billy soon picked it up and joined in.

The sun shone down and the afternoon shadows lengthened. Nobby Stiles was dancing a jig along the touchline and as he grinned he showed his missing teeth. Alex found himself jogging close to Gordon Banks and right in front were Geoff Hurst and Martin Peters, the goal scorers, together with Captain Bobby Moore holding the World Cup. There was something about this scene that stirred Alex. He had seen it before somewhere, he thought. Maybe his childhood had hinted forward to this single moment. When the realisation dawned on him, he almost fell over at the revelation.

He'd had a vision. He remembered. Yes it was Bobby Moore who had come to him. Alex had been summoned. As he'd stood upon some verdant grass, the champion had revealed himself. For it was there that he'd heard the prophecy: *One will divide our last defeat and bring victory. That one is coming.*

As Alex ran behind the three players he saw that the numbers they each bore on their crimson shirts were in the order: *ten, sixteen* and *six.* 10166. *One will divide our last defeat.* The last English defeat had been at the hands of the Normans in 1066. It was a date Alex knew well. He realised right then that the infamous date had been cleaved in half by *one.* In that defining instant he understood the sign heralded the completion of their task.

His dream had been fulfilled.

Just then, Bobby Moore's steps slowed and as he turned his eyes fell upon Alex following behind. For a second he levelled his gaze at the ball-boy and smiled faintly. It was the confirmation Alex needed, and he suddenly remembered that England's maestro would lose his life to cancer at the age of fifty-one. It would be a tragic end to an illustrious career. For one last time Alex watched him lead the team on their lap of honour.

'Let's go,' Alex said. 'We've done what we came for. Our bags are over there.' He pointed to the cinder area behind the goal. Britannia took his cue and led them over. She knew it had now fallen to her to get them away.

'There you go Billy, grab your bag.' Alex hauled it up and gave it to his friend. 'Blimey mate, feels like you've got a ton of bricks in there. Hey, I gotta show you this.' He pulled out the *SpEx* device Britannia had shown him and put them on. 'You can call up any match you like.' For several seconds he was silent as he looked and moved his head around, but then he said with surprise, 'I see people all over the place. We're infested!'

It took Britannia almost no time to find her own visor and slip it on to see what he was talking about. Amidst the head-up display of a future Wembley she saw Alex standing beside her, but scattered round the empty terraces were other avatars. They stood out like black rats in a bath tub.

'It's Trinity,' she said, almost in a panic. 'They're up there. Looks like more of their henchmen. They must be linked by a system compatible with *SenseSurround*. They can see us Alex. Turn it off. We have to get out of here.'

'What's she talking about Alex?'

'No time – I'll tell you later.'

In the Royal Box, Prime Minister Harold Wilson applauded politely as the England team passed by below. He turned to someone and said, 'The linesman must be protected. Grant him asylum if he requests it.' His aide nodded and pushed his way out of the enclosure.

54

The car park surrounded the stadium like a vast concrete beach around an island. Alex noticed straightaway that something was missing.

'The Mini's gone!'

'Bo's taken it.'

'How're we gonna get away then?'

Alex knew he was being hunted and gave an anxious look behind. He remembered the man selling the Big Issue and realised they were being trailed even as they had arrived at Wembley – and maybe before that. *What about the busker*, he thought.

'In that!' Britannia said.

They climbed into the ambulance and she started the engine and pulled away.

Only a handful of stewards could be seen but it would not be long before the place would be over-run by supporters. They reached the high-street and sped south along Harrow Road.

It wasn't the traffic that held them up, but revellers coming out of front doors and flocking across the roads singing and shouting. The fans soon got out of the way when they heard the tinkling bell coming down the road. Celebrations were breaking out all the way into central London.

'Where we going? Alex said turning to Britannia.

'It's time to get you boys back.'

'What, the train?'

'Yes.'

'But we're nowhere near Moorgate.'

'Trinity will expect you to go back to where you arrived – *but* – there's another way.'

'How do you know?'

'Don't forget, my hindsight stretches back further than yours. I know more.'

Alex stared at the young woman in the St John uniform and was doubtful.

Britannia drove through the borough of Chelsea and Westminster and on towards the looming Elizabeth Tower, home to Big Ben. Alex looked out at the passing skyline and an idea came to him. There was a paradox that had been playing on his mind.

'Hey Brit, pull over. There's something I must do. I'll only be a few minutes. Trust me.' Alex was insistent.

'No way. Trinity'll be all over us like a rash.'

'I need to stop a deviation before it causes a parallel timeline.'

'*What*?' It was the first time Alex had seen Brit looked puzzled.

'You know – all that time shit you told me.' He started to open the door even though they were moving.

Britannia took the cue and parked beside the pavement; she didn't want him falling out. She frowned at him with suspicion. Alex took an object from his bag, jumped down and ran over to a narrow cutting just off the high-street.

'You've got two minutes,' Britannia called out. 'No longer.'

'This is a mistake,' Billy said as he watched him go. 'What does he want?'

Alex disappeared between some tall Edwardian tenements and was quickly out of sight.

55

The old horology shop looked unchanged. The passing decades had made little impression since he'd last seen it a few days ago. It bore the name over the window: *Time After Time*. Underneath he saw when the original dwelling had been built: *Established 1666*.

Alex peered in through the dark window. He saw shelves full of clocks; hundreds of them ticking with a complex rhythm. *Not a digital in sight*, he thought.

From his pocket he pulled out the tobacco tin and a scrap of paper. With a blunt pencil he leant on the window and scribbled a rushed inscription. But then looking at the door his plan quickly fell apart. No letterbox! *Shit*. He would not be able to leave it for some future legacy.

For a second he considered breaking a window, but then thought that would bring unwanted attention. In the end Alex had to admit it was no use, he would have to take it with him. In frustration he thrust the tin back into his pocket and walked away. Britannia would be waiting, he thought.

'Can I help you Sir?'

Alex jumped with surprise and turned round. He saw a man, much taller than himself, dressed in a dark pin-striped suit. He had long straw-like hair that fell to his shoulders; his eyes were a piercing blue. From his jacket he took out a pair of gold-rimmed glasses and put them on.

'Perhaps I can take that for you Mr Bell.'

Alex was shocked. 'How d'you know...'

'Harry Hunter.'

'How did you know I'd be here?' Alex suddenly realised the man he was talking to was the same person he'd met when he'd taken his Rolex to be repaired. *But that was impossible.*

'I come and go,' Harry Hunter said. 'Like you, I get around.'

'Who *are* you?'

He rubbed his chin. 'I'm interested in *clocks* Alex. All kinds of clocks and time-pieces. Many years ago I worked in the Serjeant of Arms' department at the Palace of Westminster.' He pointed towards the landmark of the Elizabeth Tower. 'I was responsible for the Great Clock. It slowed once and I had to add a farthing to correct the balance. More recently, I've been holding down a small job at Greenwich. That's the place from where the world's time is set. And sometimes, I'm here.' He waved his hand theatrically in front of the window full of clocks. 'So Alex, maybe I can take that item for you.'

'Um, yeah okay.' Alex had not understood what he said but gave him the tin. The chime of Big Ben sounded across London.

'Ah, six o'clock.' Harry Hunter checked his pocket watch.

'*Six o'clock*!' Alex repeated. The peal of the bells seemed to spur him into action as he remembered Britannia. 'I've gotta go. People are waiting,' and he began sprinting.

Just when he became all alone in a back-street he suddenly felt lost in time. He wondered if he would ever get back home – his home in the future.

The ambulance was still there beside the main road, much to his relief. The engine was running.

'Get in Alex,' Britannia shouted. 'We need to be moving.'

'Shit Alex, what you up to?'

'Unfinished business!'

Billy scowled at him.

They came to Parliament Square beside the Houses of Parliament. Harold Wilson would be back at the Despatch Box on Monday. Whether there would be any questions about a linesman from Azerbaijan remained to be seen. There would certainly be an announcement of England's win recorded in Hansard, the Parliamentary register.

Above them loomed the Elizabeth Tower housing the famous bell. Alex remembered it signalled a mile to go on the London Marathon course. He had run the scenic route once and finished in a worthy 3 hours 29 minutes and vowed never to do it again.

As they approached Westminster Bridge they took a left into Victoria Embankment and pulled up sharp opposite the Thames. London was still devoid of traffic. On the other side of the road was a statue of Boadicea the Celtic queen who had led an uprising against the Romans after their invasion of Britain. She was riding in a chariot and being charged on by two prancing horses. It was their rendezvous point.

'Across the road. Quick. We need a faster way to go.' Brit was already out of the ambulance.

Alex and Billy grabbed their bags and dashed over the road. Weaving between parked cars they crossed the wide pavement and looked out across the grey-green river. The tide was high.

'Down there,' she pointed. Alex detected a nervous flutter in Britannia's voice.

Waiting by a jetty was a sleek powerboat. Twin Mercury outboard engines were whipping the Thames into a white froth. At the controls was Boadicea with her blond hair trailing in the breeze. She waved them down the steps as a sparkle of light caught the gold brooch on her powder-blue suit.

Seconds later the sharp bow on the speedboat lifted out of the water as the engines thundered, driving them forward with a surge. Almost straightaway they passed beneath Hungerford Bridge. The river was choppy but the boat sliced through the turbulence forging a foamy wake behind them.

'We'll be there in a few minutes,' Bo said, raising her voice above the roar of the engines.

'Where?' asked Alex, thinking her voice sounded identical to her twin.

'*The Tower.*'

As soon as she had spoken there came a pulsing throb that punched a sonic wave through the sky above them. Turning round Britannia saw a black object rising into the air and coming over the Houses of Parliament.

'*Trinity,*' she gasped. 'They've got a Wessex.'

The helicopter took on a sinister appearance, like some giant black locust intent on ravage. Boadicea revved the engines to full power but the bulbous chopper was clearly gaining. They breached Waterloo Bridge, then coming to Blackfriars, Alex picked out the dome of St Paul's Cathedral on their left and he knew the Tower was not far away.

On top of the long bow in front, Billy saw two Lambretta mopeds strapped to the deck. 'What're they for?'

'We're going to need those,' Britannia said. 'Have you been on one before?'

'No, just a mountain bike.' Billy wondered what she meant.

The helicopter sounded like a machine gun. Alex turned and saw that the Wessex bore no markings. They passed under Southwark Bridge and then they could see coming into view ahead of them were the dark walls of the Tower of London. It was an imposing structure that had shaped the city's skyline since the days of William the Conqueror in the eleventh century. The citadel was solid, impregnable, and Alex could not imagine why they were heading so quickly towards it.

'Hey, it looks different here,' Billy observed.

'Yeah, there's no HMS Belfast. You know – the *battleship.*'

'It's still in service,' Britannia added.

The noise from the Wessex was so loud it was hard to hear what she was saying. Alex looked up and saw that the helicopter was directly overhead. The rotors were spinning against the evening clouds and exhaust belched from the fuselage filling the sky with a dirty trail.

'Hold tight,' Boadicea screamed.

She slung the powerboat into a sharp left turn and aimed the bow towards the embankment straight in front of the Tower. Alex could make out tourists walking along the front above the Thames; some were looking towards the boat and pointing. The ramparts loomed high and the square battlements of the White Tower higher still. A Union flag unfurled in the breeze. Boadicea continued to steer them on a collision course towards the embankment. But then Alex saw an arched opening in the high stone wall that lined the Thames. It was then that he realised where they were heading: *Traitors' Gate.*

Seconds later they slewed into the watery opening and Boadicea cut the power and the engines chugged and sputtered and fell silent. This was the entrance through which hundreds of traitors had made their final journey before being imprisoned in the Tower and their ultimate execution. Alex shivered at the thought.

Then they lost sight of the Wessex.

56

Inside the high-arched entrance to Traitors' Gate was a flight of steps that rose out of the water up to a platform. The Thames slopped around and splashed over the worn stones covered with slippery green slime. There was a rank odour that seemed to suffocate Alex's every breath.

'Throw your bags out,' instructed Britannia. 'We need to get these Lambrettas off.'

Billy jumped from the powerboat and climbed the steps. 'Alex, push one of these bikes up. I'll grab it.'

'Why do we need these bloody scooters anyway?' With a pained expression Alex hauled the bike onto a step.

It was tricky as the boat bobbed and lurched and was always swinging away from the jetty. Boadicea fired up the engines and kept them turning slowly to stop the boat drifting. Eventually with a bit of push and heave they managed to lug both scooters onto the walkway at the top.

'Now what?' Alex asked breathing heavily. Somewhere nearby he heard the whirring blades on the Wessex slow and finally stop.

'We're getting out of here.' Boadicea wrenched open a wooden door near to where they were standing. 'Get them in here. We're under Wakefield Tower, this leads down to a tunnel that goes north from Lanthorn Tower.'

'Oh yeah,' said Alex, 'and where does that go?'

'Moorgate.'

It smelt damp and felt squelchy underfoot. The passage was pitch black until Boadicea switched on the lights on her bike. They saw a cobbled slope that led downwards. Britannia closed the door and they began descending. After a few minutes they came to a ninety-degree left turn where the gradient levelled out.

'Let's go,' Boadicea said. She was keen to get moving. 'One on the back of each scooter.'

Billy squeezed on behind her and Alex held on to Britannia and they eased away along the tunnel. The shaky beams from the scooters shone ahead but all they could see was the narrow tunnel stretching away in front of them. In the distance Billy could make out nothing other than the grimy walls that sped by.

'How do you know about this tunnel?' Alex spoke into Britannia's ear as her flaying hair brushed his face.

'It's been here for hundreds of years. I heard about it while working for Trinity.'

'So if Trinity knows about it, then they might be following us.'

'I'm guessing they're not far behind.'

'Can't these bikes go any faster?' A sudden surge of adrenalin began coursing through Alex.

'Yes, downhill.'

If the scooter had not been making such a buzz he would have heard his own heart pounding rapidly.

Britannia's quip did nothing to allay his fear. Again it came to his mind: *She's my granddaughter*! He still found the idea impossible to comprehend. He put his hands round her slim waist and held her close and he remembered her saying that she had come to make sure nothing would happen to him. *What does she know*?

'Couldn't we have gone into Moorgate the way we came out?'

'No way Alex. Bo told me they're building on it.'

Alex looked over Britannia's shoulder and could see Billy on the bike about fifty yards in front. They had been travelling for several minutes and still the tunnel continued in a straight line. Then there came a sound that caused panic to rise inside Alex. Far behind he heard a roar.

'What the hell's that?'

'Sounds like a two-fifty,' replied Britannia. 'We've got company.'

The deep growl of the motorbikes' engines travelled at the speed of sound along the length of the tunnel and overtook them. In a few minutes they would be right behind them. As if things couldn't get any worse, Alex caught sight of huge black rats scampering along the tunnel in the glare of the headlights. They zigzagged and scattered and disappeared into the darkness. Then Alex lost sight of Billy and Boadicea.

'Where've they gone?'

'They've turned off. We're there now.'

No sooner had Britannia spoken when she turned a corner and they arrived through a concealed entrance that led onto an Underground platform that had been built one hundred years ago. Alex saw Billy and Boadicea dismounting. He recognised the place; the squalid concourse, the old posters and the Moorgate sign. It all came back to him. But there was something missing.

'*No train*!' His voice echoed along the length of the platform. Then from behind there came the deep vibration of approaching motorbikes. Alex shot a look both ways, 'Typical, the bloody train's been cancelled.'

Two bikes thundered onto the platform and stopped just yards from Alex. On one machine was Warwick Vane. His tyres squealed sharply on the concrete and he got off.

'Ladies and gentlemen,' he said in his gravelly American accent, 'you really have put up some chase. I think you remember my colleague.' He turned and gestured to the other bike. The passenger swung a leg over and stood up. The person wore a tight leather outfit and a black helmet. But as she walked towards them, clicking stilettos gave away her anonymity. It was a traitor's gait. Victoria Trevelyan removed her helmet and her dark hair fell over her shoulders. Her deep green eyes and her smooth brown skin looked as immaculate as ever.

'Alex and Billy, you've had quite an adventure, and I think you will agree, it has been a success. I'd like to congratulate you. Once you had tested the machine we were able to follow you, for we also had a purpose for being here. But for the moment that avenue has been closed. We may come back for Benjamin Janus one day. But I think there is a greater prize within our reach.' She took a step closer to Alex. In her heels she stood much taller. 'Yes, there's something that we want that is very dear to you. I think you know what I'm talking about, don't you Alex?'

He took a step back. 'I don't know what you mean.' He wondered if they knew as much as he did.

'Oh but you do Alex. I think you've discovered something you didn't know you had.'

He took another step back and felt Britannia standing behind him.

'There's so much knowledge here. It would take Trinity to a whole new level of understanding. We could discover so much about the future – and if necessary, augment it. We wouldn't think twice.'

'Sod you Victoria. What're you talking about?'

'I'm talking about Britannia and Bo – your *grandchildren.*'

The Controller of Trinity snapped her fingers and Warwick Vane stepped forward with the rider from the other bike. But as they did, lights appeared in the tunnel, and with a metallic screech and a harsh grating noise the tube-train arrived beside the platform. The two carriages were fire-engine red. They came to a stop and the doors juddered and opened with a hiss. The destination on the front displayed *Moorgate.*

'Front coach,' Britannia called. In a flash she was running. Alex and Boadicea followed her while Billy knocked over the two Lambrettas which acted as barriers to obstruct the members of Trinity just a little longer. They sprinted along the platform and flung themselves in through the door. Billy arrived last just as they closed. Alex jammed the doors open with his bag and dragged Billy in.

Warwick Vane had fallen headlong over the mopeds but managed to pick himself up just as the train began to move.

'Get on it,' Victoria Trevelyan screamed.

Vane made a desperate lunge and caught his fingers in the crack of some closing doors. His boots scuffed along the platform as he scrambled to get a footing on the step. In the next moment the train entered the darkness of the tunnel and rattled away from Moorgate station. Bright flares erupted from the tracks and seared along the tunnel.

Billy stood up and grabbed a black rubber handle dangling from the ceiling to steady his balance. 'That was close,' he said playing it down. 'This is the only train I know that runs on time!'

Looking out they saw the blackness changing to a deep emerald with flashes of scarlet pulsing like a severed artery. Golden sparks like fireworks fizzed into existence and vanished instantly. Alex watched mesmerised and felt a static sensation in the air that seemed to attract the hair on his head.

'*Event horizon*,' yelled Bo. 'Brace yourself.'

Suddenly the connecting door between the two carriages burst open with a splintering crash and there stood Warwick Vane. His eyes stared unblinking like a man possessed; his fingers were cut and bleeding. He staggered forward as if he were carrying an injury.

'Get out the way boys. You're of no interest now. There's a bigger prize to be had, and look, I've got a choice. There's nothing like killing two birds with one stone.' Without warning he pounced on Britannia who screamed and began clawing at his face. 'When we get out, I'm gonna call Trinity, then we can, um, interrogate you. It'll be very interesting finding out what happens in the future. We could be one step ahead of the game. You and me Brit.' Spittle began to dribble down his stubbled chin.

Warwick Vane held Britannia vice-like in a head lock. She let out a stifled whimper. Alex could see she was in agony; her face was becoming flushed. He threw himself between them and Britannia fell to the wooden floor. Alex clenched hold of the lapels on Vane's long black coat and they both became pinned to the glass door. Through the window, he caught sight of a whirling violet pattern that began to spiral like a vortex. His cheek flattened against the glass. The pressure suddenly snapped the door open with a rush of noise revealing an immense nothingness beyond.

The Underground tunnel had vanished. Britannia watched in horror as both men fell into an endless chasm.

'Alex...Alex...'

In a moment he was gone. He had been hurled towards eternity and a trillion, trillion stars.

57

A vast emptiness consumed Alex. The recesses of his memory conjured a multitude of life experiences that came to him all at once.

Alex cried.

No one knew his name for it had not yet been chosen. Nearby, but unseen, a tall and radiant figure stood beside his mother as she cradled him in the drab maternity ward.

Alex embraced his Dad. He was ecstatic.

'*Shearer...Shearer...*' The boy jumped for joy, and punching the air on the Wembley terrace sang like never before.

'Happy birthday Alex.'

Day turned to night. The breeze calmed and the birds became silent. The time had come. For two minutes Alex watched in awe as the eclipse hung high above him. *A circle of fire*, he thought. Then the sun burst through like a diamond ring and the crowd on the French hillside gasped at the wonder.

Lily lay asleep in her mother's arms. Alex was too excited to get into his sleeping bag. He glanced along the length of The Mall and saw thousands camped out between Buckingham Palace and Admiralty Arch. A pale sky wrapped around London as the sun rose that September morning. In a few hours' time Princess Diana's cortege would pass by just yards away.

'I've got a surprise for you Alex,' his Dad had said on the phone. 'You'll see tonight.'

He never did find out what it was. Six hours later Alex was in his grandfather's shed.

'There's been a terrible accident Alex,' his grandfather's eyes were raw. 'Your Dad...'

Why?

The school auditorium was full. Not a spare seat anywhere. A stage light picked out Lily as she began to sing. Alex watched; something burned deep inside him.

'*Somewhere over the rainbow, way up high...*' Her voice was enchanting.

Alex was choked.

Why did she have PH? It was so fucking wrong.

His tiny fingers trembled as he picked up the shards of glass in Grandpa Bell's greenhouse.

Had he heard? What will he say? Fear came over Alex and he began to snivel.

He threw the catapult over a wall and made his way to the backdoor. Floods of tears filled his eyes. The football results came from the front room.

'Arsenal 2, Newcastle nil...'

They sat together on her quilted duvet. Both were nervous with excitement. Each saying nothing. The TV flickered in the corner. Alex put his arms around her; Abby felt so warm and soft. He caught a whiff of perfume that lingered on her neck. Alex let his fingers slip gently round her waist. Her skin felt smooth like porcelain. His other hand explored her long dark hair. Holding Abby's slender neck he drew her closer until he felt her breath upon his face. Her mouth was warm and his pulse began to race. Abby sighed.

In a flash the goalkeeper saved the penalty. Alex fell to the ground and covered his face. He had to hide from Abby. Oh the sweet, sweet smell of freshly cut grass.

The radio crackled. 'Forties, Cromarty, Forth, Tyne, Dogger…'

The paper crinkled. Dr Raja peered over his gold-rimmed glasses.
'Who are they Alex?'
'They are Shadows.' *We know, don't we?*
The man's cufflink sparkled like Sirius and Alex smelt the sweet ether hanging in the air.

He heard a voice inside the shell. Distant. Faint. There was a message but he couldn't make it out.
The tiny golden fish teased him and darted out of sight. Then the chilly water came and engulfed him. The place was cold and alien.
The face he saw was purity personified. He had seen her during the first moments of his life. Then a power came and took him and in a breath he saw the wide blue circle of the earth below.

There came a shudder of thunder and in the blackness beyond all the stars sang together.

58

Alex stood on a beach of golden sand that stretched in both directions as far as the eye could see. Each tiny grain twinkled in the glancing sunlight like the multitude of stars that filled the cosmos.

Behind him he could hear the incessant ocean lapping gently along the shoreline. By his side was the one who had borne him to this paradise. Alex knew he had met her before. He had seen her once in a cemetery and then again beside a deep blue sea like the one he now looked out upon.

She stood tall and graceful and her countenance was bedazzling. The length of her sword fell from a belt woven from fine silver threads of bdellium and dug deep into the crystalline sand below. Her wings of white iridescence glistened and many facets sparkled as they came down and folded behind her with the faintest rustle.

'Who are you?' Alex held the gaze of the seraph's sapphire-blue eyes. Inside, an uncontrollable nervousness welled up and caused his whole body to shake. He tried to keep the tremors in check, but failed. Her beauty was terrifying.

She looked down upon the mortal. 'Do not worry Alex. Like you, I was once human.' Her voice was clear and tender and in no way betrayed the hidden power she had at her disposal. Her skin was pure and her hair fell in flowing ringlets over her shoulders.

'For a while I served a king and stood at his right hand and waited at table. In battle I wielded an iron sword in defence of the realm.' She paused and her eyes strayed for a moment. 'Yes, my name was *Freya Aylwin*. Now I have a new name – a name that means *Radiance of the Everlasting Day – Eloeth-Elohim La-Lothrandir*. And I serve a new king. When you most needed me I came to you. I have brought you here for a reason.'

After she had spoken, Radiance looked to the sky and began to sing. Alex heard that the luminary's melody was joined by a vast choir whose harmonies were so rich and tantalising and intricate that no human voice could sing with such purity or reach so high or sing so deep. Like piccolos and bird song and crashing waves and organ pipes.

As Alex looked across the sea, what he took to be the billowing clouds of rising nimbus now appeared full of golden seraphim. They were a host beyond number, towering upward ever higher towards the zenith overhead; a never ending well of souls singing songs of victory. They filled the sky; a mighty celestial army with stringed instruments and sounding brass and thunderous drums. The anthem they sang was so haunting that giddiness overcame Alex and in a swoon he fell to his knees in the soft sand. In submission he covered his ears. He had never heard such loveliness. It was a symphony so enchanting and awesome that he would not forget it in a thousand years.

But then he heard just one voice speaking to him with a gentleness he had never known.

'Stand up Alex. I must take you into the garden. There, you will find something you hold very dear.'

Alex raised himself from the sand and followed Radiance from the shore, and walking over the camber of a grassy bank they came to a secluded wood. There he saw a veiled waterfall cascading from a rocky cleft into a placid lake of deepest turquoise. A rainbow shimmered in the spray. He passed a tree with foliage that seemed one moment the colour of bronze and the next of silver-grey. And as he walked below it, he touched a bough. With a flutter, a myriad of resting butterflies took to the air with the slightest fanning breeze from tiny wings that flickered between both bronze and silver. Silently they rose, spiralling like a cloud of gold-dust scintillating in the sunlight. Tears began to flow down Alex's face. Never before had he known such wonder or felt so deep a joy.

They came to the foot of some giant red sequoia reaching high above them. With a metallic zing, Radiance drew her sword and pressed the blade into the earth. She leant upon its hilt and spoke to the young man standing beside her in his grey cotton track suit.

'There is someone you are to meet Alex. Take the path into the garden. I will wait.'

Suddenly he realised that she had always been near, but just out of sight. She was a *Shadow* – a Shadow of the day.

Alex did not question Radiance, but took the track through the wood which led to a clearing. There came a wonderful aroma which wafted through the meadow and drifted on the gentle breeze and reached Alex. It reminded him of home. He breathed deeply and inhaled the intoxicating smell that filled the air. *Breakfast!*

A man was kneeling nearby planting vegetables in a freshly dug allotment. Alex was drawn towards him. He knelt there poking with a dibble; his back to Alex. He wore a baggy cream-coloured cricket jumper, blue denim jeans and scuffed brown boots with a deep rugged sole. The man was tall with an athletic build. He ran his hands through his dark mop of hair and stood up. On turning, his eyes fell on the ball-boy standing there in his grey track suit.

'*Alex.*'

'*Gramps!*'

'Come here Son.'

For a second, Alex thought he must be dreaming but his senses tingled with vibrancy. He felt alive – more alive than ever before. He ran to his grandfather and held him in a firm embrace as he had done so many times before. Alex felt safe at last. They said nothing for a long time. Eventually Grandpa Bell spoke.

'Alex we must talk. I have lunch ready.'

The idea of food sounded like music to Alex's ears. Only then did he discover how hungry he was. He followed his grandfather across to where a barbeque was smoking close by. Sizzling above grey coals were portions of fish and large succulent mushrooms seasoned with herbs and drizzled with olive oil.

Alex looked longingly at his grandfather. *Had he been expecting me?*

Grandpa Bell appeared to be in his early thirties but was still unmistakeably his grandfather. His hair was dark like Alex's and there was a youthful twinkle in his eyes. He was full of vitality and brimming with energy. An emotion began to rise inside Alex. Here was his hero who he'd lost and now had found. He tried to stifle a whimper and felt in his pocket for a handkerchief. But all he could find was an article from a newspaper he had forgotten about. He had stuffed it into his pocket when getting changed at Wembley. It seemed like a lifetime ago.

'There are no tears here Alex.'

Alex tried to control the sobbing he felt rising inside him.

'I've got this paper,' he said taking it from his pocket.

His grandfather took the torn page of the Sunday Telegraph.

'I should have died.'

'It's all a lie Alex.' His grandfather read the article. 'It will not happen.'

He screwed the paper into a ball and tossed it on the burning embers. It burst into flames.

'There, it doesn't exist. Never did.'

Grandpa Bell plated up the cooked food and placed them on a wooden tray. Then setting the feast down on a park bench beside him he turned to Alex and smiled.

'See that oak tree over there?'

Alex laughed. He knew exactly what his grandfather was about to say. It was a contest they had played many times when Alex was growing up. He'd almost forgotten that phrase used so often by his beloved Gramps. The beat of his heart began to quicken with expectation. But it was Alex who spoke next as if by gamesmanship to outwit his grandfather.

'Race you!'

302

'Go!' yelled Grandpa Bell.

As if a gun had been fired to start a race, in a flash they were sprinting across the wide meadow just as Alex had done as a boy.

The large oak was about a quarter of a mile away and it seemed to Alex to take an age to reach even half-way. Together they ran, side by side, the wind in their dark hair.

'You're getting better!' his grandfather shouted, knowing he had trained him well.

'I've grown up Gramps.'

'Yes you have.'

The thought came to Alex that, although his grandfather had been a toned athlete, somehow he had always let him win. As a boy, Alex was unaware of his grandfather's subtle diplomacy. But now he knew. They were both flat out, neither giving way to the other. Fleet of foot they paced in unison over the verdant pasture.

'Come on Gramps!' Alex teased, even though his lungs were bursting and he knew he could go no quicker.

'I'm right with you.'

With just a few strides to go they lunged for the trunk and together slapped their hands on the rough bark.

Alex slumped upon the gnarled roots that spread out around the tree. He could not remember the last time he'd run so fast. Between gasps he laughed, and looking up at his grandfather he saw him beaming and noticed he was not even out of breath. *Could he have beaten me?* Then he realised that within his own body he carried his grandfather's genes, and maybe his personality.

The tall man bent down, grabbed his hand, and hauled his grandson to his feet.

'You've still got it Son.' He looked pleased. Then he glanced back across the meadow. 'I know a place you will love Alex.'

59

There was a familiar dusty smell inside the wooden potting shed. It was just as Alex remembered.

A heady concoction of paint and thinners and glue were mixed with odours from wood shavings of pine and walnut and mahogany. It was a rich aromatic cocktail that Alex had only ever known in Grandpa Bell's shed. The curious blend had all been part of his childhood. As he had grown from toddler to teenager, so it seemed had the assortment of objects inside.

In one of the wooden slats he saw the small hole through which he used to look for hours on end. It was an opening left from a knot he had poked out. And through the hole he would have spied the unseen dwellers, the invisible college, that used to come and go and haunt his early years.

Alex picked up the shiny brass steam engine and spun the wheel.

It seems like yesterday!

And then he saw, etched into one of the legs of the sturdy workbench, his own handiwork. He ran his fingers over the design and his mind crossed the years.

'*Abby Hart*,' he whispered, not quite believing it could still be there. It was his little engraving, roughly scratched into the wood using a screwdriver. Her serene face came to him; her dark eyes, soft voice and her sweet *Paris* fragrance she wore. 'Where are you Abby?' he mused.

Then his stomach tightened, he felt a wrench and a sudden paroxysm of panic. The door had flung open that day and there was Grandpa Bell framed in the entrance. His eyes were sore, his voice rattled.

'Beer, Alex?'

The image in his mind's eye was swiftly quenched like the action of an analgesic targeting the hurt of many years. The pain of losing his father still lingered.

There was a chink of glass as Grandpa Bell reached to a shelf and handed Alex a green bottle containing his homebrew. Alex gladly levered off the cap with an opener.

'Good health,' his grandfather said.

'Cheers! It must be Christmas.'

Alex looked at Grandpa Bell and saw the youthful glint in his eyes and the toned frame of an athlete he had once been.

He sipped the beer and could not remember drinking anything so refreshing. *Nectar*! It was golden in colour, light and malty and smooth, and he wanted more.

'Mm, this is the best homebrew you've ever made!'

'I've had some practice.'

It was while Alex was relishing the barbecued mackerel and mushrooms and the olive bread Grandpa Bell had brought into the shed that Alex happened to see something that evoked a far deeper memory. He reached to a high shelf and lifted the object out of a glass jar and as he did his eyes strayed to his grandfather's gaze. Like an arrow piercing his heart, the shame returned once again.

How could it be here? I got rid of it.

The catapult he held seemed like an exhibit on display at a court hearing. It was evidence of his guilt. An embarrassed flush warmed his face.

'Grandpa,' he began and faltered. 'I always meant to say sorry.' He remembered all too clearly the pane of glass he had smashed in his grandfather's greenhouse when he was just a boy. It was a wayward shot.

'I know Alex. It was a long time ago and it doesn't matter now. Anyway, I'd forgotten all about it.'

His grandfather took the catapult and threw it into one of the bench draws and slammed it shut.

'Why am I here Grandpa?'

'I will tell you soon. Look, I want to show you my star charts.'

Alex had already noticed the ream of papers spread out over the bench. They were strewn haphazardly and his grandfather shuffled them into some order. The pages were of all sizes, from scraps to large sheets. Alex could see they were covered with scrawled inscriptions, diagrams, arrows and all manner of cryptic writings.

'I've spent some time studying the stars. You remember those nights when we used to stand in the garden and I would tell you the names of the planets and the stars and show you the constellations?'

Alex nodded. He had treasured every moment he'd spent listening to his grandfather's knowledge of astronomy. Through his reflecting telescope Alex had seen the ragged craters on the moon, the Jovian satellites and the rings of Saturn. His mind had been opened to the vastness of space and just how small and precious the earth is by comparison.

'I've found something quite remarkable.' He smiled.

His grandfather traced his finger across one large sheet showing star maps and annotations. Alex glanced and read some of his grandfather's notes.

Draco will be cast out and Rastaban shall be trodden underfoot and seized by Ophiuchus. A woman, Coma, bearing a child destined to rule the nations will bring forth Orion the prince. Libra will show the price that he will pay.

Alex frowned. It made no sense to him. Then under the pile of papers he saw something half concealed. It was a blue tobacco tin like the one he had been keeping safe. Just as he went to pick it up his grandfather spoke.

'Let's go for a walk Alex. I want to tell you a secret.'

60

Dusk had fallen leaving the wide horizon hemmed with a hazy light of deep magenta. High above, a flock of swallows scattered in a frenzy and were lost amongst the lofty sequoia, the tips of which glowed an autumn copper in the last rays of setting sun.

Grandpa Bell put an arm round his grandson and took him by a path that climbed a gently sloping hill. After all the dizzying events that had happened, Alex felt safe at last.

To his amazement he suddenly heard the laughter and chatter of tiny voices. Out of the woods ran twenty, maybe thirty boys and girls; Alex couldn't tell for certain. They were young and their voices seemed to sing and babble like a bubbling brook as they danced and chased each other in playful amusement. Alex found their faces captivating and their warm smiles a delight. Then quickly they vanished beyond the curve of the hill and the sound of their laughter ebbed away until solitude returned once more.

'Who were they?' He was enthralled; he had never known their like.

'These are they who were lost in innocence.' His grandfather had seen them before. 'Like them, there are many others. But it's not for you to know.'

Alex held his hero's gaze and for a moment felt as if he were a boy again back in his grandfather's garden. His memory was clear.

One night his grandfather had shown him Mizar, the double star in Ursa Major and they had traced across the sky and found Andromeda; a fuzzy smudge of a billion stars. Alex had remembered his grandfather's words: 'And who knows Alex, maybe in that galaxy there could be a grandfather and his grandson looking across the sea of space to our Milky Way galaxy.'

A secret, Alex thought, and he heard his grandfather's voice again.

'The secret is a story!' Grandpa Bell said at last and his eyes strayed towards the constellations above. One by one the stars began to adorn the deepening darkness. An expansive swathe, like a river flowing, spanned the depths of space in a high arc overhead. It was the heart of the galaxy.

Across the blackness of night there came a ribbon of aurora that began to colour the sky with swirls of emerald and violet that drifted and painted the atmosphere with a shimmering veil. Alex watched and his heart missed a beat. Then as soon as the display had arrived it ebbed and melted away showing the brightness of the stars beyond.

'You came to me once Alex, and you have come to me again – and for a reason.' He lifted his hand from his grandson's shoulder and scanned the pathway ahead. 'We must go higher. To the top.'

Alex wondered as his grandfather studied the sky now peppered with countless stars. *What does he mean: The secret is a story?*

A short time later they stood on the broad summit and there below them was the lay of the land stretching to a great distance. Alex was breathing heavily from the climb, but his grandfather, who looked like an athlete at peak fitness, seemed undaunted. In one direction Alex now saw a crescent moon low in the sky reflecting on the distant ocean. It was a world filled with blue seas and white clouds and green continents. A faraway tapestry embroidered with pastel shades and framed in black.

'*Beulah*,' Grandpa Bell said and turned to face his grandson.

'Where am I?'

'You're in extra time Alex.' His grandfather paused for a moment and then began his story. 'A long time ago, everything we know about was squeezed into something so small it was no bigger than nothing.'

Alex looked into the eyes of his grandfather and was instantly spellbound.

'Inside was stuff that would seed the emptiness of space and ultimately become the matter that would make up you and me and many, many other things. We were there Alex, being readied on the first day.'

Alex could feel his pulse hasten; somehow everything his grandfather said seemed to make sense. He couldn't wait to hear what he would say next.

'The bang started the story with the biggest moment of all, but that event passed swiftly. Order took charge and the universe and everything in it spawned to fill the vastness. On that day, time was born when all the stars rushed to fill the heavens and the centre of immensity was embellished with the host of bright suns.

'And here we stand Alex – beneath this celestial sky.' His grandfather raised an arm and swept it slowly in a circle. 'The story has been written in the stars for all to read. It's right there Alex and no one knew it – written long before it ever happened.'

Alex pulled a face, 'I don't understand.'

'I'm not surprised. It's taken me ages to fathom it.' His eyes sharpened with an intelligence Alex had not seen before.

Transfixed by his grandfather's explanation, Alex listened like the child who'd once sat upon Grandpa Bell's knee. His voice had the same strength and resonance he remembered. He spoke with a cutting edge, yet often softly and with an air of authority. His diction was perfect unlike George, Alex's father, who often got tongue-tied and became choked by an involuntary stammer.

What fatherly example had *he* ever shown? Alex thought. *Nothing* – nothing that had left any lasting impression.

Except for those dark days when he would drink endlessly and enter his bedroom and beat him until he almost lost his mind. After all, his father could not deal with his mother in the same way. Alex had been the whipping boy.

That was how the nightmares had begun.

He had become susceptible to wild imaginings and the infrequent visits of other entities. They were the Shadows of day and night from a world out of sight and just beyond the horizon. But it was a place very close. They would come through a crack in the fabric of space, like going from one room to another.

Grandpa Bell's voice sliced through the air and brought Alex's fleeting thoughts back to the present.

'The stars are for signs and seasons, from the chains of the Pleiades to the belt of Orion. They are the Mazzaroth.'

'The *Mazzaroth*?'

'The Zodiac. The patterns that make up the constellations and the message they tell. Let me show you.'

He shot a finger to the sky.

'There, that group is Serpens, the serpent, who came to lead astray man and take the royal crown, Corona.

'And that's Virgo, the woman who gives birth to the promised one, followed by Crux, the cross, which tells of the price paid so that the lost may be saved.'

As his grandfather pointed to each constellation in turn, it seemed to Alex that their shape and identity came alive standing out against the velvet blackness of the cosmos. When he was a boy he had struggled to make any sense from the random clusters of stars in the night sky, but now each one took on a distinct form and were plain to see.

Grandpa Bell was still talking.

'...The constellation of Auriga, the shepherd who cares for his flock. And in that direction is Cepheus the king who is coming for his bride and to establish his kingdom rule, and further still there, you can see Eridanus, the river of life, along which everyone must pass to be judged.

'These are the Mazzaroth Alex, and this is their story.'

'But there are so many more stars.'

'Yes and there's so much more that they tell. The story goes on. Who knows Alex, maybe there's a star out there with your name on it!' He laughed. 'In a universe that is infinite, everything is possible. Even God.'

It was just as if a tarnished mirror had been brightly polished to show a hidden image. His grandfather's revelation was like the missing piece of a jigsaw that filled an empty space in his life. Alex could only stand and stare.

'All these stars are set at different distances from us and their light has taken different times to reach us. Each star we see a thousand years in the past, ten thousand, a million.' He pointed to a distant hazy galaxy, 'Yes, a billion years ago. Everywhere you look you can see creation as it was in years gone by. The universe is the ultimate time machine Alex, one vast involution displayed for our wonderment.

'And this is what I want to tell you. You came to me for a reason: to have your mind opened and to discover that you can do so much more.

'Through life's journeys many are called but few are chosen.

'You have been chosen Alex. Other tasks lie ahead which only you can fulfil. You will do greater things than I have ever done.'

'But I am nothing. What can I do?'

'You can do anything if you only apply your mind.' His grandfather thought for a moment. 'Look at that rock – can you pick it up?'

Nearby there lay a dark grey boulder about the size of a football.

'I think so.' Even so, he doubted his ability.

'Show me.'

Alex didn't question his grandfather, although it seemed a strange request. All his life he had trusted him. He went to the rock and squatting down placed his arms under its bulk to get a firm grip. Then with a sharp intake of breath he gritted his teeth and stood up straight using the strength of his quadriceps. It was heavier than Alex had estimated and after a few seconds he found himself breathing heavily with his arms shaking from the strain. His face began to flush, but he held it.

Just as Alex felt he could hold it no longer his grandfather said, 'Let it go.'

The rock fell to the grass and landed with a thud and he let out a sigh of relief.

'Well done Son.'

He turned to his grandfather with a blank expression as his heart rate began to slow to a steady rhythm.

'You lifted that rock and yet the whole earth was pulling with all the force it had. And you won! Your strength is greater than the earth. You have the ability to overcome the hardest challenges you will ever meet.'

For a moment Alex thought about the notion that, yes, he had lifted that weight and the world beneath his feet could not overcome his own strength.

'Come here Alex. You passed a trivial test of mine, but there are other tests that lie ahead.'

Alex stepped forward and his grandfather embraced him with his strong arms and held him tight. He saw a tiny smear appear in the corner of his grandfather's eyes and noticed a tremor in his voice.

'There're no tears here Gramps.'

His grandfather held him close for a moment and then released him. They looked longingly into each other's eyes.

'Alex, your past has gone. In front of you are many futures. Make sure you choose the right one.'

'Will I see you again Grandpa?'

His grandfather smiled.

John Bell gently touched his grandson's forehead and deep inside the young man's soul was roused.

His voice was a whisper, 'Time to wake up Alex.'

61

In a twinkling, a glorious light came and vanished.

62

With a blinding flash the darkness was gone and there was Moorgate once again.

The train lurched and slowed and with a deepening hum, came to a grinding stop. After a sudden snort of compressed air, the doors slid open and Brit and Bo stepped onto the platform. Billy followed and humped the bags down. He found the twins sobbing and holding each other. They seemed inconsolable.

'What's going to happen to us?'

'I don't know. We may cease to exist!'

'Without Alex, what future do we have?'

'What past do we have?'

'What shit you talking about?' Billy still hadn't grasped their relationship to Alex.

Britannia turned to him; mascara had streaked from her eyes. She was about to speak, but Boadicea interrupted.

'…We could go back for him.'

'No not from here. We need a more stable link. We could end up months out of place.' Her shoulders dropped and she hid her face in her trembling hands. Bo placed a slender arm round her sister.

Their despair was interrupted by a strong voice. Billy thought it sounded familiar.

'Damen, you're going precisely nowhere.' A Teutonic accent travelled along the length of the underground station. They turned and saw someone they recognised.

'*Schneider!*'

'Yes Billy, welcome home. Although I can't say that for your lovely companions – can I ladies?'

'What's he mean?' Billy shot an alarmed look in their direction.

'Simply this Billy. This is not home to your friends Britannia and Bo Bell, because they come from somewhere completely different. Yah, decades in the future.'

Billy couldn't speak. He was trying to comprehend what the German was talking about. It wasn't just that they seemed to come from a different time, but he was also perplexed because they shared a common name with his lost friend.

Before Billy could say anything Ralf Schneider clapped his hands. From the tunnel that led onto the platform came a dozen men dressed in black overalls. Britannia thought they looked like those she'd seen inside Wembley Stadium.

'See, I have brought some friends from Trinity to celebrate your return.' The men in black spread along the platform and several went inside the train with monitoring devices. 'It seems you have left Alex behind. That's a shame...'

'He loved it so much he wanted to stay,' Billy spat out the words with more than a hint of sarcasm.

'Never mind. I'm not here to share the Wembley gig with Alex. Instead, I'd like to extend the contract that Miss Bell and Miss Bell once had here at Trinity. If I remember correctly, it was a contract you did not complete.'

'We don't want an extension.'

'This is not negotiable my dear Bo. It's mandatory.' He clicked his fingers, 'Gentlemen.'

Some of the men stepped forward and surrounded Billy and the two sisters.

'You see ladies; we could make such a good team. You know so much. You know the order of events to come. Together we could stop a war – together we start a war. We could bring down a government – we could raise one up. We could make the timeliest economic investments. We could gamble and win. We could even place a bet on the day

William's son becomes king. All *you* have to do is remember when it happened. And then Trinity will rival the Illuminati.'

'You're insane Dr Schneider,' Brit snapped.

'On the contrary Fräulein, as you know, Trinity has already flexed its influential and far reaching muscles. I'm sure you are aware of some of our projects: Princess Diana, Jerusalem, The Vatican. Need I say more?' He stared at them sternly until a wry smile spread across his face. 'Take them.'

The black-suited men held each of them in a firm arm lock and began to man-handle them towards the tunnel that led to Trinity. Billy remembered the dark walk he had made before and the huge rats that scuttled along its stinking length.

He struggled and resisted and kicked out, and as he did there came a deep thundering sound that reverberated somewhere inside the station. Ralf Schneider spun round to see a horde of leather-clad warriors spilling onto the platform. They had grim faces etched with anger and they beat their iron swords against shields and screamed something unintelligible. Three or four abreast, the soldiers emerged onto the concourse, and as they spread out there seemed to be thirty or more in number. Ralf Schneider snatched out a radio, but in a split second it was knocked from his hand by a warrior, sending it spinning across the platform. Another stamped on it with a heavy boot and splintered it into many shards.

'Let's get out,' Schneider hissed. 'We need reinforcements.'

The men from Trinity began to disperse and quickly disappeared into the tunnel.

Billy realised he had seen these soldiers before. It was when he was with Alex in a corridor deep inside Trinity. He remembered hearing them speaking a dialect of French. *Perhaps they'd escaped*, he thought.

They stormed onto the train and ran along the gangway. When Billy looked round he was relieved that Schneider had vanished along with his henchmen. But then he saw a lonely figure standing beside a large advertisement. At first he didn't recognise him but then he realised it was someone he thought he'd never see again.

Alex waved a hand and the entire troop came out of the train. It seemed they responded to his command.

On seeing Alex, Britannia ran to him and flung her arms around his neck and kissed him. Her heart leapt.

'What happened?' she sobbed. 'We thought we'd lost you...' her voice trailed off.

He held her tight and said nothing for a long time. His eyes glazed as he whispered softly into her ear, 'I dreamed I saw...the face of an angel of war...It was a near death...' He could say no more but stood there while Britannia embraced him.

When he looked again, the battalion had assembled on the platform like a troop on parade. Alex composed himself and went over to inspect them. He placed his hand on the shoulder of one of the warriors as if to thank them.

'What's going on?' Suddenly Billy's emotions began to spill over. 'Where the fuck have you been – we could have done with you here. Schneider nearly took us out!'

'I went to Trinity and released these men. They don't belong here. Come on; let's get out of this place.' He began striding through the station with a sense of purpose.

Billy went chasing along the platform. 'How did you get them out of Trinity?'

Alex stopped, 'I don't know. I had an inclination. And maybe I've discovered stuff that's been hidden from me. I've seen so much since I left you.' His stare focused.

'You weren't meant to blow the bloody doors off!' Billy said in his best Michael Caine impression.

'Good call!' Alex laughed and pointed, 'this way.'

Their on-screen chemistry was as slick as ever.

Behind his eyes there seemed to be a different persona Billy had not seen before.

Alex took them to the end of the platform where he found a door shoddy with age and covered with flaking paint. Rattling the handle, he saw it was held by a rusty padlock.

'La porte,' he levelled his gaze at one of the strongest warriors.

The soldier knew what he had to do. He stepped forward and with one hefty blow, smashed the lock with his sword. A metallic clang echoed through the disused station and the door swung open. Beyond, Alex could see a passage.

'Let's go.'

He sent in some of the French company and Alex and Billy with Britannia and Bo followed on behind. Then came the entire battalion clumping along in single file. It was dark, but they could just make out a long corridor. It stank as if no fresh air had flowed through it for years. Billy took out his mobile phone and held it up; its blue glow was enough to cast a pale light in the passage way.

'Who're this lot?' Billy asked.

'Don't know, but I'm guessing Trinity somehow managed to retrieve them from another age. At least, they seem to be on our side.'

'That's gotta be a first for the French!' Billy was beginning to relax.

They walked for several minutes and came to a flight of stairs that led them upward. Alex sensed the air begin to freshen, and looking up he saw a faint light coming from above. When at last they reached the top, Alex found he was breathing heavily. He dropped his bag and looked around. The staircase had emerged into what seemed a large store house. Alex saw wooden crates, boxes, and machinery covered in tarpaulins. But what interested him most was the slither of brightness filtering in beneath two large doors.

'I think we've found a way out.' He turned to the soldiers. 'Open it.'

The doors were huge, but as the men began exerting their weight, the doors started to rock and buckle and after a minute they burst open with a grating noise. The stale air was replaced with a freshness that wafted in and chased away the musty smell. It took a moment for their eyes to adjust, but when they did, they couldn't quite believe the spectacle outside.

They looked out onto a road full of people passing by. There were hundreds of men and women dressed in bright and bizarre clothes of all colours. Many wore very little and others had painted skin. Some carried placards; others sang and a number blew piercing whistles and juggled. Motorised floats came by blasting out music while dancers cavorted along behind. There was a whole cavalcade and amongst them walked police in a stream that spread out for a mile or more.

'It's a march!' Billy couldn't believe it.

Alex read one of the banners being carried by two men dressed in shiny turquoise Spandex. '*Gay Pride*!' He laughed and looked at Billy, 'Perfect, we can merge in. Trinity won't find us here.'

'Sorted!' said Billy, as he often did.

But it seemed some of the French warriors were already entering into the spirit of the occasion. Someone from the procession came over to where they were standing and taking a soldier by the hand pulled him into the march.

'Bondage works for me,' he said with a broad grin.

Then more of the troupe joined the pageant, waving their swords and cheering. '*Allez...allez...allez,*' they called out and eventually the whole battalion took to the street and followed the gala.

It had been a most unexpected welcoming party.

63

Jack was pouring a pint as soon as he saw Alex and Billy stepping into The Moon.

The place was empty as usual. Alex scraped a chair across the wooden boards and sat back exhausted while Billy flung his bag on the floor with a loud clump.

Alex felt relief as he looked round at the familiar mementos that decked the lounge. He was thankful not to see Warwick Vane sitting in the corner. Apart from his own flat and his grandfather's shed where he used to hide, The Moon was like a second home to him.

'Ain't seen you boys for a few days. You been outta town?'

'Yeah, you could say that.'

'*Outta time*, more like it,' added Billy.

'Look at this Jack,' Alex said, walking over to pick up his beer. He held out the cup final programme. 'See that,' he said, 'that's a genuine Tofik Bakhramov signature. You know – the Russian linesman.'

'*Azerbaijani*,' corrected Billy.

Jack squinted at the squiggles on the page. 'Nice one. Where'd you get it?'

'Um, Selfridges. And I bought this poster which is going up over here.' Alex went to the wall of photographs and unrolling the picture, pinned it on. 'There you go Billy, how does that look?'

'Perfect.'

The photograph that hung on the wall showed Captain Bobby Moore raising the Jules Rimet trophy and he was being held aloft on the shoulders of Geoff Hurst and Ray Wilson. Alex and Billy looked smugly at the headline across the top: *30th July 1966 England 3-2 West Germany.*

'Shame Geoff skied that last shot; *four* would've been so much better. Still, who cares? We won. And this, Billy me ol' mate, will take pride of place in The Moon.' With reverence he balanced the orange ball on the table and gave Billy a wide smile. 'How good does that look?'

'Yeah, great smell of dubbin.'

'We can get that slash repaired. Let's get a tune on.'

Alex went over to the juke-box and selected something. It was a Pink Floyd track full of synthesizers which eventually gave way to David Gilmour's silky vocals.

'Welcome my son – welcome to the machine
What did you dream?
It's alright we told you what to dream
You dreamed of a big star – he played a mean guitar
He always ate in the steak bar – he loved to drive in his Jaguar
So welcome to the machine...'

Alex remembered the surprise encounter with Syd Barrett and the original Pink Floyd. One of their early gigs in the Post Office Tower had been a humbling experience. It had not gone well. Alex wondered if he had indeed influenced the course of their music when he gave them his iPod with a version of *The Dark Side of the Moon*. He knew Brit would not have approved.

The song was interrupted by a chime from Alex's mobile phone. The screen flushed brightly and he touched the pad bringing up a text.

'*Abby Hart*! I haven't heard from her for a while.'

'You alright mate? Looks like you've seen a ghost.' Billy could sense his friend had been caught out.

'Listen to this: *Alex, it was good to see you last week. I really enjoyed the Shiraz. Can we meet again? Abby, xxx.*' His brow furrowed.

'So you've got a date. Sounds good to me.'

Alex was quiet for moment. 'I've got a feeling that some of those changes we made at Wembley have had a knock on. I don't remember seeing Abby…' His voice trailed away.

Billy could see that Alex was troubled so he tried to deflect his thoughts.

'Oh yeah, I got a couple of things we can put on display.' He dug into his bag. 'We could make this place into an exhibition – you know, like a shrine to football. Mind you, when people find out, Jack might get swamped with customers.'

Billy slammed a metal object onto the table with a thump.

'Yeah, I forgot you bought a World Cup souvenir.' Alex picked it up. 'Blimey, it's heavy. Good copy.'

He set it down and looked at the inscription on the gold plate and saw a list of names neatly inscribed: *Uruguay, Italy, Italy, Uruguay, West Germany, Brazil, Brazil*.

Alex looked up and suddenly had a most awkward feeling. 'Is this what I think it is?'

Billy hesitated, 'Er no…um, yeah. It is.'

'…Oh, shit!'

The Jules Rimet trophy stood there on a table in The Moon. It was just twelve inches tall. The slender figurine of Nike, the goddess of victory, held an eight-sided chalice on top of a blue base made of lapis lazuli. Her long pleated robe fell to her feet and her out stretched wings were wonderfully spread above her head. Her face portrayed a calm serenity. And the longer Alex stared at the exquisite gold trophy the more he was reminded of the seraph called Radiance who had rescued him and carried him to a far paradise on wings of steel.

'I thought it would look good on Jack's bar, next to the pumps.' Billy didn't sound convincing.

Alex could say nothing. He opened his mouth but no words formed.

'It was really easy. I met this nerd at Wembley who insisted on showing me the trophy. He had a replica as well, just in case the real one got lost. I had one in my bag and…'

'...Billy, you said you had a couple of things.'

'Yeah.'

'What else have you got?' A deep uneasiness was welling up inside Alex.

'It's not much,' he said, placing a small object next to the gold trophy.'

'What is it?'

'Nobby's teeth.'

'*Nobby Stiles*?'

'Yeah, it's his dentures. I thought I could put them on eBay.'

'You're gonna have a job convincing anyone that these are Nobby Stiles' gnashers. They could be your Nan's for all I know.' Alex sat up and ran his hands through his dark hair and let out a long sigh. 'If this is the real Jules Rimet and you left behind a replica and a plastic one you bought in Carnaby Street, then that means the Queen presented Bobby Moore with...'

They looked over at the photograph on the wall showing the England captain proudly raising the World Cup.

'...A *fake*,' someone else said.

The door had opened and there stood Britannia dressed in knee length boots, a mini skirt and a Union Jack top. She walked into the lounge followed by Boadicea who was wearing her pale blue courier suit with the gold brooch.

'Bobby Moore was given a *fake*. It's in all the pictures.'

Alex slumped forward and held his head in his hands as the sisters came over.

'What's going on Alex?' Jack called out seeing his friend in some dismay.

'Um, nothing Jack. These are some girls we ran into. A couple of Pinots for Brit and Bo.'

'Not now Alex. This trophy shouldn't be here. If we don't return it, there could be some catastrophic bifurcation in the retrograde timeline.'

'What does that mean?'

'It means we've gotta get it back. Small changes lead to big changes as time proceeds.' Brit said. 'Big changes are not good! Our best option is to unload it somewhere not too close to the day of the final. Let's hope it goes synchro!'

'*Synchro*?' Alex pulled a face.

'Synchronicity.'

He was none the wiser.

'Let's go fellas,' Bo added. 'It's the *Butterfly Effect*. Haven't you read Ray Bradbury?'

Alex looked over to the barman who had a blank expression. 'Jack, it's just a rehearsal. You know, a sketch we're working on for the next show.'

64

Outside The Moon, the late rays of evening sun slanted down the length of the cobbled street casting a warm glow. The four stood there for a while just as a black people carrier rounded the corner and approached them; its diesel engine rumbled in the quiet backstreet.

Britannia turned to Alex, 'There's something we need to tell you.'

'What's that?'

'It's about you – and it's about us.'

Alex had experienced more shocks in a few days than he had in his lifetime. Surely nothing could surprise him now.

'Go on.'

'Technically, it's not quite true that we're twins.' Alex stared at them. 'We're much closer than that. I was able to go back in time one day and meet myself. It was quite a scare for both of us. We're actually the *same* person! You really have just one granddaughter.'

'We weren't separated at birth,' said Bo.

'We were separated by time!' added Brit. 'We're each other's Doppelgänger.'

'And I had to change my name,' said Bo. A trace of light caught her QT brooch.

'Ah, here's our lift.'

Brit tenderly slipped her fingers into Bo's identical hand and gave her a kiss. 'I love you,' she whispered.

Alex stood there rooted to the spot; his face showed a blank resignation. He turned to Billy, 'Why is life so complicated?'

'Shit happens!' his friend shrugged.

Billy clutched the Jules Rimet trophy close to his chest. In retrospect, he thought, it seemed a mistake to have duped Bob into swapping the cups. But getting it back sounded a better option than a *bifurcation*, whatever that was.

A tall, distinguished man got out of the Mercedes Sprinter. Alex recognised him straightaway.

'You've met Harry Hunter,' Brit said.

Alex remembered the conversation he'd had with him in the little watch repairers: *Time After Time*. Looking at him once more another train of thought fell into place.

'It was *you*, wasn't it? That time when I was mugged by those time gangsters. You were there – and so was,' he looked at Bo, 'a blond woman!'

Bo smiled. 'All part of the service.'

'I've got something for you Alex.' Harry Hunter's voice was smooth and calculated. He took an object from his pocket and handed it to Alex.

'My *Rolex*!' Alex was delighted; he'd forgotten all about it. A broad grin curled across his face. 'And it's working.' The sight of his favourite watch brought an image of his beloved grandfather to his mind. He felt comforted to have it back.

Brit began to speak. 'Now I told you there was more than one machine.' She turned to the horologist. 'Take us to Greenwich, Mr Hunter.'

Harry Hunter lifted a pocket watch from his waistcoat by the gold chain attached and tapped the glass face. 'Time to go,' he said.

'Where?' Alex asked.

The tall man levelled his gaze at Alex. 'Whatever is has already been, and what will be, has been before!'

A confused look creased Alex's face, '*What*?'

'Ecclesiastes!' Harry Hunter's eyes narrowed.

Bo rested a manicured hand on her grandfather's shoulder.

'Welcome to Quantum Tours Alex. We hope you enjoy the ride.'

Epilogue

Sunday 27th March 1966

No one knew for sure how it happened, but the following day the papers would be full of it.

The wireless crackled in the front room and a voice spoke in hushed tones.

'…Viking, North Utsire, South Utsire, Forties, southeast seven to severe gale nine, becoming variable, three or four in south Forties; rain, moderate. Cromarty southeast six to gale eight, becoming variable, three or four in southwest; occasional rain, moderate or good. Dogger, Fisher, southeast, becoming cyclonic seven to severe nine, decreasing four or five in Dogger; rain, moderate or good…'

David Corbett switched off the radio with a click and shouted upstairs, 'I'm just popping out love. Back in a mo.'

He closed the front door of his house in Norwood, South London, and walked down the garden path towards the road.

'Come on Picks. Here boy,' he called.

A black and white mongrel wagged his tail and scampered up to the Thames lighter-man who fastened a lead. It was Sunday evening and David Corbett wanted to phone a friend he hadn't seen for a few days, so opening the gate he made his way to the red telephone kiosk across the road. Earlier, the news on the radio had brought a report from Belfast about the activity of the IRA in Northern Ireland. It would play on his mind and influence what he would say next.

As they passed a neighbour's car, Pickles suddenly pulled up sharp and began sniffing at a package on the ground.

'Hey Picks, what you found, a *bomb*?'

Pickles continued to sniff and scratch, so David Corbett looked closer at what his dog was finding so interesting. It was an object wrapped in newspaper and tied with string. Corbett bent down and picked it up; he was surprised to find how heavy it was. For a moment he weighed it in his hand as if it were a dumbbell.

'What's this then Picks?'

Pickles cocked his head and stared up at David Corbett with an inquisitive look.

David felt the package and couldn't imagine what it could be. Then tearing away the paper he saw an object glinting in the evening light. As he peeled back the paper, he saw something that took his breath away. He found himself looking down at a golden statue of a beautiful angel holding a bowl above her head. Shifting its weight in his hands he let the paper fall and he saw the thing in its full glory. Raising the object closer he saw a turquoise plinth and a gold plate on which were engraved the names of several countries: Germany, Uruguay, Brazil. When he realised what it was, he could not believe what he was holding. He had never seen anything so wonderful or held anything so precious. He would have a hard job convincing the Police, but at that moment he didn't care.

David Corbett stood there beside the road and laughed, then in a moment of spontaneous celebration he held the trophy aloft.

'Hey Pickles, we've won the bloody World Cup!'